TYGER

JULIAN STOCKWIN

TYGER

HODDER

First published in Great Britain in 2015 by Hodder & Stoughton
An Hachette UK company

First published in paperback in 2016

1

Copyright © Julian Stockwin 2015

Maps by Sandra Oakins

A CIP catalogue record for this title is available from the British Library

Paperback ISBN 978 1 444 78542 5
Ebook ISBN 978 1 444 78545 6

Typeset in Garamond MT Std by Palimpsest Book Production Limited, Falkirk, Stirlingshire

Printed and bound by Clays Ltd, St Ives plc

Hodder & Stoughton policy is to use papers that are natural,
renewable and recyclable products and made from wood grown in sustainable forests.
The logging and manufacturing processes are expected to conform to the
environmental regulations of the country of origin.

Hodder & Stoughton Ltd
Carmelite House
50 Victoria Embankment
London EC4Y 0DZ

www.hodder.co.uk

To Keith

SWEDEN

Skagen

Gothenburg

THE SOUND

DENMARK

Karlskrona

60°N

Yarmouth

Texel

London

Amsterdam

POMERANIA

THE
NETHERLANDS

PRUSSIA

FRANCE

THE WHITE SEA

Archangel

St. Petersburg

Reval

RUSSIA

Riga

Moscow

Memel

LITHUANIA

Konigsberg

N
W   E
S

~England and the Baltic~

0   200
miles

30°E

~The High Arctic~

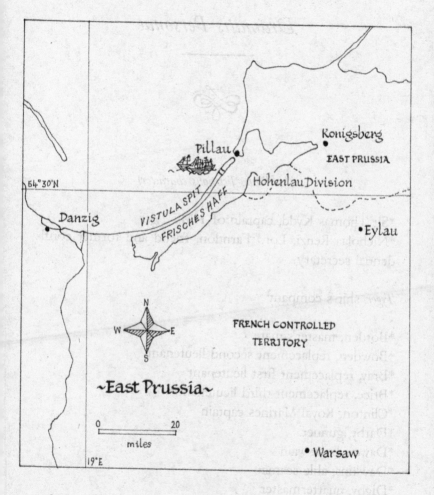

Konigsberg

EAST PRUSSIA

54°30'N

Pillau

Hohenlau Division

VISTULA SPIT

FRISCHES HAFF

Danzig

Eylau

N
W   E
S

FRENCH CONTROLLED
TERRITORY

~East Prussia~

0   20
miles

19°E

Warsaw

Dramatis Personae

*(*indicates fictitious character)*

*Sir Thomas Kydd, captain of HMS *Tyger*
*Nicholas Renzi, Lord Farndon, friend and former confidential secretary

Tyger, ship's company

*Borden, master's mate
*Bowden, replacement second lieutenant
*Bray, replacement first lieutenant
*Brice, replacement third lieutenant
*Clinton, Royal Marines captain
*Darby, gunner
*Dawes, boatswain
*Dawkins, able seaman
*Digby, quartermaster

*Doud, seaman
*Flynn, steward
*Gordon, carpenter's mate
*Haffner, able seaman
*Halgren, Captain's coxswain
*Harman, purser
*Herne, replacement boatswain
*Hollis, first lieutenant
*Jemmy, ship's boy
*Joyce, replacement master
*Le Breton, sailing master
*Legge, carpenter
*Maynard, master's mate
*Nowell, third lieutenant
*Oxley, surgeon
*Paddon, second lieutenant
*Payne, lieutenant of marines
*Pinto, seaman
*Pollard, bosun's mate
*Smyth, master's mate
*Stirk, gunner's mate
*Tully, master at arms

Others

Adams, master shipbuilder of Beaulieu
*Bazely, captain, *Fenella*
Bellingham, British prisoner in Archangel
Bennigsen, Count, commander of coalition forces in East Prussia

Blücher, Generalleutnant, aide to King Friedrich

*Blunt, Muscovy Company

Bourne, secretary of the Treasury during Pitt's office

Browne, former master attendant at Cape of Good Hope

*Cecilia, née Kydd, Lady Farndon

Collingwood, admiral, commander-in-chief Mediterranean

Davout, French general

Dundas, first lord of the Admiralty

*Engelhardt, subaltern friend of Gürsten

Essington, rear admiral

*Felkins, London solicitor

*Gürsten, Flügelleutnant, staff lieutenant in Prussian head-
quarters

*Hohenlau, Generalleutnant, Prussian commander under
Bennigsen

*Horner, Arctic pilot

*Hozier, captain, *Lively*

Jervis, Earl St Vincent

Jervis, Mr, nephew of Earl St Vincent, crown prosecutor in
Popham court-martial

*Knowles, reporting agent

Labanoff, Russian cavalry general

*Marceau, captain, *Preussen*

*Maynard, master's mate

*Miss Sophy, young London socialite

Mulgrave, first lord of the Admiralty

*Parker, former captain of *Tyger*

Phillip, rear admiral, Impress Service

Popham, Sir Home, senior post captain

Popov, mayor of Archangel

*Purvis, butler
*Rogers, captain, *Stoat*
Russell, vice admiral
Scharnhorst, Prussian chief of general staff
Soult, French general
*Stuart, foreign office
Victor, French general
Voronov, Kapitan, port captain of Archangel
Wilkinstone, rear admiral
Young, admiral, president of court-martial

Chapter 1

L'Aurore was new-moored off the legendary Plymouth Hoe. After so long at sea, and the strangeness and allure of foreign shores, it was gratifying to take in the deep green softness of England.

'Do excuse my not seeing you ashore, Renzi old fellow,' Captain Sir Thomas Kydd said, taking his friend's hand warmly. 'You know I'm bound to sail back to Cádiz to rejoin the fleet and—'

'Dear chap, allow that I've a modicum of experience in the sea service and do respect your bounden duty. To be borne back to England in your inestimable bark has been more than my deserving.'

Kydd's commander-in-chief, Admiral Collingwood, had been generous in allowing the frigate that had rescued this peer of the realm from a Turkish prison to continue on to England. Now they must part – Renzi to his seat in Wiltshire and Kydd to restore HMS *L'Aurore* to the blockading fleet as soon as possible.

'You'll give my respects to Cec— that is, your noble wife,

won't you?' That his young sister had married an earl and was now a countess was still a thing of wonder to Kydd.

'I will. Providing I have your promise that you'll honour us with a visit just as soon as you're able?'

'You may count on it, Nicholas.'

He watched his closest friend swing over the bulwarks and, with a last wave, descend into the boat hooked on alongside. He heard his coxswain Poulden's gruff 'Bear off – give way together,' and saw it stroke smartly off.

It had been this way before: a boat bearing Renzi shorewards after far voyaging, once after the near-mortal illness that had ended his naval career, and again after his high-minded but doomed attempt to start a new life in New South Wales, Kydd himself, as a lowly sloop commander, heading ashore to social ruin after spurning an admiral's daughter for a country girl. But now he and Renzi were immeasurably different creatures.

The first lieutenant broke in on his thoughts with a discreet cough.

'Yes, Mr Curzon?'

'The carpenter asks if he might have a word.'

The mild and obliging Legge came forward with a worry frown fixed in place and touched his hat. 'Sir Thomas, m' duty, an' I begs to know how long we'm here at all.'

'Why do you need to know that, Mr Legge?'

'Me an' m' mates had another look at that garb'd an' I has m' strong doubts about 'un.'

'Go on.'

'It's druxy timbers, I'd swear on it.'

Kydd's expression tightened. This was not good news: the carpenter suspected rot, and in the worst part of the ship – the garboard strake was the range of planks that met the keel, all but impossible to get to from inboard. It was, as well, the natural resting place for bilge water. In those dark and secretive spaces, ill-ventilated and never to be kissed by sunlight, it would be the first to yield to the insidious miasma that would turn to rank decay.

It was said to have been the cause of the loss of *Royal George* at anchor in Spithead, with the deaths of her admiral and nine hundred souls – the bottom had dropped out of her. And so many other ships had put to sea to disappear for ever, meeting a lonely fate far out on the ocean when rotten timber deep within their bowels had given way under stress of storm.

'Very well, Mr Legge. I'll send for a dockyard survey.'

They arrived promptly and disappeared below with their augers and probes but came back up with dismaying haste. The extracted sample told it all: instead of tough, dark timber, this was spongy, white-veined – and spurted foul water when squeezed.

Kydd went cold.

'We recommends you comes in f'r a better look, like,' the shipwright surveyor said impassively.

L'Aurore went to the trots in the Hamoaze opposite the dockyard, joining the long line of pensioned-off vessels and others for repair to await her fate.

A frigate, however, was worth every effort to retain for service and no time was lost in bringing out the master shipwright and his team. *L'Aurore* was heeled and investigated and the contents of her hold discharged into lighters along-side. Then her footwaling, the inside planking, was taken up to expose her innards.

There was no doubt. An area on the starboard side,

extending from midships right to her forefoot, was condemned.

'Middling repair, great repair – either way it's a dry docking as will take a lot o' months,' the master shipwright pronounced.

Kydd slumped back in despair. It was almost too much to bear – he knew the navy would not allow them to spend the period in idleness. The expense of maintaining a ship and officers all this time was out of the question – and, besides, the country needed every man jack it could find in its desperate grappling with Bonaparte. *L'Aurore* would be taken out of commission and her ship's company scattered throughout the fleet.

He had to face it, however much it hurt. The beautifully forged weapon that was his crack frigate was now no more. The trust and interdependence that had grown between captain, officers, men and ship, the precious bond stemming from shared danger, adventure and achievements, was broken for ever.

All in a day.

Lieutenant Bowden's features were troubled as he entered the great cabin. 'Sir, you've had word?'

'Yes. *L'Aurore* is for repair. Docking. Months. I rather fear this will mean the end of the commission.'

Bowden stepped back as though he had been slapped. 'I – I . . . Shall you tell . . .?'

Kydd nodded gravely. There were formalities: the Admiralty to be informed, and by return, orders for *L'Aurore*'s decommissioning and paying off would arrive. The master attendant would have to consult his docking schedule but soon it would be all over. 'Yes, the people have a right to know.'

The young lieutenant turned to go.

4

'Mr Bowden – Charles! Please stay.'

It came out before he could stop it. Years ago, as a lieutenant, Kydd had taken him under his wing as a raw midshipman and had seen the lad develop into a man. Bowden had witnessed Kydd's reading in of his commission to his first command and their destinies in the service had interwoven ever since.

'Sir?'

'I'd take it kindly should you tarry to raise a glass to *L'Aurore.*'

'That I'll do right gladly, sir, should we drink as well to the Billy Roarers.'

A pall hung in the air as the news spread. *L'Aurore* had been a happy ship and lucky with prizes under the legendary captain they called 'Tom Cutlass'. She was a barky to boast of in sailors' haunts and wherever seamen gathered to spin yarns about daring and enterprise on the seven seas. From the shores of Africa to South America to the turquoise waters of the Caribbean. The monster guns of the Turks. Trafalgar to empire. Glory and prize money.

Kydd was determined he would see them right: they would be paid off and no guardo tricks with the pay tickets. It was the least he could do. The men would have one glorious spree and, after it was all spent, return to sea, necessarily to give their allegiance to another ship.

Nevertheless, there were duties that had to be performed before they could be discharged ashore. The first was de-storing: the landing of all the provisions and war impedimenta a frigate needed to sustain herself at sea. All to be noted up in due form – a painstaking task to enable Kydd to clear his accounts with the Admiralty.

Even with the assistance of the ship's clerk and the purser it was going to be a long and arduous job, and the day wore on while all the time unaccustomed jarring and strange thuds told of the dismantling of the life-essence of his lovely frigate.

There were tasks of special poignancy: his duty at the end of a commission was to render to the Admiralty his 'Observations of the Qualities of His Majesty's Ship *L'Aurore*', which detailed her sailing capability. Form questions had to be answered: how many knots does she run under a topsail gale? What is her behaviour in lying to or a-try? In a stiff gale and a head sea?

How much more revealing it would have been to tell of her heroic clawing from the path of a Caribbean hurricane, her exquisite delicacy in light airs so close to the breeze that none could stay with her – that endearing twist and heave in a following wind . . .

A subdued Dillon, his confidential secretary, brought the completed copy of the captain's journal for forwarding to the Navy Office.

This was not the ship's log, maintained by the sailing master and replete with plain and practical observations of course and speed, weather and incidents, it was an account of what her captain had done with *L'Aurore*. In it were such details as the various gun salutes fired and with what justification; reasons for condemning three barrels of salt pork, and why he had authorised the purser to purchase petty victuals, viz, five quintals of green bananas, from a port on the African coast.

The most explicit of all were accounts of the actions *L'Aurore* had fought. In carefully measured tones the whole course of each engagement was laid down – the signals passed, the exact time of opening fire, the dispositions of the enemy. Its dry recounting would never stir the reader's blood but Kydd would remember every detail to the day he died.

It was all so sudden, and before the shock of the situation had ebbed he found himself sitting down in the gun-room with his officers for the last time. Tried in the fires of tempest and combat, now, through no fault of their own, they were unemployed and on half-pay.

There were more officers in the navy than appointments available and their fate would assuredly be a dreary waiting on the Admiralty for notice and a ship. Even if they were successful, the chances of a frigate berth were scant; more to be expected was to be one of eight lieutenants walking the quarterdeck of a battleship on endless blockade duty.

'Well, at least I'll be able to see through a whole season in Town.' Curzon's attempt at breeziness was met with stony looks. With his blue-blooded family he would not want for an easy life, but money could not buy preferment in the sea service.

'And you, Mr Brice?' Kydd prompted his taciturn third lieutenant.

The man flashed him a dark look. 'Should I not get a berth quickly I'll sign on with the Baltic trade as a merchant jack out of Hull.' He'd joined *L'Aurore* in somewhat mysterious circumstances and was close-mouthed, but with his experience in the North Sea his seamanship was excellent and he was a calm and fearless warrior.

Bowden was next. 'And I shall hold myself blessed that I saw service in the sauciest frigate there ever was,' he said, adding, with a forced gaiety, 'and so will be content with anything after that swims.'

The master and gunner were standing officers and would remain with *L'Aurore* during the repair.

Kydd was unsure of his own future. His whole being demanded he stay by the ship he loved but his fate was in the hands of their lordships of the Admiralty.

The meal passed off miserably. There was no singing or yarns and the toasts were proposed into a funereal silence. Then they left with awkward goodnights.

The next day HMS *L'Aurore* paid off. The clerk of the cheque arrived on board with an iron-bound chest and the ship's company was mustered by open list in divisions. It was the last time her people would be assembled together and for Kydd, standing to one side, it was an almost unbearably poignant moment.

The ship's clerk called each man's name and rate from the muster roll. The shore clerk sang out his entitlement as he approached the table, cap in hand: the amount was carefully counted into it from the chest and the man returned to his shipmates.

Kydd remained to see every one of *L'Aurore*'s some two hundred-odd men step up and receive their due. Some touched their forehead; others, avid for a spree ashore, hurried off, but he knew each man and could place them with entire trust in any one of a hundred situations, fearful or challenging, dire or victorious.

And now all were lost to him.

In the afternoon the boats started heading ashore, carrying them and their sea-bags filled with treasured possessions – curios from far parts of the world, beautifully worked scrimshaw and tiny model ships. Soon, all over England, there would be delighted reunions: wives, sweethearts and families, children awestruck at the exotic being that was their sailor-father.

Village taverns in the summer evenings would crowd around the homecoming mariner, pots of ale pressed on him, and in return they would be regaled with tales of the high seas and confusion brought to the King's enemies by one who could claim to have sailed under the knighted hero of Curaçao.

Kydd took refuge in his great cabin but some came to pay their respects before they left. He found words for each of them: Poulden, his coxswain, Doud, Stirk, others. Most were tongue-tied, overcome by the final parting, mumbling their farewells and blindly turning away.

And then the ship was empty.

Echoing mess-decks, no watch-on-deck, the helm abandoned. A chill wind, a flurry of rain and endless stippled grey water.

The actual ceremony of decommissioning was a subdued affair. With only the standing officers, a few dockyard workers and his officers witnessing, Kydd's pennant was struck from the main masthead where it had flown night and day since from that time before Trafalgar when it had proudly mounted up. It was solemnly presented to him, and then, in accordance with the immemorial custom of the sea, the ship's cook went aft and lowered the ensign.

It was finished.

9

Chapter 2

'So kind in you to call, Sir Thomas.' The first lord of the Admiralty was in an affable mood and had quickly found time for a now legendary frigate captain. 'I heard about *L'Aurore*. Hard luck, old fellow.'

'Thank you, my lord. It will be quite some months, I fear, before *L'Aurore* is fit for service. We'll know more after she's docked.' Mulgrave was a not unsuccessful army general and therefore could not be expected to feel the void in Kydd's soul.

'Yes, yes. I heard you brought back a travelling earl caught up in that business in Constantinople.'

'Lord Farndon, sir.'

'And jolly grateful he must have been, undoubtedly. Well, now, and you'll be taking some time to be with your family, no doubt. Pray don't neglect us here, Sir Thomas – you are at some eminence in the public eye and the government is always proud to be associated with such a one.'

'I will, my lord, although I do feel I should stand by my ship as she repairs.'

'Well, yes, we've been giving thought to that. You are, of course, unemployed as of your pennant being struck.'

'Yes, sir, but it doesn't signify. I shall wait for *L'Aurore* to be made good, however long it takes.'

'Ah. Don't you consider a trifling twelve-pounder of the breed just a little beneath the notice of a distinguished captain such as yourself?'

'Why, no, my lord. She's tight and true and I'll wait until——'

'Nonsense. The public would never stand for it. There is a better course – I'm appointing you to a brand-new heavy frigate. A thirty-eight no less, and all eighteen-pounders! From the best shipyard in the country, Buckler's Hard, and to the latest design. What do you think of that?'

So there was no waiting for his ship's restoring: now he had lost his dear *L'Aurore* altogether and another would know her and her sweet ways. 'I . . . I thank you, my lord.'

Mulgrave's brow creased. 'I would have thought such a prospect would bring more joy than you show, Sir Thomas?'

'Oh, I'm deeply honoured, my lord,' Kydd said, adding hastily, 'I'm merely thinking of the much greater responsibilities a heavy frigate brings.'

The frown cleared. 'Good. I'm sure you'll be equal to the burden. Then you'll accept?'

'I . . . Yes, sir.' It felt a betrayal, like casting off an old love to run with a younger.

'Excellent. I shall immediately let it be known in the proper quarters. The broadsheets will love it.'

'Sir, what is her name, at all?'

'Name? She has none! Only at the launching, I'm told. I'm sure the Navy Board has a right fearsome-sounding tally to an ocean-bounding beast such as her. Why don't you go down and sight your new command?'

There was a lot to take in. The most immediate was that the ship was still building, and while the launching was set for five weeks hence, with fitting out and trials it could be anything up to half a year or more before he was once again at sea. The pace of his life had, in one stroke, fallen to an amble.

So he would have more than enough time to visit Renzi and his sister at their estate. His spirits rose at the thought – he hadn't even seen their castle or whatever it was that Lord and Lady Farndon called home, and it tickled his fancy to think to see his sister topping it the countess.

There were details to attend to first, however.

This was a complete break with the past in so many ways. His shipboard possessions must be landed and stored – or should he take the opportunity later to outfit his cabins entirely anew?

And what of the two last remaining of *L'Aurore*'s complement still with him? Dillon, his confidential secretary, had so ardently wanted to see the sea and the world. Now there was no more for him to do and, reluctantly, Kydd must let him return to where he'd begun, lent by Renzi from his estate. Guiltily he pictured the tanned young man, who'd come so far and seen so much, now having to revert to being a country-house under-secretary.

And the other, the devoted Tysoe, his valet, who'd looked after Kydd since his early days as a lieutenant.

No – he couldn't do it to the man!

Of all *L'Aurore*'s company, only Tysoe would follow him into his new existence.

It was time to spy out his new ship. He took a leisurely coach to the south coast, first spending a day or two with his parents in Guildford, his blind old father and plain-speaking mother, neither having any conception of the world he lived in but fiercely proud of him – and now so immeasurably distant from his present being.

Buckler's Hard was on the west side of the Beaulieu river, which met the Solent opposite the Isle of Wight. A private yard, it was at the edge of the ancient forests to the south, the slipways of the shipbuilders occupying a gentle slope down to the river with buildings of the humbler sort on either flank.

There was a large vessel on the stocks nearly complete and several smaller, one unmistakably a brig-sloop like *Teazer* and another mere gaunt ribs reaching for the sky. It was a busy scene – shipwrights and their quartermen, apprentices, shipsmiths, labourers, on stages and underneath the vast hulls.

As Kydd walked closer, the rich stink of wood shavings, bubbling tar, varnish, and the smoke from charcoal braziers enveloped him, and the faint sounds of industry became more insistent: the rhythmic *thock* of shores being set up with mauls, the muffled thud of an adze, the buzz of saws, all set against a discordant background of taps and clunks of hammer and chisel, caulking irons and persuaders of every kind.

He made his way towards the larger construction, knowing from the row of empty gun-ports that this was his ship – *his* ship!

Out of uniform, nobody paid him any attention and he guessed that the yard would be a local sight-seeing attraction. He strolled as close as he dared to the rearing colossus. He would never again have the opportunity to see the vessel like this but, oddly, it felt like an intrusion, much like catching a lady half undressed and not at her best.

He walked slowly along. The squared-off hances, so typical

of British construction, the no-nonsense sheer and the fat bow. But everywhere there was naked wood, raw gaps at timber edges, giving a curious disappointment – betraying that this was merely a work of man, not a divinity. He tried to shrug it off, then realised it was a consequence of the sailor's belief that his ship was a living being, with all her likes and dislikes, humours and fierce loyalty, and that she would bear him in her bosom to far places and return him safely to the place of his birth.

This before him was only an 'it', not yet a 'she'.

'What can I do for you, Captain?'

The soft-spoken voice made him wheel around. A man of years gazed at him shrewdly.

'How do you know I'm to be her captain?'

'As you're alone and the smack o' the sea about you,' the man replied. 'Those who's just a-looking always comes in families an' so.'

'You're in the right of it. Captain Sir Thomas Kydd, appointed to this ship.'

'Edward Adams, shipbuilder.'

They shook hands.

'The Admiralty has a good opinion of your work, sir.'

'When it suits 'em,' Adams said, with a small smile. 'Still an' all, we've given satisfaction, I believe. You know the Lord Nelson's favourite ship?'

'*Agamemnon*? A very fine sixty-four.'

'From this yard, over yonder slip. And his frigate captain, Blackwood?'

'*Euryalus*. He often spoke of her – I knew both men, Mr Adams.'

'The same. Her keel was laid at that very slipway over there. And *Swiftsure*?'

'The seventy-four-gun ship-of-the-line?' This was impressive work for a small private yard. 'I had the honour of seeing all three ships at Nelson's last battle,' Kydd added.

'So you were at Trafalgar, Captain?'

This prompted an invitation to a charming house near the water. Over a flavoursome local ale, Kydd spent an agreeable few hours discussing the qualities of the oak of Old England, the fitting of iron tanks for water in place of the traditional leaguers, the merits of seasoning on the stocks.

But he also learned there was no possibility that the completion date could be advanced. This was the way it was done and always had been.

Chapter 3

'Thomas! You've come!' Cecilia squealed delightedly, running down the steps of Eskdale Hall to hug her brother.

'M' lady,' Kydd said, with an exaggerated bow.

'How long can you stay – or is your ship lost without her brave captain?' she asked breathlessly.

'A sennight at the least, Cec.'

As his baggage was swung down Kydd looked up at the noble edifice. The coach had come along a driveway a full quarter-mile long, through spacious formal gardens and tree-studded green lawns. 'A rattlin' fine mansion you have, sis,' he murmured, impressed to the point of astonishment at its seemingly endless windows and imperious ornamentation.

'Why, thank you, Captain,' she answered demurely, then looked back and said happily, 'And here's Nicholas!'

Renzi emerged, accompanied by footmen, and hurried down to greet him. 'My dear fellow,' he blurted, 'welcome! Welcome, indeed!'

16

Inside, in a small, intimate drawing room, they caught up with Kydd's news over tea.

'A stout thirty-eight, then,' Renzi enthused. 'And eighteen-pounders all. Enough to give pause to the finest Boney possesses. English-built, too. Your first, then, as I'm obliged to remark.'

'True,' Kydd agreed. His initial command, *Teazer*, had been Maltese and *L'Aurore* was a French prize. 'And at over a thousand tons, it's spacious enough for the most dainty sybarite,' he reflected with satisfaction.

'It?' Renzi asked.

'Oh, doesn't have a name yet,' Kydd replied defensively. His friend, it seemed, still had the blood of a mariner. 'And you, old trout, dare I ask if you're settled in at all?'

'Of course he is, silly billy!' Cecilia chided. 'As this is his ancient family seat. But, Thomas, there's always a welcome for you here, at any time –'

'I do thank you—'

'– recollecting that it's customary among our station to send ahead before you arrive,' she teased.

'I'll try to remember, sis.'

'Now, dinner is at five sharp. You'll want to refresh after your journey and—'

'Thank you, but first I beg to ask Nicholas to give me a sight of his grand estate.'

'Farndon has a meeting with his tenants this afternoon,' Cecilia said, 'as cannot be put off.'

Kydd shot a look at Renzi, who gave a saintly smile.

'Therefore it shall be myself who will take you around. Like you did for me over your *Artemis*, Thomas,' she added softly.

There was a warm rush of remembrance. 'And so far have we come since then – the both of us.'

* * *

They sat down to dinner in the blue dining room, *en famille*, just the three of them. It was, nevertheless, at a substantial polished table with silver and adornments, Renzi taking his place at the head. Purvis the butler stood solemnly behind him, footmen nearby.

The candlelight was soft, its tawny gold barely reaching the richly decorated ceiling, with its goddesses and painted satyrs, but throwing the sculpted picture frames and bas-relief into high contrast.

'I think a hock?' Lord Farndon suggested. 'The 'ninety-four Rheingau, if you would, Purvis.'

He'd brought to mind a time when they'd all been together at sea, long ago in a place far away, in the little cutter *Seaflower* – Renzi had served this same hock to an important passenger, Lord Stanhope, whom they were urgently transporting to Barbados to take ship for England on a matter of high diplomacy.

Cecilia picked up his meaningful glance and laughed delightedly, turning to her brother. 'You were steering the boat, Thomas. You couldn't have any!'

It set the tone, and by the time the venison arrived they were in a full spate of reminiscence.

'Oh, Thomas. It nearly broke my heart to tell you of Papa's sight failing, that we needed you to leave the sea and return to Guildford . . .'

'And there and then, sis, on this heathen beach in Van Diemen's Land, a thousand miles from anywhere, Nicholas wept to think he was letting you down . . .'

'All the time I thought he'd run away with a loose woman . . .'

'. . . then we threw out the euphroe and the driver took up, would you believe it? We had steerage way before the

18

hurricanoe and . . . Why, what's wrong, Cec?' Kydd asked, in sudden concern, seeing the glitter of tears in her eyes.

'It's nothing, Thomas. I'm just so happy, that's all. Do continue with your story.'

Kydd finished his tale and, in a warm glow, turned to Renzi. 'I'm thinking you're main pleased to be atop such a splendrous pile, Nicholas.'

'As it must be, dear chap. Like you – do you question your elevation to the great cabin at all, to rue the day that sees you as lordly seigneur over some hundreds of doughty souls – which is more than I can claim to, old fellow?'

'But you've got—'

'I may have land and tenants, but nary a one may I put to the lash, as I've seen my captain do on occasion.'

'Then—'

'Yes. I'm captain of the good barky Eskdale Hall and, like all captains, I have my duties and my paperwork and, as I must, I'm to concern myself with my stout crew and their liberties.'

They toasted their respective commands with all due ceremony.

Then Kydd asked, 'And can it be said you're restored after your . . . travels, Nicholas?'

Cecilia flashed Renzi a warning glance. 'If you'd leave the brandy, Purvis . . .'

The footmen quietly retired as well.

'It was—' Renzi began, but Cecilia interrupted him, leaning forward, 'Nicholas suffered dreadfully. Thomas, he told me everything – but now he's home and we're together again.'

She reached across to squeeze her husband's hand, her piercing look both pleading and of the utmost love.

An unexpected wash of envy at the intimacy between

them took Kydd off-guard. 'Ahem. So you've no plans for another . . .'

'Dear fellow, allow that I've earned a measure of repose, which I fully intend shall be spent in my library,' Renzi said firmly.

Cecilia brightened. 'Oh, I nearly forgot! Thomas, it's the county ball next week – we're host this year. Please say you'll attend, dear brother?'

'Why, of course, Cec.'

'You'll be the toast of the evening – a true hero who graces us with his presence on our little occasion.'

'You shall want me in uniform, then?'

'With star and sash both! And I have in mind just the lady you'll squire,' she added. 'The Honourable Arabella Fortescue, an accomplished beauty and most delightful woman . . .'

Chapter 4

It had been touching to see Renzi and Cecilia together, but Kydd had still not quite grown used to seeing his friend at such an elevation.

Renzi had changed. He was wearing the honour and noble bearing as though born to it, which of course he was, but now he carried himself differently: serious, listening more, saying less. Kydd suspected he'd gone through some private hell in Constantinople in his clandestine efforts to stop it falling into the hands of the French, but was not letting the world see how it had affected him. The healing was a task for Cecilia alone.

For himself it was different. He'd lost *L'Aurore* – but in her place had been given a plum prize: a brand-new heavy frigate of the latest design, the envy of every red-blooded captain in the navy. The price? Months of patience in idleness.

Since his first command, dispatch had been the watchword, and sloth a vice. Now he was being asked to kick his heels, with nothing to do other than graciously accept the reputation and eminence that was now his.

After making his farewells to Renzi and Cecilia, it was off to London – with leisure time and freedom to make foray into the entertainments on offer in the world's capital.

Kydd settled into his accustomed chair at the White Hart Inn while Tysoe dealt with the baggage. He realised he needed someone who could provide a fashionable steer, give him an *entrée*, and thought of Edmund Bazely, the jolly commander he had first met among the Channel Gropers in those feverish times of Bonaparte's threatened invasion.

He'd heard that the man had just returned from a particularly fortunate cruise in the Caribbean. A determined bachelor, he was above all a knowing man about town in London.

Impatient to taste the delights of the capital, Kydd soon found himself outside Albany in Piccadilly.

The doorman took his card and before long a tubby man stood before him, not fully dressed but beaming with pleasure.

'Why, damme if it ain't Kydd the Frog-slayer! Or is it t' be Sir T at all?' he added, with a teasing grin. 'Do come in, cuffin. M' cabin is all ahoo but ye're welcome, very welcome!'

The rooms, or 'set' as they were termed in Albany, were modest in size but well appointed and quite the thing for their chief function, bachelor quarters for the comfortably off.

'A snort o' something?' Bazely called to his guest, from the bedroom, as he completed his attire. 'Jus' touch the bell.'

Kydd nonetheless politely waited until he emerged. 'You've done well at prize-money then, dear fellow.'

Bazely grinned. 'Pewterising is the solemn duty of any in a blue coat, m' friend.' He looked at Kydd shrewdly. 'Last I saw ye, you'd run afoul o' Admiral Lockwood, somethin' about his daughter, wasn't it? Now I sees before me a cove who's made post, got his name in *The Times*, shipped a star, an' who everyone says is today's hero. I honour ye for it, Kydd. And thank 'ee for noticing an old frien' like this.'

'Damn your eyes, Bazely – I came of a purpose, man.'

'Oh?'

'I'm to get a frigate – but not yet. She hasn't completed, I have to wait it out. Months. And I've a yen to make the most of it, take m' fill of what London can offer a weary mariner, if you see my meaning.'

'Ha! Jack Tar on the ran-tan in the Great Smoke?'

'Just so.'

'*Fenella*'s in for small repair, I think I c'n see m' way clear to a mort o' frolicking. Cards? High table? Theatre? Ladies – or all four on 'em?'

After an agreeable discussion on which to do first, Bazely reflected lazily, 'Weren't ye in that Buenos Aires moil at all?'

'Yes, I was. Why do you ask?'

'As it might put a crimp in your little spree – the court-martial. I take it y'r not bein' charged?'

'No, but I'm to witness.'

It had been a relief to hear that only one man was to face the court: the instigator of the failed expedition, Commodore Popham. Kydd had received the formal notification only very recently that he was being summoned as witness, with the instruction to hold himself in readiness for the date of convening, to be announced.

'Should be interestin', I'm persuaded.' Bazely chuckled.

'Maybe, but I think it a miserable thing, and to be honest with you, m' friend, I don't particularly want to dig it up again.'

'No? Then you've been out o' Town too long – every codshead scribbler tryin' either to roast the man or cry up the hero. Here y' have the Admiralty, righteous an' frowning, saying as how he left his station to go a-venturing without leave. An' over there you've got Johnny Public – he adores a scrapper who sees th' enemy an' goes for him.

'And it's gone political. Popham was a Pitt's man, an' when he was gone, he lost his friends. He's a cunning old fox, but where can y' stand with a closet Whig like Portland? Not t' say the Tories at each other's throats and ready to see their allies go hang. It's a right shambles an' the whole world has an opinion. I'd say ye'd better have your story tight an' pretty, Kydd. You're in the centre o' the storm.'

It cast a pall, but not for long.

Bazely beamed. 'So we're for the tiles. Now, m' knightly friend, if I'm to introduce ye to ladies o' my acquaintance then I'm not t' be shamed in the article o' dress. Here in Town we has t' be taut-rigged an' in fashion or we don't stand a chance against y'r strut-noddies prancing about as calls 'emselves the *ton*. I know a tailor t' be trusted in Old Bond Street. Shall we . . .?'

Kydd had been overseas for so long that he hadn't appreciated just how much things had changed. Gone were the colourful and ornamented waistcoats and breeches of the eighteenth century and in their place was a mode laid down by the upcoming society dictator Beau Brummell, avidly followed by the Prince of Wales – a plain, studied elegance that owed everything to cut and quality.

'Sir has a fine figure,' the tailor declared, holding Kydd at arm's length. 'We can make much of this. Buckskin pantaloons, perhaps?'

In the next few days Kydd was transformed.

He stood in front of a mirror in admiration. Over a cream

24

waistcoat he wore a double-breasted dark green tailcoat, relieved by two discreet lines of brass buttons. Its high collar felt awkward but it served its purpose in confining a gushing white cravat, starched and finished with the looser but fashionable mailcoach knot. The tight-fitting pantaloons were tucked into gleaming hessian boots, sporting tassels and ending with beautifully shaped pointed toes.

In his hand was his latest purchase, a narrow-brimmed hat, flat on the crown and all of twelve inches high but with a wicked curve to the edge. It felt so impractical compared to his service bicorne, which could be folded flat in an instant and tucked under the arm in confined spaces 'tween-decks. He hesitated to put it on, especially as he'd paid a barber an extortionate sum to style his hair in the latest mode, the Titus, shorn everywhere but the front where his dark curls were swept forward in imitation of classical statues of a Roman emperor.

'Bang up t' the mark,' Bazely enthused from behind. 'As will f'r a surety have the ladies all of a tizz, you devil!'

A visit to the glover followed. Kydd blinked at the mounting cost but, then, if he was to be taken for a gentleman about town, why hold back?

It was a gratifying experience to promenade in Hyde Park in the bright summer sunshine, swinging his cane, noticed with a tip of the hat by gentlemen of consequence – he raised his own to passing ladies to their barely concealed delight.

A parade of soldiers, regimental band thumping away, marched past; Kydd and Bazely respectfully stood still with doffed hats as they passed and were awarded a smart salute from the young subaltern in command.

Spotting Kydd, a curious Curzon and his lady hurried over

to pay their respects. Too well-bred to remark his astonishment at the vision, he made much of introducing his companion to the famous frigate captain and, in return, Kydd was gracious and fulsome. Finding his old lieutenant still without a ship, he extended an invitation for the pair to accompany himself and Bazely to the theatre the following evening.

Kydd had mentioned that he'd heard the legendary Sarah Siddons had expressed a desire to leave the stage: he would be mortified, he'd said, to miss her performing. The obliging Bazely had made the necessary arrangements, even down to the provision of a pair of pretty sisters, awed to be seen out in such company. And he'd managed to secure extra tickets for Kydd's guests.

The great actress did not disappoint. Covent Garden was packed for her *Isabella, or, The Fatal Marriage* and from their box Kydd delightedly took in the sweeping grandeur of her gestures, the agony of her portrayal of the torn woman – and lustily joined in the storm of applause that followed.

At the supper afterwards he was at a loss to remember when he had been last so contented with life.

At breakfast Tysoe appeared with a silver tray. 'For you, Sir Thomas.'

It was a personal card with a folded sheet of paper. He recognised the name instantly: Essington, rear admiral, his former second lieutenant's uncle. Many years before he had put Kydd forward as acting lieutenant, starting him on the journey that had led to where he was today.

The note was short and to the point.

My dear Kydd, or should I say, Sir Thomas.

On seeing you at the theatre last night I conceived it my duty and pleasure to invite you to an evening with my friends in retirement, some of whom I'm sure are old acquaintances of yours. Should you feel able to attend, then shall we say tomorrow eve at seven at my club, Brooks's?

Kydd was delighted. If Essington thought it proper to esteem him as a guest at the distinguished Brooks's Club, he was most definitely on the rise in society. Not only had it been many years since they had met but Kydd had a soft spot for Bowden, Essington's nephew, a clear-thinking and resolute young man. With a twinge he reflected that, now unemployed as a lieutenant, Bowden was at that moment probably at the Admiralty begging for a ship. But that was the way of the navy.

He took especial care with his dress, Tysoe fussing with the fall of his cravat, the lie of the satin knee breeches against white stockings and the correct ribbon ties on his silver-buckled black shoes.

Later, with a surge of nervousness, Kydd stepped out of the carriage and looked up at the frowning Palladian façade of the club in St James's Street. An expressionless doorman took his hat and cane and led him through to the Small Drawing Room.

Half a dozen gentlemen sat comfortably, some alone with newspapers, others together in conversation, and he saw that almost to a man they were in blue, the coats cut severely, with plainly wound neckcloths and close-cut hair. However, the man who rose to greet him wore a white cravat, his hair tied back with a ribbon in the old way.

It was Essington. 'So pleased you could come, old fellow,' he said, with a warm smile. 'You'll take a glass of something?'

One or two looked up curiously.

'Kind in you to invite me, sir,' Kydd said politely. 'After so long out of hail.'

'Ah – that's because you've been away at your adventures. You're much talked of, Kydd, you know.'

'I've been lucky, sir, this I'll admit right readily.'

'And you'll oblige us at supper with an account of each and every one.'

He raised his glass to Kydd, then turned to one of those sitting. 'Reginald, you'd like to meet Captain Kydd of Curaçao, at all?'

The man nodded pleasantly.

'This is Admiral Gardner from the San Nicholas Mole affair, old chap.'

Kydd shook hands, aware of a keen look of appraisal. He recalled hearing of the engagement as a young quartermaster.

Then it was Wilkinstone, lamed at the Glorious First of June but who had gone on to command a frigate in a bruising fight in Quiberon Bay, and others, some of whom he remembered from his days as a common sailor when he had seen them as god-like figures on their quarterdecks. To be among their number as a guest now gave him a rush of pleasure.

One stood up to ask him about the taking of Cape Town and soon more came over to listen until Kydd found himself in the middle of an animated throng. He kept his accounts guarded and modest – for all that this was a social occasion, there were at least two serving admirals present.

They were interrupted by the call to supper and sat down with other club members for the informal repast.

Kydd introduced himself to one opposite, a gentleman of years with a shock of white hair, who turned out to be a banker from the City, interested in his observations on trade prospects with South America. On his right, a younger man with a world-weary look was the Member of Parliament for Weymouth; he slumped back cynically as Kydd finished his story of a naval engagement up an East African river among lions and crocodiles.

Past Essington on his left, at the head of the table, there was an empty chair which no one seemed inclined to inhabit. Shortly, the conversations died away as a stooped, elderly man with fierce eyes shuffled painfully in to assume the seat.

With a shock Kydd recognised him: John Jervis, 1st Earl of St Vincent – and first lord of the Admiralty at a crucial time for both Kydd and England. In command of a man-o'-war since the long-ago victory at Québec, a queller of mutinies, the unflinching enemy of corruption and legendary commander-in-chief of the Channel Fleet, he had only recently retired.

Just in time Kydd stopped himself scrambling to his feet as the great man was merely greeted affably and offered the claret. He grunted a pleasantry to one side, then addressed himself to the crumbed veal cutlets.

'My lord, we have a guest tonight,' Essington said smoothly, 'whom I've no doubt you've heard about in recent times. May I present—'

'No, let me guess,' Jervis interrupted gruffly, staring steadily at Kydd as he ate.

Nervously, Kydd wondered whether he should prompt the aged sailor.

'Ah, yes. Kydd with a *y* amidships, a Nelson *élève* before Trafalgar, if my memory serves.'

'Why, yes, sir—'

'And a damned odd way of demanding a ship!'

Kydd reddened at the recollection of the muddle that had allowed him, as a post captain, to beseech the command of a lowly sloop. At the same time he glowed: the illustrious admiral remembered him! 'I have to thank your lordship for your kindness.'

It seemed to mollify.

'You've seen service since, Kydd.'

'I've been fortunate, my lord.'

'You have. Curaçao was a well-done thing, but where does it leave us? Another Caribbean liability for not much revenue.' Jervis reached out and poured more currant sauce dismissively.

Essington politely interjected: 'Captain Kydd had a significant role in the conquest of Cape Colony, my lord.'

'Did he?' He looked at Kydd coldly. 'Then he must have followed that damned popinjay Popham on his hare-brained and insubordinate adventure against Buenos Aires!'

'Yes, sir, I did.'

'For which the coxcomb must explain himself before a court-martial, hey?'

'My lord, do you not think there might have been circumstances that—'

'Sir, there is no conceivable state of affairs in creation that allows a junior commander to take it upon himself to leave his lawful station to go adventuring,' Jervis said acidly.

Kydd knew he should not press the matter with so fabled a figure but couldn't help murmuring, 'All the same, it does seem a hard thing to me that a man be punished for being active, when the safer is to do nothing.'

Jervis slammed down his fork and glared at him. 'Are you trying to excuse the man's actions? If so, you fall far short in my estimation, Mr Kydd!'

Kydd burned. 'Commodore Popham thought to do his duty to the larger interests of Britain, which he saw—'

'How dare you lecture me, sir?' Jervis barked. 'Are you to be counted in that poltroon's camp? Then you're sadly misguided! The Admiralty can brook no insolence from mercenary venturers such as he and they'll show him no mercy when the verdict's given.'

He leaned forward and, with a look of deadly intensity, went on quietly, 'So have a care, Mr Kydd. If you shackle yourself to that mountebank I will not answer for your future. You understand me, sir?'

Afterwards Essington took Kydd aside. 'That was not a wise thing in the circumstances, my dear fellow. He may now be retired but his word counts for much in the high councils.'

Kydd smiled ruefully. 'I honour the old man with all my heart, but I'm persuaded there's two sides to the business, and this being a social affair I thought I could—'

'St Vincent cares deeply for the staunch, true ways and will be merciless to those he sees failing to conform. You're sailing close to the wind, my friend.'

The next day Kydd had other concerns, chief of which was the rendezvous to go riding with the winsome younger sister he had accompanied to the theatre, Miss Sophy.

He and Bazely had rented hacks, passable high-steppers, and Kydd was conscious of the fine figure he made as they cantered out to the broad perimeter roadway around Hyde Park, known as Rotten Row.

They were far from alone: there were carriages of every degree of opulence, tooling along with ladies twirling parasols as their beau held the reins, weaving in and out of knots of dandies 'on the strut' and promenading couples. Others passed by, their riders eyeing them to see if they were to be ignored or deferred to.

The sisters were waiting for them, sitting demurely side-saddle on matching brown mounts. The four set out together at a sedate walk, conversations light and gay. It was a perfect day and Kydd's blood rose at the sight of the girl beside him in her fetching blue habit and prim *chapeau*.

'I do declare,' she said, with a pout, 'it's so perfectly unfair that you men do hold to yourselves all the excitement!'

'Why, what must you mean, Miss Sophy?' Kydd chuckled.

'You're soon enough going back to the sea, to a great big ship searching for prey to fall upon, and after a huge battle you'll take it, then come back to land with hatfuls of guineas in prize – and all the time your intended must wait alone for your return . . .'

'Ah,' Kydd said, aware of the prettiness of her downcast eyes. 'The sea service does not always yield such, I'm persuaded. Have you not heard of storms and tempests? And what if the foe is bigger – what then?'

She looked up winningly. 'The brave captain I see will not be dismayed by great odds!'

Bazely leaned over and said with a piratical chuckle, 'Aye, this is true 'nuff. I've seen Tom Cutlass here stand with bloodied sword on his quarterdeck when all around—'

'Do stow it, Bazely, there's a good fellow. I've a mind to enjoy myself. Where shall we victual, do you think?'

They finished the day with a promise of a visit to the races. If this was what he had to put up with while he waited for his new command, there were worse fates, Kydd mused.

But returning to the White Hart he found the post had brought a complication. The court-martial of Commodore Popham was to be held at HMS *Gladiator* in Portsmouth in three days' time and his attendance as a witness was thereby required.

Chapter 5

❧

Kydd penned a quick note to Bazely, then he and Tysoe took the next coach for Portsmouth. No doubt the business would be concluded in a few days and he could be back in Town. Unlike the protracted deliberations of a civil case, court-martial proceedings consisted of naval officers trying their peers. There would be no need for lengthy explanations and all would be judged in the stark light of the Articles of War. It was incontrovertible that Popham had left his station without orders. That alone was sufficient to condemn the man, whatever mitigating circumstances were brought before the court.

Kydd knew the road well and gazed through the window at the garden-like countryside passing by, idly considering possible future entertainments with Miss Sophy when his life of leisure resumed.

The prospect of the old naval port loomed and the coach clattered over Portsea Bridge and into the busy town. In the matter of accommodation the Star and Garter was for lieutenants, the Blue Posts for midshipmen, so Kydd would be lodging at the George, Nelson's favourite.

It seemed unusually crowded and it was some minutes before he was attended to.

'Staying for the trial, sir?' the innkeeper asked, summoning a porter. Kydd was in plain brown dress but he'd clearly recognised the bearing of a naval officer. Without waiting for an answer, the man added, 'Then you'll be interested in the newspapers, sir. We have them all in the parlour for your convenience.'

While Tysoe saw to the unpacking, Kydd sat in the bow window for the sake of the light and picked up the *Portsmouth Post*. Although ostensibly just reporting the facts, there was malice behind the words. 'The Trial of Sir Home Popham . . . upon the most serious charge of abandoning his station . . . the unfortunate failure of the unsanctioned enterprise . . . must now answer for it before his peers . . .' In three dense columns the writer had laid out the essentials. The article began with the British army's near-run conquest and subsequent control of the Dutch-held Cape of Good Hope, at six thousand miles distance of England, leaving the victorious army in control but the Navy's small squadron under Popham on guard against a vengeful counter-stroke.

The narrative ran on: it was the 'unaccountable desire of the naval commander to cross the Atlantic without orders on a brazen attempt to invade South America, which notwithstanding that the capital Buenos Aires had actually been captured in no way excused the action, still less the consequent shipping back of millions in silver bullion'.

The piece pointed out that the adventure had failed, with the ignominious surrender of the British forces to the rag-tag Spanish colonial forces, which was greatly to be regretted. Then, in ponderous, elliptical prose, it scouted the rumours that the entire venture had been for the personal profit of this distinguished officer.

Kydd threw the paper aside. The author had not even mentioned the immense strategic advantage of detaching Spain from her colonies and their sustaining wealth – if successful, it would almost certainly have thrown her out of the war.

The *Hampshire Register* took a different and more sympathetic tack, wondering if the entire affair was the work of Popham's enemies, seeking to destroy his reputation. The undoubted benefit to British commerce of opening up the Plate river trade in hides and grain and as a market for industrial goods, it claimed, was never going to be recognised by stiff-necked Tories intent on bringing down Popham.

That was the daily newspapers. The radical Cobbett in his *Annual Register* had ranted against the expedition as having 'originated in a spirit of rapacity and plunder' and even questioned whether Popham 'had ever been placed in a situation to have had a single shot fired at him'. There had been pamphlets too, some making direct accusations of avarice and corruption and others of sordid dealings in India.

What was it about Popham that roused such emotions? Kydd shook his head and decided to take a stroll in the warm evening air.

There were many about, some no doubt on their way to Governor's Green to an open-air meeting on the trial he'd seen posted up, so he shaped course towards the seafront with its view of the fleet at Spithead.

He hadn't gone far when he heard a cry and saw a figure hurrying towards him. It was his former second lieutenant.

'Good day to you, Mr Bowden. What brings you here?'

'The trial in course, Sir Thomas. As I have a certain interest

35

and . . . and I find myself at leisure at the moment,' he added.

They began to walk together.

'Your own presence I gather, sir, is rather more than a passing curiosity?'

'I'm summoned as witness. A sad business.' Then Kydd said offhandedly, 'Look, if you've nothing better, shall you wish to sup with me? The George is famous for its lamb cutlets, as I remember.'

They dined together in a quiet corner, the young man respectful and attentive.

But Kydd needed someone to whom he could speak in confidence. It was the inevitable consequence of the sea service: at any time the odds were that his friends and fellow captains were away in their ships, scattered over the globe in the vast oceanic arena that was now modern war.

'You knew Commodore Popham well,' prompted Bowden.

'As far as any man can penetrate his character,' Kydd replied. 'A vastly intelligent fellow – you remember Fulton and his submarine boats, his inventing of the telegraph code we used at Trafalgar, the catamaran torpedoes, his raising of the Sea Fencibles – he's a fellow of the Royal Society and knows more about conjunct operations than any man alive.'

'Conjunct?'

'Where the navy and army join to effect some blow against the enemy that neither may achieve on their own. He was with the Duke of York in Flanders, and that successful destruction of the sluice gates at Ostend in 'ninety-eight? It was his plan, not to mention his transport of Indian soldiers across the Red Sea to take the French in the rear when we were hard-pressed in Alexandria.'

'Then why . . .?' began Bowden, carefully.

'I can't answer that. I've got along with him well enough but I can see how his superior ways could upset some of the blue-bloods. He's a genius for making enemies – and friends, for that matter.'

'So the charge is leaving station, sir.'

'A very severe one, young fellow. If the Admiralty thinks you to be in one place, and makes plans to use your fleet in that belief, then finds too late you're off somewhere else, can you blame them for feeling peeved?'

'Our talk in the gun-room was that he had secret intelligence he was acting upon. Did you believe him, sir, or should I not be asking this of you?'

'No, you should not, but I'll tell you, as it has to come out in the trial. He told me at the time, without any evidence about him, that he was in thick with the prime minister and others and that they'd together devised a plan of attack on South America and that this was interrupted by Trafalgar. This means that the whole thing against Buenos Aires could have been an official move, not his own idea.'

'Ah. I see that the only way he can prove this is to call the prime minister as witness, but he's—'

'Quite. Pitt dying is a big blow to his story. That is, if it wasn't all a bit of a stretcher from the beginning.'

'Sir, can I ask you a personal question, as bears on the trial?'

'You can – but I'm not bound to answer it.'

'Sir, can you tell me why you fell in with his proposal to quit station?'

'I . . . I judged it more in keeping with a naval officer's

duty to do something in a rush of events than sit idle waiting for orders. I conceived that there was an opportunity of strategical significance that, if missed, would be a betrayal of the higher cause.'

'Sir, there were those in *L'Aurore* who observed you close to him, even as his special confederate in the whole matter. I hope you will excuse my plain speaking, but they might be forgiven for wondering why you are not standing next to him at the trial.'

'Do *you* think I should be?' Kydd asked.

'No, sir,' Bowden said. 'You showed loyalty to your superior as so you should. And, besides,' he added, with a twist of a smile, 'were you not following orders, as you must?'

'You'll go far in the service, young whipper-snapper.'

'Then may I know what position you'll take in court?' Bowden persisted.

'Position? There's only one possible, as you should know.'

'Oh?'

'I tell the whole truth.' Kydd paused, then said with a slow smile, 'That is, I answer every question put to me, neither more nor less than the matter being asked. If certain questions are not put, then . . .'

'And if they require to know whether you believe Commodore Popham was right to—'

'That is a matter of opinion, not evidence, and has no place in a court-martial,' Kydd barked.

He had thought hard about his position and this was the only one he could square with his conscience. On the one hand he felt sympathy with what the man had been trying to achieve in the larger picture, but on the other he did not want to be seen in the ranks of those trying to tear him down.

Yet there was still one niggling concern: might he eventually find himself accused of being an accomplice and arraigned?

In the morning, at eight precisely, a single gun thudded out from *Gladiator* and a Union flag mounted to her masthead.

The court-martial of a senior officer of the Royal Navy in what some were calling the trial of the age was beginning with the summoning of the court.

The majority were admirals and, as was the custom, mere captains took boat first from the man-o'-war steps. There was a sizeable crowd to see them go, held back by redcoats from the garrison, and an excited buzz rose. Kydd was in his full-dress uniform, his star and crimson sash marking him out as one of the sea-heroes so talked about, and he gravely acknowledged the cheers.

In the boat were other witnesses of like rank, with two older captains who were to sit in judgment. They avoided each other's gaze until they reached the venerable ship's side and disembarked one by one.

An immaculate side party in white gloves piped them aboard, then the captain of *Gladiator* welcomed them and saw the witnesses aft to a special area where they would wait until called.

The great cabin was arranged with a long table and chairs, several side-chairs and small tables for officials and attendants.

One by one the members of the court filed in, in strict order of seniority, the glitter of gold lace and the steely gleam of the sword of the provost marshal adding to the solemn majesty of the moment.

Last to enter was the president of the court, Admiral Young, who took his high-backed chair with ponderous deliberation. Next to him was the judge advocate who would advise on points of law and procedure. At one end was a bewigged civilian supported by another, the prosecuting counsel for the Admiralty; at the far end two others stood beside an empty chair, Popham's legal counsel.

After a muttered consultation the president was ready.

'Carry on, the Admiralty marshal.'

This was the warrant for proceedings, under the signature of the highest authority possible.

A clerk took up a paper and read, in a thin, reedy voice, "'Whereas Captain Sir Home Popham left the Cape of Good Hope without orders to attack the Spanish settlement on the Rio de la Plata, now this is to command you that you take the said Sir Home Popham under arrest preparatory to his trial by court-martial for his said offence.'"

Each of the members of the court were then individually put on oath.

'Bring in the prisoner.'

Popham wore a faint smile as he stood erect before the court.

His sword was produced by the provost marshal and handed to the president.

'You are Captain Sir Home Popham?'

'I am.' The voice was calm and even. 'Mr President, I have thought it advisable to seek legal assistance upon this occasion and I beg leave to ask permission of this court to have this assistance attend me during the trial.'

'Sir Home, any assistance you may require, the court is very willing to allow you.'

Popham gave a slight nod in acknowledgement, and the opening gentlemanly play was over.

Although he was not in the great cabin, Kydd knew what would be happening. A court-martial was a straightforward affair: the precise charge facing the prisoner would be read out, then the prosecution would make its case, producing the entirety of evidence in support of the charge. Following this, the defence would begin with its own evidence, then witnesses would be called and examined by both sides. On completion, after the customary closing address by the prisoner, the court would be cleared for deliberation to a verdict.

On more than one occasion Kydd had sat on courts that had opened in the morning and concluded before midday; evidence presented, witnesses heard and verdict arrived at – a man condemned to hang at the yardarm.

The president turned to the judge advocate. 'The letter of complaint, if you please.'

The archaic practice was for the charges to be framed in the form of a grievance from the Admiralty to be addressed by the assembled court.

Rising to his feet and adjusting his spectacles, the learned gentleman outlined the case to the court: '"By the commissioners for executing the office of Lord High Admiral of Great Britain and Ireland, etc., to William Young, Esquire, Admiral of the Blue, and second officer in the command of His Majesty's ships and vessels at Portsmouth and Spithead. By command of their lordships, William Marsden, first secretary to the Admiralty."' The words rolled out with a practised delivery.

'"Whereas, by an order . . . Sir Home Popham, then captain

41

of His Majesty's Ship *Diadem* . . . was directed to take under his command . . . for the purpose of capturing the enemy's settlements at the Cape of Good Hope in conjunction with the troops of Major General Sir David Baird . . . and whereas it appears from letters from the said Sir Home Popham that he was proceeding to Rio de la Plata with a view to attack the Spanish settlements for which he had no direction or authority whatsoever, and he did withdraw from the Cape the whole of the naval force which had been placed under his command for the sole purpose of protecting it, thereby leaving the Cape, which it was his duty to guard, not only exposed to attack and insult . . . all of which the said Sir Home Popham did notwithstanding that he had previous information of detachments of the enemy's ships being at sea . . . And whereas it appears to us, that a due regard to the good of His Majesty's service imperiously demands that so flagrant a breach of public duty should not pass unpunished."'

He flashed a glance at Popham. "'We send herewith, for the support of the charge, the following papers, viz:

"'The copy of an order from the lords commissioners of the Admiralty . . . to Sir Home Popham, to take the ships therein named under his command, and to proceed to the Cape of Good Hope . . .'"

Some eighteen orders and instructions were cited, and after a small cough to signify a change of tempo, the reading concluded with, "'And we do hereby require and direct you forthwith to assemble a court-martial; which court (you being the president thereof) is hereby required and directed to enquire into the conduct of, and try the said captain, Sir Home Popham, for the offences with which he is charged accordingly. Given under our hands . . .'"

The judge advocate turned to the president. 'Further, sir, I have here a letter directing Mr Jervis, counsel for the affairs of the Admiralty and navy, assisted by Mr Bicknell, to conduct the prosecution on the part of the Crown.'

At the opposite end of the table to Popham, a thin, predatory figure in legal robes rose and bowed briefly to the president. Before sitting he fixed an intent look on Popham.

It was crowded in the witness waiting area. Several left to stretch their legs on deck for a space. A seamed old captain sitting next to Kydd leaned sideways and whispered, 'They're no doubt making sure o' things. That legal cove prosecuting can call old Jarvie "uncle", did ye know?'

Kydd felt dismay. Was St Vincent really going to such lengths or was it merely coincidence that his nephew was leading the prosecution? Either way, however Kydd answered as a witness, his words would doubtless be known to the implacable old admiral the same day. When under examination it would be wise to weigh what he said very carefully indeed.

'This court now sits. Pray read to the court the evidence in support of the charge.'

'Very good, Mr President. Document One. Copy of Instructions to Sir Home Popham.

'"By the commissioners for executing the office of Lord High Admiral of the United Kingdom of Great Britain and Ireland, etc., the Lord Viscount Castlereagh, one of His Majesty's principal secretaries of state, having, with his letter . . ."' He read aloud the actual instructions to Popham in the matter of preparation for the descent on Cape Colony in all their meticulous wording.

'Document Two. Copy of a letter to Sir Home Popham . . .'

One by one the orders and strictures that had passed out of the Admiralty from hopeful beginning to disastrous end were revealed, a damning avalanche of evidence that took nearly two hours to complete. Included were intelligence appraisals from military commanders in the field, advisories from the new governor of the colony and correspondence between the secretary of state for war and the Admiralty.

It finally ceased.

Popham had been listening politely, his faint smile still in place, but as soon as the judge advocate sat down he spoke crisply: 'Mr President, I beg leave to point out that Document One is in error, sir.'

Admiral Young blinked in perplexity. 'Sir Home, these are Admiralty documents. How can they possibly be in error?'

'May I draw the court's attention to a significant omission? If you'll note the passage relating to the governor having information concerning where the French had prosecuted their voyage, here we read "the Indies", which is clearly in error.'

'I don't really see—'

'Sir, the accompanying dispatch makes clear that the "West Indies" is signified. If this document is to be received as it stands I shall have been sorely calumnied, for if understood as the "East Indies" a most improper impression of my motives for proceeding would have been deduced. Sir, these are copies. That a clerk may have omitted the word is to be regretted, but worse would be to let it stand. I must insist that the word "West" be inserted to correct the error.'

'This is most untoward. Mr Jervis, do you wish to speak to the matter of this omission?'

'Sir, I am not prepared, not having the original dispatch by me.' The prosecutor glared down the table. 'I'm not disinclined to admit that there might be such a mistake alluded to by the honourable captain, but without the original I cannot state positively.'

'Then—'

'The matter is trivial. This dispatch is not entered in as evidence against the honourable captain but read in the statement of the charge only.'

'Sir Home?'

'I am aware that the document is not admissible evidence against me, but I allow I'm desirous that every document laid before the court should be correct in its particulars. Indeed, sir, I'm anxious that everything should transpire, as concealment is not in my interest.'

'Mr Jervis?'

'This conversation is very irregular, sir. As the paper is not adduced in evidence, any mistake in it cannot be considered material.' He shot a venomous look at Popham. 'However, I would have no objection to accede to the honourable captain's wish.'

The correction was so entered.

'Mr President,' the judge advocate intoned, 'all papers that compose the charge have now been read.'

'Sir Home, do you now accept the receipt of these documents on to the court's records?' the president asked heavily.

'Certainly. I do admit every document referred to in the charge that purports to be written by me, also such as were received by me.'

'Thank you. Then we may go on to—'

'Such as were received by me. This cannot include Documents Three, Four and Five.'

'Pray why not, sir?'

'These Admiralty instructions sent in dispatch by *Belle Poule*

45

packet were captured by the enemy. Their duplicates, by *Lyar* cutter, never arrived on station as she did not touch at the Cape. In fine, sir, I cannot be held to account by anything specified therein since I did not receive them.'

Jervis came back instantly: 'May it please the court, the dispatches do not form evidence to affect the honourable captain as knowing their contents. They are adduced merely to show to the court the orders issued by the Admiralty in the belief he was still on station.'

The president frowned. 'As there is no evidence of the receipt of these orders, of course no charge of disobedience can arise out of them. However, let them be so received.'

Popham smiled wolfishly. 'Then for what purpose are they laid before the court, if they are not meant to affect me? I really cannot perceive the object the learned counsel has in view. I do not wish to argue a point of law with the eminent gentleman but I am advised that naught may be entered save it is legally admissible as evidence.'

'Sir! Are you questioning the prerogatives of the court to rule upon a question of law?'

'Sir, I have been asked to accept the entirety of a total of eighteen documents brought forward today when but three were served on me when arrested. There are here papers I have never seen or heard of. I hope the court will feel it natural that I should seek to be fully prepared and therefore grant an adjournment.'

'Sir Home. There are officers here today called away from various stations where they are engaged in the service of their country. Therefore every degree of expedition is desirable. I shall adjourn, and trust you are ready with your defence shortly.

* * *

46

Bowden was waiting for Kydd after he had braved excited crowds to return to the George.

'Sir, you'll think it awfully impertinent of me, but—'

'You want to hear about the trial.'

'I do, sir. Everyone's talking of it and—'

'I'm bound not to speak of proceedings until they be over, Lieutenant.'

'Oh. Well, I do understand then, sir. I'm sorry to have troubled you.'

Kydd relented: all would be made public eventually. 'If it was known I'd been speaking to you, I'd be indicted for contempt of court, and you wouldn't wish that upon me, would you?'

'No, sir.'

'Then we'd better not let it be known. The cards room, one hour.'

'Aye aye, sir.'

They found a pair of winged chairs near the fire, the noisy play at the tables ensuring they could not be heard. Kydd appreciatively sipped the brandy he had demanded as fee for his tale.

'Well, do you know the usual watch and station bill for a court-martial?'

'I've never attended one, sir.'

'Now, this one's nothing like it. It's held in *Gladiator*, a paltry new-hulked forty-four-gun fifth rate of the last age, thirty years or more old. Can you conceive of it? Seven admirals, four captains and all the court lackeys, jammed into a great cabin not much bigger than *L'Aurore*'s?'

Bowden shook his head.

'So they made as though clearing for action – tore down

47

the bulkheads so the bed-place, coach and great cabin were all one.' He smiled ruefully. 'Well, of course, witnesses aren't allowed in the court except when they give their evidence, but through – shall we say? – *various means*, we did get the drift of what was going on . . .'

'And?'

'First of all Popham is brought in to hear the charges read, as cool as may be. And I should tell you that the prosecutor is old Jarvie's – that is to say, Earl St Vincent's – nephew. And then all kinds of legal backing and filling. By any standard, Popham was a taut hand at the business, dishing Jervis like a good 'un. Not a wise notion to bait such a one, I'm thinking, or debate law with the president of the court.'

Kydd smiled briefly. There was no doubting the man's courage, or his intelligence.

'Then they read out the prosecution evidence, all of it, and a shocking hill of it there was. I really can't see how he can tack around it. He did sail for South America without orders, that's the truth of it, and they're going to hang him for it.'

'Court will come to order. Sir Home, are you now prepared to defend the charges brought against you?'

'In so far that in the small time allowed me to draw up my defence, I am now ready to answer, yes, sir.'

'Then do so, if you will.'

'If it please the court. Sir, after having devoted the greater part of my life to the service of my king and country, I am brought before you to vindicate my conduct upon a charge so extraordinary in its nature as was ever submitted to the interrogation of a court-martial – that with means placed at my disposal for a successful attack against the possessions of the enemy, instead I should have suffered my command to remain inactive.

'Notwithstanding this singular view, it is my intention to demonstrate to the court that, far from being a rash adventure conducted on an impulse, this has been an operation of long consideration, carefully planned and authorised at the highest level, the prime minister himself terming it his "favourite object". I shall bring to the attention of the honourable members of this court memoranda and dispatches that reveal my actions to be sanctioned by ministerial knowledge and approval.

'In this, was I not doing my duty in the interest of my country? As to the accusation that I quit my station without leave, I can only point to more illustrious commanders than myself who, in the recollection of members here sitting, have seen with the daring spirit of enterprise an opportunity to further gallant achievement beyond a passive acceptance of their situation.

'I beg leave to mention the *coup de main* of Admiral Rooke who, having no orders to do so, in bold enterprise seized Gibraltar for the British Crown. And in the late war, in 1793, Lord Hood took it upon himself to enter Toulon and move upon Bastia. That we had insufficient force to hold them does not diminish his achievement. Neither was he made subject of imputation.

'At a later date we find Lord St Vincent, then Sir John Jervis, sent the heroic Nelson to attack Tenerife in the mistaken belief that treasure ships were sheltering there, which as we know met with dolorous consequences. This was undertaken without orders from any superior authority and outside the limits of his command. Certainly no judicial inquiry or public censure ever followed the enterprise.'

The shot hit home: the prosecuting counsel's face tightened but Popham went on in measured tones.

'And I need hardly remind the honourable members of the action of the gallant Lord Nelson himself in leaving his station to pursue Villeneuve to the West Indies. I quote from his letter at the time from Martinico. "I had no hesitation in forming my judgement, and I flew to the West Indies without any orders, and I think the ministry cannot be displeased." I believe it unnecessary to state that the country as a whole rejoiced at his so doing.

'In short, it is that officers with independent command cannot be fettered by the literal tenor of the orders given them. A command such as mine is, from its very nature, discretionary in the very comprehensive meaning of the word.'

He accepted a sheaf of papers handed to him by his counsel. 'Honourable gentlemen, I have here sufficient evidence for my stand. That my project was known at cabinet level and that I acted with due discretion in the discharge of my duty. May therefore these be read into the record.'

'And this is the documentary evidence for your defence?'

'It is, Mr President.'

'Very well. Judge Advocate?'

One by one they were read out in open court, Jervis in ill-natured debate challenging their legitimacy as evidence, demanding corroboration, sarcastically questioning their relevance. But it appeared that Popham indeed had had the ear of the greatest in the land.

The picture they gave was of Popham moving in the very highest circles – accounts of his dealings with Miranda, the Venezuelan revolutionary, and early plans for a joint attack on Spanish South America. Letters from Pitt demanding more details, military estimates to meet secret plans, correspondence with the Admiralty and, in fact, the first lord himself on the subject.

'We will now call witnesses.'

The president of the court picked up his list and made play of consulting it.

'Call Henry Dundas, First Viscount Melville.'

There was an immediate rustle around the court – this was none other than the reigning first lord of the Admiralty at the time, who could be relied upon to have been privy to every naval confidence.

It took a little while, for the noble lord was being accommodated ashore until summoned. A tall, imposing figure, he appeared with his flag lieutenant.

As soon as he was sworn in Popham wasted no time. 'Will your lordship have the goodness to relate to the court the circumstances respecting the communications I held with Mr Pitt and your lordship upon the subject of a proposed expedition to South America?'

A respectful hush descended. If a first lord of the Admiralty supported Popham's claims, then the court-martial was all but over – who sitting there in judgment would dare to press the issue?

Jervis waited in a forced rigidity, Popham with an air of supreme confidence and polite patience.

'I . . . feel some difficulty in answering this question,' Melville began, with a deprecating gesture. 'I have no doubt it can be answered but for any allusion to confidential secrets of state, and this . . .'

Popham's smile slipped a little. 'Nothing can be more foreign to my wish than a disclosure leading to the improper publication of a state secret. No – let my reputation suffer rather than such a consequence be risked.'

'Then I shall endeavour to answer to the best of my recollection.'

Dundas began by telling the court how Popham had introduced General Miranda with a plan for a simultaneous descent on the southern continent, at the successful conclusion of which Britain would be rewarded with preferential access to the newly opened market.

'Did Mr Pitt accede to this plan?'

'We had several conversations on the matter but did not immediately proceed.'

Jervis scribbled something that was handed to the president, who held up his hand. 'Can your lordship indicate to the court why this was so?'

'I may say that a higher political purpose prevented it.'

'Sir, if at all possible, the court would be interested to know it.'

'Very well, as any pretence at secrecy in the matter is now no longer practicable. It is that until the events off Cape Trafalgar it was held that any attempt on the Spanish colonies would provoke a more fierce adherence to the French cause, at hazard to our diplomatic exertions in Madrid to detach them.'

Swiftly Popham gave over a paper. 'Does your lordship recognise this letter?'

'I do. It is one sent by me directing you to attend a meeting with Mr Pitt upon the subject.'

'And to produce a memoir upon the matter.'

'That is so.'

'Which resulted in a warm discussion between us.'

Jervis had waited for his moment: it was now.

'Mr President,' he said, in a voice silky with menace, 'this is neither here nor there in the charge before the court. We accept that the honourable captain was engaged in dealings with the noble lord and Mr Pitt in the matter of South America. There is really but one question that interests us: does his lordship confirm or deny that orders were given to Sir Home Popham specific to an attack on Buenos Aires?'

'Let the question be put.'

'No orders were given in that tenor.'

Smoothly, as if nothing had happened, Popham continued to examine the first lord. Cabinet meetings, dry detail of fleet assembly, intelligence pertaining to Spanish colonial conditions but nothing to stand against the damning disclosure just given.

Melville was stood down with every expression of gratitude for his time graciously given.

Popham then called William Sturges Bourne, Esquire.

He took position before the court and was duly sworn in.

'Is it possible, Mr Bourne, from the situation you held, you should be acquainted with the secrets of government?'

'I am not aware of the extent of your question.' The man was reticent, defensive.

Popham seemed nettled. 'Were you one of the secretaries at the Treasury during the administration of Mr Pitt?'

'I was.'

'Then do you recall, sir, confidential information received by your office relative to the situation obtaining in Buenos Aires?'

'I have a faint recollection only.'

'Come, come, sir. Of such import, and bearing so on the—'

'I object – leading the witness!' rapped Jervis.

'Quite. Sir Home, in any case the witness has further admitted only an unreliable knowledge of this. I rule the question disallowed.'

53

'As the court pleases. Mr Bourne, do you recollect the confidence Mr Pitt reposed in me in respect of secret matters pertaining to South America and in particular the situation in the Rio de la Plata?'

'He mentioned you in cabinet discussions on the subject,' he said carefully.

'And did he not in your hearing seek my personal opinion on the officer to command the Cape expedition?'

'I have some remembrance of it, but not sufficiently strong for me to speak positively on it.'

Admiral Young interjected, 'Sir Home, where your questioning is headed is not altogether clear to the court. I have but one question to put to the witness: Mr Bourne, in the conversations at which you were present with Mr Pitt and Sir Home Popham, was it determined or proposed to attack the Spanish settlements in South America after the assault on the Cape, in the event that it proved successful?'

'I recollect no proposal being made in any conversation respecting a descent on the Spanish settlements in South America.'

'Thank you. Have you any more questions for this witness, Sir Home?'

Bourne was stood down and William Huskisson was sworn in.

A young, intense individual, his prominent forehead and alert eyes gave an impression of high intelligence.

'Were you one of the principal secretaries in Mr Pitt's government?'

'I was.'

'Do you recollect my taking leave of Mr Pitt in your room at the Treasury, immediately prior to my sailing for the Cape?'

'I do.'

54

'Was the impression at all on your mind that I had at that time a conversation with Mr Pitt on South America?'

Jervis objected immediately. 'The question is illegal. How can the witness testify to what transpired when he was not present?'

'Sir Home?'

'Mr President, I cannot understand distinctly what the learned prosecutor means when he calls this illegal evidence. Unfortunately for me and the country, Mr Pitt is no more and I am therefore under the necessity of seeking that from others he could prove by himself were he alive. In the absence of this testimony I now adduce one of his most confidential friends in order to show the wish and views of that illustrious man.'

'We will allow the question.'

'I had the impression that the conversation related to South America, yes,' said Bourne.

'Sir, did you have any discussion with Mr Pitt yourself upon the subject of South America, particularly Buenos Aires?'

'I did have, as I was directed to take certain steps by his desire concerning Buenos Aires.'

'And what was the nature of this direction?'

'In that instance it was to explain the existence of a map or chart of the approaches being lately taken from the King of Spain's depot in Madrid, being afterwards copied for the French military.'

'For what purpose, pray?'

'It was believed to form part of a design by the French for their own incursion, a likelihood which was not thought much of.'

'Sir Home,' the president came in, 'I find myself under

the painful necessity of intervening once again. Let the witness answer: did Mr Pitt at any time communicate to you any orders of a nature requiring Sir Home to attack Buenos Aires upon successful conquest of the Cape?'

'I certainly never understood from Mr Pitt that Sir Home had such positive or provisional orders, no, sir.'

'Sir Home?'

'Sir. It could be said that plans were well advanced for the reduction of the Spanish colonies when I sailed for the Cape. Were they not put in train to take effect once news of the successful taking of Cape Colony was received? That is to say, orders from Mr Pitt would have been issued if I had not exercised my discretion in view of rapidly advancing events?'

'I cannot speak to that. At this time there was no communication between myself and Mr Pitt, he being upon his death-bed.'

Popham's hands clenched, once, and in a thick voice he asked, 'How long have you been in post?'

'In a situation with the Admiralty? Why, sir, we may say above twelve years.'

'In a long experience as chief secretary to that board, can you state to the court whether in the trials of Admiral Byng, Lord Keppel, Sir Robert Calder, Admiral Duckworth –'

'Pray what is your question, Sir Home?' the president asked testily.

Popham went on doggedly, '– whether the charge was framed in such a manner as to call the court, ahead of the trial, to punish the individual to be tried?'

The witness looked helplessly at the president, who frowned.

'Sir Home, I'm at a loss to understand where this is leading.

Kindly explain to the court what you expect the witness to disclose by this line of questioning.'

Popham breathed deeply. 'I demand a precedent for the scandalous pre-judging of my case, by which I mean the charge, which contains an incitement to punish the defendant even before tried!'

'I cannot know what you mean by that, sir!'

'I quote from the charge, sir, read out in open court at the outset of this trial. It plainly states: "Whereas a due regard to the good of His Majesty's service imperiously demands that so flagrant a breach of public duty should not go unpunished!" This is not to be borne, sir!'

'I beg to know what we have to do with that,' the president rapped. 'The Admiralty have the authority to word the charge as they please. They are not to be arraigned for wording the charge as they see proper. I have sat on fifty courts-martial or more and never heard such quibbling.'

Jervis looked sorrowfully at Popham. 'And as learned counsel, my earnest advice is that censuring the Admiralty is not a way for the prisoner to defend himself.'

'Quite, quite,' the president rumbled. 'This seems a good point to end the day, I believe.'

'What he said today didn't help him, apparently,' Kydd said, tucking into more collops of fish. 'Talk about Nelson and other great men leaving their station.'

Bowden reached for the sauce. 'He has a point, surely. They quit their rightful station without orders – this is a precedent if ever there was one.'

'Not so! Consider the charge – it's wonderfully crafted. They want to make sure of it, see him nailed to the bulk-head.' Kydd hesitated to say more in front of a former lieu-

57

tenant in his ship. But he knew the young man could be trusted not to repeat what he said. 'The charge is not for leaving station, it's not for attacking South America, it's not even for failing at Buenos Aires. It is that he's guilty of sailing off and leaving the Cape undefended.'

'So . . .'

'You see, Nelson and all the other commanders had a battle-fleet, which is meant to chase after the enemy. Popham had a fleet of sorts but its job was to stay in one spot to defend a territory, not sail off into the blue.'

'Ah. Then what about his talking of Miranda, bringing in Pitt, the others?'

'He nearly did it – pulled the court around, humbled 'em by showing how he'd been hobnobbing with high politicals. He even called Lord Melville and other grand ones to witness how he'd been thick with Billy Pitt actually planning an attack on South America.'

'And it didn't work?'

'If he could show he'd orders or instructions for the taking of the Spanish colonies he'd be able to argue he was only being impatient – but none of 'em would say he had positive instructions to that effect. It really destroyed him and he ended up losing his humour.'

Kydd leaned back. That such a brilliant mind was being slowly ground down was a sad spectacle, but how much was he bringing on himself? This talk of how he, a lowly post captain, had had the ear of the highest could only provoke resentment and fear among those his superior, and there was not much doubt that his disgrace would bring much satisfaction.

The trial had gone on for considerably longer than the usual court-martial but the end must be soon. Unless Popham could meet the central charge with an unanswerable argument it would be all over for him.

'Sir Home. Before we begin proceedings, I think I must mention, sir, you will feel that this court has listened to you with patient attention while many papers were read and examinations put that were wholly irrelevant to the question immediately before it. It has done so out of consideration of what you have alleged to be unfavourable prejudices in the public at large, which have gone abroad. With such the court has nothing to do. Thus I trust you will confine yourself to points necessary to defend against the charge now before us.'

Popham was now back in possession of himself and spoke in a cool, wary manner. 'I shall most anxiously endeavour to comply with the wishes of the honourable court and I beg to present thanks for the indulgent attention I have received.'

He glanced once at the silent Jervis, now poised like a vulture awaiting its chance to fall upon a weakened prey.

'I do call Mr Thomas Browne Esquire.'

A bulky man entered and came forward.

'Mr Browne. Were you master attendant at the Cape directly after its capture?'

'I was.' The voice was husky and indistinct.

'Speak up, if you please,' the president snapped.

'I was that, sir, yes.'

'Do you remember when I sailed for South America?'

'I do, sir.'

'At that precise time, were the defences of Cape Colony in such a state as to offer sufficient security against any attempt of the enemy to retake the Cape – in your opinion, of course?'

'Opinion has no place as evidence, if it please the court,' Jervis said, with heavy patience.

'Sustained.'

Popham smiled briefly. 'Then it becomes necessary to lay before the court in detail the facts of the situation obtaining at the Cape in order they shall make their own appreciation.'

'Is this really necessary, Sir Home?'

'Sir, as you have made abundantly clear, the heart of the charge against me is that I left the Cape undefended to prosecute my attack on the Spanish settlements. By this I will show that it was far from the case.'

Without waiting for an answer he launched into a detailed examination of the fortifications and other works one by one.

The litany drew on.

Jervis was attending with an air of superior confidence. Finally, he spoke. 'If I could be permitted an observation?'

'Of course, Mr Jervis,' the president said with relief.

'The honourable judge advocate might correct me, but surely what is being attempted to be established is entirely beside the point. Whatever the honourable captain brings forward in military facts does not address the central issue: that it is for the Admiralty to adjudge the level of defences due a station, and in their wisdom they had appointed him and certain forces they deemed necessary to defend Cape Colony.

'I would be interested to know what grounds the prisoner has for disputing the judgement of their lordships.'

It was a savage blow and, for the first time, Popham's face betrayed a stab of despair.

'A valid and cogent remark, Mr Jervis. Sir Home, this line

of defence is worthless to you. I strongly suggest you find a more reliable one.'

'Very well, sir. Stand down, Mr Browne.'

And then it was time. 'Call Captain Sir Thomas Kydd.'

Kydd entered and made his way to the table to be sworn in, conscious that every eye was on him.

'Sir Thomas, how long have you been an officer in the Royal Navy?'

He raised his eyes to meet Popham's and saw only a controlled wariness.

He braced himself: if the questions following attempted to implicate him as principal in the offence then not only would he most certainly earn St Vincent's ruthless enmity but he might well end up with his own court-martial.

'Since the year 1797.'

'When you earned a field promotion at the battle of Camperdown.'

'Yes.'

'Your subsequent service saw you at both the Nile and Trafalgar?'

'That is true.'

The president interrupted: 'Captain Kydd wears the star of a knighthood, Sir Home. We accept that he is a distinguished and gallant officer if that is your purpose.'

'You were under my command as part of the Cape squadron.'

'I was.'

'Were you present at the capture of the French frigate *Volontaire*?'

'That is so. I took possession of the vessel per your orders.'

'Were you with me at the examination of her papers?'

61

'I was.'

'Did they indicate that the vessel was part of a battle squadron?'

'They did – but of the Willaumez force, bound for the West Indies.'

'Thank you. Later you took the corvette *Marie Galante*. You returned with valuable intelligence. Pray tell the court its nature and the circumstances of its discovery.'

'It was reliable information that the vessel was not part of any fleet at large in the Indian Ocean and that all other squadrons had sailed for France.'

'And how was this intelligence obtained?' Popham prompted.

'I had a Guernseyman in my crew who I set to be sentry over the prisoners. They talked freely before him, thinking him English. They revealed that—'

Jervis raised his hand. 'Sir Thomas, what rank was this Guernsey seaman?'

'An able seaman so far as I can remember.'

'And whose testimony may therefore not be acceptable in a matter of high intelligence.'

The president raised his eyebrows. 'The court will consequently ignore this last. Have you any more questions for this witness?'

'Sir Thomas, at the time we sailed for South America did you at any time take the view that the Cape was open to descent from the French?'

'Objection. The evidence takes the form of an opinion and – I beg pardon of the honourable captain – from a junior not to be expected to know the strategical situation.'

Popham returned hotly, 'This was the captain of a frigate entrusted with the responsibility of several independent

62

cruises touching upon the defences of the Cape. I know not any who could be more cognisant about the reigning situation than such a one! Sir Thomas?'

'In the knowledge of the quitting of all French squadrons from the adjacent seas I saw nothing to indicate there were hostile plans to be directed against the Cape.'

'Did you have any reason to suppose there was on the other hand any internal threat obtaining?'

'Objection! How is it at all possible that a naval officer, however distinguished, might be in a position to make comment on that?'

Popham gave a tight smile of condescension. 'The court may not know that this officer was centrally involved in the suppression of a French-inspired rising of the natives, the last threat of consequence to our holdings in the Cape.'

'Sir Home, I fail to see—'

'Now, Sir Thomas. You were present, were you not, when the American trader Waine arrived in Cape Town with information concerning the current state of Buenos Aires, its defences and politics?'

'I was.'

'Kindly tell the court your conclusions following our interview with him and the examination of the Buenos Aires newspapers he offered.'

Kydd went cold. He remembered this well as the turning point when the fantasy Popham had conjured became a practical reality. There and then he had offered his support. Yet if it were taken that as a consequence he had thrown in his lot with the prisoner before the court things could turn very ugly.

The inner truth was, of course, that he had gone with the scheme for its audacity and prospects but—

63

'Sir Thomas?'

He was only too aware of Popham's intent gaze as he waited for the reply.

'My conclusion at the time was that should orders be given for a move on Buenos Aires it would be difficult to conceive a better time.'

Jervis struck like a snake. '*Should orders be given* . . .' Then pray tell the court, Sir Thomas, what your objections were when an attack on the Spanish was formally proposed.'

It was a loaded question and Kydd floundered for a reply. His very nature rebelled at anything other than a faithful account, but this would be to say that he did not in fact object and therefore he was in favour of an expedition.

His next words could . . .

'If it please the court, I found it difficult to object to the *practicality* of what was being put forward, which as we know did result in a success for His Majesty's arms.'

He dared a glance at Popham and from the slumped shoulders and bowed head realised that he'd failed him. It clutched at his heart. That long-ago time in the old *Diadem*'s cabin when they'd talked of being left to rot in a backwater station, the boredom and lack of a chance at distinction, then an opportunity for both of them – and now this.

He opened his mouth to say something but nothing came.

The president snapped, 'Sir Thomas, thank you and you may stand down.'

'Are there any further witnesses?'

It seemed there were not.

'I rule therefore that you should now look to closing your defence, Sir Home.'

It was all but over.

Popham had only a brief closing speech to make before the court retired for deliberation to a verdict.

'I here close my defence and I throw myself on the wisdom and justice of this honourable court. My feelings and character have suffered severely but I trust to your judgment to relieve the one and rescue the other.

'If I have, in the exercise of my zeal, exceeded the strict bounds of discretion, I hope it will be evident that I have been actuated solely by a desire to advance the honour, glory and interest of my country . . .'

It was noble, uplifting rhetoric and concluded with a Shakespearean quotation from *Othello*, defending the Venetian state: 'That the very head and front of my offending hath this extent – no more!'

A stirring among the members of the court seemed to show that they were not unmoved, and as the prisoner was led away by the Admiralty marshal they all rose to their feet.

'Clear the court.'

As with all who had been present for the days of the trial there was a reluctance to leave the ship before the verdict was reached, and Kydd found himself pacing the upper deck with them, engaging in awkward small-talk as the time passed.

It was not until hours later, when the sun was going down, that a sudden excited buzz from the cabin spaces indicated that the moment had arrived.

They crowded into the great cabin where the president sat with a grim expression, flanked by the gold lace of the seven admirals who had made their judgment.

'Bring in the prisoner.'

Popham entered, his face pale but giving nothing away.

'The court, having maturely considered the nature of the

charges, heard all the evidence and having deliberated upon the whole of this case, are of the opinion . . . that the charges *are proved* against the said Captain Sir Home Popham.'

He waited for a wave of murmuring to die then continued: 'The court is further of the opinion that the conduct of the said Captain Sir Home Popham in withdrawing the whole of the naval force under his command from the Cape of Good Hope and proceeding with it to the Rio de la Plata was highly censurable.

'In consideration of the circumstances, however, the court doth adjudge him to be only severely reprimanded, and he is accordingly severely reprimanded.'

This time there was no holding back the excited babble as a stunned Popham was handed his sword and taken to the door.

As he left, he looked once at Kydd but his expression was unreadable.

The George was abuzz with excitement and speculation but Kydd wanted no part of it.

He called for Tysoe. 'I'm returning to London tomorrow. We leave on the first stage.'

'Very good, Sir Thomas.' He moved forward to help Kydd out of his heavy full-dress uniform into the plain brown attire he'd come down in.

'And if you'd find me a whisky . . .?'

The dull roar from below wafted up in eddies. This had been the court-martial of the age and everyone had a view on it.

He closed the window and sprawled in a brown study.

His thoughts were disturbed by the arrival of Bowden. 'The town's in an uproar, Sir Thomas, and I'd hoped you'd—'

'Come in, dear chap. Care to join me in a whisky?' Kydd said, with false gaiety.

'That's kind in you, sir,' Bowden said, and took his place in the chair on the opposite side of the fire.

'They're in quite a taking out there,' he said sombrely, picking up on Kydd's mood. 'Half are declaring it a victory and the other cry it down as a guilty verdict.'

'Ah, yes.'

'I'd be beholden should you share your views with me, sir.'

'My views?' Kydd paused. 'Naught that should be shared with a young officer who's warm to daring and enterprise.'

'Sir?'

'No matter. I've the blue devils after that trial.'

'You're an admirer of Captain Popham, sir?'

'In fine, I'm not. The man is manipulative, uses his cleverness to excess, is too slippery by half. Yet I find any who seizes the chance and dares to reach for glory to the benefit of his country one to applaud.'

'Then how do you accept the verdict?' Bowden asked.

'It's contrived and it's political and it's very neatly done. To his friends he's weathered the storm – not cashiered, dismissed the service, worse. To his enemies is thrown the satisfaction that he's found guilty. Has he won? Not at all. The Admiralty have their verdict – and our Captain Popham will, very quietly, never be employed again.'

Bowden looked shocked. 'As if he'd been sentenced . . .'

'Quite.'

Tysoe silently freshened their glasses as they stared together into the fire.

'If I might remark it, sir, at least your yardarm is clear, if you'll pardon the expression,' Bowden observed.

'As is no credit to myself. After my showing it seems I'm not to be made an accomplice, neither numbered among Captain Popham's followers, and therefore have my hopes the doughty St Vincent will be contented.'

'To be devoutly desired, I believe.'

'Well, that's the way of things, young fellow. I'm for London and society tomorrow.' He tossed back the whisky, then remembered that Bowden's own future was now more than a little problematical. Without a ship . . . 'I do wish you well in the article of finding a berth as lieutenant,' he said, with a twinge of sadness. 'You've a good record but there's others, of course.'

'Thank you, sir. I'll always remember my service in *L'Aurore*, whichever ship I end in.'

'I'm sure you will. I'd offer you a place in my new frigate but it doesn't even kiss water this year and that kind of time in idleness would not be good for your record.'

'I understand, sir. I . . . I do have friends in high places,' he said lightly, 'who will I'm sure bend every effort. I now bid you farewell, sir,' he said formally, 'and pray we will meet again.'

Kydd took his hand. 'I'm sure we will. Take care of yourself, younker.'

Chapter 6

It was a relief that the court-martial was behind him. Arriving back at the White Hart, Kydd wanted nothing more than to leave it all in the past and re-engage in the agreeable socialising to be had in London before duty reclaimed him.

He took an early night and was up promptly. A note to Bazely was quickly returned with a reply: he'd be delighted to rendezvous at the Quill and Wig with a view to planning further capital delights.

Tysoe laid out the tailcoat and pantaloons and took pains in seeing him as taut-rigged as every fashionable man-about-town. The hessian boots were tight and caused Kydd to wince as they were fought on, but a glimpse of his figure in the long mirror showed the trouble was worth it.

They were interrupted by a knock at the door.

'A gentleman as begs Sir Thomas should spare him a minute or two,' the landlord said apologetically. 'Said as how it's a matter of urgency.'

'Very well. Five minutes,' Kydd answered, easing his cravat a trifle.

A scruffily dressed individual with his hat in his hands and an ingratiating air appeared. 'Sir Thomas? So kind in you to see me.'

'Your business, sir? As you see I am in haste.'

'Sir, I'm Josiah Knowles, you may have heard of me.'

'No?'

'May I introduce myself? I'm a reporting agent for the very respected *True Briton* newspaper.'

'What's that to me, sir?'

'It's my honour to cover the biggest story this age, the court-martial of Sir Home Popham.'

'And?'

'This is my difficulty, Sir Thomas. I attended at Portsmouth and followed the trial with great diligence, but there are certain matters that are still obscure to me. I know you were with Sir Home at the Cape, Buenos Aires and similar, and beg to say my readers would welcome your views on this dolorous proceeding.'

'You were there? Then, sir, you must report what you heard. I've nothing to add to what I said as witness.' The man was demented if he thought he would share his private opinions with a reporter.

'The daily trial transcript is a dull enough thing, Sir Thomas. You'll know that the affair has seized the fancy of the public and they want more – the politics, the people, the plots. Are you sure you've nothing further you can tell me, sir?'

'I have not. Now, if you'll excuse me, I'm off to an important appointment.'

'Sir Thomas, we can go so far as to—'

'Good day, Mr Knowles. Show him the door, if you please, Tysoe.'

* * *

'This'n is Parlby, o' *Wyvern* sloop as was – you do remember, old trout?'

'Channel Groper, smart hand against the smuggling sort, of course I do!'

It was now some years in the past, a fellow commander on small ships in the front line against Bonaparte, but Kydd quickly recalled those feverish days. Parlby beamed at being remembered by one who had done so valiantly since.

Bazely waited until the ale came, then leaned back expansively. 'So. It's got all London a-spin. An' you're one who was there. Tell me, cuffin – how did it go for ye?'

They were in high-backed chairs away from the others, so Kydd described the sight of seven admirals and five captains arrayed against just one man: Popham's unquenchable verbosity; Jervis's lethal questioning. Then he told them of his own testimony, all the time having been conscious that St Vincent would seize on any sign that he'd taken sides. And he ended with the seething crowds insisting their hero had been vindicated when in fact the verdict had undeniably been guilty.

'I'm thinking it all would've been a mort different if he'd held fast to Buenos Aires, o' course. We'd all be dancing t' quite another tune!' Bazely said. 'I wasn't there, but you were,' he went on. 'What do you say, if he'd had the men and guns in the first place, we'd be talking about our South American empire? After all, see what he achieved wi' just two thousand against forty thousand . . .'

Kydd smiled bitterly. 'There you have it. Damn it all, he took Buenos Aires, and God knows, while we suffered under siege for so long, hoping every day to see our reinforcements come, we did have our views.'

'That?'

'That if the Admiralty had seen fit to get off their arses and move smartly with the reinforcements when they got Popham's dispatch in the first place, it would have been quite another story.'

'Why did they not?' asked Parlby.

'Not so hard to fathom. Popham's a genius for making enemies. My taking is that there's plenty he's annoyed in the Admiralty, and they made sure of it that he'd fail.'

Bazely cocked an eyebrow. 'You're probably in the right of it, Sir Thomas. God forbid I start makin' enemies among their sacred lordships.'

'Nor me,' Kydd said fervently. 'I kept a close reef on my jawing tackle – that you must believe – and, in course, our conversation here is just between ourselves, hey?'

The two nodded.

'So. What of the morrow? You said . . .?'

'Ha! A day at th' races, just the ticket wi' the ladies. Never seen a one didn't adore the gee-gees with a gent o' fashion. Will you be—'

There was a sudden scraping from close behind their high chairs and as they looked around curiously a figure scuttled away.

By the end of the day Kydd was five guineas richer and in possession of a solemn promise from Miss Sophy respecting a grand assembly at Almack's in the coming days. They dined well and Kydd went to bed with a light heart.

In the morning he suppressed a stab of guilt. In ships of war at sea they'd be meeting the dawn at quarters, fearful of what the light of day might bring, the captain alert on his quarterdeck at the head of his men.

Here, the question of greatest weight was whether to rise now . . . or stay abed.

He lazed a little longer until his conscience overcame him, then ate a hearty breakfast, nothing to do until he met Bazely later for an evening out on the town.

Tysoe answered a knock at the door. It was the landlord, who made much of offering a morning paper.

Kydd saw that it was the *True Briton*.

As was usual for the quality newspapers the front was all advertisements, the meat always inside.

Curious, he turned the pages. There was a sizeable leading article in big print and—

He jerked upright, frozen in horror.

Legendary sea hero accuses Admiralty of betrayal

It continued:

Sir Thomas Kydd, recently ennobled by our good King George for his gallantry before Curaçao, was heard to reveal publicly that a dastardly plot by the Admiralty saw Commodore Popham, lately victim of a vengeful court-martial, made sacrifice to the political prejudice of a small circle of evil-minded superiors. He went on to say . . .

For God's sake, where had all this come from?

. . . and this newspaper, as ever unflinching in its support of the intrepid Commodore Popham, warmly applauds Sir Thomas's courage in speaking out upon the base iniquity of their impregnable lordships in failing to send due reinforcement to Sir Home, then fighting for his life and the honour of his country . . .

73

His mind reeled.

. . . therefore we demand, on behalf of the people of this great country, that a stern investigation be made at the highest level . . .

He let the newspaper drop to the floor. All over London, these words were now being read by the great and good, lieutenant to admiral . . . and Earl St Vincent. Now everyone would think he'd taken side with Popham against the Admiralty – and he'd never be forgiven.

It was calamitous.

He shot to his feet and started pacing. The other night – in the Quill and Wig when talking to Bazely – the *True Briton*'s reporter, Knowles, must have been hiding behind their chairs, damn his blood!

The urgent question now was what to do – how to find some way to undo the damage.

The only acceptable course was to get the newspaper to apologise, print some sort of article that they'd got it wrong and put it all right.

But how? Go storming in and demand it of the editor? No, it had to be tight and legal – and binding.

He left hurriedly.

'Sir Thomas, a great honour!' The elderly solicitor, Felkins, was mild-mannered but with flint-like eyes. 'How may we assist you?'

It took only minutes to outline the situation.

'Ah. To bring an action against a national newspaper. This is within the competence of these chambers but we will require additional legal counsel. It will not come cheap, sir, and the case will not be heard for some months, a year or more possibly. Are you certain you wish to proceed?'

'Yes, Mr Felkins, I do!' If it was heard that he'd immediately entered legal proceedings against the newspaper, it should go far in assuring interested parties that he'd been misquoted, calumnied.

'Then we shall open the formalities. You are aware that it is the usual practice to post bond, a surety against the expenses of the case?'

'I see. In what amount?'

'Let us first explore for a moment the scope of the action. I understand you wish to prove libel, a traducing in respect of this article, such that upon a judgment in your favour a suitable retraction is published. Am I right?'

'Exactly so.'

'To the essentials, then. Did you in fact utter words in substantial agreement with what is alleged to have been said by you in the article?'

'Well, I . . .'

'I must press you to answer, Sir Thomas.'

'I may have done, but this was in private, in strict confidence among my naval friends.'

'So the article does in fact reflect your views. Hmm. And you spoke before more than one of your friends. This is hardly a private talk. Where in fact did this take place?'

Face burning, Kydd admitted that it was in the Quill and Wig.

'I see. Well, sir, a jury would find it difficult to accept that a common tavern is not a public place. Sir Thomas, I'm grieved to say that I find I'm unable to proceed in the matter. The case has no merit and it would be wrong of me to persevere in its prosecution. I'm sorry.'

'But . . . but what can you advise? Perhaps buy a large advertisement in another newspaper and strongly deny the—'

'I cannot counsel you to do this. It is in effect admitting you are unable to refute the offending article by an action in law against the newspaper in question and would be worse than useless, drawing more attention to the situation. And possibly creating a public furore resulting in factions for and against you, which I'm sanguine you would not desire.'

'There must be something I can do – anything!'

Felkins gave a sad but kindly smile.

'There's no way out, then.'

'Sir, my advice is to take patience. These newspaper squibs have a habit of slipping from the public view and all will be forgotten after the next scandalous revelation appears.'

Kydd clamped a hold on his growing despair. 'I'm grateful for your time, Mr Felkins, and won't bother you further.'

'Thank you,' the solicitor said politely, 'I'm always happy to assist the heroes who defend us so valiantly against the Tyrant.'

Kydd rose to leave.

'Oh, and my clerk will have my fee invoice in hand by now. On your way out, perhaps?'

'Have you seen this'n?' Bazely said, waving the paper. There was no trace of his usual light-hearted manner.

'Yes, I have.'

'You're aware what it means? You're a marked man, cully. People's hero or no, at the Admiralty they'll never let it go.'

'I know,' Kydd said wretchedly.

'They'll not forget what you've said about 'em – they've a long memory.'

'Yes, damn it!'

'And don't think you'll get away with it. They'll find some way to get back at you.'

'I've got my ship, they can't take that away.'

'Tom,' Bazely said soberly, 'something'll happen, and soon – you'll see.'

Kydd felt sick. 'This evening, old trout. I don't think I can—'

Bazely stopped him. 'Let me be straight with you, m' friend. You're now one o' the damned, you've the mark of doom about you, and all the fleet'll know it. I'd take it kindly if you'd understand that I'm not to be seen with ye any more. I'm truly sorry, but I've m' own career to think on.'

Chapter 7

Kydd returned, much chastened, to a concerned Tysoe. Time was ticking by: if he failed to come up with some public gesture of repudiation of the article he'd be damned for a Popham admirer. But by evening he'd reached the conclusion that there was no chance of a resolution.

He retired to bed with the forlorn hope that it would blow over in time and that he'd be well advised to keep away from everybody until it did.

In the morning four letters arrived. The first he opened was from a complete stranger.

> . . . *why should we not believe that yourself and the notorious Captain Popham made assault on the Spanish colonies for reasons of personal plunder? At the sacrifice of lives and honour . . . by turning on the Admiralty who employ you, in the basest way, in that they cannot reply, you have betrayed your comrades and your country . . . the name of Kydd will for ever be associated with . . .*

The others would no doubt be in the same vein. He hadn't the stomach to read them. It was now becoming clear that, far from dying down, the affair was heating up.

In the days that followed there was a riposte in the government-leaning *Review*, attacking him personally and asking why the Admiralty did not take certain measures against him. Worse was the *True Briton*, which ran a feature that listed all the merchants, liberals and others who were loudly supporting Kydd in his comments.

By the fourth day he'd accumulated more than fifty letters. He took harsh delight in not giving the writers satisfaction by reading them, but he knew there would be an accounting. The blow would fall, as Bazely had warned.

Then a letter bearing the Admiralty cipher came. He tore it open.

> *You are hereby required and directed forthwith to repair on board* Tyger *frigate and take upon you the charge and command of Captain in her accordingly . . .*

This was nothing less than a formal letter making him captain of a ship!

> *. . . strictly charging the Officers and Company of the said ship with all due respect and obedience . . . for His Majesty's Service. Hereof nor you, nor any of you may fail, as you will answer the contrary at your peril, and for so doing this shall be your warrant.*

An enclosed slip of paper briefly informed him that the said ship was lying in Yarmouth Roads, of the North Sea squadron under the flag of Admiral Russell, and was ready for sea. No reason was given for the sudden change of captain – or why his prestigious new heavy frigate appointment was being overruled.

Was this the blow he'd been dreading? That he'd been given an inferior command?

But the correspondence carried no implication of retribution. It would have been easy to find some excuse to withdraw the offer of the new frigate and simply let him rot, unemployed.

Why another ship? Was it simply that they wanted him out of the country, back at sea where he'd be out of the way? Or was there a more sinister motive? The only course to find answers and clear up the mystery was to brave the den of lions that was the Admiralty.

As he took his seat in the captains' room it fell silent. Then a whispering began that Kydd pointedly ignored but his face burned.

The clerk hurried away with his card, but there was some delay before he was called.

When he entered the first lord's room Mulgrave greeted him with awkward geniality. Two grim-faced admirals, whom Kydd did not recognise, stood behind him.

'Ah, Captain Kydd. So glad to see you again. Are you well, sir?' He did not introduce the senior officers.

'Thank you, sir. Yes. My lord, I've come this morning to beg explanation of my letter of appointment. It appears to contradict the understanding I'd been given concerning command of the new heavy frigate now building and—'

'Quite. The reason is simple, Sir Thomas. Under advice by my sea lords you're to be given an immediate important appointment, your good self being highly commended by them for the post.'

'May I know the reasons, my lord?'

'Why, your record of service to His Majesty, Sir Thomas. It has been distinguished and meritorious but has certain . . . characteristics that single you out for the post.'

Unease began to spread in Kydd's vitals. 'For this particular ship, my lord?'

'Yes. HMS *Tyger*, frigate.' He went on, avoiding Kydd's eye, 'You see, er, she was lately taken in mutiny and we rather thought a firm hand is what is required to bring her back to fitness for war.'

'And my new heavy frigate? After this may I look forward to—'

'I'm afraid that won't be possible, Sir Thomas,' he said awkwardly. 'It's been promised to the Lord Faulknor.' Mulgrave's manner softened a little. 'Believe that I'm truly sorry to have had to rob the victor of Curaçao of his reward.'

One of the admirals coughed meaningfully, but was ignored.

'If there's anything I might do . . .?' Mulgrave added.

Kydd tried to gather his thoughts. He knew the unwritten rules: if he refused the appointment without good reason nothing would be said, but he would never be offered another command.

There was one thing he could ask. Captains were entitled to 'followers' if they went on to another ship. These were usually midshipmen, coxswain, others, all of whom in *L'Aurore* had long gone on to who knew where. But . . .

'There is, my lord. I desire that I might name my officers.'

There was an intake of breath from the admirals.

This first lord had an army background, which Kydd was bargaining on to work in his favour. He looked surprised but assented quickly enough. 'If it is convenient to the gentlemen concerned, you shall have them.'

To his credit Bazely did come on Kydd's hastily penned request to meet.

'So you've taken a broadside from their lordships,' he said, when Kydd outlined what had transpired at the Admiralty.

Kydd nodded while Tysoe dealt with the drinks. 'I'm to have another frigate. And to sail immediately. I'm supposing it's to get me away to sea.'

'You got off very lightly, m' friend, don't ye mourn it.'

'The ship's been in mutiny and they want me to cure 'em.'

'Ah.'

'Name of *Tyger*, lying at Yarmouth. Don't know else.'

Bazely sat bolt upright. 'Did ye take her? Tell me ye didn't!'

'I did – why not?'

'I heard fr'm Parlby, she was in mutiny well enough. Bloody business, two men dead. Court-martial in Yarmouth found three ringleaders and set 'em t' dangling at the fore yardarm. Kept it as quiet as they could, but there's talk. An' it ain't pretty, m' lad.'

Bazely sat back with a cynical smile, cradling his brandy. 'Neatly done. Very neat – can't ye see it? You've been trussed up like a turkey dinner!'

Kydd glowered, then downed his brandy savagely.

'They offer you a swine of a command on th' strength you're from afore the mast and a hero both. If ye refuse, ye're finished and off the books. If ye take it, there's no chance in Hell you'll succeed.'

'Why not?' Kydd snapped.

'M' friend, think on it. The barky must've been in sad shape to think on mutiny, worse to rise in one. They got

82

three leaders an' made 'em suffer for it. That means the rest get away wi' it, and that's where they stand now, your declared mutineer agin them as were too shy to join 'em, mess an' watch split down th' middle, shipmate agin shipmate. Your petty officers too scared t' keep discipline, the officers in fear o' their lives.'

'I know what a mutiny is,' muttered Kydd, icy memories of his part in the great fleet mutiny of 1797 flooding back.

'Then ye'll know as a ship out o' discipline is a useless fighting machine. They'll not fight for you, an' ye needs must haul down y' flag to the first Frenchy ye sees. Kydd, m' sad cock – ye're meant to fail!'

Kydd scowled at his words. In '97 the ships at the Nore had not been part of a combat fleet, being a reserve of vessels under repair and press-gang receiving hulks. This was different. He was being expected to take a front-line man-o'-war lately in open mutiny out to face the enemy – like a gladiator wearing leg-irons.

'The mouldering bastards,' he said thickly, realising that the proof of what Bazely was saying lay in the fact that it was practice for a ship in mutiny to be taken out of commission, the crew scattered among the rest of the fleet and a new ship's company brought in on a fresh commission.

Tyger would be putting to sea with the mutinous crew unchanged. There was precious little he could do to bring about anything miraculous before the first deep-sea encounter. Bazely was right, damn it to Hell!

It stung. The Admiralty was now against him and seeking vengeance.

He motioned to Tysoe. 'Leave the bottle, if y' please.'

With a troubled glance, the valet left.

Kydd downed his glass in one and poured more. This was

not the pleasant sharing of libations with a friend, it was a furious need to deal with the frustration and anxiety that had built up over the few days past.

'Mulgrave was decent enough. Granted me leave to name my officers while all the time these gib-faced admirals gobbled away.'

'I've not heard o' that ever given, cuffin. It'll make it easier for ye.'

'Ha! Don't know why I asked for it, really. I'm never going t' involve my fine fellows of *L'Aurore* in this stand o' stinking horse-shit!'

Bazely nodded. 'This I c'n understand o' ye, Tom.'

Kydd found himself recounting his brush with mutiny in his first ship as a young seaman but stopped short of telling all of the fearsome days at the Nore when as a master's mate he had sided with the mutineers.

Bazely listened with sympathy.

With exaggerated politeness born of alcohol, Kydd turned to him. 'I'm t' thank you for your concerns, Bazely. As I'm qui' capable o' dealing with this'n.'

'O' course ye are, old trout.'

Befuddled with drink, Kydd felt the anger coming back. It was so bloody unfair. That scuttish reporter had had no right . . .

The evening wore on until it didn't matter any more.

Kydd woke blearily to a disorienting jolting and swaying. It seemed he was in a coach. Opposite sat Tysoe, with a blank expression. Next to him a plain woman was wearing a look of extreme disapproval, her yeoman farmer husband sitting beside him, trying to keep as far away as possible from him.

With a parched mouth and throbbing head Kydd tried to

make sense of it all. Tysoe and Bazely must have bundled him aboard the coach to Yarmouth; he was on his way to take command of *Tyger* – his punishment ship. The other passengers must think him a rake or worse, but at least he wasn't in uniform.

He shied at the thought of stepping aboard in his condition, and rising emotion took him again at the low ploy of the Admiralty, the image of the craggy but malevolent Earl St Vincent thrusting before him.

To go from hero of the hour to this in so short a time was hard to bear and he gulped back his feelings as they entered the outskirts of Yarmouth.

They were dropped at a mean inn and Kydd collapsed wearily in his room.

His head still swam but it didn't stop the thoughts that stampeded unchecked.

One in particular grew. Why not quit while he was still on top? As far as both the public and the navy were concerned he was still a fresh-returned hero, victor of battles and a name to conjure with. If he put to sea in a fragile, mutinous ship and lost to the French, he would never be forgiven by those who had celebrated him before.

It was an attractive course: he wouldn't get another command, but the public would assume he'd left the sea to rest on his laurels, like many had done before him, and Sir Thomas Kydd would find an admired and respected place in society where he would be valued for his experience and achievements.

All this could be thrown away if he meekly took what the Admiralty was dishing out and it went badly.

A maudlin rush of memories came. His translation from foremast hand to King's officer – he'd made the conscious decision to take the harder route, not to be a tarpaulin officer but learn to be a gentleman, enter society on their terms, not his, and it had paid off handsomely. It had been a hard lesson and dear Renzi had been crucial to both the deciding and the accomplishing, so here he was, a figure in the quality and a hero to boot.

Cruel self-doubt mocked. A hero? Was he really . . . one like Nelson?

At Curaçao he'd been consumed in the mad onrush of events and could not have acted differently if he'd tried. And back at Camperdown, where he'd been singled out for the quarterdeck by his courage, there he'd done only his duty, harshly driven by previous events, the great mutiny at the Nore.

Other times: in *Tenacious* at the Nile? He'd taken away the ship's boat in deep pity for the men struggling for their lives in the water. It was only common logic that they themselves would not be in peril so close to *L'Orient*'s gigantic explosion – the wreckage would go up and over them.

It was early dawn when he woke. He threw off his bedclothes and went to the pitcher to slake his thirst.

Tysoe noiselessly appeared with his robe.

'Thank ye,' he croaked. 'I'm not playing their game, Tysoe. Pack the gear, we're leaving.'

The man stood unmoving, his face sagging.

It goaded Kydd. 'Didn't you hear me?' he raged. 'I said I'm not going through with it. Be damned to that parcel o' stinkin' shicers but I'm not falling for it.'

Tysoe's expression turned to one of devastation.

'Get out! Be buggered t' your wry looks! Get out, damn ye!' Kydd roared.

Hesitating, the man gave a dignified short bow and withdrew.

In a paroxysm of fury, Kydd seized the pitcher and smashed it to the floor.

Breathing deeply, he crossed the room, threw open the window and stood there, letting the fresh morning air do its work.

There was a fine view of the sea with the first tentative rays of light tinting it, the sun's orb just beginning its lift to full daybreak. And inside the sandbar a gaggle of ships at anchor, prettily silhouetted against the dawn – King's ships.

Could he turn his back on this?

Yes, he could – and would!

He spotted one anchored apart from the others, like a cast-out leper. It had to be *Tyger*. Waiting for one who could cure a mortal sickness. Could he just leave her to her fate? Damn right he could!

About to close the curtains on the sight he stopped, remembering what he had seen in Tysoe's face. To him Kydd's decision was nothing less than a betrayal: his master was diminished, a coward – no longer one to admire, to serve with pride and respect. Kydd had let down the only person still with him from his early days as an officer. He'd been found wanting – and it hurt.

He balled his fists as a deeper realisation boiled to the surface. If he retired from the navy his public would be mollified, the Admiralty would be robbed of his humbling – but he would have to live with the surrender for the rest of his life.

He couldn't do it. It wasn't in his nature to run – and, by God, he wasn't going to do so now!

'Tysoe! Where are you, man?' He found him in the other

room, listlessly filling the trunk. 'What's this, laying out m' shore-side gear? I said to pack, we're leaving, and that is, I'm to board and take command o' frigate this day – but not in those ill-looking rags!'

Chapter 8

Kydd threw on a boat-cloak and took coach for the naval base. It was only a short distance, near where the Yare river met the sea, an unassuming building with blue ensign aloft. The establishment was the smallest Kydd had encountered, with a modest stores capability and accommodation for the senior naval officer who had charge of a local force of sloops and brigs guarding the coast.

A single marine sentry snapped to attention at Kydd's sudden appearance.

He didn't care how he was received for there was only one objective in his sights: to fight and win in this unfair contest. Nothing else mattered.

Captain Burke rose to greet him with a look of polite enquiry.

'Captain Sir Thomas Kydd, to take command of *Tyger* frigate.' He handed over his warrant.

'Ah. We've had word of you, Sir Thomas.'

Burke was of the same rank as he. In the normal course of events, Kydd could expect to know only the company of lowly sloop captains, mere commanders. He felt the tug of temptation to unburden, but his mood was too bleak.

'I intend to assume command and put to sea with the least possible delay,' he rapped. 'What is *Tyger*'s condition, pray?'

The man's expression was guarded. 'You'll know she's been in mutiny, and that only very recently?'

'I do. That's in the past – I desire only to proceed to sea with all dispatch, sir.' Kydd's instinct was to reach open water, then let sea air and ship routines do their work.

'Very well. She was near completing stores when it . . . that is to say, the mutiny happened, some eight days ago. In all other respects she's ready.'

Like the majority of mutinies this one had broken out just as the ship was preparing to leave – very few happened on the high seas. And as was the way with mutiny, it had been met with instant justice: corpses at the yardarm only days after.

'My orders are to join the North Sea squadron off the Texel. I should be obliged if you'd honour my demands on stores and powder with the utmost expedition, sir.'

'As you wish, Sir Thomas. I should point out the ship is in . . . a parlous state, the people fractious and confused. And not having had liberty –'

'What is that to me, sir?' Kydd said tightly.

'– she's grievous short-handed.'

He went on to add that in Yarmouth there were few trained seamen to be had as protections were insisted upon by both colliers and fishermen.

'Is her captain available to me?'

'Captain Parker? He is – but you're not to expect a regular-going handover from him. The man's in a funk over events and is ailing.'

'I'll see him directly. Do send to *Tyger* that I'm coming aboard by the first dog-watch, if you please.'

Some hours later Kydd was in possession of a pathetic and disjointed account of a passionate rising, put down bloodily and untidily. Parker was a crushed man and Kydd had to come up with his own reading of what had happened.

A weak captain, hard first lieutenant – it had happened so many times before. He didn't need much more. This captain was out of touch with his men, unable to read the signs, and had lost the trust of his officers.

As well, it had been a miserable year or more in these hard seas without action to relieve it, except for one incident. One day, out of a grey dawn, they had come across a French corvette. Finding themselves inshore of it, and therefore cutting it off from safety, it should have been easy meat. They had gone for it, but before they could engage, *Tyger* had missed stays and it had escaped. They had botched the elementary manoeuvre of going about on the other tack.

This could only speak of appalling seamanship – difficult to credit in a frigate after a year at sea – or a command structure that was fractured or incompetent. The effect had been a destructive plunge in morale and men deserting. With the inevitable suspending of liberty ashore, trusties suffered with the disaffected. A fuse had been lit in the prison-like confines and it had detonated when the ship received orders for sea.

God alone knew what he'd meet when he went aboard, for nothing was changed, nothing solved. The men were the same, as were the conditions that had sent them over the edge.

Kydd presented himself at the headquarters of the Impress Service. An aged rear admiral greeted him with respect and politeness but told him there was little hope for men in the shorter term. There was no receiving ship at Yarmouth to hold the harvest of press-gangs, and in the near vicinity pickings were slim from merchantmen unless a Baltic convoy had arrived.

The old sailor suggested that his only hope was to wait for the next periodic sally by his gangs in the north but that was not due for some weeks yet.

Kydd accepted the news without protest, knowing that it was well meant, and from a man retired who had felt it his duty to return to the colours to do what he could for his country, and who had been handed this thankless task. It was only by accident as he was leaving that he found he had been talking to Arthur Phillip, the man who had led the first convict fleet to establish a settlement at Sydney Cove in New South Wales.

There was no point in putting it off for much longer. He would take command of *Tyger* this hour.

But when he returned to the naval base he found waiting not a ship's boat but a local craft: there were not even sufficient trusties in *Tyger* to man a boat.

They put out from the little jetty and shaped course for the ship. She was anchored far out, a diseased ship kept away from the others. It was a hard pull for the men at the oars but it gave Kydd some time to take in her appearance, her lines. A bulldog of a ship. Bluff, aggressive, there was no compromise in her war-like air.

And as far different from *L'Aurore* as it was possible to be. Where before there had been grace and willowy suppleness, it was now power and arrogance, the masts and spars thewed like iron and the gun-deck in a hard line, with guns half as big again.

Yet it reached out to him: this was a British ship, her stern-quarters without the high arching of the French, her timbers heavier – she was built like a prize-fighter.

As they drew nearer he could see other details. She was shabby, uncared-for. Her black sides were faded, and there was no mistaking an air of sullen resignation. Her figurehead – a spirited prancing tiger wearing a crown, its raking paws outstretched – was sea-scoured and blotchy.

Along the lines of the gun-ports boarding nettings had been rigged to prevent desertion and two shore boats pulled around lackadaisically in opposite directions on row-guard.

They shaped up for their approach and Kydd could see other signs of neglect: standing rigging not with the perfect black of tar but with pale streaks of the underlying hemp showing through where worn, the running rigging hairy with use where it passed through blocks and not re-reeved to bear on a fresh length. Even her large ensign floating above was wind-frayed, the trailing edge tattered and decrepit.

A side-party of sorts was assembling and Kydd prepared himself for the greatest challenge of his life.

The pipe was thin and reedy. The man wielding the call – presumably the boatswain – looked as if he'd be better off cosily at home by the fire.

Kydd stepped over the side and on to the deck of HMS *Tyger*.

There was no going back now.

The line of side-party glanced towards him as he came aboard: some with a flicker of curiosity, most impassive and wary. All individuals, all strangers, every one tainted by past events in one way or another.

A tall officer was at the inboard end of the line and took off his hat. 'Hollis, first lieutenant, sir. May I present your officers?' he said formally, in clipped tones.

Kydd would have rather he explained why his boat had not been properly challenged but decided to let it pass.

The second lieutenant, Paddon, seemed mature enough but returned his look with defensive wariness. The third, Nowell, was young, barely into his twenties, and appeared lost and frightened.

An equally young lieutenant of marines, Payne, nervous and edgy, completed his commissioned officers and it was time for the ceremony.

'Clear lower deck, if you please, Mr Hollis,' Kydd said crisply, and while the pipes pealed out at the hatchways and companions he walked slowly aft to take position and waited, watching while the ship's company of *Tyger* came up to present themselves to their new captain and hear him formally take possession of his command.

Kydd had done this before and knew what to look for in an able and trustworthy crew but he did not see it. The men came slowly, resentfully, hanging back, surly and suspicious, crowding the upper deck but with none of the half-concealed banter and out-of-routine jollity of seamen in good spirits. He could feel in the stares and folded arms a dangerous edge of defiance and he tensed as he took out his commission and stepped forward.

"'By the commissioners for executing the office of the Lord High Admiral of the United Kingdom of Great Britain . . .'" He read loudly and forcefully, conscious of an undercurrent of muttering that the dark-jowled master-at-arms did not seem to notice.

The time-honoured phrases, rich with meaning, rolled out

in a measured rhythm ending with the customary '. . . as you will answer to the contrary at your peril.'

It was finished. At the main masthead his pennant broke out, taking the wind and streaming to leeward where it would stay night and day until it was hauled down at the end of the commission or . . .

Now was the usual time for a new captain to address his ship's company, to set the tone, inspire and give ground for confidence in the man to whom the seamen must trust their lives.

But this ship was on the edge and he knew nothing of the men or their mood.

'Officers and warrant officers, my cabin, fifteen minutes. Carry on, Mr Hollis.'

He left the deck, feeling a need to claim at least some part of the ship as his own.

The great cabin, with a table big enough to seat eight, was broad and spacious, the sweep of stern-lights square-patterned and plain, the curve of side timbers restrained but massive.

Pathetic traces of its last occupant remained: a wistful miniature of a woman in lace, an amateurish landscape, a side-table with unremarkable ornaments. On one wall there was a needlework sampler with some doggerel beginning, 'Tyger, tyger, burning bright . . .'

The bed-place still had the cot and wash-place trinkets – it would all have to go. His personal effects from *L'Aurore* were in store and this space would be achingly bare but it couldn't be helped.

His gear was a change of linen only: Tysoe would be arriving in the morning with his remaining baggage and what cabin stores he could lay hands on at this notice.

There was only one chair at the table – it seemed that Captain Parker expected his visitors to stand. He sent for wardroom chairs and settled to wait.

They came together. Kydd motioned Hollis to the opposite end of the table and let the others find their places.

The next few minutes could make or break him. Much depended not on what he said, but how he said it. Should he come in hard and single-minded, tough and unbending – or was it to be understanding and forgiving, willing to give them latitude?

'Mr Hollis, be so good as to introduce the warrant officers.'

The gunner, Darby, came across as professional enough but bit off his words as though he paid for each one.

The boatswain, Dawes, did not inspire. Defensive and fidgety, he did not seem to know the condition of *Tyger* as well as he should, and Kydd sensed an element of mistrust in the attitude of others to him.

The sailing master was of another stamp entirely. In his thirties, young for the post, Le Breton was from Guernsey, its countless reefs and currents a priceless school in seamanship. Soft-spoken and quiet, he let others make the running and only then offered intelligent comment. Kydd warmed to him.

The surgeon and purser were not present, having sent their apologies.

'I'm Sir Thomas Kydd, late of *L'Aurore* frigate,' Kydd began. There was little change in their expressions but he knew what they were thinking: what was a knighted sea-hero so lately in the public eye doing in a contemptible mutiny ship?

'I'm sent here on short notice to relieve Captain Parker.'

They listened in watchful silence.

'I know of this ship's past. Mutiny. I don't care about the details. I don't want to know about it. There's only one thing I care for – that *Tyger* is restored to the fleet as a fighting frigate and in the shortest possible time. Is that clear?'

There were indistinct murmurs.

'I'll not accept anything less than your full duty to that end.'

He paused significantly. 'Their lordships have done me the honour of allowing me to name my officers. That's as may be, but know thereby that if there are any who fail me, I swear I'll have them turned out of the ship directly.'

As soon as it came out Kydd knew it was the wrong thing to say. After their searing experience, and now being virtually imprisoned in an unhappy ship, they'd no doubt welcome any chance to get out.

'We'll start shortly. I'll desire each of you to make report individually and alone, no need for formality. Mr Hollis to begin, other officers and warrant officers after.'

They made to rise and he added, 'I take it the ship is in routine. I've no wish to interrupt. Please continue watches as usual.'

Kydd was left alone and he leafed through the existing captain's orders. There were no surprises, no concessions or idiosyncrasies that he could see. Almost certainly these had been inherited from the preceding captain unchanged. He'd leave it a while before he—

There was a knock and a face appeared around the door. 'Sir?'

'What is it?'

'Ah, then, oi'm Flynn, y'r steward, sir,' the man said, letting himself in. 'Just thought how ye might fancy a bite, like.'

Unusually, Kydd preferred his manservant to attend at his

meals as well. Tysoe was one of nature's gentlemen, quiet and unobtrusive, and knew him and his ways completely. 'Not at the moment, Flynn. I'm very busy. We'll have a talk about things later.'

'The ol' cap'n, why he—'

'Later.'

Hollis arrived soon after and began to lay out the quarters bill. Kydd asked him bluntly, 'How's *Tyger*'s manning at the moment?'

'Complement of two hundred and eighty-four. We're seventy-one short-handed.'

Kydd nearly choked. This amounted to the loss of one in every four men at every gun and station. How could they possibly . . .?

'I see. Are you able to—'

'Watch and stations are complete, quarters one side of guns.'

There was something hostile about his manner, a holding back. Probably he'd considered it reasonable to be promoted to command but instead must stay where he was while an Admiralty favourite had been put in over his head.

A twisted smile surfaced on Kydd's face: he'd find no ally or friend in this officer.

'Well done then, Mr Hollis. I'll take it that we're ready for sea.'

There was no response. The man sat rigid, tense.

'Tell me, what's your feeling of the people at the moment?'

Hollis gave a thin smile. 'Whatever ails the rogues is still there, cankering, festering. They're in an evil taking and are not to be trusted. Nothing that a taste o' discipline won't cure in the end.'

'Very well. I'll take your views into account,' Kydd

98

responded. But this was confrontation, not enlightened leadership – and he'd noticed not a single 'sir' in the whole exchange.

The boatswain was visibly sweating when he lumbered in. He had his books but Kydd waved them aside. 'I see much that needs attention, Mr Dawes. How can this be?'

'Why, sir, and how this ship's bin in a rare state for months. I dursn't come hard on 'em, if y' gets m' meaning.'

The man was cowed and intimidated – broken by the mutiny?

'Mr Dawes, I desire you as of this moment you take survey of this ship. Any line or spar as can't stand up to a North Sea blow, do tell me directly.'

The gunner was brief and to the point. Short near half the quarter-gunners and with a sick armourer, he could not vouch for the condition of their armament, although in the absence of any past engagement with the enemy they retained a full complement of powder and shot.

It would have to do.

Then the sailing master came in.

'Sit down, Mr Le Breton. I've a notion you'll know your nauticals, a Guernseyman like you. I had service there in a brig-sloop some years ago and well do I remember the Little Russell at low water springs.'

'Sir.'

'You've long service in *Tyger*?'

'A little over a year, Sir Thomas.' As with many of his countrymen there was the quaint tinge of a French accent in his words.

'Then you'll know her little tricks. Do tell me something of her, if you please.'

He deliberated before he answered. 'A strong ship, full

bow and clean tail. Likes a blow but needs a firm hand always. Stays about reliably, up to twelve knots on a bowline, and tends to sail stiff, so sky-sails will not be impossible. Deep in the hold and so plenty of endurance.'

Kydd was a little disappointed that for some reason Le Breton had not shown anything like affection for his charge, describing the ship as if standing outside her. But then he reasoned that, after going through what he must have during the mutiny, he could be forgiven for holding *Tyger* at arm's length.

'Fair weather?'

'Prefers a fresh, quartering breeze is all I can say.'

'Foul weather?'

'A good sea-boat. Dry.'

Again, distancing. 'Would you say she's ready for sea?'

'Yes, Sir Thomas.'

'Confidentially, Mr Le Breton, what is your opinion of our ship's company?' It was an unfair question but he could glean much from his answer, both about his crew and the man himself.

'They've been through a serious mutiny, sir. They're melancholic, down-hearted. For myself . . .'

'Yes?'

'I believe there's no better medicine than the open sea. Work to do, a different view each morning. Idleness at anchor can only breed . . . unhappiness.'

'My feeling exactly, Mr Le Breton.'

At last a principal in *Tyger* he could rely on!

As he left, Kydd heard the faint strike of eight bells. The men would be going to their grog and evening meal – he would give a lot to hear what was being discussed over the mess-tables.

The thought of this brought on a pang of hunger. In his anxieties he hadn't eaten since breakfast. And pointedly there had been no invitation from the wardroom to dine.

'Flynn!' he called.

There was no response. The man was probably at his own meal and grog, and Tysoe was still ashore.

Kydd was suddenly overcome by a wave of desolation as he looked about his bare cabin, shadows deepening in the evening gloom. Would he still be standing at the end of it all?

His steward finally appeared, resentfully wiping his mouth.

'You mentioned a bite?'

'Officers' cook ain't victualled for youse . . . sir, and y' didn't bring yer own.'

'Then I'll take a dish of mess-deck scran.'

Flynn blinked and looked at him as though he hadn't heard right.

'Now!'

In theory Kydd was, as any officer, entitled to take ship's food, but the captain?

He ate slowly by a single candle, listening to the timber creaks and muffled groans as the ship lifted to the slight swell and snubbed to her anchor. Every vessel had a different pattern, which varied as well with the direction of the roll. How long would it be before *Tyger's* characterful sounds became familiar?

There was little more he could do before morning but so much would face him then.

Paperwork by the mountain was needed to complete the handover. He was expected to sign that he accepted the state of accounts of the three main figures: purser, gunner and boatswain. In the usual formal procedure he would have taken the time to have them mustered before him, and the outgoing captain would have an interest to make sure it went smoothly.

Now he was being asked to sign for them unseen and take personal responsibility for deficits.

And, crucially, did he have sufficient confidence in his officers that he could take *Tyger* to sea? He had grave reservations, but unless he went with what he had, there would be endless weeks of soul-destroying idleness.

If he ordered them to up anchor, would the hands obey or would it trigger a bigger, final, mutiny?

He pushed away the remains of the pottage, unable to finish. His time among the indulgences of London had spoiled him but these were now but a dream in the face of what threatened.

The empty cabin smelt alien and musty and he felt another wave of bleakness clamping in. He got up and made for the open deck. It was dark and, except for a lanthorn suspended in the rigging above the huddled watch, there was nothing but the dimness of a cloudy night and the occasional fleck of foam.

A figure among the watch group straightened in alarm. It was Nowell, the third lieutenant.

'Why, Mr Nowell, what brings you up on deck?' Kydd asked mildly. 'Is there any complication at all?'

While at anchor it was quite in order for the officer-of-the-watch to spend time in the warmth of the gun-room, on call by the mate-of-the-watch.

'N-no problems, sir,' the young man stuttered. 'I thought as I'd, er, take the air for a space.'

Kydd sensed agitation. 'That's well, Mr Nowell. It's my invariable practice to take a turn around the deck before I retire. Shall we walk together?'

He waited until they were out of earshot and opened, 'Your first ship as lieutenant?'

'Y-yes, sir.'

'A hard enough thing to face a mutiny, then.'

There was no answer, and Nowell stared obstinately out into the blackness.

'I was once in a mutiny,' Kydd continued. 'At the Nore in 'ninety-seven. Not as I'd wish to go through it again. We were five weeks under the red flag and—'

'It's not over, I know it. They're talking, whispering and I'm . . . I'm not easy moving about the ship at night. They look at me without saying anything but when I pass by, give me a cruel smile as if . . .'

Kydd felt for him. The young lad, so recently a midshipman, was having to find his place as an officer and had been pitchforked into the worst kind of situation to be found at sea.

But the fact that he was confiding in his captain was disturbing: it meant that his fellow officers were not extending a comradely understanding, were keeping aloof. Had they retreated into themselves, separate islands, as the vital officer corps of the ship fell apart?

'It'll be better for everybody once we get to sea, Mr Nowell, just you see.'

There was a question he had to ask: 'If you say the mutiny is still threatening, that means the ringleaders were not all caught. Have you any notion of who it could be that's causing unrest among the men?'

'None, sir,' he said miserably. 'They don't talk in front of me.'

Shunned by the men, left on his own by the officers, the young man was going through Hell.

'Well, I don't expect trouble but if you do hear anything, don't hesitate to let me know.'

'I will, sir. And . . . thank you, sir.'

As he returned below he tried to put the young officer's troubled admission aside, but it stayed.

'L'tenant Payne to report.'

The young marine officer came in hesitantly. 'You wanted to see me, Sir Thomas?' He looked as edgy as Nowell had.

'This is a ship lately out of mutiny. I don't want to know what happened, but it would oblige me should you tell me your dispositions for the night.'

He gulped nervously. 'Oh, er, the same as Captain Parker posted up.'

The man had obviously been left on his own to take responsibility for the ship's main recourse in time of mutiny, and he without even the time at sea that Nowell had had.

'So where . . .?'

'Magazine, your cabin, spirit room, gun-room door, hour-glass—'

'Very good.' These were the usual postings but if more were added this would not only goad the sailors to see themselves under guard but would reveal that their captain was afraid.

'Look after your men. We may have need of 'em.'

A brief flash of terror showed. 'Yes, sir,' he replied faintly.

Last Kydd saw the master-at-arms, making his routine report that the silent hours had begun and that all lights had been doused. 'Come in, Mr Tully,' he called, to the dark figure in the doorway. His corporal stayed outside with the lanthorn.

'I want you to tell me the temper of the people,' Kydd asked quietly.

The man's face tightened. 'Nuthin' to report, sir.'

'That's not what I asked. It's your opinion I'd like to hear.'

'Not for me t' say, sir,' Tully said, in a flat voice.

'Well, are they, who shall say, reliable?'

'Can't answer that, sir.'

The gaze was steady, the replies quick. This man stood between the seamen and the officers and in normal times his allegiance was a given. But Tully was a survivor: things could go either way.

It was disquieting. It could only be that subversion was so widespread and imminent that Tully couldn't now risk being seen on the wrong side. Not only did it imply that his loyalty was in doubt but it also appeared he had certain knowledge of a conspiracy that had every chance of succeeding. Why did he not tell of it?

'Very well,' Kydd said. 'You'll inform me if you hear anything.'

'Sir.'

Kydd lay awake, every strange noise and playful slap of a wave jerking him alert. At last he drifted into a troubled sleep.

The night passed without incident and the ship met a cold dawn with little ceremony. If there was any defiance or rebellion brewing they were probably biding their time until they knew more of their captain.

Kydd took a quick breakfast of burgoo and went up to see the change of watch.

It was a sullen, listless show. The oncoming officer-of-the-watch, Paddon, seemed disinclined to stretch them and contented himself with the minimum necessary. Was he concerned that if he had them knees down deck-scrubbing it would provoke a rising?

Now would be the right time for a taut captain to come down hard and lay out just how he wanted his ship run, but Kydd had a bigger problem: how to get *Tyger* to sea.

At ten a shore boat brought the welcome sight of Tysoe, imperturbably seeing his baggage and stores up the side.

'The boat to lay off,' Kydd ordered.

To his credit, there was only a moment of wide-eyed disbelief as Tysoe entered the bare cabin. Kydd had ordered all of Captain Parker's personal ornaments and knick-knacks to be placed in the cot and taken ashore by the waiting boat. For some reason he kept the needlework but everything else went.

'Sir Thomas,' Tysoe said, troubled. 'You have no bed.'

'Draw a hammock from slops, there's a good chap,' Kydd replied instantly.

The morning went quickly. He put off seeing the purser with his accounts but asked for the master, telling him they would be going to sea in the near future. 'To join the North Sea squadron. Do you have good charts from the Texel to France? I rather think that's where we'll be employed, Mr Le Breton, and I've never served on that coast.'

'Ah, I'd feel happier were I to have the new "Antwerp approaches", sir. May I send for one?'

Kydd nodded, distracted. Sooner or later he must complete the paperwork and put to sea. If anything, this would be the thing to bring it all to a head. But it couldn't be delayed for much longer – all the time they lay at anchor they were consuming victuals and water and the canker of idleness was spreading.

Then he had an idea. An outrageous idea that fitted the bill perfectly, solving several other problems for him but which was fraught with unknowns. In the privacy of his cabin he penned a quick note, sealed it and asked the officer-of-the-watch to signal for a shore boat. When it came he handed over the message with the instruction to deliver it to the senior naval officer, Yarmouth Roads.

Too late to change his mind now.

He slowly paced the quarterdeck, sniffing the wind, a fresh westerly breeze. 'Mr Paddon.'

'Sir?' There was wariness in his manner.

'Hands to stations to unmoor ship.'

The officer goggled. 'W-what did you say, sir?'

'Am I being unclear? I ordered stations to unmoor ship. Carry on, Mr Paddon.'

When a ship put to sea there was a notice period – known as being under sailing orders – that warned all that the ship was about to leave port. The Blue Peter was hoisted to signify it.

Men on liberty ashore would repair back on board, mail would be quickly written and consigned to the mailbag, last-minute stores and various to-ings and fro-ings would occur before the final ceremony of closing up the ship's company for departure.

Kydd had cut through all that: they were going to sea with no warning period whatsoever. If there were troublemakers, they had no time to plan anything and could not, for they would be closed up at stations.

Tyger had no men at liberty ashore, no ties, no port admiral and ceremonies: there was no need of a notice for sea.

A frigate generally victualled for a six-month voyage – three months in home waters – and, stored not so long before, *Tyger* had all the sea endurance she needed to join the squadron.

In his note he had explained that his orders had stressed

his losing no time in joining the North Sea squadron and this had priority over petty matters such as signing for stores accounts and the like.

They were on their way.

There was utter confusion for the first ten minutes or so as men below had to be convinced of what was happening but eventually they took station.

He didn't ease the pressure and, with the capstan manned, he gave orders to get under weigh.

In rising feeling he saw that he'd been right: in the controlled chaos that was putting to sea there was no one point that gave chance for a banding together in refusal.

In well-worn sequence the anchor was won clear, sail dropped from the yards and, with a gentle sway to leeward, *Tyger* got under way for the open sea.

'Set sea watches, Mr Hollis. I'll be below.' It would be some time before things settled down, and he allowed himself a grimace of sympathy for the hapless officer-of-the-watch.

But it was done! *Tyger* was safely to sea and the healing could begin.

Chapter 9

It took hours only to reach the rendezvous line of the squadron on the front line of the defence of Britain.

Vice Admiral Russell's force of a handful of sail-of-the-line came into view off the treacherous and hostile Texel and Scheldt. Their task: to keep the seas in all weathers and deny Bonaparte any chance to break out. A no less vital role was the tight blockade on the Netherlands coast and all the enemy ports either side to choke off trade in this new economic war.

The squadron was part of the strategic North Sea Fleet under Admiral Keith, with responsibility for the entire eastern approaches to Great Britain. With the Channel Fleet they'd succeeded in keeping England inviolate for more than a dozen long years.

Admiral Russell was welcoming. A frigate with its multi-plicity of possible roles was the most valuable reinforcement a lonely commander might wish for. And at this remove Russell seemed not to have heard of the turbulence following Popham's court-martial.

'You'll stay for supper, my boy?'

'I thank you, sir, but there's a matter of urgency I need to discuss with you.'

'Oh?'

'My ship *Tyger* was lately taken in mutiny.'

'I know about that. I'd hazard you're going to tell me you've an entire new ship's company and wish to train 'em to satisfaction. I can give you a week, that's fair enough.'

'No, sir. Her company is the same as rose up.'

Russell frowned. 'Not dispersed among the fleet at all? A rum do, that. The Admiralty knows b' now what's needed in such. I'm supposing they're hard pressed for men – ha! Ha!'

'Ah, yes, sir. It's just that—'

'I do apologise, Kydd. I didn't mean to make light of such a drear affair. So all the officers the same, Captain Parker sent away and you hoisted in to sort it all out?'

'Sir.'

'So. I don't envy you, old fellow. Are they settling, at all?'

'This is what I wanted to speak to you about. They're as fractious and discontented a crew as ever I've seen and show not a sign of being reconciled. I don't wish to revile Captain Parker's commanding but—'

'You can take it I understand what you're saying, Kydd. And a hard thing indeed when you know not a soul of your seamen, their temper.'

'I should tell you now, sir, that my judgment was to get to sea as quick as I could, and sadly therefore had to put aside much in the way of paperwork – handover accounts and similar until I'm in better position to give them attention.'

'Quite right.'

Relieved, Kydd went on, 'Sir, what I ask is that you give orders as will see *Tyger* in action against the enemy just as soon as we may.'

'Done!' Russell agreed. 'The inshore flotilla. Hard sea conditions but you might even snap up a prize or two, you never know. First, you'll have to satisfy me you're in a right and proper state for it.'

'The ship's new stored, no powder and shot expended, and my boatswain's survey gives me no concern for her sticks. It's her crew only – that they'll fight when called on. If they do, I can't think of a more sovereign medicine for what ails 'em.'

'And if they don't?' Russell frowned. 'I admire your spirit, Kydd, but you're taking a risk, m' boy. Can I interest you in taking a fair-sized detachment o' marines who—'

'Thank you, sir, no. They'll not pull together if they see they're under guard, and when they finally do, they're to see it's all their own efforts.'

'Well, anything I can do, give me a hail. Go now, you've things to attend to. I'll have Flags get your orders and signals to you as soon as I can. Then it's up to you.'

Unfamiliar with the waters, Kydd carefully scanned the charts. He had a frighteningly short time to get to know them enough to risk throwing his frigate into action.

The Texel, their nominal blockade station, was an island with the naval base of Den Helder that lay strategically across the main entrance to Holland's inland waterways. North of it were the Frisians, an endless stretch of sandy islands in a continuous chain to Prussia, nothing but low dunes and mud-flats. South of it were the fertile plains and main population centres of the Netherlands – Amsterdam was beside the waters of the Zuider Zee, safely inland halfway to Rotterdam in the south, itself not far from the great port of Antwerp and the Scheldt river.

He summoned the master, the only one in the corrosive atmosphere he felt able to turn to. 'Mr Le Breton. As you know, I've not seen service in these waters and I'd value your advice concerning likely objectives for our operations.'

'Of course, sir,' he said politely, but with an odd avoiding of Kydd's eye.

Was this a reluctance to be drawn into the often dehumanising confidences of preparations for warfare? What Kydd was asking was irregular: a master had no part in operational planning and he was in effect opening a discussion about a course of action, a matter more properly for his lieutenants. But Kydd didn't feel inclined to rely on them at this time and continued, 'I have it in mind to give the men a taste of action, a chance to pull together.'

'Sir.' The guarded reply gave nothing away.

'And what I'm thinking is, to do the Dutch a mischief on their own doorstep. Tell me, how does shipping go about its business in these waters?'

Le Breton rubbed his chin thoughtfully. 'The larger ships may never put to sea for fear of the blockade and cruisers offshore, and only a gale of wind from the south-east will release them. The smaller – well, with the coast so risky for ships as we, these are really meat for our inshore squadron, the sloops and cutters.'

'I know that, but times are strange and we've a need to prove ourselves. So – what game is there for the taking?'

The master looked away, then turned back with an aggressive gleam in his eyes. 'The coast trade, this is in sizeable fluyts, which are flat-bottomed with leeboards and can take

112

to shallows that vex our sloops. They are then safe, for no lesser draught cutter or similar dare approach a vessel of such size.'

'So these then sail up and down the coast without being troubled by our cruisers?'

'A considerable trade. When they sight same they head inshore where we cannot follow and continue on. But if we could just . . .'

'I can see what you're saying, Mr Le Breton. *If* we could . . .'

He traced the depth figures for the coast south of the Texel. It was certainly hazardous: sandbars marked that were twenty miles or more out to sea, reversing tidal currents and worse, but if they were bold and conditions were right . . .

Nearly halfway down, the five-fathom soundings closed with the shore until at one spot they were within three miles. If they dared everything they could be within full view of any watcher ashore.

It was what he wanted.

Kydd had at one time been a privateer master and knew the tricks. Now what he was after was a nearby cove, an inlet, perhaps, or a creek. There were few but there was a small river issuing out at a place called Breesaap and well within the area.

'Here,' he announced, tapping the chart. 'And this is what we'll do. I mean to cruise along the five-fathom line, give 'em all a fright, as we'll be plain within sight. They'll think it a lunatic captain to bring a frigate in so close, and to take no chances with such they'll go to ground somewhere safe, which I'll wager will be this pawky river here.' He smiled. 'And then it turns into a cutting-out expedition.'

'Sir. The hazards are many. We draw twenty-two feet aft

and in anything of a sea . . .' In a five-foot swell, at the lowest point there would be just the length of a man's arm depth of water under their keel.

'Indeed so. But mark that we have at the moment a slight swell only, a fair sou'-westerly as goes with the coast, and not forgetting that these depths are chart datum only. Should we have the tide in our favour I do believe we must attempt it.'

The full moon would bring spring tides, in this part of the world a good six, seven feet.

They had a chance.

'We go in, Mr Le Breton. Keep it quiet for now while I complete plans – and thank you.'

'You'll be acting soon, sir?'

'That you may believe,' Kydd said firmly.

'Yes, sir. Then might I know what you have in mind until then?'

'With these winds, I'd think to press on north. Why do you ask?'

'Oh, just that I'd give it thought for anything I can suggest to you, sir.'

It didn't take long for Kydd to work up the plan and he asked the first lieutenant to come to his cabin.

'This is by way of a bracer, Mr Hollis.'

'Sir?'

'I've a notion we'll be seeing some action against the enemy this night. We've some preparing to do.'

The man jerked upright in astonishment, banging his head on a deck beam. 'You can't be serious, sir!'

'Why not, pray?'

'The – the men, they're near mutinous, out of discipline!'

'All the better to find something to give 'em heart, don't you think?'

Hollis looked incredulous. 'How can you know they'll fight? This is rank lunacy and—'

'Yes, Mr Hollis?' Kydd said dangerously. 'Am I to believe you're not in favour of taking the war to the enemy?'

'Well, I—'

'Then don't you think we'd better begin our preparations, sir?' He pointed to the chart. 'We close with the coast to the five-fathom line and cruise north. Then—'

'To . . . to five fathoms?'

'Yes. Tide's with us from into the dog-watches – there'll be fifteen feet or more under us. The Dutch run their fluyts inshore – you knew that, o' course . . .'

'As you say.'

'We give 'em a fright by being so close, and they go for the nearest bolt-hole to wait it out until we're past. That's just what we want 'em to do, for that night we go in with the boats, cut out any we find and . . . What is it ails you now, Mr Hollis?' Kydd finished irritably.

'I can't help remarking it,' the first lieutenant said stiffly, 'we're officers in the boats without marines, trusties? This is begging for calamity! The ship's in a state of mutiny and we're inviting anarchy. Have you never suffered mutiny? I have, and—'

'Enough!' Kydd grated. 'There's one damn good reason they'll follow and you've not the wit to see it, sir!'

'Oh?' Hollis's face was now a mask of hostility.

'This is not a yardarm-to-yardarm smashing match with a butcher's bill to follow, all for the honour of the flag. No, sir! In this little exercise they stand to make a fat bag o' prize guineas each, but only if we return to write their tickets.'

Kydd had the satisfaction of seeing the dawning of respect and continued, 'I want the barky on a long board to seaward, to return on the starb'd tack to meet up with the coast at fifty-two twenty latitude where we'll begin our cruise north.'

'Sir.'

'Carry on, then, Mr Hollis.'

After the lieutenant had left, Kydd reflected on what had been said. He, too, had suffered mutiny, the biggest the navy had ever experienced, but this was quite another species. At the Nore there had been good and clear reasons for the rebellion but here in *Tyger* . . .

He couldn't put his finger on it; this was not how he'd foreseen things developing once they'd put to sea. There'd been no healing that he'd been able to detect. The same closed faces, silent and sullen working together, whispering, off-watch hours spent below instead of the usual hum of companionship on the fore-deck – all was profoundly disturbing.

Having served before the mast himself, Kydd knew what it was: the dire portent of a deeply riven ship's company, the sign of 'us and them' that was at the root of the most violent surges of discontent.

And it was unbridgeable. The worst thing he could do was address them with words to try to allay it, for that would be admitting his anxiety. Through his lieutenants he might have been able to spread a message that things were on the change for the better but with Hollis in open confrontation with them, his second, Paddon, retreating into himself and the third, Nowell, terrified and next to useless . . .

This united front against him, undiminished and sustained, implied that ringleaders were still at large, planning and co-ordinating. If so, what in Hades did they expect to get out of it? The most probable was that his sudden dash to sea had caught them by surprise, but that would suggest the rising was just to be deferred, almost certainly to when they got back to port. There was precious little time left to him to bring about a miracle.

None of it made any sense. But what he was about to do was the best course: to conjure some prize money for them.

So much hung on the next few hours. If his reasoning was wrong and they came away empty-handed, it would be a serious matter. But in his bones he knew he was right: this was the way merchantmen behaved under threat.

Sitting alone in the bare great cabin, he hailed for Tysoe. There was no refinement such as a summoning bell yet. He waited. 'Tysoe – ahoy there, you rascal!'

His manservant appeared at the cabin door. 'Sir Thomas?' he said thickly.

Kydd started in surprise. Tysoe had a bloody scrape on the side of his face, his nose was battered and he moved awkwardly. 'You've . . .'

'A disagreement only, Sir Thomas, not to concern yourself.'

'Who did this?' Kydd demanded harshly.

'As I said, sir, there's nothing that may disturb you. Is there something I can do for you?'

'This is abominable. I want to know who did this to you, understand me?'

In dignified silence Tysoe made ineffectual gestures of tidying up; Kydd knew he was going to get nothing from him.

They closed with the coast and began their cruise northward soon after midday. Tension rose as they took up parallel to the shore. A handful of miles distant only, the low and

117

featureless coastline was plainly visible and, pitilessly revealed by any with a telescope, near useless for navigation.

Here the shape of the seas was disordered, toppling and confused as they passed over the notorious sand-waves below, mighty tide-shaped subsea hillocks that directed surging currents vertically as well as to the side.

The day was perfect, however, and the wind fair and brisk. Sail was seen up against the shoreline but their rig quickly identified them as small fry.

What Kydd was after were the substantial two- or three-masted vessels seeking to break blockade. Hopefully *Tyger* had been quickly sighted and they had scuttled in haste to their hideaways. Or was he was wrong in his reasoning? After all, the Dutch had their spacious inland waterways and canals: why risk the open sea?

And would his men obediently man the boats for the dangerous pull inshore on a hostile coast, or would it bring on what he feared most? As far as he could see, preparations were going ahead without the men balking, even if there was still that same surly reluctance. Was the prize-money bait working? He allowed himself a stab of hope.

Later in the afternoon a sharp-eyed lookout swore he'd seen a three-master close inshore in the haze far ahead but it had then disappeared. This was in the area more or less up with Breesaap but the vanishing act was worrying. It might indicate anything from sail being doused, to invisibility as it snugged into its bolt-hole, to the casual alignment of the masts of two lesser craft.

He would have to take the chance.

For their expedition the launch and red cutter would make the assault and the barge and blue cutter would lie off to seaward, with extra men if needed.

What had been a simple enough drill in *L'Aurore* was turning into a gravely difficult task. In any close-quarter fighting it was vital to have good fighters to the fore, to press on courageously and without hesitation so others would follow in good heart. Weak or timorous men leading would hang back at the first opposition and all would be lost. Where was he going to find these good men?

He'd decided he would lead in the launch and Paddon would follow in the cutter. It was usual for the captain's coxswain to take the tiller and stand by him in the action to follow. Aboard *Tyger* none was yet rated, but Kydd knew whom he wanted. And he'd tell him to muster a boat's crew he could trust. It would be very much in his interest to go for good men to fight beside him – and thereby Kydd would have his picked men.

The one he had in mind was a fair-headed giant of a man, part of the fo'c'slemen and therefore a tried and reliable seaman. He was quiet and, like so many big men, moved lightly. He carried himself with dignity, almost aloofness, which Kydd put down to his Scandinavian origins. It would be too much to expect him to be completely unaffected by the malign influence of whatever was behind *Tyger*'s malaise but at the least he could be relied upon to be steady.

He entered the great cabin warily to stand before Kydd, shapeless cap in hand but with a direct and fearless gaze.

'You're Halgren. A Dansker – Norwegian, perhaps?'

'Strom Halgren of Kristianstad. A Swede, sir.' The voice was deep but soft, the manner wary.

Kydd had an instant taking to the man, the silent strength in his character reaching out to him. This was a seaman who would be an asset in any man's watch.

'Halgren, I've a mind to rate you up. To captain's coxswain. How does that suit?'

To his surprise, the man dropped his head and shuffled his feet without answering.

'You don't want the rate? I can't force it on you.'

Halgren remained doggedly silent and didn't look up.

'Very well,' Kydd said, trying to keep the bitterness from his words. 'Carry on.'

Nonetheless he'd see that Halgren was at the tiller when they went in.

As dusk settled, any anxious eye ashore would have spied *Tyger* giving up her audacious but fruitless inshore cruise and making for the open sea. But Kydd knew that no master worth his salt would hazard his ship by resuming his voyage among the shoals in the hours of darkness – their prey would still be where they'd been driven.

The frigate sailed hull-down offshore in the gathering dark, then hove to. Conditions were unequalled for what they were about to do: calm seas, a little night breeze and complete darkness until they struck. Then there was the rising of a full moon to aid their carrying to sea a strange vessel.

The only unknown was *Tyger*'s men.

Boats were manned, arms handed down and stowed, a massive axe new-sharpened for cutting the cable. Paddon in the red cutter embarked and lay off, a shapeless shadow on the gloom of the sea. Kydd couldn't help noting that there'd been none of the familiar nervous bravado and black humour as they boarded, only a sly and secretive murmuring. But, thank God, they had obeyed his orders and were on their way.

For all that, he was taking no chances, waiting until the barge and other cutter had been filled and pushed off. Then he swung over the bulwark and dropped into the sternsheets of the launch.

It was too dark to make out faces properly but he felt reassured at the sight of Halgren's bulk at the tiller and the stolid mass of men at the oars.

'Give way,' he ordered, then added loudly, 'And stretch out – we've a purse o' Dutch gold each to collect this night.'

This brought an immediate ripple of comment and the occasional chuckle. He'd been right: there was no doubting what had them obediently at the oars now. Dare he hope that this was the turning point?

The boats headed in; he was following a compass bearing to Breesaap and the unnamed little river.

With all his heart he willed there to be a fluyt lying there . . .

Dimly ahead he could see the occasional line of white at the edge of the sea and he strained to make out features in the low coast, anything that pointed to a river mouth. He couldn't see one that did – and there was no time to be flogging up and down looking for it. When the full moon rose, the alarm would be raised and then there would be no chance.

They had to turn either up or down the shoreline. Which was it to be? It couldn't be far off – the compass bearing would set them in the right area – but if he chose the wrong side they could be uselessly pulling away from it.

He concentrated furiously. The bearing was right but if the slight breeze from the south-west had taken more effect over that mile or two, then . . .

'Larb'd, follow the coast,' he snapped.

The tiller went over and, snatching a glance astern, he saw the other boats conform. If he'd guessed wrong—

There! A clump of bushes and another distant from it and nothing between.

Heart bumping, Kydd made motions for the other boats to come up.

'Lay off. I'm going in to reconnoitre,' he whispered urgently.

It was a modest enough river, easing out to sea through the dunes but with depth of water enough to take a reasonable-sized vessel.

There was a bend to the right; they eased up to it to see around and – lights!

Not one but two ships lay at rest by the bank, quiet, unsuspecting.

'Back!' Kydd growled, hoping his elation didn't show.

Quickly he came alongside Paddon's boat. 'Two of 'em and I want both. Merchantmen, shouldn't cause you problems. I'll take the further, you the nearer. Be sharp about it – moon rises in half an hour.'

'Aye aye, sir,' Paddon said, with irritating detachment.

The men bent to their oars and the launch surged forward, the cutter not far behind. Pulling like madmen they entered the river and started around the bend. There was no time for stealth or elaborate cunning – this was an assault by storm!

It worked. Only when within a hundred yards or so did an urgent cry go up from the nearer vessel and dim figures boiled up from below.

'Lay out like good 'uns, lads!' Kydd roared, slapping his side with the intensity of his feeling.

They passed the first ship as several muskets banged off, a derisory defence in the blackness. They came up fast on the further one, hearing harsh shouts behind them as Paddon's crew prepared to board.

It was happening: they were going to do it!

Forcing coolness, Kydd concentrated on the approach. There were figures active on the quarterdeck but none forward – they'd board by the fore-chains.

The launch curved in and in the same moment that the bowman hooked on the rest were swarming up, screeching and yelling, effortlessly swinging over on to the little fore-deck. Caught up in the excitement, Kydd did likewise, adding his battle cries to the others.

At the sight of the boarders the Hollanders wasted no time. In a body they splashed into the water and struck out for the shore.

They had the ship! Against all the odds, they had taken a prize.

Something caught his eye. A rocket soared from Paddon's ship and burst overhead with a huge lazy sparkle. What did it mean?

But Kydd had no time to think about it.

'Cable party – do your duty!' They loped forward with the big axe.

Inland and not so far away came an answering rocket, curving balefully across the sky. And another, further away.

'Topmen, lay aloft!'

There was canvas bent on the yards as he'd known it would be – with a small merchant-service crew it would not be a popular move to send it down when they'd be putting to sea the next day.

He sniffed the wind. A cast to starboard should do it. At this rate they'd get away well before . . . An indistinct figure was standing before him. 'Sir, can't cut the cable.'

'What? Get on with it, man!'

'It's made o' iron. Shackles an' all.'

'Well, cast it off, damn it!'

'As it's secured t' a strongback an' we can't make it out in the dark. Two on 'em, too!' said the unknown voice, resentfully.

Kydd tried to think.

In one stroke the tables had been turned. Even if they found the tools it would take hours to cut through a wrought-iron cable link and this showed forethought: the cable would be doubled around the bitts and taken ashore again with its final securing hidden in the darkness. But if it were not released . . .

On the night air came the faint but urgent sounds of a martial drumming. Somewhere a militia had been called out to resist the English pirates.

He should have known! The inshore squadron of sloops and others would have made this coast a fearful place through cutting-out expeditions of their own. This was only the Dutch taking measures to deter them, and he had blundered into it.

Gulping down his bitterness he bowed to Fate. He must abandon their prize and return empty-handed, and with the militia on their way, he would not even have the satisfaction of properly setting fire to the ship.

'Into the boat,' he said dully.

Was there nothing he could do? Valuable articles to be seized at all costs were the navigation charts and papers that could provide precious intelligence.

'Keep alongside until I get back,' he called down to the launch, and hurried below.

The master's cabin was easy to find but in the darkness impossible to ransack. He lunged outside to find a lanthorn but the haul was miserly. Outdated coastal charts and papers in Dutch that could mean anything.

He clattered up the companionway to the deck – already there was an appreciable ghostly lightening as the moon began lifting. Running to the ship's side he—

The boat was not there!

He looked about frantically and spotted it disappearing into the murk after Paddon.

They had deserted him, left him to be taken or killed! The realisation shook Kydd.

A trumpet call sounded in the blackness, much nearer than the other.

He had to do something! But . . . what?

If he made it to the shore and blundered about looking for a path he'd quickly be found by the locals. And in full uniform what chance did he have in the open country?

Seething with rage and hopelessness, he could do nothing but wait for capture – or some militiaman cutting him down with a musket.

Then, with a catch in his throat at the unfairness of it all, he saw a miracle: out of the same blue river haze, the launch, pulling fast for the ship. They had come back for him – but, in God's name, why?

Now was not the time to question it and he swung down into the fore-chains and when the bows of the launch touched he jumped in, knocking the bowman aside.

'Back-water!' It was Halgren's voice, now harsh and commanding.

Kydd made his way aft clumsily through the rowers just as shouts erupted on the opposite bank.

'Hold water larb'd, give way starb'd.'

Through the reeds there was a vivid gun-flash of a musket and then another.

The launch was curving around and unavoidably nearing

125

the bank. Half a dozen gun-flashes came at once, the *whuup* of a ball close, but Kydd knew that they had destroyed their night vision by firing too early and there was little to fear.

He thumped into the sternsheets seat and sat back, breathing deeply with tension and relief.

He got back aboard no wiser as to why they'd come back for him. Was it Halgren, or was it a general consensus with his agreement? The big seaman disappeared quickly and Kydd decided against calling him back for explanations.

But he felt a tiny stab of hope. At least someone cared about what happened to him.

On the other hand, there was no denying the mood was ugly. In the darkness he heard savage shouts, sour rejoinders.

Hollis barely concealed his contempt and Paddon needed prodding to admit the fact that he'd even had one deserter, leaping ashore to vanish into the night. He'd pleaded confusion as to why he'd left Kydd to his fate. Most likely he'd made away without seeking orders just as soon as the situation had become plain.

Only the sailing master showed any kind of sympathy, asking for details and commiserating quietly.

The boats were hoisted in and the ship reverted to sea routine, heading out under easy sail.

Kydd took a cold supper, still shaken by events. Too keyed up to sleep, he decided to take his customary turn around the upper deck even though it was well into the night.

It was chilly and he hugged his coat to him as he left the group around the helm and made his way forward.

The ship heaved at an increased swell. Cloud had come up to blot out the moon – there'd be heavy rain before morning.

Jumbled thoughts raced through his mind as he slowly paced along, the darkness now near absolute, the white of wave-crests almost luminous out in the blackness.

He reached the fore lookouts and returned down the opposite side, trying to come to a conclusion. But nothing made sense and things were getting worse.

Turning at the taffrail aft he began another pace forward.

The officer-of-the-watch, Nowell, and the quartermaster stood silently, watching in blank curiosity.

Passing the boats on their skids amidships Kydd felt the beginnings of despair. There was only a short time to pull off a miracle and he didn't have anything. If he couldn't . . .

At the sound of a sudden scuffle behind him he twisted round. A blow aimed at the back of his head took him on the side instead. Disoriented, he fell to his knees – and they were on him.

Instinctively he seized a rope and clung to it, lashing out viciously with both feet, which connected solidly with two of the assailants. They staggered back, the third irresolute.

Kydd let out a choking cry, then a shout.

His attackers turned and fled but in the dark he hadn't been able to see their faces clearly.

Gasping, he waited for help – but then, in sudden dawning realisation, he understood: he was succeeding. He now had conclusive proof that there was an evil mind behind the whole thing, holding his crew in thrall by some means but now so desperate to stop him that he'd taken the grave risk of having him attacked on his own ship – because he was getting through to the seamen.

In a haze of relief that overcame his pain he heard running feet and the quartermaster, followed by Nowell, arrived.

'Sir – what . . . .?'

Kydd was ready for it. 'Oh, it's nothing, Mr Nowell. I tripped and hit my head. That's all. A bit of a sea tonight, don't you think?'

If he could just find this devilish plotter and put an end to him – he'd cleanse the ship of the man's malign sway over the Tygers.

Chapter 10

Nowell stood down from his watch at midnight, handing over to Paddon, who listened with barely hidden contempt to his recitation of sail carried, course and weather conditions before dismissing him without a glance.

The young third lieutenant left the deck, desolation descending on him, as it seemed to so much these days. The ship was a nightmare of contradictions, a parody of what he had learned of sea service as a shy but eager midshipman.

The men were unreadable, their looks calculating and hostile, and he sensed a dangerous, edgy undercurrent. Their captain, the acclaimed Sir Thomas Kydd, didn't seem to have any notion of how to put an end to it.

He reached the bottom of the ladderway and turned aft for the gun-room when Smyth, a master's mate, emerged out of the gloom. 'Begging y'r pardon, sir,' he said, with a sketchy salute. 'The master wonders if he can have an urgent word wi' ye.'

At this hour? But it was the courteous Le Breton, who,

of all of the quarterdeck, was the most calm and reliable. No doubt it would be for a good reason.

'I'll come now.'

'Ah, not in the gun-room, sir. In the boatswain's storeroom, like.'

Nowell thought this odd, but then assumed that the problem was in the odorous recesses of the orlop, forward.

Smyth carried a lanthorn, and as they approached the store, Nowell saw several figures outside, waiting.

'The master?'

'Inside, sir.'

Nowell entered cautiously. Le Breton was sitting on an upended barrel at the far end among the hanging tackles, blocks and tools. A lamp on the deck cast a ghostly light up at him in the gloom. The reek of rope and Stockholm tar was almost overpowering.

Smyth followed him in. The door closed quietly.

'Do sit,' Le Breton said politely, indicating another barrel near him.

Nowell hesitated. 'Master, is there something you wish to discuss? I've just come off watch and—'

'There is. A matter of great importance to us all.'

Nowell sat and waited uncertainly. There was a gleam in the master's eye, which unsettled him with its uncharacteristic fervour.

'What I have to tell you is a fact that you must accept here and now, for there is no changing it. It will happen and there is not one thing anyone can do to stop it.'

'Go on,' the third lieutenant said, as a chill stole into his vitals.

'Tomorrow there will be a rising of the hands and this vessel will be handed over to the French Navy.'

Nowell gulped. 'How do you know this, Master?'

Le Breton smiled thinly, 'Because it will be my doing. I will not bore you with details but it's sufficient to tell you that my allegiance lies with the people, not their rulers.'

'You're French! An agent sent to—'

'It doesn't really signify. What does is that tomorrow a frigate will rendezvous with this vessel, summoned by Mr Paddon's "deserter". It will be the signal for us to complete our task and take charge of this ship. It will then be handed over and carried in to port.'

'I – I don't believe you! The men would never—'

'My dear sir, they will – and I'll tell you why. I have five other agents to spread my tidings that every man who stands on the right side when called upon will then be the possessor of a purse of gold, together with safe passage to any country or territory they so desire. Those who do not . . . well, let us say they must take their chances.'

Nowell tried to think. It must have been in the planning for some time, awaiting a suitable victim, and they had found one in *Tyger*. Le Breton was masquerading as the sailing master indicated on his warrant, the actual one removed. And with a grave shortage of seamen it wouldn't have been too difficult to insert those five others – ostensibly volunteers of foreign extraction – into *Tyger* to plan and supervise the disaffection and poisoning of the crew to the point at which they could be relied upon to rise in mutiny at the right time.

A climate of fear would have been easily generated by the simple means of keeping secret the identity of his agents. In this way any who tried to raise the alarm could never know if he had been seen and betrayed. It explained the fear and distrust that had driven the Tygers into a fragmented mass.

A sudden jet of terror came. It made no sense for them to let him in on their plans unless . . . 'Why are you telling me this?' he croaked.

'We need an officer.'

'Why me?'

'Mr Nowell, it doesn't take much discerning to mark you out as a very unhappy man,' Le Breton said softly, looking up at him in a kindly way. 'You've suffered more than most at the hands of those who call themselves your betters. You deserve a new start.'

With a numb inevitability Nowell saw where it was all leading.

'As an officer, your share of the proceeds in gold would be much larger, undoubtedly sufficient to set you up as a gentleman of affluence, of leisure. In Portugal, the Caribbean, even America, you could be sure of a welcome and a place in society as a respected figure of means. Who knows? A good marriage, a family . . .'

A vision grew and matured, an intoxicating one of dignity and esteem, of repose and peace in a country far away from the madness of war.

Le Breton smiled. 'You're considering your position. That is good. But you're wanting reassurance that you're coming over to the winning side and I can appreciate that. Let me tell you more of what's planned and why it cannot fail.

'It requires only a dozen or more to declare themselves ready to act and I can state positively that we have more. These are merely the active players – many others will join us when they see how swiftly we succeed when my order is given, and how much they stand to lose if they don't.' He spoke as if he was giving a lecture, calm, reasoned and persuasive.

'You see, we have surprise on our side. While attention is on the enemy frigate none will suspect us. All men will be at their guns – you'll know how grievous short-handed we are. At my signal – well, I'll leave the rest to your imagination.'

There was more to it than that, obviously, but the essence was there. On the next day *Tyger* would be carried over to the French. This was now a foregone conclusion. The question was, where did he stand?

'What assurance have we of our reward?' Nowell found himself saying.

'If the word of a gentleman is insufficient for you,' the master said reproachfully, 'then might I ask you to conceive of the gratitude to be expected by a government presented with the gift of a most valuable ship of a thousand tons? You can be sure it may be measured in gold.'

From behind him there was a fruity chuckle from Smyth.

'And may I point out to you that this whole proceeding is ordered, with decorum and completely bloodless. What more can you ask of me?'

Nowell realised that in less than twenty-four hours he could be on his way to a new life, an end to this nightmare. 'What do you want me to do?'

'Merely to assist me in making the affair bloodless. When my order goes out it will be with moves that are intended to prevent retaliation. Our gallant captain will be taken by surprise but will order the crew to resist. Your job is to countermand his orders and advise the men to stand down and accept the situation. At best they will do so, you being an officer and one they are accustomed to obey. At worst there will be confusion, which will enable us to consolidate our position. You understand me?'

133

It made sense and Nowell would seem to be trying to pacify a dangerous situation. With this one act he would secure his golden future!

'And this is all I'm called upon to do?'

'Only this. A small enough thing, I would have thought.'

His mind blazed with feeling. To have sweet revenge on Paddon, Hollis and all those who'd made his life a wretched misery! To be quit of this existence for ever and— 'I'll do it.'

'Good. It's no discredit in any man to bow before the inevitable. Go to your rest now, Mr Nowell, and we'll speak more of this tomorrow.'

Was that all?

'Yes. Well, good night, Master.' He left.

Le Breton motioned briefly. Two men immediately detached from the several waiting outside and followed noiselessly.

Nowell lay in his cot, his mind racing with possibilities and fears. When next he slept, it would be in a very different world, one that until an hour ago he could never have dreamed of.

Could he find it in him to shout down Captain Kydd when he roared out at the seamen to stand by him? He quailed at the thought, then realised that this wasn't what he was meant to do. His would be the voice of reason, of sorrow to have to bow to the twist of fortune that saw them all at the mercy of a higher force, to which it would be no dishonour to yield.

Yet Kydd had been the only one who'd been good to him, walking the deck and hearing his anxieties with sympathy and understanding. He wasn't like the others. And he was a hero, a real one, and had bothered to speak to him kindly when he must have been distracted beyond imagining by the condition of his ship.

It troubled him. This man had accepted the mission to go to *Tyger* and make her whole, and it was not his fault that he was being invisibly thwarted from within.

What would happen to him? Like all those who remained steadfast and true, he would be condemned to rot his life away in a bleak fastness somewhere. The seamen would be taken to a wretched prison or put to hard labour in some ancient port. None would have any chance of release or exchange – Bonaparte knew that British sailors were preventing him achieving his destiny and would never let them go.

All the while he himself would be taking his ease in a far country on the proceeds of his . . .

A surge of shame burned inside him.

He couldn't do it. Not to Captain Kydd – and the true-hearted seamen who stood by their ship.

In a rush of determination he threw off the covers and found his watch-coat, drawing it on over his nightshirt. Inching open the door of his cabin he peeped out into the gun-room. It was steeped in the darkness of the silent hours and he tiptoed out.

He was ready with his excuse to the marine sentry at the gun-room door but the man was standing glassily upright and didn't even blink as he passed.

It was only three steps to the aft companion up, carefully avoiding the rows of hammocks stretching away in the gloom, swaying gently together with the easy heave of the ship. As his head rose above the level of the hatchway he paused. This was now the gun-deck, open to the sky forward, and close by, under the quarterdeck above, the captain's cabin spaces.

Nothing moved.

Reassured, he stepped out on to the deck and went quickly to the door of the cabin where a marine sentry stood.

'To see the captain,' he said in a low voice.

The sentinel hesitated, then stood aside.

Nowell made to open the door – it wouldn't open. He tried again. It was locked!

'Why—'

He never finished the question. The smack of the musket across his skull, in a blinding flash, ended his purpose there and then.

'Look again. He must be somewhere, damn it!'

Even as he spoke Kydd was caught in the chill of a premonition. Nowell was cruelly dejected and it was not unknown for men to suicide by throwing themselves over-side during the night watches – or might there be the more sinister explanation that he had had wind of a plot and been silenced?

Either way a ferocious tension now gripped *Tyger*. Hardly a word was spoken as men padded about with animal wari-ness, some deliberately keeping their gaze turned away forward, others stopping to stare back at the quarterdeck as if to be the one to witness a descending catastrophe.

Whatever cataclysm was threatening would not be long in breaking.

Turning out the marines was useless. They could not stand to indefinitely, and in their pitiful numbers were a pathetic deterrent even if they could be fully relied on.

There was only one way to deal with it: to stand fast and confront whatever evil finally burst out.

The shadowy organising genius must show himself, and then at least he'd know who his adversary was and what he was up against. An end to the ominous stormcloud of dread and foreboding. No more—

'*Deck hoooo!* Dead astern – a frigate!'

Nobody moved. It was already topsails up from the quarterdeck. For some reason the main-top lookout had not sighted it until almost too late. One thing was sure: it could not have come at a worse time.

Tyger went to quarters in an agonisingly long time – but there were men at the guns, others at their station. Kydd vowed that if it was an enemy they'd make a fight of it.

The sailing master appeared beside him.

'Ah, Mr Le Breton,' he said, with as much spirit as he could muster. 'There – a frigate. An enemy, do you think?'

Calmly the master shielded his eyes to look. 'A Frenchman you may believe, sir.'

Its profile lengthened as it altered course to come up on them from seaward. It was now possible to make out the tricolour – it was the enemy right enough, a heavy frigate with many more men than *Tyger* if it came to boarding, which, of course, was the last thing he intended.

Kydd smiled grimly. If it was thinking to cut off their escape to seaward then it wasn't the first to misread a British opening manoeuvre.

He considered his tactics. The Frenchman had the weather gage and was positioning to cut across any move by him to reach the open sea. The land was under his lee to starboard and the winds going large. Unless he wanted a prolonged chase, with his ship as the prey, there was only one alternative. 'Helm up, hard a-larb'd!' he ordered crisply.

By hauling to the wind he was going to throw his ship across the bows of the other in a raking broadside, or if

Tyger couldn't reach there in time, at the very least he could bring about a close-range combat.

Obediently, as the yards were braced up their bowsprit swung across the horizon and they began closing fast.

'We'll give 'em a what-for they'll remember!' Kydd said to the master.

'Stand to your guns, lads!' he roared, as they came up on the enemy – who unaccountably shivered sail and slowed as if in welcome.

Kydd glanced across at the master, puzzled . . . Then the whole world went insane.

Le Breton darted to Paddon and snatching his speaking trumpet, bawled something in French to the deck in general.

A dozen or more men wheeled about, snatched pistols from the open arms chests, then returned to stand behind each gun, a pistol trained steadily on the gun-captain.

Another half-dozen took position along the centre of the deck, their pistols roving about, alert for the first to make a move among the crew.

'Any who moves – any at all – will be killed instantly,' bellowed Le Breton, his own pistol trained on Kydd's belly. 'Stand still by your guns and no one will be hurt. This vessel is now in possession of the French republic!'

Kydd let out his breath. It was Le Breton. The calm Guernseyman had master-minded the whole thing in as neat a coup as may be conceived. There could be no man who would sacrifice himself to certain death by being first to resist – and all the time they were racing on to come under the guns of the French frigate and ignominy.

'Douse that rag, Gaston!' the master snarled.

A man loped to the halyards and swiftly hauled down their colours.

An appalled paralysis gripped the ship. Pale-faced, Hollis stared at Kydd in supplication while Paddon stood motionless, his expression blank.

'She acknowledges, comrade,' came a voice to one side.

'Very good,' snapped Le Breton, and his eyes flicked to the frigate in triumph.

At this Kydd flung himself away sideways and down, rolling with it in a frantic dive. The pistol banged but it missed and he was up, in one fluid movement yanking his sword out and lunging for the master, the point just an inch from his throat, stopping him in his tracks.

Kydd's blade held him while he circled for what he wanted – a pistol from the arms chest. He brought it up and held it under the man's jaw, letting his sword slide to the deck.

'Move!' he hissed, jabbing, crowding, until his back was safely against the main-mast.

'I have your leader, you mutinous dogs!' he bellowed. 'He dies if you move an inch!' His mind raced. It was unlikely they would throw down their weapons to save his life. He had a desperately short time to turn the tables.

'You! Haul up our colours,' he barked to a nearby sailor.

The man hesitated so he ground the barrel of the pistol into Le Breton, bringing a cry of pain.

Tyger's ensign rose again.

'Bear away,' he snapped at the stupefied helmsman. 'Do it, damn your hide!'

Kydd's eyes never left Le Breton's.

Now there was a chance.

'Listen to me, all of you!' he roared. 'Our colours are a-fly again and we're running free, heading out. The Frenchy thinks he's been tricked. He'll never come for you now!'

In the tense stillness he shouted, 'You're outnumbered, damn it! How long can you stand there like that? For ever?'

He saw Le Breton's arm stealthily creeping up and grinned mirthlessly as he viciously ground the pistol barrel into him again.

He might have the ringleader but he was faced with a standoff without resolution.

It could go either way and all it would take would be—

'I'll give you a chance!' he bellowed. 'Stay where you are and take your chances at a court-martial – or go overside now and let your friends pick you up!'

His talk about the French seeing trickery might or might not be true but these men would see it as a done deed. The whole rising was designed only to hold *Tyger* in a state of suspension for the few minutes until the ship was safely under the guns of the other. Without the enemy guns, there was no threat.

First one, then another ran to the side and plunged into the sea. The rest broke and raced to follow.

It was too much for Le Breton. With a screech he threw himself at Kydd, the sudden movement catching him off-balance, his pistol discharging harmlessly into the air.

They fell to the deck, the Frenchman gouging, smashing, bludgeoning in a demented frenzy that Kydd couldn't stand against until, quite suddenly, it was all over.

A giant of a man had snatched the crazed attacker bodily off him and held him aloft.

Dazed, Kydd could only watch as the Swede swivelled and threw the man down directly across the iron barrel of a gun. The sound of his maniac shrieking snapped off in the same moment that Kydd heard the sickening crack of a broken spine.

The last of the mutineers had flung themselves over the side and were now just a straggle of dark heads in the white of the ship's wake. Kydd breathed deeply. With their guilty fleeing he had cleansed *Tyger* of the evil that had been infecting her.

Chapter 11

'Well, 'pon my soul!' Admiral Russell sat back in admiration. 'And I honour you for it, m' boy! It was the thing to do, to be sure. You'd never have irons enough to keep 'em all under eye, an' without you knew who was a rogue, well, that was a rattling good catch to root 'em out, I'm bound to say.'

'Thank you, sir. I was concerned that without prisoners for the court-martial it would—'

'Never fret, sir. There'll be no court-martial, conceivably perhaps a quiet court of inquiry. Admiralty don't like it known there's unrest, let alone Frenchy agents abroad.'

He reflected for a moment. 'You'll be grievous shorthanded then, and lacking a third lieutenant.'

'And a sailing master, sir.'

'Quite. I see nothing for it but a quick return to Yarmouth with my note of encouragement to the Impress Service. You shouldn't suffer botheration over a new third – there's enough young sprigs around kicking their heels.'

'I'll sail this hour, sir – and thank you for your understanding.'

When the anchor went down in Yarmouth Roads Kydd could not suppress a shuddering sigh. He knew so little about any of his company: both they and his ship were still largely an unknown quantity.

But now there were other things to see to.

The first was to send off his official report of events to the Admiralty, including a mention that his actions had had the complete approbation of the admiral commanding the North Sea squadron.

In a separate cover he took up their commitment to allow him to name his officers and asked for Bowden and Brice – he didn't want to see Paddon again. And more in hope than expectation, while acknowledging that even as the rate of his ship did not warrant it, the appointment of one Clinton as acting captain, Royal Marines, to stand by his current raw lieutenant after his ordeal would be much appreciated.

There was one other he would give a great deal to secure: Dillon, his former confidential secretary. He hurriedly penned a note, regretting the lack of notice and urging him, if interested, to lose no time in joining.

There was no question of liberty ashore for the Tygers. 'They have to earn it first, Mr Hollis!' he had said loudly, on deck, within the hearing of nearby hands. He wasn't going to risk losing even more men in the nervous, febrile atmosphere that followed recent events and before he had had a chance to pull the ship together.

The first lieutenant was treating him with something like hero-worship – or was it that it was in Kydd's power to have him replaced as well? He'd decided to keep Hollis because he knew the ship and seamen well and would probably be amenable to Kydd's ways in the future.

Kydd stormed ashore to the impress office, leaving Tysoe

to do what he could to ransack local shops and chandlers in an attempt to make his living spaces comfortable, and to lay in cabin stores as he saw fit.

'Not much of a catch locally,' he was told, on showing Russell's letter of encouragement, 'but with this authorisation, I can send to Sheerness for you. Can't promise you'll get your full entitling but . . .'

Back on board Kydd publicly railed at the purser for not moving faster in securing the sweets of the land for his ship's company: 'soft tommy' – baked bread in place of hard tack – beer, fresh beef, greens and all the little things that went far in making a sailor's life a modicum more bearable.

When that had been put in train he called for the big Swede and put the question again.

'Aye, sir,' Halgren said slowly. 'I'd like it right well, sir.'

He now had a captain's coxswain.

On the third day the press tender arrived with barely satisfactory numbers, and later Bowden and Brice reported aboard, recounting how they had suddenly been plucked from the disconsolate crowd of petitioning lieutenants in the Admiralty and told to join HMS *Tyger* that very day.

Barely suppressing his delight as he welcomed them, Kydd told them briefly what had happened and they handed over orders they were carrying.

Kydd was a little taken aback as he was under the command of the North Sea squadron and therefore not normally at the disposal of the Admiralty.

In his cabin he opened the packet quickly: a single page only. It seemed it was convenient to their lordships that *Tyger* lay at Yarmouth at this time, for they were minded to detach her for a short but important service: he should hold himself at readiness. In the event a Mr Stuart of the Foreign Office would make contact with him in the near future for a mission of great discretion.

His eyes narrowed. Was this to be a malicious complication to crowd in on *Tyger* before he had worked the ship up to something like effectiveness?

But it was no use worrying about it: this Mr Stuart would reveal all when he came. Meanwhile he had other matters to attend to.

There was the mountain of paperwork he had necessarily set aside. If only Dillon . . . but might he be expecting too much? So little notice and the young man might have decided that the comforts of Eskdale Hall were to be preferred to the stern realities of sea life.

He took a deep breath and set to on the pile.

When the Foreign Office emissary arrived in Yarmouth he insisted he saw Kydd in the office of the senior naval officer ashore, with no one else present.

'You come highly recommended, Sir Thomas,' he said, studying Kydd with interest, 'for this mission, which is of a singular importance, I might say.'

'Thank you, sir. Yet I should warn you that my ship is untried, many of her crew having newly joined. In the article of fighting I cannot be sanguine that—'

Stuart smiled thinly. 'It should not come to that, Captain. A straightforward assignment but one that touches on the very core of England's struggle against Bonaparte.'

Kydd felt irritation. 'I've had my share of hard service, Mr Stuart. Be so good as to tell me the details directly.'

'Very well. What I'm about to tell you is for you alone. Not another soul, you understand me?'

'Yes, sir, I do.' Kydd sighed.

'Then this is the essence. It is of the utmost importance to keep Tsar Alexander in the war against the French. Since the fall of the Third Coalition after Austerlitz, Russia is the only power of significance left on the continent of Europe to oppose the tyrant. At all costs we must preserve relations or we stand on alone – none other by our side!'

'I see.' This much was common knowledge and Kydd had only recently returned from a close liaising with Admiral Senyavin of the Imperial Russian Navy.

'Captain, we want you to convey to Gothenburg a subsidy due the Tsar, in the amount of one half of a million pounds in specie.'

Kydd caught his breath. Never in his life had he heard of such an amount mentioned anywhere. With his own pay recently raised to fifteen pounds and eight shillings a month, he'd have to serve something like a thousand years and more to see its like. 'That's a great deal of responsibility, Mr Stuart.'

'Your ship is the only one of sufficient weight of metal available. Now, please to pay particular attention. At seven in the morning a detachment of the Royal Horse Artillery will arrive in Yarmouth with their field pieces. In the limber of every odd-numbered gun will be concealed a number of cases labelled "Explosive Shot". These will be taken directly to the jetty where your boat will be waiting under guard from the Yeomanry. Clear?'

'I understand.'

'Once aboard you will treat the cases as experimental ordnance, to be stored in the ship's magazine.'

'Yes.'

'On arrival at Gothenburg you will be approached by a

member of the British Embassy, who will be identified by a paper that you will now sign.'

'Presumably sent ahead by dispatch boat.'

'Quite.'

Kydd scrawled his signature on the paper.

'You will then follow any instructions you are given. Do not fail, sir, upon your peril!'

The next morning the men in *Tyger*'s launch and a cutter lay on their oars and precisely on time two carts, guarded importantly by the Norfolk Yeomanry, ground to a stop by the jetty.

A mystified gunner stood by Kydd's side on the rain-swept pier.

With a flourish, the subaltern in charge produced his paper and considerately held his cape over Kydd while he signed: never again would a fabulous treasure such as this be in his charge.

'Strike the cases into the launch – and be damned careful of it!' he snapped nervously.

Half a million pounds, it seemed, required seven stout chests, and as they took their place along the centre-line of the big boat, Kydd suffered a moment's giddy vision: halfway to *Tyger* the weight of the gold becomes too much for the planking, which gives way and sinks the launch, putting the fortune out of reach for ever.

But he was being paid freight money, awarded to the captain of any naval vessel charged with the carriage of bullion in consideration of the worry at its presence. Lately the amount had varied, a small percentage of the value, he'd heard. And on half a million that stood to be a useful sum.

In heartfelt relief he saw the cases swayed aboard and

carried forward by the gunner's party to the main magazine. Fending off murmurings from the gunner, he turned to greet a welcome figure.

'Mr Clinton!' He started in mock surprise at the brand new epaulettes. 'Or should it be Captain Clinton?' He shook hands warmly, touched to see the man who had calmly done his duty in the final days at Buenos Aires only to be cut down with a near-mortal wound at Constantinople. 'You are well?'

'Perfectly recovered, sir – that is, Sir Thomas,' he added, with a broad grin.

There was no sign of Dillon but Hollis was waiting with a surprise. 'The pressed men mustered and rated, sir. No prime hands but the Sheerness draft has a few that look promising.' He waited a moment, then added, in an odd voice, 'And when shall you rate the volunteers?'

'Volunteers?' Kydd said, in amazement. Who the devil would sign up to join a ship recently in mutiny? Nevertheless he promised he would see them shortly.

In his cabin Tysoe was distracted with the unpacking and stowage of the new furniture and stores. Kydd left him to it and returned on deck. 'So. Where are these volunteers, Mr Hollis?'

They were brought before him . . . Toby Stirk, gunner's mate and fine *L'Aurore* seaman. Next to him, Doud and his inseparable shipmate Pinto, shuffling their feet bashfully.

'You're right welcome, all of you,' Kydd said, conscious of Hollis's curiosity. 'As I'd never wish for a better parcel o' hands. But how . . .?'

'Heard you was shipping out, thought we'd join ye, sir! Wouldn't be right, puttin' to sea without we looks after the barky.'

Kydd knew there would be no further explanation given.

Pinto and Doud would certainly find a petty officer's berth but for Stirk this was another matter. He'd been a gunner's mate, which could prove difficult as *Tyger* had one already, a wizened old sailor who was apparently a friend of the gunner. A comfortable situation like yeoman of the powder room would serve for now.

A little later a jolly man of some years in a characterful tricorne of a past age clambered aboard. 'Cap'n Sir Thomas?' he breezed, snatching off his hat. 'An' I was tipped the wink b' Mr Burke as y' might be in need of a sailing master. I introduce m'self – Nehemiah Joyce, master o' the *Ramillies* as was, come t' offer m' services.'

Kydd had reservations at the man's age. 'What recent service have you, Mr Joyce?'

'Why, not three years afore – *Queen Caroline*, ninety-eight.'

'I thought she was a guardship at Sheerness, and hulked?'

The man's face fell. 'As it was m' last ship before I swallowed the anchor t' be with m' lady wife in Yarmouth.'

It was the way of it for a long-service warrant officer, given a soft berth in his final post in the navy before retiring. For all that, he looked spry enough.

'You've seen your share of service, I'd wager.'

His open features creased with remembrance. 'Aye, sir! Started in *Ferret*, cutter, removed into *Terrier*, sloop, and after . . . No, I tell a lie, it were *Crescent* first, then *Terrier* – rare sailer, she! Nothing from Ameriky could stay with her on a broad reach. Then it was—'

'Frigates?'

'Sir,' Joyce said, affronted. 'First one I has after I gets m' paper from Trinity, an' it were *Quickmatch*. Naught but a sluggard, whatever we does. In *Lacadaemon* 'twas another story. Why, when we had bowlines up—'

'Thank you. So now you think to abandon your good wife to return to adventuring at sea.'

'Oh, but that's me answerin' the call t' duty, sir!'

'I see. Very patriotic of you, Mr Joyce. I can only offer you an acting position.'

'That'll do me, sir.' His joyous smile couldn't help but bring a twitch to Kydd's lips.

'We sail shortly on a voyage to Gothenburg. See we've charts to suit, if you will and welcome on board!'

With the secret freight in her bowels he had no intention of delaying and, despite the hour, by the first dog-watch, stations for unmooring ship was piped.

Kydd watched discreetly. There were no visible signs of discontent among the seamen but on the other hand neither was there the peculiar mix of exuberance and rueful acceptance that usually went with a ship outward bound.

It was now entirely up to him. The heart and soul of *Tyger* was his to win.

Then as they tripped their anchor, just as it had happened in *L'Aurore*, the last boat from the shore brought Dillon, a cheery figure standing perilously in the sternsheets of a fishing smack.

It was their first night at sea and Kydd's invitation to the gun-room came promptly. Their heads turned respectfully as he entered and took his place at the end of the table.

'So kind in you to invite me,' he said formally, to Hollis on his right, the mess president.

A subdued murmur was his polite welcome from the rest.

Kydd looked forward keenly to this time: it was the only occasion aboard ship that he could reach out and make sociable contact with the officers who would run his ship for him – and, of course, for them to take measure of the captain who would rule over them.

'Our pleasure, sir,' came the first lieutenant's equally formal reply.

Down the table faces steadily looked his way, expectant or apprehensive, curious and guarded.

He motioned to the servants who stood behind their chairs. 'Gentlemen,' he began genially, 'I'd be interested in your opinion of this Frontignac from my private stock. It's much cried up in London, these days.'

When they were served, Kydd tasted his and went on pleasantly, 'I rather think I should introduce to you Tygers the strangers we see here tonight. On my larb'd side is Mr Bowden, a gentleman of long acquaintance, who was with me at Menorca when we entertained the Dons with our patent signal method of pantaloons and bloomers.'

It was gratifying to see the goggling eyes at this admission from the legendary Sir Thomas Kydd.

'And opposite is Mr Brice, who's no stranger to the North Sea, preferring more of a blow than is offering now. It was diverting indeed to see him standing forrard in *L'Aurore*, scornful of the Turk that they had no bigger shot to throw at him than a marble ball a fathom around.'

This brought admiring chuckles and a tangible easing around the room.

'And at the end there you'll find Master Dillon, my confidential secretary, a scholar and staunch landlubber, whose ancient Greek confounded not only the treacherous Ottomans but also the ship's entire complement of midshipmen.'

This was met with relaxed laughter.

'Captain Clinton sits yonder, new-rigged and splendid, but

I remember him best as a pox-doctor flamming the Spaniards in South America.'

Incredulous looks flashed across the table at the pink-faced Royal Marine.

'And, finally, our newest member who seems set fair to be our oldest – Mr Nehemiah Joyce, sailing master, who I'm sure if pressed could conjure a yarn or two.'

A babble of talk rose as the evening progressed, and while the conversations ebbed and flowed, Kydd discreetly took in the others.

Dawes, the portly boatswain, was clearly out of his depth, fiddling with his glass and confining his talk to the tight-faced gunner, Darby, who held back from the growing merriment.

Oxley, the surgeon, a portly but sharp-eyed individual, sat back with an expression of distaste, listening to a laboured tale from Harman, the shrewish purser and across from them the absurdly young lieutenant of marines, Payne, who sat petrified and mute.

There would be many more miles under their keel before this company became one.

With the arrival of the lamb cutlets, Kydd judged the time right and gave a smart *ting* on his glass to call their attention.

'Gentlemen – Tygers all! A traditional first night at sea. But this one – this is out of the ordinary run and by any man's reckoning a special one. It marks a dawning, a new life – a fresh beginning. We've been through a fierce time, when no man may trust his shipmate, fear and dread stalking our decks – who can say where it'll all end?'

He let it hang for a space before he continued. 'But it's over! Finished – the canker purged! Never more will this King's ship need hang its head in shame. I for one refuse utterly to bring it to mind ever again and will hear nothing from any who can't let it go. We're outward bound, shipmates, to adventures and challenges we can't possibly dream of, and I'm here to tell you, this world holds more in store than ever we can imagine.'

'Shakespeare,' murmured Dillon, and was immediately silenced with a glare from Bowden.

'Gentlemen, we're all on notice. We in England lie under such peril as never was, since even before Trafalgar. Boney stands astride the whole of Europe, and if we in *Tyger* are to play our part we're going to have to be a damn sight better than we've been. I'm sure we will, but each one of you must haul and draw alongside our company with a whole heart and to one purpose.'

It was reaching most, but not all.

'In token of which I can tell you that we're on a mission of national importance, their lordships having seen fit to entrust this to *Tyger* and no other.'

This brought a ripple of interest and, despite himself, the gunner dared, 'This special ordnance, sir. An' what is it exactly, as must be kept from us?'

'Shame on you, Mr Darby!' Kydd came back without hesitation. 'Are you not aware that Swedish iron makes the best guns there are? And what better to trade with than . . . I cannot go further, you must understand.'

The gunner subsided, satisfied. The *Naval Chronicle* had been detailed in its descriptions of all manner of new inventions, from Captain Popham's catamaran torpedoes to Major Congreve's war rockets, and it was not outside the bounds of possibility that a two-way exchange was taking place, with *Tyger* in the centre.

Kydd drew the table's attention again. 'So I ask you to

charge your glasses, gentlemen, and drink a toast. To *Tyger* and the Tygers! And the future that both will share!'

Kydd woke early. The passage to Gothenburg was not long, some four days or so at most, but he was eager to take the earliest opportunity to put *Tyger* through her paces. Although he was anxious to deliver his cargo as soon as possible, he decided to take advantage of this short voyage to make acquaintance of his new command and at the same time shake the vessel down into an effective fighting force.

He knew already that she was a sturdy, no-nonsense British-built ship, with all the advantage this gave in foul-weather sailing, endurance and sheer strength of timbers, but there was more to it than that. How did she stay about in a gale? Was she a witch in a quartering breeze, like *L'Aurore*? What was her best point of sailing? In a fight, how much could he rely on her clawing up to the wind under topsails, true and staunch? Only a thorough exercise of her qualities in the open sea would reveal this, with other eccentricities left to discover in due course. And it would be his pleasure to bring them to light.

He was up with the morning watchmen in the last hour before daybreak, his mind alive with ideas for the day. It was a simple, straight-line course across to Gothenburg, in this south-westerly able to be done in one board. It would be comfortably far from the hostile northern European coast and it was vanishingly unlikely that they would run into anything capable of troubling a well-muscled frigate like *Tyger*.

Light was stealing in over the cold grey seascape, picking up the startling white of seagulls, a suffused gold in the morning haze promising a broad sunrise.

The first thing he needed to do was a series of timed

staying-about manoeuvres: tack and wear, in these brisk breezes a useful indication of what could be expected in winds both greater and less. To follow would be an hour at the guns, in slow time in deference to the first lieutenant's new quarter-bill. Then back to sail-handling – and the vital knowledge of just how close to the wind *Tyger* could manage with all possible measures taken.

It would be interesting as well to—

'*Deck hoooo!*' came an urgent hail from the main-top lookout. 'Sail – three points on the st'b'd quarter!' A careful scan of the horizon as the dimness of night lifted had revealed something in sight.

Should he go after a potential prize at the small risk of his precious freight?

'I see a frigate two, three miles, an' she's alterin' towards!'

The probability was that she was British but there was no harm in taking precautions. Automatically his mind meshed with the elements. The stranger was downwind from them: by now there was no land cramping their room to manoeuvre and no change in weather threatened.

'What's her colours?' bawled Kydd, through cupped hands.

After a space a reply came back: 'Don't see none!'

This was odd. A British frigate on sighting another would fly the private signal, then, if necessary, fire a gun to leeward, inviting a correct response – and this was wasting no time in shaping course to intercept.

'Bear away, our private signal and a gun!' he snapped.

Out of consideration for the ship's company, and assuming that their course through British waters would not meet with an enemy, he hadn't followed the usual war precautions by meeting the dawn at quarters with all men at the guns.

'Turn up the hands, if you please.'

If the stranger was a forgetful Britisher there was no harm done but if—

'There's another! Two points t' larb'd, an' heading us!'

Kydd's senses tautened. It could be a classic French tactic, a pair of hunting frigates, and they had found prey. As they lifted above the horizon he fumbled for his pocket telescope.

He saw immediately: the new stranger running for them was big – and with its larger beam and heavier spars must be a razée. These were ships-of-the-line levelled down one deck to form powerful frigates and were rare in British service. It had to be an enemy.

Another cry came down from the lookout: the other was not a frigate but a corvette, lighter than they but rigged similarly and still of significant force.

'Clear for action!'

Kydd sniffed the wind: steady from the south-west. A bit of a lop to the sea but nothing to worry about.

It was unusual for the French to show such aggression, even at odds of two to one. Their reason for being was commerce raiding and they had every incentive to avoid unnecessary damage in a frigate duel.

The corvette was further off, more evidence that they were in a line of search but, whatever the situation, he couldn't risk his precious freight. They would run for it.

Then everything changed.

'A frigate!' cried the fore-top lookout with an out-flung arm pointing ahead.

There, at speed, a full-rigged frigate was closing with them to cut off any escape.

This was now deadly serious. Their precautions of secrecy in Yarmouth had been in vain. Somewhere in the chain of arrangements the shipment had become known about and word had got out.

Their course from Yarmouth to Gothenburg was a direct line. Simplicity itself to mount an ambush, and the French had made the most of it, boxing him in.

Three of them: the corvette alone he could be confident of handling, include the new frigate and it would be a hard-fought match, but with the razée as well he was up against a terrible foe.

And with an untried crew. It was impossible – in some way he had to even the odds.

Far spaced on either quarter astern were the first two, still some miles distant but the one ahead was only a mile or two away, close-hauled across their course to cut off his retreat.

'Go for the Frenchy ahead,' he instructed the conn, and concentrated on his tactics.

The first thing to do was give the opposing captain something to think about – which was that while *Tyger* was running downwind with every choice of course, the other was hard into the wind to cross their bow.

Its captain would therefore be anxious to avoid a fatal move: that Kydd would time his approach such that at the last minute he would put over his helm and pass behind, delivering a devastating raking broadside into the unprotected stern. While it was possible to choose any direction moving forward consistent with the wind, no square-rigged ship could ever sail backwards to rectify a wrong move.

Nonetheless there was going to be one lunge only with this advantage and Kydd couldn't afford to make a mistake.

Hollis reported the ship cleared for action. 'To quarters,' Kydd ordered.

They raced over the pretty morning sea, wavelets exuberant

at meeting the new day, the sky now blue and cheerful, a lone seagull wheeling and keening.

'Keep our bowsprit square on his main,' Kydd grunted. He wasn't going to make it easy for his opponent. *Tyger* was under all plain sail with full manoeuvrability but the other had to think about shortening sail or risk what he most feared.

It all came down to this one pass.

They neared, the enemy now in plain sight, colours streaming and men along her deck staring at them.

The Frenchman opened fire – but *Tyger* end on was a difficult target.

Nearer – firing became general now and holes appeared in *Tyger*'s sails.

Kydd smiled grimly: his opponent was inexperienced. Any upcoming interchange would be savage and swift, leaving no time to reload the guns that were now blazing futilely.

The bowsprit spearing for the exact centre of the enemy frigate, Kydd sent his orders forward. 'Helm down!' he rasped.

The long spar began tracking the length of the enemy in a give-away move towards that unprotected stern.

The reaction was immediate – expecting it, the French captain rapidly fell away off the wind, his intention to circle around to bring his broadside to bear in place of his stern-quarters.

But Kydd was one step ahead. Instantly he countermanded his order and *Tyger* stopped her swing and began rotating the other way – and there presented to him was the enemy stern. In aimed shots, the raking storm took the frigate in a blast of destruction down her length that went on and on.

Kydd was not finished – as their guns on that side ceased their carnage he brought the ship over and delivered the

158

other broadside, now at close range, into the appalling swathe of devastation.

For the first time he heard the Tygers roar in an ecstasy of victory that had been long in coming.

When the smoke had cleared and they swept past, the hapless frigate was left in a tangle of wreckage and defeated, only the fore-mast standing. If their captain survived he would have learned much of the importance of the weather gage in frigate warfare, Kydd mused grimly.

Now the remaining two in chase had this advantage themselves and after witnessing what had happened to their confederate there would be no easy deceiving.

Bonaparte would be merciless to any who shied away with such stakes to be won. They wouldn't give up, that much was certain.

It was time to flee: there was no question of risking their cargo on the chances of close-quarter combat, but for this he hadn't even the elementary knowledge of *Tyger*'s sailing qualities. The one best placed to advise was her sailing master, but he'd been aboard for less time even than himself.

Kydd turned to the first lieutenant. 'Mr Hollis. In your experience, what is this ship's best point of sailing?'

Hollis looked uncomfortable. 'Sir, with our previous captain there was no stretching out, he not wanting to risk her sticks. I'm sorry, but I can't advise you.'

They had to find out, and quickly, or their pursuers would catch them.

Kydd looked soberly out at the distant sails of the two.

It had been an exhausting day, under chase the whole time and, it had to be accepted, the two French appreciably nearer. *Tyger* had not disappointed him but she was no flyer in light winds as *L'Aurore* was, and while he now knew a lot more about her, it had not been enough.

He'd tried everything, from fashioning watersails under the stun'sails while running large, to all the lore he could muster about dangerous clawing to windward as close to the wind's eye as he dared contrive.

Night was coming on – some time in the morning there would be a reckoning and *Tyger* would be brought to bay.

With darkness came the opportunity to slip away – but this would be known to the French. It was another classic situation: if he turned away in the night a pursuer had a one in two chance of guessing which side he had taken. With a pair in chase they could cover both sides, and at a minimum *Tyger* would find herself at daybreak in a full-scale action with one, the other then attracted to join in by the gunfire and smoke.

Which direction to choose? It made little difference. Unless . . .

It was a desperate gamble but would be the last thing they would suspect. Just as long as they were not sighted in the act.

Evening came, and with it the last chance for the French to catch them that day.

Every rope and sail taut they barrelled into the dusk, the picture of a desperately fleeing vessel not daring to take in sail by the smallest amount. Close to midnight a cloud-driven sky brought the blackness Kydd craved. It was a frightful risk but there was no other way.

Working fast, one by one, first the stunsails, then the topgallants and topsails were struck and *Tyger* straight away slowed dramatically, to the consternation of those not in the know.

But this was only the first act. The second was to wheel

about – and as closely as possible to sail back down their own wake!

Necessarily they would pass between the two hunters but by dousing high sail they had avoided the glimmer of white canvas in the crepuscular gloom, and the headlong speed of the chase past them would ensure the danger period would not be long.

He'd given orders that not a sound was to be made. No orders shouted, no watch bell, no careless knock. Their speed was now painfully reduced to ensure there would be no betraying swash of white wake.

At one point Kydd caught a brief sight of a pale smudge out on their beam but he couldn't be sure and held course for another breathless hour before he took his last action. Setting full sail on once more he put over the helm – for the enemy coast, the Netherlands, which was somewhere to the south and which he knew would be the last place of refuge they would think he would take in preference to the open sea.

At eight or nine knots he needed a good two or three hours southward before he could be sure he was out of sight of a masthead lookout and alter course eastwards – to ease around the vainly searching pair.

Then, as dawn broke, eyes strained across the waters and . . . they saw an empty sea. They were alone.

Gothenburg was Kydd's first sight of Scandinavia.

With a pilot on board, insisted upon by Joyce, who had been in these waters in the peace, *Tyger* wound through an uncountable number of islands of rough cliffs and sea-dark barren rocks that completely obscured the harbour until the last mile or two.

Keyed up to be rid of his special cargo he took little interest in the unfolding seascape, the ancient medieval clock towers and waterfront bustle.

They came to anchor and, without a moment's delay, Hollis was on his way ashore to alert the embassy. He was back within the hour, accompanied by a young man who introduced himself as Beckwith, under-secretary at His Majesty's embassy.

'You have something for me?' Kydd asked.

'Oh, you'll be meaning this.' It was the signed paper, all present and correct.

'Very good. You'll oblige me by taking this freight off my hands, Mr Beckwith. It's caused us no end of vexation.'

'I suppose it has. Well, let's see if we can't take delivery in the next few days. We're awfully busy with the visit of Prince Gustaf—'

'The next few days?' Kydd exploded. 'I'm damned if I'll wait, sir! I want it all ashore this day or I'll know the reason why!'

'Oh dear – it'll mean extra tides for someone but don't worry, I'll see to it. Be ready to load it on the barge when it comes. Good day to you, sir.'

The 'Explosive Shot' was mustered under guard by the mainmast well before the flat barge began creeping out from the wharf, watched over by a square of marines, a mystified gunner and a fuming Kydd.

There was no one on it to take delivery so Kydd himself and the guard went into the barge for the journey inshore.

With great care each case was landed and conveyed to a warehouse where they were lined up in order of the number painted on each, and a full guard posted.

Where the devil was the reception escort? The functionaries with documents and receipts? Anyone?

A little later a puffing Beckwith arrived, mopping his forehead. 'So sorry, old chap. Didn't realise the prince was bringing his mother as well.'

'I'm having a signature!' Kydd mouthed dangerously.

'Oh, yes, I suppose you do.' He snatched Kydd's form and threw off a huge scrawl on it. 'There. All done now!'

Just like that. Well, on return he'd now be able to claim his bullion freight money – after his junketing in London it would be a welcome easing of finances.

'Where's your escort then, Mr Beckwith?'

'Escort? I don't think we'll bother with that right now. You can tell your brave fellows they can leave.'

Kydd could hardly believe his ears. 'No escort? It's your worry now but . . .'

The young man gave a lopsided smile. 'Captain. Have you ever wondered what a half-million in specie looks like?'

He didn't wait for an answer but went to the first case, prised apart the wooden slats on the top and stood back.

Gingerly Kydd went over to see, probably his only chance to take a peek at an unimaginable fortune.

Inside, neatly stacked together, were two neat rows of best Yorkshire furnace bricks. 'You see, we took delivery of the real subsidy two days ago. A fast post-office packet that your most creditable decoying allowed to reach here in perfect safety.'

Chapter 12

Tyger rejoined the North Sea squadron in light rain and a listless grey calm, which barely lifted the signal flags that indicated their station in the line.

Kydd left the deck to Brice and went below to his cabin. He looked about. Tysoe had contrived a certain homeliness with a scatter of small Swedish landscapes and a charming miniature of an unknown young lady. A modest collection of silver now graced the bluff sideboard and colourful covers hid the shabbiness of the two armchairs. His new heavy frigate being denied him, this would be his home for some time. But it didn't speak of him – it didn't proclaim that this was where Sir Thomas Kydd lived.

'Come!' he called, in reply to a hesitant knock. It was only the weekly accounts due the flagship regularly each Friday at the routine captains' meeting. He toyed with the paperwork, his mind straying to the hundreds of men and officers under his command.

Was he winning their souls? After the brief taste of action he'd noticed a distinct loosening of attitudes, and there was a pleasing hum from the mess-deck at meal-times that could be heard through the hatch gratings. But the mockery of the gold shipment had destroyed much of what had been won. At best there was now only a respectful wariness, at worst a cynical turning away.

Nothing like an effective ship's company should be. They were doing a job, nothing more. How could he bring them together, infuse and inspire them with the spirit that drives men to heroism in storm and battle for the sake of their ship?

Kydd saw there was now no chance of seizing a prize, and the prospects for action were dim, with the enemy retiring to lick their wounds. Ahead lay only the boredom of blockade as summer moved into the miseries of winter.

Two days later the usual cutter from Yarmouth fussed up to the flagship and Admiral Russell's routine dispatches were transferred into it. No doubt a bag of pettifogging Admiralty and Navy Board correspondence would pass the other way but there would be very little in it to disturb the motions of a crucial blockading squadron.

On Friday captains were signalled aboard the flagship as usual and their small business conducted quickly and efficiently. Kydd had been greeted politely but for some reason the admiral avoided his eye, and when boats were called alongside, Russell quietly asked him to stay behind.

'Sherry?'

Kydd declined politely.

'So you've men?'

'Pressed is all, and a few volunteers.'

'And the barky's tight-found an' all a-taunto?'

'Not all as I'd wish yet, sir,' Kydd answered carefully.

Russell found his chair, patting the one that faced it. 'You've done well, m' boy. Damn well. Can't imagine how you did it, an' I honour you for it.' He fiddled with his glass. 'So it grieves me more'n I can say to have to tell you this.'

A sudden stab of alarm shot through Kydd.

'Y' see, I've orders to tell you that when you make Yarmouth again you're to give up your ship.'

There was a moment of disbelief, then a wave of anger. He'd been pitchforked into an impossible situation and when, against all the odds, he'd succeeded, they'd cast him ashore?

'No mention of another, I'm afraid.'

Kydd stuttered his acknowledgement in sick dismay. They'd not succeeded in their object of seeing him fail but now they were turning over what he'd achieved to another.

'I've heard from one o' my officers about your falling athwart St Vincent's bows over the Popham trial. A sad thing when a sea officer like y'self gets drawn into politicking.'

'That cursed rag! I never said what—'

'Doesn't signify – it was published an' that's that.' Russell gave a small smile. 'I've a guinea to a shilling that this'n is their way o' thanking you for your labours. I'm sorry, Kydd, truly I am.'

It was extraordinary that an admiral would criticise the Admiralty before one of his captains and Kydd was touched. But now he had to come to terms with the fact that his remaining sea service in the navy was to be measured in weeks only.

'M' dear fellow, we both came aft the hard way. If 'n there's anything I can do . . .?'

'That's kind in you, sir, but I can't think what,' he muttered.

After an awkward pause, Russell said doubtfully, 'If you've a mind t' stay in your ship for as long as y' can before . . .'

166

Kydd's first instinct was to get it over with, put it behind him, but he knew in his heart he had to keep the seas for as long as he could, before the inevitable caught up with him. 'I'll stay with *Tyger* – she needs me.'

'As I thought, m' boy. Well, I'm a mort reluctant t' put it to a first-rank cap'n as you are, but it's in my gift to extend your cruise a while longer. Just a trivial bit o' work – I'd normally send a sloop or such, but my orders say "send a vessel", which leaves the choice to me. Nothing to set before a prime fighting captain but—'

'I'll take it.'

'It won't be without its interest, but don't think on prizes, or sport with the enemy.'

'Sir. Where?'

'North. As far as you may go. The High North.'

Blinking in surprise Kydd waited for him to continue.

'Through the Arctic circle to the polar regions. Their lord-ships wish a man-o'-war sent right around the north o' Norway into the Barents Sea and to the Russian port of Archangel.'

'Wha'?'

'There's good cause, while the season allows, to make a neighbourly visit, simply to assure ourselves that His Majesty's interests in the area – which're pretty slim, incidentally – are safe and in order, but mainly t' reconnoitre if the French have made any moves into the region.'

'I see.'

'We know for a fact they've not been spotted, but that's not the point. This is only to give good public reason for you being there while you get on with a much more important and discreet task.'

Kydd listened quietly.

'You probably don't know it, but less'n a century past,

Russia had only one port connected directly to the outside world. Just the one, and that was Archangel. Then your tsar, Peter the Great, built St Petersburg, and it took most o' the trade. Why? Because it's mainly ice-free and Archangel is locked in pack-ice anything up to eight months in the year. And Petersburg is much closer to Moscow and the heart of Russia.'

He gave a grim smile. 'Well, now we've got a problem. While we're allies of Russia we've a concern to keep their ports open and trade flowing free, but Boney's latest victories are giving us a parcel o' worries.

'St Petersburg is at the head of the Baltic. When he's finished with the Prussians there's little to stop him sending his army north into Denmark – and then he'll have seized the entrance to the Baltic and can choke off all access. We stand to lose our vital naval stores and Russia will be isolated – unless she can find another port. This is really why you're going north. To see if Archangel can again be that port.'

Kydd shook his head in disbelief. 'I can't just—'

'Easy enough, really. All they want is a report on the depths mid-channel, working length of wharves, repair, warehousing – you know the sort of thing. It's not your job to make judgement – there'll be people in London to do that. So, no more'n a week or two at most – don't delay leaving, you wouldn't want to be iced in for half a year.'

'No, sir.'

'It's a useful exercise you'll be doing but it probably won't come t' much. Even Bonaparte would hesitate over attacking a strict neutral like Denmark, but we have to look to all possibilities.'

'Sir. May I – may I thank you for—'

'Be damned – it's little enough! Off with you, m' boy. I've

a notion I'll be receiving my letter concerning you tomorrow, too late to stop you going . . .'

Kydd decided to tell nobody of his personal blow. It was hard enough to face up to it himself, let alone to bear any awkward sympathies. In any case, it would not be in *Tyger*'s best interests to learn that they would have yet another change of captain.

For him their mission would be a tough challenge: to penetrate the God-forsaken wilderness between the extreme north of Russia and the polar regions where very few naval vessels had ever been – but for the seamen it would mean the harshest conditions that sea life could throw at them and *Tyger* was not prepared for it.

He'd keep quiet about where they were headed until he had to admit it and trust he could carry the men with him.

His orders were brief and to the point. They required him to put into Gothenburg where he would take aboard an Arctic pilot provided by the British consul. He was further authorised to secure a limited amount of clothing deemed advisable at that season for a voyage to the daunting latitude of seventy degrees north.

The rest was up to him.

The outlines of the Swedish town hove into view. They moored in the outer roads and Kydd wasted no time in getting ashore.

The British consul was fat and expansive and read the admiral's request with interest. 'Well, now, and I won't enquire what in Hades the navy's doing in the far north but I've got just the fellow. Greenland whale fisheries, married to a Finnish lass. He's a knowing cove but won't stand for nonsense. I'll see if he's available to you and send him out.'

It was no use delaying any further. The man's arrival on board would give the game away and there was much to do.

He summoned his officers to his cabin. 'Gentlemen, I'll not have you in doubt any more about our detached service. It's to the north – the High Arctic!'

Briefly he explained that they were on a mission to show the flag and assure themselves there was not a French presence, without mentioning the real reason.

There was an immediate ripple of dismay.

'Sir, we ain't equipped! I've charts for naught but—'

'Then get some, Mr Joyce,' Kydd said bluntly.

'It'll be mortal cold, we'd best lay in some—'

'We've tickets to ship enough foul-weather gear for all the people. Any more questions?'

Bowden looked concerned. 'As far as I'm aware, Sir Thomas, there are none aboard who've been to the Arctic regions. How are we to navigate in ice and similar?'

'A pilot is on his way out to us, who will also be in the character of a guide in these matters.'

'He'd better be good,' muttered Joyce.

'The man is from the Greenland whale fisheries and is accounted a taut hand, well experienced. And he'll be berthing with you, sir.'

The man standing in the door of his cabin was of an age, wiry but with a steady gaze from his soft grey eyes. 'Cap'n? Kit Horner, an' I hear you're wanting a pilot.'

Kydd motioned to a chair. 'Tell me of your experience in the High North, Mr Horner.'

'As I'm spliced to a Sami,' he said, as if it explained everything. Then he added, 'An' thirty years on the Greenland coast, I know the north . . .'

'Very well, I'll take you on. You'll be—'

'Ah, it's four shillun' a day, an' five after we crosses the Ar'tic circle.'

Kydd agreed with a tight smile. 'You don't come cheap, if I might remark it.'

'An' all found.'

Then it was down to details of the voyage.

Horner rubbed his chin. 'Archangel? Bit late in the season, but shouldn't be a hard beat. Merchant jacks do it every year, o' course. Could meet wi' some ice islands but you'll find the White Sea clear o' drift ice this time o' the year.'

'At seventy north?'

'Cos there's an up-coast current from the Atlantic passes right round an' into the Barents. We'll be snug if'n we sail soon.'

His quiet certainty was reassuring and Kydd encouraged him to go on.

It seemed greenstuffs were essential, although scurvy grass could be collected on some islands Horner knew of and provisions were to be had if necessary at certain remote Norwegian coast settlements.

There would be no need for real Arctic clothing for this voyage but a chaldron or two of coal in place of firewood was a good plan to ensure a hot breakfast for the hands – and spirits were a sovereign cure against the cold of a night watch.

Horner had his own rutter, which he would bring with him, and there were charts available from the chandlers, the Dutch being the best. As to the ship, no particular mind need be paid to her fitness in view of the small likelihood of ice but if the cap'n wished he might consider bringing along the makings of a Baltic bowgrace, reinforcing at the bows to shoulder aside small floes to save a constant battering at the hull.

But Archangel was a run-down parody of its glory days. Timber and furs – and not so much of those. Located at the mouth of the Dvina river, it would be beset by ice in a few weeks and then there would be nothing happening for at least six months.

Despite this, Kydd felt a thrill. Few naval officers would ever see what he was about to: the very top of the world!

'Sir, eight have deserted,' Hollis reported, with an expression of rebuke at Kydd's having granted liberty to men who hadn't earned it.

Kydd looked away, frustrated. This was more than an offence, it was a violation of trust. Were the Tygers still in a defiant mood, disaffected and hostile? 'Who?'

Hollis named them.

All good men, no dregs of the press. And gone off in a body – this was no idle straggling. There would be more soon, for Gothenburg was a lively international port and they would have no trouble finding a berth on an outgoing merchantman.

'Stop all liberty,' Kydd said heavily. This was punishing the innocent but he couldn't risk losing more. He knew the reason: their destination had got out and they wanted no part of the hardships of an Arctic voyage.

Only one of her company was rejoicing – Dillon, whose desire to see something of the world was about to be fulfilled beyond expectations. On ship's business ashore he'd picked up more worthy tomes, some in Russian, for despite having the tongue he'd never heard it spoken in its native land.

* * *

They sailed two days later, into the teeth of a north-easter straight from the Arctic, a bitter foretaste of worse to come.

Leaden skies and white-streaked grey seas added to a feeling of unease at leaving the world of men for the boreal realm where they did not belong. With winds dead foul, only a hard clawing far to seaward would clear the long and formidable Norwegian coast, to be followed later by a board inwards to high latitudes to clear North Cape and into the Barents Sea.

Tyger heaved and laboured, the spray driven aft, spiteful and stinging. A bitter wind cut into the muffled figures about her deck and the watch hunkered down behind the weather bulwarks. With canvas taut and hard as wood, the straining rigging strummed fretfully, a mournful drone rising and falling, like a funeral dirge.

Kydd could feel the old canker. Them and us. The tyrants and the slaves. But in these conditions, at the very time it was needed, there was no possibility of bringing the officers and men together in traditional ways – at divisions, a church service, light-hearted competition mast against mast, an impromptu entertainment around the fore-bitts for seamen and officer guests.

Instead there would be weary and bone-chilled men going below to take out their frustrations in cursing the fate that had sent them to *Tyger*. There was little he could do about it and virtually no chance of the ship's company coming together as one to face the enemy. *Tyger* was as divided as ever.

As the latitude grew higher, so did the ceaseless, long and immensely powerful seas charging out from their polar heart, a strength in them that made it a folly to confront. Taking them on the starboard bow one after another, *Tyger* reared and writhed to avoid their punishment, but in relentless,

173

heedless succession they seethed past in a roar and clamour that had her twisting back as if in pain.

It was hard, bruising work. Then they reached the same latitude as Iceland, out there far to their lee – but this meant only that they were less than halfway on their northward odyssey and now in waters near unknown to men.

And further still, with the same battering onrush, on and on, until three things happened.

During the night the seas eased and in the morning, like a miracle sent by gods relenting of their savagery, the skies cleared to a vast, innocent blue. At midday meridian altitudes were taken and, after careful correction for height of eye and refraction, the word came out: during the night they had passed the defining limit of their familiar world, the north polar circle, and were now firmly within the Arctic regions.

But it was so unreal and unexpected – a placid, glittering sea and the sun with real warmth in it.

The watch shed their coarse dark wadmarel pea-jackets for gear more in keeping with the south; fair-weather habits took over and, in wondering relief, *Tyger* surged on into the north.

Now there was a hard, actinic edge to the light, a glare that had men shielding their eyes as it was reflected up, and the blue of the sky had a strange remoteness, an unearthly purity.

The most eerie of all was after the last dog-watch was relieved and the sun began to set – but then it slowed and stopped. The middle-watchmen had the singular experience of seeing it rise again without setting.

Kit Horner remarked drily, 'The midnight sun – you'll not see a shadow o' night for another month or so. I'm thinkin' you'll save a bushel o' money on candles an' such.'

Joyce came up from below, shaking his head. 'The glass at thirty an' a half. It ain't Christian, begob!'

The weather held. In a week they'd reached seventy-five degrees north and Horner allowed that it was safe to go about, to round North Cape.

When at last they raised land it held everyone in thrall.

A steel-hued row of massive headlands and bluffs with not the tiniest scrap of vegetation visible, or any hint of humankind. A stark, petrified wilderness with only the unceasing fringing white of the sea's assault on the iron-bound shore.

North Cape appeared out of the blue haze one morning, vertical cliffs plunging into the icy-green sea and desolate flat-topped mountains, but it was the turning point: they were leaving the Atlantic to pass into the Barents Sea. On their right was the great continent of Asia, on their left nothing but the frigid polar sea until it met the edge of the ice-pack reaching all the way to the fabled North Pole.

That night they crept along under reduced sail to be ready in the morning to make entrance to the White Sea.

The barren shore was riven with dark fjords, white streaks of snow showing stark in the fissures of desolate cliffs and peaks as they entered. The winds turned fluky and unfriendly, a frigid bullying down from mountainsides, which had all hands reaching for greatcoats and mufflers.

Picking up the opposite shore it was then a matter of shaping course for the south-east and the head of the White Sea, where the drab brown of a great river delta appeared. Horner refused to leave the deck for hours as he conned them into the right channel, anchors ready for slipping fore and aft and a leadsman in the chains.

Here at last were signs of man: cleared expanses of corn,

recognisable orchards among wild flowers and birch woods down to the water's edge, even grass, a thing of wonder after so long at sea.

It brought other things: insect clouds, the rich stench of peaty vegetation, the fetid miasma of barely thawed bogs – and the first settlements of low, shabby huts.

They rounded a point, and as it opened into a bay, Kydd saw at least thirty vessels at anchor. They glided in, the biggest ship by some margin.

'Mud'yugsky, and as far as we go, Cap'n,' Horner said laconically. 'There's a bar an' shoal water stops us going to Archangel, as is another four mile. Get the hook down an' wait for our welcome.'

A boat detached itself from a jetty at the tip of the point and bustled up to them.

'Two to come aboard, Mr Hollis,' Kydd said, noting the florid officer standing in the sternsheets staring up at the big ship, another beside him.

The little man spoke up immediately in passable English. 'The Kapitan Voronov. He want your business, pliss.'

While the dragoman translated, Kydd tried to think of an expression of military courtesy. There were no forts visible with flags proudly flying to receive and return gun salutes but neither was there a single warship in sight.

'We are honoured to visit this port and, as an ally of Russia, His Majesty wishes me to pay our respects to the – the governor in charge.'

It was received with puzzlement and dismay but Horner came to the rescue. 'There ain't any such thing in this place. A mayor or such, but nothin' else as would stand next to youse.'

It was apparently so outlandish for a warship to appear

176

that there were no procedures the good *kapitan* could think to apply. Port clearance, merchant papers, manifests and, of course, Customs appraisal were the usual but in this case . . .

'Kapitan, he say welcome an' he report to his superior.'

It was clear there had been no French or any other naval visit of significance here for some time. The open reason for their voyage therefore was answered, but he had the other discreet task to complete – and for that he had to get to Archangel itself.

The boat put off and Kydd turned to Horner. 'I'm supposing I should pay a visit to your mayor or someone.'

'He won't thank you for it.'

'Pray why not?'

'Cos he's a Dutchman an', like most of 'em, hates your kind.'

'How can this be? They're an enemy of Russia as they are of us.'

'They's merchants who sit on all the trade hereabouts and t' stay loose buys their papers as a Russky.'

Kydd's heart sank. What with shoals, a bar and channels unnavigable by vessels of size, the prospects of Archangel as a port to rival the Baltic were not promising before he'd even started, and with the Dutch in a position to obstruct and disrupt he might as well sail for home now. 'Nevertheless, I'm going. Mr Hollis, my barge.'

'That's not how it's done here, Cap'n. They likes you should use their traps. Hoist a red flag on the fore an' see what happens.'

It brought a peculiar craft beetling out from the shore. A wide, shallow-draught boat, it had a flat railed-off area raised on posts above the rowers with banks of seats atop.

Coming alongside, a hinged gangway swung out neatly and Kydd could step directly from his ship to the platform. In the shadows beneath the anonymous figures of rowers were still and bent, in pitiful rags. Were they convicts or serfs?

'Carry on, Mr Hollis,' he instructed, and took his place at the front, Bowden beside him and Dillon in his best secretarial garb behind. He'd had to refuse Clinton's offer of a ceremonial marine guard: in any foreign land it was a provocative act to land an armed party without due permission.

Their progress through the marshy landscape was slow but methodical. They finally turned around the last point to reveal Archangel, port city of the High North.

A mile-wide peninsula set out into the confluence of count-less muddy streams and rivers of the delta, it was perfectly flat. The waterfront was lined with warehouses and at one point there was a lengthy grand building with a fat white tower. Further inland, Kydd could see a peculiar lofty building of many storeys, sharp curves, rickety balconies and a spire, and to the left a quaint five-domed church with a distinctive bell-tower.

He looked about carefully. A number of ships were working cargo but all were of a modest size, and as they drew nearer the high, angular jetty, the whole prospect resolved into one of shabby decay. Any thoughts of diverting the great Baltic convoys were rapidly dwindling.

Kydd wondered whether it might be possible to dredge a channel for deeper-draught ships. The wharfage looked capable of some hundreds of ships, especially the timber yards to the left. Could they separate in- and outbound?

They stepped off to the stares of labourers and nearby

stall-keepers, heading for the long white building, Gostiny Dvor, or Merchants' Court, that Dillon had been assured was every captain's first port of call.

Kydd was thankful he'd thought to wear sea undress uniform without star and sash: with their naval accoutrements they stood out enough already. But then they quickly discovered to their dismay that everywhere was a sea of dark-brown mud.

There were no paved avenues – only roads laid with timbers along which carts with tinkling bells jolted and swayed. Peasants trudged by with impossible loads and a boy in bare feet driving geese stopped to stare at them.

It was a strange, forbidding place.

Their entry into the Merchants' Court stopped the hum of activity and half a hundred eyes stared at them from behind tall, ancient writing desks.

'Tell 'em it's Sir Thomas Kydd of the Royal Navy come to pay his respects to their mayor.'

The man Dillon addressed looked at him in consternation, then let it be known that Mayor Vasiliy Popov was not to be troubled on minor matters as he was a figure of some consequence in the town.

Kydd explained that he was in Archangel on matters touching on trade and would appreciate a little of his time.

Doubtfully, the man got up and went to an office at the back. There were angry words and suddenly at the door stood a giant of a man with a monstrous black beard.

'Come!' he roared, beckoning to Kydd. 'You're Ingliss?' he said, in a voice of thunder. 'Vot you doing here?'

After an elaborate courtly bow, Kydd suggested they discuss matters further in a more private situation.

Popov hesitated, then pushed past and led them to a low

room with dark, varnished panels and smoke-grimed portraits. It smelt of boiled cabbage and strong tobacco.

They sat at an old-fashioned meeting table and Popov boomed something unintelligible out of the door, then closed it and took his seat.

'Now. You come in man-o'-war? Why?'

Kydd explained their mission to uncover any French threat, careful to refer to him as our good Russian ally.

The door opened and two others entered, glaring suspiciously at Kydd as they sat opposite. Close behind, a servant came, bearing a coarsely made brown glass bottle and small glasses.

'No French here,' rumbled Popov, leaning back to let the servant pour out the colourless liquor before each man. 'None since the peace finish. So?'

He glared about him, growling, '*Za zdorovje*,' and downed the contents of his glass in one savage gulp.

Kydd was not going to be caught out and took just a sip of the rough potato liquor.

'Drink!' Popov demanded, miming a full toss.

Kydd replied, 'Sir, this is far too good a potion to down carelessly,' peering up at his glass as if it were a rare claret. Bowden and Dillon followed his lead.

'So, no French. You sail now, *hein*?'

'Perhaps later. My orders are to let the flag of His Majesty be seen by any of his subjects in Archangel as a comfort and support in a foreign land.'

'None. No Ingliss here.' Swift looks were exchanged between the two others.

It had to be a lie: somewhere in the trading community there would be seamen or merchants. Was Popov too anxious for them to leave?

'And, of course, after such an arduous voyage my ship requires repairs, water, victuals.'

'You get – you go.'

'My men will be grateful indeed to take liberty ashore,' Kydd enthused. 'To spend their hard-won coin on the simple pleasures.' He got no response beyond a glower. 'I do believe I'll take rooms for a day or two and enjoy a promenade around your beautiful town.'

Popov looked as though he would object but fell to muttering. He rose to his feet. 'Season nearly finish. Ice come, you trap!' he said, through gritted teeth.

'Thank you, I'll bear that in mind.'

It wasn't hard to locate the usual seafront hostelry catering to ship's captains that could be found in every port. Dingy, reeking of the ever-present cabbage and tobacco, it would serve.

Kydd sent Bowden back with instructions to the first lieutenant to award liberty to half a watch under the direst penalties for behaviour. He knew Bowden was intelligent enough to let slip that offenders taken in riot by the locals would find themselves choked up in a Russian gaol as *Tyger* sailed. It would give pause to the most dedicated joyster.

It was not simply a humane gesture on Kydd's part. In this hostile and uneasy place he wanted men within hail about him – those who, like Stirk, could be trusted to see that the hot-headed were kept in check.

He had a duty to complete his mission, as unpromising as it was turning out to be. The alternative was to return with nothing. And he supposed he should find any Englishmen here and let them know they were not forgotten.

In the absence of a British consul how was he going to

locate them? In any other port the sheer presence of a smart frigate anchored offshore would signal his presence, but *Tyger* was well out of sight.

Then he remembered an offhand remark by Russell's flag lieutenant while rounding up the paperwork: it was not impossible that the venerable Muscovy Company might still have representation there.

He sent Dillon out to enquire, and his secretary returned quickly. 'Still here, Sir Thomas, but at a remove.'

They set out for the southern part of the town, an older but more picturesque district of quaint timber dwellings with sharply inclined roofs and parquetry eaves, tradesmen's workshops and tiny vegetable plots.

Set back from the muddy road, a larger dark-timbered building had seen better days – but over the low doorway there was a sign with a faded shield that incorporated a galleon with an inscription in Latin.

Inside they found an Aladdin's cave of goods piled here and there in glorious confusion in the gloom, with a pungent whiff of hides, raw mahogany and the dust of ages.

A man emerged from behind a counter to come to a stop, wide-eyed.

'You – you're English!' he managed. Elderly, he was in a well-worn long frock-coat, breeches and an old-fashioned wig.

Dillon stepped forward. 'Sir Thomas Kydd, captain of His Majesty's Frigate *Tyger*. And you, sir?'

The man bobbed hurriedly and spluttered, 'Jeremiah Blunt, proprietor.'

'Of?'

'Oh, the Muscovy Company of Merchant Adventurers Trading with Russia.'

'The very man we seek,' said Kydd, encouragingly. 'I'd be obliged should you tell me of the British in Archangel as you know of them, sir.'

Blunt ushered them to a back room as cluttered as the store and flustered about until a tea samovar appeared, borne by a curious beady-eyed woman in traditional dress.

Sipping black tea, Kydd knew there was no hurrying the man and sat back to listen.

Most improbably, Archangel had been founded not by the Russians but by the English. In 1551, in the last few years before Elizabeth I came to the throne, two courtiers, Willoughby and Chancellor, had set up an enterprise: the Mystery and Company of Merchant Adventurers for the Discovery of Regions, Dominions, Islands, and Places Unknown. The first voyage selected was to uncover a trade route to north-east China and a small fleet had duly sailed to the top of the world.

Only Chancellor reached safe haven, here in the maze of muddy channels where the green of larch and willow beckoned, while Willoughby, beset in ice, froze to death.

Alert for any mercantile possibilities, he saw that the lucrative fur trade was being hauled south overland all the way to Moscow, and knew that here was an opportunity. He made the journey himself, arriving to great astonishment at the court of Ivan the Terrible, introducing himself as an ambassador from Queen Elizabeth of England. Chancellor left the tsar well satisfied with a sea route now to Russia, and when he returned home he was granted a monopoly on the market. The Muscovy Company was born.

Apart from one distraction, when Good Queen Bess had unaccountably declined Ivan the Terrible's proposal of marriage, the Muscovy Company went from strength to strength, dealing in furs, English wool and other profitable lines.

But when in the next century it was heard that Charles I had been executed the then tsar expelled all English merchants, except those in Archangel. Into the vacuum stepped the Dutch, who by the end of the century had toppled the British monopoly.

It was the establishment early in the eighteenth century of Tsar Peter the Great's grand Baltic port of St Petersburg, open to all, that finally relegated Archangel to a backwater.

Where before the bashaws of Elizabeth's day had held court, now all that remained was a little emporium of knick-knacks from Britain's industrial enterprise. The Dutch held the town, with the still considerable timber trade and the White Sea Company whaling concern, and did not welcome outsiders.

'For our gewgaws we take by return seal skins, walrus tusks and down of the eider duck. Some flax and hemp, a trifle of tallow, on occasions wax and pine resin.'

'And furs?'

'Ah, the sable and ermine,' sighed Blunt, 'and, of course, your glorious Arctic fox. Grey-blue over-hair, soft and deep, much prized by the knowing. In times past Archangel shipped the best there was, but now . . .'

'Finished by over-hunting?'

'I'm supposing so. There's been none at all shipped from here for some years, even if the prices in London are beyond a prince's commanding. In these dolorous times of revolution and the mob, you might think such fine trappings would be frowned upon but, no, they must have their—'

'Mr Blunt, I really came to discover whether Archangel today possesses subjects of His Majesty as would welcome the sight of the flag at all.'

'Very few, and those only of a quality not to be noticed.'

'Then I thank you for your—'

'Ah, there is one. A respectable merchant on a failed venture here. A Mr John Bellingham of Liverpool, a factor in timber and iron.'

'Where might I see him?'

'In the Solombalsky prison.'

'Did you say . . .?'

'Yes. A difficult man,' Blunt came back, 'not to say vexatious. Yet he has reason. He defied the Dutch cabal and paid for it. I cannot tell of the details. In truth I feel sorry for him – he has a wife and little ones who even now are in St Petersburg praying for his release, and I visit him when I can. If you could find it in your power to show that he's not forgotten it would be a mercy.'

'I shall do so. I thank you for your hospitality, sir.'

On the way Dillon expressed reservations at visiting a Russian prison, but as a civil debtor, the man was apparently entitled to a better class of confinement.

'Mr Bellingham, I believe?' Kydd said mildly, as they were ushered in. The small room had a window, high and barred, that shed light on worn furniture and faded carpet.

'Good God! I never thought to see you!' A painfully thin man scrambled to his feet, his face working. 'They've heard my petition? That damned crew of politicals finally moved, did they? Justice at last—'

'Mr Bellingham, I'm sorry to say I'm not here to attend your release.'

'Then why did you come?' The fevered eyes narrowed. 'You wouldn't be here without you had a reason. Who are you?'

'Sir Thomas Kydd,' Dillon intervened. 'Captain of *Tyger*, frigate, of his own good will come to visit an Englishman in reduced circumstances, sir.'

'Ah, but what's he doing here in Archangel?' Bellingham leered. 'Never seen hide nor hair of any nob worried about this arse-hole of a place.'

'I'm in this port to assure myself that the interests of His Majesty are respected, sir,' Kydd said stiffly.

'Ha! Then you've found the Dutch-run Archangel – precious little interest left to His Knobbs hereabouts.'

'I see my presence is not welcome to you, sir. I'll take my leave if I may.'

'You're like 'em all, aren't you, Sir T?' he sneered. 'Come here, see nothing of notice and get out as fast as you can.'

Kydd made to go.

'Wait! I know what goes on here, all of it! And there's something afoot as I can tell you of!'

'What is it?'

'Ah, well. Come here, we don't want to be heard now, do we?'

Kydd sat reluctantly at the small table as Bellingham leaned across. 'Archangel, the town's run by the Dutch, in with the mayor and all on 'em.'

'I know that.'

'What you don't know is that it's a cesspool of corruption. They run fancy schemes between 'em and split the cream.'

'What's this got to do with—'

'The whole town is in on it. All of 'em!'

'Mr Bellingham, this has gone far enough. You—'

The little man gave a confident smile, which turned into a smirk. 'Nobody knows, but I do!'

Kydd got up to leave.

'They're trading with Napoleon Bonaparte hisself!'

'What did you say?' Kydd said sharply.

'Knew that'd get you! Yes, indeed. See, I know what they're doing.'

He leaned back and cocked his head to one side. 'Ever wondered why the fur trade dried up? Great shame – some of those blue-fox pelts would sell for their weight in gold, should they ever get to London. Why, ermine at—'

'Yes, sir. I know about this,' Kydd said, with heavy patience.

'Don't you feel for the lords and ladies, paying a ransom for their precious furs? They do, you know. Smuggled in from the continent, prices that'd set your eyes to watering.'

'So what are you telling me?'

'That the fur trade is never better! I heard it from the timber loggers – they've seen cartloads of furs heading here. Don't it tell you something?'

'Well, Mr Bellingham?'

'The Dutch have cornered the market, taken the lot, none left. They're shipping 'em out to their kin back in Holland and making a hill of money outfitting Boney and his crew! Any that's left over he lets go over the Channel to the fools in England who can be relied on to pay any price. See?'

If this were true it would be at a prodigious loss to the City traders and a serious breach of Britain's blockade, let alone the wealth being diverted to Bonaparte's coffers.

'How do they do this?'

'As I said, the whole town's in it together, the mayor and all the officials, and they keep it secret, all to 'emselves.'

'So you don't know.'

'I didn't say that. What I can tell you for certain is, the furs arrive here, they're stored and then get shipped out.'

'How can you be sure?'

'One of my runners thought it proper to tell me of furs he saw stowed in a shed. I went there on the sly and saw for myself. Next day they were gone. They never came on the market – and there's no sense sending them back to where they'd come from, so they must be shipped out.'

'Where is this shed?'

'Hard by the whalers. There, it stinks so much nobody's going to wander by 'less they have to.'

'Did you spy furs being loaded aboard any ship?'

'And let the world see what they're up to? I tell you, they're all in it, mayor, Customs, military – all of 'em taking a share. Stands to reason they want to keep it out o' sight.'

'It only happened the once?'

'More. When they've got a shipment, it goes quickly. None o' my business, o' course, but it's been several times this season I've seen 'em at that shed. Like I said—'

'Thank you for your information, Mr Bellingham. I shall look into it. Good day to you, sir.'

'Sir, the man is unhinged. Surely you're not going to—'

'I'm not, Mr Dillon. Even if what he told us is true, this is Russia, their laws, and we would have to show there's been a crime committed against us personally for them to act.'

'I see, sir.'

'And if the town is all hugger-mugger together, how far do you think we'd get? No, we let it go.'

'All the same, it's—'

'Here's my lodgings. You'll want to wander abroad. Pray do so, if you wish.'

The little room with its plain furniture was dreary, as was the view of the flat marshland through the grubby window.

A wave of depression began to settle. This last venture

before he relinquished *Tyger* had turned out bleak and pointless. Archangel was humid, midge-ridden and not in the least an exotic destination.

The voyage had failed: he had shown the flag but found few English subjects to encourage. On the other matter of opening up the port to rival the Baltic, with the natural conditions he had seen, it was a lost cause.

And there had not even been the rumour of French activity in these remote parts, no prospect of action or excitement. But given what was in the future for him he wanted to spin out the remaining time as long as he could.

He threw off his coat and boots and lay on the wooden bed.

The first men on liberty would be arriving soon – the least he could do was stay another day to give the other watch a chance to go on a frolic. Then he would have to leave.

As if in rebellion his mind began casting about for a reason to delay.

What if Bellingham was right, that there was in fact clandestine fur smuggling going on? It would be a fine thing indeed to put a stop single-handedly to the business, return with something of real value achieved. But here in Russia he was powerless to interfere.

His mind refused to let go. Just how could such smuggling be organised?

Ironically the biggest single obstacle was breaking the Royal Navy's blockade of the continent. Even if they got to sea Russell's vigilant inshore squadron would pounce and the valuable cargo would be seized. This had never happened that he'd heard of, so there must be another way.

It had to be by ship – but how the devil was it done that none could see?

A faint raucous cheer came from the first Tygers arriving. There'd be sore heads in the morning if there was nobody to tell them of the potency of Russian liquor.

Idly his mind wandered back. If *he* were in charge of the fur smuggling he wouldn't trifle with piecemeal shipments, any one of which could tip off a naval boarding officer to the existence of the operation. But only small brigs and sloops could make it up the Dvina as far as Archangel. Transship at sea? Too risky and open to spoilage.

It was a conundrum . . . but then something Bellingham had said flickered into an idea. He'd said that the shed had been near the whaling-ship grounds, the White Sea Company, controlled by the Dutch. What if . . .

Yes! It made sense. The whalers returned from their hunting grounds with their oil, which was landed, and then they went back to their hunting grounds – with clean, empty vats! If the furs were stored in those, suitably protected, who would think to stop a whaler on its way out?

So this was a method to get the furs away – but what advantage did it give? Whales were taken at sea and brought to their shore station to be flensed and tried. What better than to use this base as a depot to consolidate the shipment? If so, they could be picked up all together by a ship of size only once a season with much-reduced risk. And at such a place, necessarily remote and inaccessible, they would be perfectly safe . . .

He sat up suddenly. All this was quite possible – but that didn't prove a thing.

He could do nothing in Archangel. Once at sea he could stop and search a whaler on its way out, but that had two problems: those ships were flying the flag of Russia, an ally, and any such interference would cause an international incident – and if he did board one, he would get only a small part of the trade. It made more sense to find the base and, with it, the entire shipment.

However, he had no right to set one of His Majesty's valuable frigates charging about searching for a fairy-tale haul of furs without solid evidence. All he had were the ramblings of a deranged prisoner of the Russians.

He had to have more.

A passing burst of noise showed that the Tygers were not wasting time. He gave a twisted smile in acknowledgement of times long ago when he had stepped ashore with his shipmates in foreign parts. They'd found the grog-shops and roystered happily with mariners from all the seven seas regardless of creed or language.

He remembered once when he and Stirk had . . . That was it!

Impatiently he waited until his confidential secretary returned. 'Mr Dillon, I have a task for you – that is, if it is not too great an imposition.'

The young man heard him out, then beamed. 'It shall be done, Sir Thomas.'

An hour later, in the third one he tried, Dillon finally found Stirk and his shipmates, gleesome and happy amid the din of a press of humanity in the smoky tavern.

The grizzled gunner listened in amazement to what Dillon was asking. Then, laughing together, they went outside and around to the back of the dark-timbered hovel.

Minutes later, Stirk returned in the company of a rollicking young Jack Tar in smart sea rig who rolled as he walked and looked right primed to blow out his gaff.

'Arr, me hearty!' chortled Stirk, slapping him on the back. 'Yo ho ho, an' a bottle o' the right true stuff!'

Inside Doud and Pinto started with astonishment. Before they could say anything, he roared, 'Mates, this skiddy cock is me old shipmate off the *Saucy Sue* as was, come t' see how we Tygers has a good time.'

They blinked at him, speechless.

'Bring y' arse to anchor, lad,' Stirk insisted, making a place for him.

A black leather tankard was shoved into Dillon's fist. 'Beer is all, we has no truck wi' the Russky cat's piss.' Leaning forward, he whispered hoarsely, 'This berth do ye? Or?'

Dillon paused, pretending to swig his beer, and decided. 'Er, I'd rather I sat in Ned Doud's place.'

'Outa there!'

Muttering, Doud was made to change places.

'Orright now, cock?'

It had worked! Kydd could barely suppress his elation. Not only did he know for certain that the furs went out with the whalers but he had the priceless additional piece of information that the last shipment of the season was about to depart!

The whaling men in the tavern would never know that among the jaunty British sailormen on the ran-tan there was a scholar of modern languages, only too eager to round out his education by overhearing what they were saying.

There was little point in staying any longer in the town so Kydd returned thankfully to his ship and Tysoe's ministrations.

In a hot tub he settled to think about what he could do with his new-won knowledge.

From casual talk with Horner he'd discovered that, while Britain kept to the Greenland whale fisheries, the Russians and Norwegians hunted in the seas around the appallingly remote and desolate icy fastness of Spitzbergen.

As a storehouse and base it would be perfect. The whalers could earn good money on the empty outward voyage and that was all they needed to do, as usual returning with oil. So far removed from the shipping lanes there would be no chance of unwelcome visitors, and the actual taking up of the furs for entry to Europe would be more than two-thirds through waters never cruised in by any man-o'-war.

The final passage through the blockade would no doubt be achieved by some means but if Kydd was to make his move it would be well before that.

The elements were clear: he could not move against the whalers. Spitzbergen was Norwegian territory, nominally controlled by Denmark and thus neutral territory. He could not land a party and seize the goods.

That left the one course. He had to intercept the ship sent to pick up the season's furs – after it had loaded and sailed, and was on the high seas.

The chances of being in the vicinity when that happened were too ridiculous to contemplate – except for one thing: Dillon had learned that the last whaling ship of the season from Archangel was about to sail, which implied that the year's haul of furs would be ready to pick up in Spitzbergen and there would be no reason for them to delay. In fact, it was more than likely that the ship was waiting there at this very moment for this final consignment before sailing.

This was now a very real possibility and a flood of renewed energy went through him.

Tysoe brought his robe and Kydd paced up and down – he was now seriously contemplating a voyage to the true Arctic, to the very edge of the ice-pack and the spawning ground of ice-mountains. Nothing in his experience had prepared him for such a venture and, apart from Horner, there was no one aboard who had been there.

If he was wrong in his reasoning the whole thing would end in failure. Did he have the confidence in his own judgement to go ahead? The worst they could do was strip him of his command, which they were doing anyway.

But would *Tyger* and her crew back him in his last great adventure?

Chapter 13

'No, an' that's m' last word on it!' Horner folded his arms and returned Kydd's gaze defiantly.

'Sir, you're engaged to be this ship's pilot in polar waters. I fail to see why Spitzbergen is not to be included in such.'

The sturdy whaleman said nothing.

'And I have a duty to the admiral to satisfy myself that there are no Frenchmen there. The only way to do that is go and find out,' Kydd added.

'Cap'n, this is y'r true Arctic. Ice floes, wind blast as'll freeze your soul, ice mountains bigger'n a ship-of-the-line – it's no place for a King's ship, I'm telling you!'

'You've been to Spitzbergen.'

'Aye. Mate of a Scowegian whaler f'r two year. That's how I knows—'

'I'll double your fee.'

'I got no charts o' the place. No one has. Whaling seamen know it by eye, hand on the lore down the generations. You have to, your lives depend on it.'

'As that may be, but—'

'Double and a half.' Horner bit his lip, hesitating. 'And a certificate sayin' as how I'm agin the voyage and I'm t' be cleared o' blame should we run afoul of the ice or such.'

'Done,' Kydd reluctantly conceded.

In the senior petty officers' mess Stirk slapped down his cards in annoyance. 'Matt, stick y'r head out an' see what all that fuckin' noise is about.'

Brewer, captain of the main-top, leaned over and pulled aside the painted canvas screen. 'Hoi! Jemmy, what's to do, as you're disturbin' the peace, like?'

A tow-haired ship's boy detached himself from an excited group and raced across. 'You ain't heard? We's going t' the North Pole an' all!'

'What's he say?' grunted Pollard, the hard-faced boatswain's mate, fingering his cards impatiently.

'Says we're goin' to the North Pole, Kip.'

'He what? Squeaker, get y'r arse in here an' explain y'self!'

'We are an' all, Mr Pollard. I heard the sailing master say as we ain't got no charts for the North Pole.'

'He's joshing, is all,' Brewer said, grunting. 'An' where's he say we're really off to?'

'T' the north, Spitsbugger or somewheres,' the boy came back.

'An' where the hell's that?' Pollard growled, looking at the others.

'Spitsbuggen,' Brewer said loftily. 'I heard on it from m' dad. Was in *Carcass* when they went explorin' in the High North thirty, forty year ago. Had along Our Nel as a younker, nearly lost the number of his mess to a polar bear an' then they all gets trapped in the ice, ready to be froze t' death, when the wind changes and they gets out.'

The thought of Horatio Nelson taken by a bear before ever he could go on to glory made them blink.

'What's he say it's like, cully?'

'Straight outa Hell!' Brewer said. 'As no man wants t' go back. Cold as'll freeze your tears, quiet calm in the forenoon, ragin' black storm in the afternoon. I could tell ye a yarn or three as'll curl your whiskers—'

'What we goin' up there for?' Pollard snarled. 'Bears an' ice – we's a frigate. Mongseers are what we're after and we ain't seen a hair o' one since we came t' this turdacious hole!'

'Stow it, Kip,' Stirk said. 'Owner knows what he's doing. Where'd you hear for sure there's no Frenchy hidin' there? Come on, mate, tell us how y' know.'

'That's not m' point. If'n it's as bad as Brewer says, they got no right t' send us inta the ice. Stap me, the North Sea oggin gets t' my bones, this'n is like to have m' balls fall off. No, mate, this is bad cess, nothin' good t' come of it and all round sailors droppin' dead wi' cold.'

'So what are you goin' to do about it, mate?'

'Me? Not just me – all on us! It's agin justice to make common sailors go where it ain't natural, like that there. We stands square up against an enemy, yeah, but not go prancin' around in the snow an' ice. Besides, we—'

'An old shellback like you, Kip, don't like the sea life cos it's uncomfortable?'

Pollard breathed deeply. 'I don't have t' take that from you, Toby! You know right well what I mean, it'd be a Hell voyage an' they got no right to force us. I say we stand fast, refuse t' sail!'

Stirk made to rise. 'If I'm a-hearing what I think I am . . .' he grated.

'Give us a clinkin' good reason, then, why we has t' go.'

197

'I'll give ye a few, cully! Ever thought why a prime fighting captain like Tom Cutlass gets removed into a piss-poor barky like *Tyger*?'

'T' sort us out, like.'

'No, y' doesn't know the half of it. It's a punishment, for talkin' wry about the Admiralty an' standin' up for his old commodore. In all the papers, 'cept you wouldn't know that. He faces down you shy cocks who mutiny and looks fair to makin' this ship a half good 'un. You do it again, he's finished.'

'A dead shame,' sneered Pollard.

'You want more? Then why d'ye think me an' Ned came aboard this rotten scow – f'r our health? No! Becos we knows Mr Kydd from way back. He's always treated us square, never shy of a mill, an' sees his men right afore 'imself. And he's a lucky bastard – I've got a tidy pile o' prize money just a-waitin' for when I swallows the anchor, thanks to followin' him. Now, you wants to throw him over for some scruffy strut-noddy as is the admiral's son?'

'Yair, well.'

'An' I tell you this, Kip. He's on to somethin' – I've seen the signs afore! Don't know what it is, but when he treads up an' down the quarterdeck with that looby quiet smile o' his, then he's got it planned. We're in for some high bobbery afore long, I promise ye.'

'Doesn't change things, mate. It'll be mortal cold and—'

'See here, y' codshead. I'm layin' a guinea to a shillun' that before ever the hook is up Our Tom'll see us right in the way o' cosy rig an' such. You on?'

'I know what you're saying to me, Mr Harman, believe me, I do,' Kydd said.

The purser sniffed as if he'd been asked to commit a crime.

'Very well. See Mr Blunt and treat with him against this list of clothing – and you'll go with a note drawn on my own account in London. Will that satisfy?'

The story given out was that the frigate was making motions to the east before returning in a broad sweep in keeping with their mission to search out any French presence.

The sailing master was cast down. 'If'n you'd told me, sir, I'd have found charts somewhere. All I has is this geographical picture o' the High North as I uses to get m' bearings. Shows your Spitzbergen but we can't navigate by it, much too small.'

'I should have given you instructions, I admit this. But if you'll get us to a few leagues off, Mr Horner will be there to tell us our reckonings,' Kydd consoled him. 'And think on this. We'll be the first navy to visit for a long time. The hydrographicals will want good observations, so know that I'll have a good journal kept to pass in at the end of our voyage.'

Joyce visibly brightened. 'I knows procedures. When I was in *Volcano* fire-ship in Halifax, back in 'eighty-one – or was that three? Before the peace, anyways. Well, we headed out—'

'Thank you. You'll want to prepare so I won't keep you longer.'

Under advice from Horner, particular stores were laid in and *Tyger* readied for the trial as well as she could be.

Then one morning the last whaling ship slipped by for the open sea.

It was on.

Their navigational objective was plain. Like a rough inverted triangle, Spitzbergen was of considerable size, some two hundred miles from its southern tip to the north, which was marked as indistinguishable from the great polar ice pack.

The east coast was even at this time still encased in ice so the whaling station had to be in the west.

The unsuspecting whaler would be sailing direct to the west coast therefore, so for *Tyger* it would be a diverging course to arrive on the east. What they did after that was not altogether clear as Kydd didn't want to let it be generally known what they were going for until after they'd made landfall, and he could see with his own eyes what conditions would allow.

He was outwardly confident but inside he was uneasy. They were headed for breathtakingly high latitudes – eighty degrees north, where ninety was the North Pole itself. The very limit of human existing – the very top of the world!

Tyger put to sea a day later and immediately met a chill north-easterly.

It eased but the biting wind brought shudders and tested their gear – oilskins with plenty of wool under them.

Horner showed them a whaler's trick: before going aloft, have a shipmate tie off the sleeves and ankles with spun yarn, together with a stout line around the waist, which was connected to another going fore and aft under the crotch. This enabled them to mount the rigging without their gear ballooning up in the fierce winds.

All hands, including Kydd, now wore Monmouth caps – warm, knitted coverings lined with felt and a tie-loop to save it if blown off.

Day by day they penetrated further into the north, the cold steadily more insidious. The first ice was seen, insignificant fragments that were beneath Horner's notice but they held the Tygers spellbound – the first tokens of the reality that lay in wait for them out there in the frozen north. Close to, most of the floes were grubby and discoloured, some with seabirds perched cheekily on them as they watched the ship pass by. Horner grimly assured them that they would see far grander ice than this before they made England again.

Sometimes the broad grey seas were transformed to a vivid blue under a vast sky, always accompanied by piercing cold of a keen purity, the white of breaking wave-crests a sparkling brilliance, and as the latitude steadily mounted, an unearthly quality took hold. It was of a harsh light almost unbearable in its intensity; the bowl of the sky now seeming more immense, exalted; their ship, lifting over the ceaseless vast swells, now so humble and insignificant.

One morning there was a strange and preternatural luminosity growing out of the sea far ahead. It intensified, a low white glow spreading to each side and even catching the underneath of the thin grey cloud, but there was nothing on the clear horizon that gave away its meaning to the wondering seamen.

'That's the ice-blink we get off of Spitzbergen,' Horner told Kydd. 'And it'll be Sørkapp Land – further on it has a dirty yellow in it where there's bare land under.'

Within hours they raised a needle-sharp peak that stood above others like it, and then the lower levels came into view, ice-streaked and increasingly formidable as they sailed through scattered floes and fragments, these now a pure white and often tinted in soft blue and green.

Further in among the waves a pair of black forms rhythmically broke surface and fell as they progressed, their glistening backs and tall fins humping in unison.

'Where's your harpoon, Mr Horner?' Kydd teased.

The old whaleman looked at him blankly. 'As they're killer whales only, not worth the stalking.'

Nearer still, the mountains took on massive form and

colour – dark rust, for there was not a scrap of green to soften the appalling desolation that was spreading before them. Nothing but a cruel majesty of iron ramparts and sweeping valleys, sheer mountains and gleaming ice.

'Well, Cap'n, an' we're here?'

Kydd pulled himself together. In the midst of this grandeur, to be contemplating an act of war. And without charts or sailing directions he was completely dependent on just one man. There was no other option than to lay the whole thing before him.

'Mr Horner. We'll go below and discuss our position.'

'Ha! Had a notion there'd be more to it than you said.'

'Then, sir, where's the whaling station?'

Joyce's atlas was produced.

'We's here,' Horner said, tapping the apex of the inverted triangle, the extreme southern tip of Spitzbergen. 'And all up the coast on the west you has mighty fjords – and some tiddlers. The Dutchy whalers are at Barentsburg, named after their hero, an' that's halfway up, a dozen miles into the biggest, Isfjorden.'

Even at the small scale of the atlas it was easy to see the repeated pattern of deeply incised fjords and it gave Kydd an idea.

'I can't take him on this territory. Now, he'll be sailing out of Isfjorden and will want to shape course south. If I lie out of sight in the next fjord below, he'll be passing right by and I'll know.'

'I'd say it's as good a plan as any. An' I can help you with that. Next 'un south is Bellsund an' tucked inside is a quiet little bay where we rides out a westerly.'

There were still many questions to answer. Was the fur transport real or imaginary? And if it was, could it indeed be at Barentsburg awaiting this last shipment before sailing?

There was only one way to find out: to sail in and see for himself — but that was impossible. The sight of an English frigate would ensure that it stayed put, snug and wary, until they left.

The boats? A man-o'-war's craft were distinctive and under sail a dead giveaway. And a quick glance at the dire landscape put paid to the idea of landing a party on the other side to climb up and observe from the heights.

Frustration built. To be thwarted at the final hurdle!

'We'll get to Bellsund, the least we can do.'

'Might think o' something, Mr Kydd,' Horner said sympathetically.

It was all of a day's sail, yet further north, past frigid bastions, blotched and veined with white, and hummocked drift ice that reached out to them, occasionally bringing a thump at the bows and a bumping passage down the side.

Their pilot stood a-brace on the quarterdeck the whole time, sharp-eyed over to starboard where the mountains met the sea. 'Squalls come whistlin' down from your ice-rivers and no warning save you catch the sea's darkling under 'em,' he muttered.

The weather was holding but that was no guarantee that it would last. The cold was mercilessly penetrating, especially for the group around the helm, who could do nothing to avoid the bitter down-draught from the mainsail and not even the sight of a long-toothed walrus staring up at them from atop an ice-floe made up for it.

Rounding the headland into Bellsund itself, so close to the iron rocks and soaring crags, the sheer bleakness and hostility of the land beat out at them: this was a place of trolls and winter ogres where man had no right to trespass.

It was as Horner had said, a secluded little bay out of

sight of the open sea. Kydd was taken aback at the visual impact of its colossal majesty – not one but two glaciers feeding into the mile-wide bay from between massive snow-capped mountain ranges that swept down to a desolate rock-strewn fringing shoreline, the bay filled from one side to the other with a dense scatter of small floating ice fragments.

'You'll want to drop hook here, Cap'n.'

They were only just within the near-circular bay but Kydd took his advice. In the lee of the mountains the wind had dropped to a whisper and the sea was glassy smooth, the stillness breathtaking. Atop slimed crags countless rock ptarmigans, malamuck, kirmew and others kept up a ceaseless din while at the water's edge seals stared at them.

The ship stood down but most men stayed on deck to gaze and wonder. Kydd felt a tug of sadness that his old sea companion and deepest friend, Renzi, was not there to witness this, Nature at her grandest and most terrifying.

'Sir?' It was Hollis, almost comical in his cold-weather gear.

Kydd knew what was on his mind. Was the frigate going back to sea or would they remain here for an indefinite time?

He didn't have an answer. 'Ah, I'll let you—'

A cry from the fo'c'sle made Kydd wheel about.

Appearing from around the headland was a small lugger with a trysail beetling seaward past them, their first sign of humanity for so long.

They were discovered – but what was it up to?

Horner said casually, 'A fisherman. There's a settlement up the fjord, for summer only. Takes seal, bear an' eider as well.'

'So he's off to his fishing grounds?'

'Can't be. They fishes in the fjords. This 'un is probably goin' to the whaling station for a bit o' trading, picking up what's needful for 'em.'

Kydd didn't hesitate. 'Give 'em a gun!'

A slight delay and the fog swivel cracked out.

They kept on and Kydd ordered another. The lugger brailed up and slewed to a stop.

'Mr Horner, will you come with me? I've a mind to do some trading of my own!'

When he returned it was with a satisfied smile and the lugger obediently following.

As soon as Kydd stepped back aboard he called across his third lieutenant and told him of the furs, adding, 'Mr Brice. You and my coxswain have just signed on as crew in this Norwegian fisherman. This is what you're to do . . .'

They were to stay with the boat as it sailed into the next fjord, there to observe closely any shipping at the Barentsburg station and report back. Halgren was Scandinavian and could communicate with the fisherfolk.

Now there was nothing to do but wait. If all went well they would be back before dark.

The lugger disappeared around the other headland.

Dillon edged up to him. 'Sir Thomas, I wonder at all, could we—'

'Just what I was thinking!' Kydd said instantly. 'Mr Hollis, I'm taking a boat ashore – on a reconnaissance. Anything at all, a gun and flag at the fore.'

The cutter threaded through the floating ice-field so close they could feel its frozen breath, the men at the oars looking out each side apprehensively. The shore approached, rock the colour of old iron and then a dense beach of light pebbles. They crunched into it just below an old hut of bleached timbers, crazily tilted to one side.

Soaring far above them were stark, sere mountains and on the opposite shore the bluff cliff of ice that was a glacier disgorging into the bay. As the fitful sun caught it, the dull white was shot through with delicate sapphire and emerald tints and with a brilliance that almost hurt the eye.

On the air was a pungency of brine, a powerful smell that seemed oddly magnified by the intense clarity of the cold.

In awed silence they trod up the beach to the hut. It was open to the sky and empty of everything, except odd cast-off human articles. Behind it was a long pile of leviathan white bones, the skulls and ribs of long-dead whales. There was a whaling slip, with a rusty windlass at its head, and beyond a row of rude graves, unmarked but for a small cairn at the head of each. They stood for a minute by them, reflecting on the fate that had brought these men to their end in this unspeakable remoteness.

Further up, the beach ended and stony precipices and writhing crags cast in shadow were interspersed with scree slopes a thousand feet high and sharp escarpments rearing from the snow-covered uplands.

It was altogether an immensely affecting presence and there in the Arctic stillness Kydd felt a profound humility.

'Sir, you were right!' Brice said, in open admiration. 'As bold as brass, lying by the jetty just along from us. A line of men coming down from some sort of ice-cave and loading.'

Kydd quickly had the essentials: that the fur transport was a full-rigged ship with gun-ports, but not a man-o'-war and inferior in size to *Tyger*. They had sighted its name: *Grote Walvis*, Dutch.

Unable to hurry the fishermen, Brice had been forced to watch the loading complete, the hatches put in place and secured ready for sea – with sail bent to the yards, it could be only a short time before it sailed.

Kydd was ready: at the outer headland with a view both to seaward and back to *Tyger*, the pinnace was waiting, concealed among the rocks. In this strange world there was no darkness and they should sight their prey making off past them to the southward in blithe ignorance of the hungry frigate lying in wait.

Their anchor was hove short and sail brought to readiness – in minutes their true purpose was known around the ship. Kydd sensed the heightened excitement but was mystified by the knowing smile Stirk gave him as he padded past.

In a distant flurry the pinnace began flying back to *Tyger*, an unmistakable signal to prepare for the chase. Four miles out, the *Walvis* under all plain sail was on her way to Bonaparte's Europe.

There was no need for haste: it was necessary to let the vessel clear territorial waters to reach the high seas before they showed themselves, at which point it would be too late – the frigate would lie between them and safety.

He gave them two hours, then *Tyger* spread her wings for the open ocean.

It was the last act. But there was still one thing that, even at this late stage, could intervene to wreck their hopes: that this ship was intended to go on to break the British blockade of the continent. For this it would need to be equipped with appropriate papers – false, cunningly prepared and proving the vessel a sacrosanct neutral.

If this was so, then Kydd could intercept and board, but would have the mortification of being forced to let it go, no matter his suspicions. Violating neutrality was not to be considered.

He kept his fears to himself as they reached out over the grey polar seas under the steady north-easterly. The course was simple – due south to Europe, and in a short time there was a welcome hail from the masthead, then distant sails could be seen generally.

'Damn m' eyes, but I'd like to be on their quarterdeck when they sights a frigate in pursuit!' chuckled Joyce, rubbing his gloved hands.

'An' he's putting about!' came an astonished cry a little later.

Instead of their view of the distant stern of the ship, now the three masts were separating in a turn-about.

Kydd watched intently . . . and the ship hardened on a course taking them at right angles away in a desperate flight close to the wind.

'Hey, now!' he couldn't help blurting in satisfaction. 'And he's a bad conscience, I believe!'

No ship confident of its flag or papers would be fleeing so. This was now a straight chase!

'Follow his motions,' he instructed, and *Tyger* heeled as she put down her helm to run parallel some miles to windward. They could never escape this way, for with her superior speed, all *Tyger* needed to do was bear down and close until it was all over. And no darkness to put an unfair end to the pursuit, either.

Horner nodded at the binnacle. 'You've seen what he's up to? Headin' north – into the pack-ice. Where no fool goes, 'less he wants t' shake hands with a polar bear.'

The wind dropped to a whisper; the two ships ghosted on, a bare two miles apart. They stayed that way for half a day, frustrating to a degree, but then, under a crystal blue sky, the horizon softened and a long white layer extended across their entire vision – freezing fog.

The image of *Walvis* wavered and disappeared into it, her mastheads briefly visible before they, too, were swallowed.

'As far as we go, I think, Cap'n?'

'Where he can go, so can we,' Kydd said stubbornly.

'That there's the ice-edge – an' worse. No place for—'

'We go in.'

As soon as they entered the fog-bank it was another world. The surprising warmth of the sun was cut off, as if a door had been closed, and the cold set in, fierce and piercing in the soft white anonymity.

The ship began taking on a fairy-tale appearance of a sparkling loveliness as the glistening fog particles froze to a rime that covered everything: deck, rigging, sails and every individual rope that ran aloft.

'You see why I said—'

'Thank you. Mr Hollis, relieve every man of the watch-on-deck one by one. They're to go below and get on every bit of clothing against the cold as can be found. Sealskin, fearnought, leather – Mr Horner will go with 'em to advise.'

The ship stole on, the lookout at the fore-masthead relieved every fifteen minutes peering into the featureless white blanket.

An ominous thud and the frigate trembled. She had shouldered aside a wicked floe bigger than their launch.

'Sir, I really don't think this is a good idea,' Hollis muttered uncomfortably.

Kydd said nothing and unaccountably the fog-bank thinned and they were through – and not a mile ahead was their quarry, nosing along the edge of the ice.

'Got him!'

'I don't think so,' Horner said heavily. 'See this?'

He waved at the scattered ice fragments. The sea they swam in had subtly changed. Between the larger floes there was a peculiar wide scattering of floating platelets in an almost oily carpet.

'Frazil ice. Temperature drops any more an' we'll have ice rind – and then you get out fast.'

Kydd said nothing, watching his prey so close. Both ships were barely making way in the near complete calm, sails hanging loosely and giving an aimless flap every now and then. If they could catch a random cats-paw of wind it would be sufficient to bring them up and, fantastic as it seemed in the surroundings, there could be gun-play and a boarding.

The small breeze was running parallel with the edge of the ice and Kydd could see now what *Walvis* was up to. She had been looking for a way into the pack and had found one. Angling behind a long floe, she eased in, the flash of wet bearing-off spars visible as her sailors poled their way past. Then they were inside some ice-lagoon and still under way deeper in.

'Don't even think on it, Cap'n!' Horner grated. 'If you does, I quit! Hear me?'

By now *Tyger* was close to the ice edge herself. In horrified fascination men watched the unending floes drifting and heard a ceaseless tiny creaking and muted cracking as they gently rose and fell on the slight swell. Delicate frost-smoke hung over the surface of the sea, playfully plucked and flurried to eddying wreaths by a polar zephyr.

Kydd's thoughts raced. The rational course was to give best to one with superior knowledge of these regions and sail away before some hideous Arctic fate overtook them. But that would be at the cost of his only chance of coming out of his High North expedition with something to show for it.

So near!

Boats?

No, boats coming down a defined lead in the ice were a perfect oncoming target. A charge over the ice? How did he know if a floe would take their weight? If it didn't, their end would be immediate and awful.

Here he was with a man-o'-war of unanswerable force and under her guns not a mile away was her prey – but he was completely helpless!

Horner was not going to let it go. 'See all them ice-hillocks another mile in? That's your ice fast to the shore. It comes out an' meets the drift ice on its way in with terrible force. If the wind's offshore, you has a chance. Wind turns onshore, why, you'll be crushed between 'em like an egg-shell!'

Ominously, Kydd could see that, just as had been predicted, the frazil ice was coming together in a continuous greasy-looking thin sheet.

They had been lucky, he knew. On mess-decks and in wardrooms he'd heard tales of ferocious storms raging out of the Arctic wilderness and if one struck here . . .

'It's freezin' in, Cap'n,' warned Horner. 'Time we was going.'

The weather was changing – Kydd felt it in his bones. How long could he afford to wait? The smaller *Walvis* could lie there indefinitely if it was equipped for long-distance voyaging in these parts but *Tyger* was ill-equipped and vulnerable. Was it right to risk her and her company for the sake of what was really personal advantage?

He shivered and pulled his coat tighter as a slightly stronger wind flaw cut into him . . . and something Horner had said returned. What was it?

The slight wind! His unconscious mind had registered that it had shifted a point or two and strengthened a little.

'Sir, we should leave while we can,' the muffled voice of his first lieutenant came, and in his anxiety he'd even gone so far as to touch Kydd's arm.

But, with a fierce glee, Kydd had seen how he could win. 'Mr Joyce, I desire *Tyger* to lie off at two cables distance. Mr Hollis, a file of marines and a boarding party to muster at the mainmast now.'

They looked at him as if he'd suddenly gone mad.

'Carry on, please!' he ordered crisply.

With a grudging smile Horner tipped his hat to Kydd and watched *Walvis* warp about and make for the open sea – and, reluctantly, into *Tyger*'s embrace.

Chapter 14

'Don't concern yourself, m' boy, your prize will be taken care of by *Whippet* when she heads off with my dispatches. Now, tell me all about it – I'm sure it'll be a rare tale!'

Kydd knew the bluff Admiral Russell would not take kindly to tacking and veering about the actuality and opened up to him, freely admitting his motives for the daring thrust into the High Arctic. The chase after the furs had been a long shot but what had he had to lose?

There was professional talk on the suitability of Archangel as a second port – regretfully dismissed – and conditions while working ship in freezing weather.

Then Russell asked, 'Tell me, why did the barky decide to give himself up from the pack-ice so conveniently?'

Kydd debated whether to claim the credit himself but answered, 'Something my pilot mentioned. He said the worst danger for navigating in the north is when the fixed ice coming out from the shore meets the floating pack driven in by the wind. Any ship between will be helplessly crushed. The Hollander was safe until the wind turned onshore. Then he had the choice of being sunk and marooned on the ice as he watched us sail away or . . .'

'You sighted his papers?' the admiral asked, clearly keen to know if indeed there was a case for condemning *Walvis* as prize, given her rich lading.

'I did, sir.' Kydd went on to tell him how he'd found the ship was merely a ferry, trans-shipping the cargo to a disguised blockade-runner waiting in Tromsø fjord in north Norway ready for the dash south. It must have seemed wildly improbable that a British man-o'-war of size would ever chance on Archangel, still less Spitzbergen, he added. Then he beamed. 'I fancy, sir, we'll soon be sharing in as rich a prize as any these last years!'

Russell gave a sad smile. 'Not as who would say. Won't even make the prize court, o' course.'

'Sir?'

'Your action must count as a considerable success – at thwarting a smuggling ring. Kydd, I have to tell you, the offence for which we take reprisal with this prize is nothing but an offence against the revenue service of Russia. See if you can find in our orders-in-council where the fur of the Arctic fox is listed as contraband. You won't. So what we see is the property of the Tsar of Russia rightfully restored.'

'So—'

'I expect the tsar will be generous in his thanks and no doubt our Dutch friends will at this moment be marching off to Siberia in chains, but as to lawful prize . . .'

Seeing Kydd's crestfallen look he gave a chuckle. 'It has its bright side. I dare to say we've a reasonable claim to salvage on the cargo, a tidy sum. And undoubtedly it affects you personally too, Kydd.'

'Sir?'

'What would our grateful tsar say if he found the Admiralty had rewarded the captain responsible with the loss of his ship? The politicals would never allow it. No, m' boy, I do believe you've *Tyger* to yourself if you want her.'

In the solitude of his cabin, thoughts crowded in on Kydd. *Tyger* was his – but for how long? Despite Russell's words, he felt it was a reprieve only. He had to go on to achieve a standing that made him untouchable by the Admiralty and restored him to favour with the public.

Actions that resulted in distinction and acclaim could never be commanded on a whim. In all his past triumphs he had been in a position that allowed various elements to be exploited to advantage – *and* he had had the freedom to act. In a fleet there would be little chance in the short term of coming on such a situation.

But, an inner voice offered, hadn't his greatest laurels been won at Curaçao, part of a squadron?

He grimaced. There was little of the far exotic about duties with the North Sea Fleet and far less likelihood of such derring-do in these waters but it couldn't be ruled out entirely. His future course was now clear: while there was even the slightest chance of distinction he would make damned sure he was ready.

He would bring *Tyger* up to a fighting pitch such as he'd achieved with *L'Aurore* – forge a blade that he could take into any contest and be sure of victory.

Before, he'd not felt a rightful captain of *Tyger*. She'd started as a punishment ship, a place of exile, and he'd not given her the interest and attention she deserved, especially with the shadow of losing her before him: then she had been a fleeting and temporary command, which it would have been unwise to take to his heart.

It was different now and he vowed he would cleave to his new ship. There were pleasing and appealing aspects of her character that reached out to him – those bluff, no-nonsense bulldog lines, the massed eighteen-pounder great guns, her willingness to brute through head seas and fearlessly carry high sail . . .

He and the ship's company had met in the worst possible circumstances and he'd not been inclined to test their limits under those conditions. Now they'd seen him in action and he'd given them a prize of sorts. It was a start but he was not naïve enough to think that this meant he'd won their loyalty – that only came with trust and that, in turn, with shared danger. But time was not on his side . . .

He began jotting down what he must do. Gunnery, sail-handling – these prime battle-winners were top of the list.

Their brush with the frigates in the 'bullion shipment' had been revealing: there'd been no flinching or hanging back but there'd been a stiffness in working the guns, betraying a woeful lack of practice compared to the fluid choreography in *L'Aurore*. He'd long learned the lesson that halving the time for the load-and-fire cycle had the same effect as doubling the number of guns, in a frigate duel effectively pitting the enemy against the broadside to be expected from a ship-of-the-line. Every split-second saved would translate in a long, close action to many more strikes, any one of which could be a settler.

Smart working of sail was far more than mere practice. Necessarily, there was a distancing in the layers of command. In a first-rate man-o'-war the captain on the quarterdeck would issue an order, which would go to the officer in charge

216

of that part-of-ship and his team; the petty officers would pull the men together and make it happen, knowing their individual strengths and weaknesses and alert to any slacking or fumbling, while the officer stood braced for any external change in circumstances. It took trust by the officer, trust from the petty officers and mutual professional respect. So recently emerged from mutiny, these strands of interdependence were frayed at best and his officers must look to restoring them as soon as possible.

Bowden understood the importance of this, he felt; Brice was gifted, his men at the foremast the only ones showing positive signs, but his first lieutenant . . .

Hollis was from a good family, but in a ship of war that was a disadvantage. Used to unquestioning obedience from servants, his instinct was to issue a stream of directions and leave it at that. Under stress of a mutinous situation he'd become more strident, distant and critical, and while at present the men took his orders, that precious two-way reliance was lacking.

There were other elements that affected *Tyger*'s fighting spirit, as Kydd remembered from his own origins before the mast. Petty tyrannies could reign when bullies gained positions of power as petty officers. This would be invisible from the quarterdeck but would corrode a sailor's loyalty quicker than anything. He knew the signs and would deal ruthlessly with any he saw. Incompetence was another real concern. The faith in authority that made men at a word go out on a yardarm in the teeth of a gale would vanish in an instant at any misgivings, and then it would be a hesitant, cautious crew.

Because he was taking over an existing ship's company he'd had to accept the decisions of *Tyger*'s previous captain in the matter of who had been rated into vital positions, and this was not something he was happy with. It was, of course, the prerogative of every captain to rate any seaman petty officer on the spot – and to disrate. If any failed him he wouldn't hesitate to act.

So much depended on the one thing he didn't have: a first-hand appreciation of the qualities of his men.

It would probably shock the common seaman to discover just how much his captain knew of him. Restraining every instinct to join in, a captain necessarily had to pass over responsibility for the execution of his order to others, then stand back and watch. He could, without them knowing, make out who were the impulsive, the stolid, the reluctant, the reliable. He could quietly observe the interplay between leaders and followers, their character and potential, and be ready to act on it – but all this took time.

Kydd balled his fists in frustration. Their testing might be upon them without warning and a frigate could expect to be first in any action.

There was only one way forward: to show no mercy to his men or his ship in the race to succeed. From this moment on, all hands could expect blood, toil and sweat until *Tyger* was as effective a fighting machine as *L'Aurore* had been. Resolved, he jammed on his cocked hat and strode out on deck.

The squadron was comfortably in a loose extended line ahead as they ploughed the seas off the Dutch coast under easy sail, and there was nothing to challenge the afternoon watch. The men at the conn were in relaxed conversation, the others around the deck going about their business in unhurried, economic movements.

Bowden detached from the group and came over, touching

his hat. 'A fine afternoon, sir, don't you think?' he said pleasantly. 'We've—'

'You think so? What's going on there on the main hatch?' Kydd demanded.

The men were sitting cross-legged on the gratings in companionable gossip with canvas spread over their knees, stitching sails, an agreeable task in the sun.

'Sir, the sailmaker asked for hands to complete our fair-weather suit of sails.'

'When the ship's in such a state?' Kydd crossed to the lee main shrouds and fingered into the deadeyes, sniffing the result. 'This is scandalous! There's been no hog's lard in here for a cat's age. How can you keep equal strain on all parts save you grease it?'

'Sir, it's the boatswain's—'

'No, Mr Bowden, it's *your* duty – to see the boatswain does his. The watch-on-deck is there to be employed when not working ship and I'll have it so while we're sadly ahoo.'

Around the helm dark glances were exchanged.

Kydd turned and glared forward grimly.

After some minutes a flustered Hollis appeared, having caught word of Kydd's mood. 'Good afternoon, sir,' he said carefully. 'I rather thought we'd—'

'Just what I was thinking, Mr Hollis! We could be up with an enemy at a moment's notice and then where would we be? Quarters at six bells, and the men may stand down just as soon as they make my times.'

In the last hour before supper the gun-crews were set to intensive drill under eye and pocket-watch.

The individual timings were dismally slow, movements awkwardly co-ordinated, and under pressure, gun-captains became flustered.

Kydd's expression grew glacial. Their rate of fire was abysmal, the eighteens served at a slower rate than he'd ever seen before. If they went up against a well-manned and resolute French frigate, their survival could not be assured, let alone a victory. Appalled, he grunted to Hollis to stand the men down and stalked off to his cabin.

Kydd waited grimly for the men's breakfast to finish and on the stroke of one bell the boatswain's calls pealed out.

'*All hands! All the hands! Clear lower deck! Haaaands to muster!*'

They came aft – the entire ship's company. Cooks and gunners, seamen and officers, carpenter and marines. In a sea of faces they crowded the gangways and upper deck, interest, suspicion and resentment in equal measure.

He nodded at the boatswain, who blasted out a 'still' on his pipe.

The muttering and murmuring died away as *Tyger*'s company waited to hear what their captain had to say.

'Tygers!' he roared. 'You're hailed aft for one reason, and one reason only. I'm captain and this is my ship – and it's yours as well.'

He let it hang for a space, looking from one to another.

'So why am I ashamed of it?

'It's not because of what happened under Captain Parker – that's over and finished. I don't give a brass razoo about it. But what I saw at gun practice yesterday was a dance of cripples! I won't have it! This is a top fighting frigate and I mean to take her into the hottest part of any battle, ready or no!'

He was not reaching them. Stony faces, folded arms and a sullen silence.

'You say we took on those men-o'-war on the way to

Gothenburg. I say we ran away! No fight worth a spit and no mill man to man. Then a cruise in the ice and never a shot fired. You're soft and useless, and if a half-good Frenchy lays alongside he'll have us.

'So these are my orders starting today. From now on, before the forenoon watch turns to, it'll be quarters and practice for an hour. And again at six bells in the afternoon. If I don't see progress, and that quickly, there'll be more in the first dog-watch, damn it.'

This was met with savage murmurs: the dog-watches were traditionally a seaman's own time, to be spent yarning and taking leisure on the fore-deck.

Kydd looked down on the gun-deck at the row of guns being exercised. Time and time again the tons' weight of gun was run out, sweating crews heaving wearily at the side-tackles, drawing it back in with the rear training tackle, ram-rod whirling as powder charges, wad and ball were fumbled towards the muzzle in a never-ending round.

He had been on a gun-crew himself and knew what he was asking of them but he took no pity on them. It had to be done.

Forward, Bowden was taking his gun exercise by quarter-gunner – four guns at a time, allowing the others to catch their breath.

'Compliments to Mr Bowden and he's to know that at close quarters every gun is served,' Kydd snapped to his messenger. 'I want to see all his guns in action at once.'

Only long familiarity born of the same crews working together could bring about the fluid, unconscious ballet that was a battle-winning line of guns. In combat each crew needed to ply their gun in the confines of the narrow space between the pieces without tangling with the next gun-crew, who could be counted on to be out of synchrony with them. It was something they had to sort out for themselves: whether the loading number took his charge direct from the powder monkey or it was passed to him by the side-tackle men; whether these same men ducked or stood aside as the long stave was reversed end for end by the rammer to become a sponge, stabbing deep into the muzzle.

The afternoon practice was even worse. Kydd took in the shuffling and lethargy, the creaking, stiff motions, the result of bone-cracking weariness and suffering from burning muscles and painful joints. These men were sadly out of condition, clearly not having been exercised in earnest by the previous captain. But who knew when *Tyger* must face her destiny?

'Feeble and pitiful. I'll have a half-hour in the dog-watches and be damned to it!' Kydd bit out.

Bowden stared at his captain for a long moment, then, expressionless, turned away.

Three days later *Alceste* frigate rejoined the squadron and in turn *Tyger* was detached to the convoy assembly anchorage at Yarmouth Roads. Russell was at pains to explain that Baltic convoy duty, however onerous, was one they all must share in.

But it was what Kydd had been waiting for. A two-day sail as an independent and no one to see! He wasn't going to waste the opportunity. Just as soon as the distant topsails of the squadron sank below the horizon he turned to the officer-of-the-watch. 'I have the ship, Mr Brice.'

Now he would find out what *Tyger* was made of.

He stood by the helm. 'As close by the wind as she'll lie,' he told the quartermaster.

'What course, sir?'

'Never mind that, do as I say.' In these well-known waters there was no concern about picking up their position again later.

The helmsman eased his wheel to meet the wind, gingerly glancing up to the edge of the topsail for the least fluttering – too close and there was every risk of slamming aback.

Kydd sniffed the wind. Not bad. Sheet in a little more on the driver and an easing on the outer jib? It was done and he was rewarded by another half-point into the wind even if at the cost of an increased stiffness in the roll.

Around the deck seamen stopped what they were doing to watch.

A little care with the trim, and he could probably get another knot out of her in this steady south-westerly but this was not a painstaking investigation – all he wanted for the present was a feel of how *Tyger* took to various conditions.

'Shall you be exercising gun-crews, sir?' Hollis said stiffly.

'Not now,' Kydd said. 'Sail-handling first. Do hold yourself ready for manoeuvres later.'

So she was capable of a workmanlike close hauling. But there was more to it than that – how did she answer while straining so? A sluggish response to a sudden helm order while in an engagement was a grave disadvantage and therefore situations involving it would need to be avoided, if at all possible, in the deadly cut and thrust that was a frigate duel.

He hesitated for a moment. 'I'll take the wheel,' he said, to the startled helmsman, taking a spoke with one hand, the age-old signal for a handover. At his nod the man released one spoke and Kydd took another, testing the pressure on

223

the wheel as the man gradually released his other hand and stepped back.

He now had *Tyger* under his hands and the memories flooded back.

The last time he had been at the wheel was as a young seaman so long ago in *Artemis* 32, defying the Southern Ocean off Cape Horn – or was that the old *Trajan* in the Caribbean?

The feel of a live helm was thrilling and satisfying, the thrum and tug connecting him directly to *Tyger*'s beating heart.

She had a surprising amount of resistance to the little corrections he made and concentrated effort was needed at the wheel. In common with most British-built ships, her rudder was broad and deep, plenty of bite – and that translated to hard work but masterly manoeuvring.

Putting real force into it, he piled on the turns, and instantly *Tyger* paid off to leeward, the sudden change in heel sending men staggering.

This was a battle-winner! As the frigate steadied, he put on opposite turns and, without hesitation, she came up to the wind, under his touch willingly stretching out ahead. He glanced up, applying small corrections until he saw the sail luff begin a fretful fluttering.

In spreading satisfaction, he took in the line of deck as it swept nobly forward to her stout bowsprit lifting and falling. He was suddenly reluctant to give up the wheel – it brought memories of times when his only cares were his grog and his shipmates.

Then his eyes took in the faces looking down the deck at him, puzzled, suspicious.

He focused on one in particular: boatswain Dawes wore an expression that was anxious, sagging. The man was out of his depth in a first-rank ship of war, his age and comfortable ways unsuited to a frigate like *Tyger*, and he was terrified he'd be found out.

'Duty helmsman to the wheel,' Kydd rapped.

With the ship reverted to the sea watch, he went to the boatswain. 'I mean to put the ship to the test, Mr Dawes. What do you say to sending down a topmast at all?'

'Sir, could be tricksy dos, the seas bein' up as they is.' The eyes pleaded with him.

'Well, shifting one of the great guns from fore to aft – that'll need cross-tackles and preventers, don't you think?'

'Ah, Cap'n Parker, we never done that, not at all, Mr Kydd.'

'You can't conceive any need to mount stern-chasers aft in a hurry? Come, come, sir, this is what you must expect in a prime frigate like *Tyger*.'

'Aye, sir.' There was resignation and dull resentment in the reply.

Kydd knew Dawes had to go but a boatswain was appointed to a ship by Admiralty warrant and could not be turned out by his captain. He had to be made to leave the ship of his own accord. 'Then we'll think of something else to stretch our stout crew,' he added.

Out of the corner of his eye Kydd saw Bowden watching with a tight face. He shifted his gaze deliberately to his second lieutenant, who looked away bleakly.

Kydd turned to his third lieutenant: 'Mr Brice. I desire to exercise the people at putting the ship about. Both watches on deck, to work sail, first one, then the other.'

'Sir.' Standing tense and wary, his expression was unreadable.

'Ready your men. Start with the starb'd watch and they're to go about on the larb'd tack at my word. I shall be timing them.'

'Aye aye, sir.' He turned away. 'Hands to stations to stay ship,' he blared.

Kydd pointedly withdrew his fob watch and held it prominently. 'Carry on, please.'

Even under pressure it was as he'd seen before. Slow and deliberate, cautious. The other watch of the hands was the same. The time was not disgraceful but neither was it outstanding.

'We'll have 'em handing sail now. Each mast separately to furl its tops'l then set it again. Begin with the fore.'

This time he could see each individual seaman at work. He didn't yet know names but he had faces. He watched intently; the character of each couldn't be hidden and now he was building a true picture of *Tyger*'s ship's company, its strengths and weaknesses.

'Mr Hollis.'

The first lieutenant came over to the weather side of the quarterdeck, guarded and defensive.

'At the mainmast. What do you think of 'em?'

They were trying hard, the young petty officer of maintop going like a demon, flinging himself out on the yard at the front of his men in his eagerness.

'Doing well, I should have thought, sir.'

'You don't see anything wrong, who's to say, a failing?'

Hollis looked up, shading his eyes and answered woodenly, 'They appear to be succeeding, sir.'

'I'm not satisfied,' Kydd said flatly.

'Sir?'

'The captain of the top. He means well but he's no leader. It's not for him to be going out on the yardarm with his men, he should stay in the tops and take charge from there. How can he see if his men are all of them pulling their weight? What if the order is countermanded under stress of battle and he needs to regroup?'

The lieutenant continued to gaze up obstinately.

'No, Mr Hollis. This man is keen but inexperienced. Better an older hand. Do you know of any such?'

Hollis glowered but did not answer.

'And the man passing the earring, do you not feel—'

'Sir! If you feel my watch and station bill is—'

'I'm saying it were well you knew your men better, Mr Hollis.'

The morning wore on. He took to asking each officer in charge names for Dillon to take down in his notebook. That knowing old salt who always tailed on to a line last so he could take it easy out of sight of his shipmates. The young and nimble lad out on the yard who was a born top-man. The petty officer at the fore-topmast staysail who for some reason was hanging back from driving his men.

As they laboured Kydd sensed antagonism rising, the dull animus of men driven hard beyond the normal – but he was not going to let up with the sceptre of defeat hanging over *Tyger*.

He was rapidly getting to grips with it, throwing *Tyger* into all points of sailing, feeling her strength and power, her breeding. There was nothing like *L'Aurore*'s delicacy in light winds but very little to complain about, and running large she hadn't that lurching long roll and for that he was grateful. He sensed she would be at her best in hard winds: a fresh gale would have her joyously breasting the combers and he looked forward to matching her up to some of the blows he'd experienced in his last command.

All in all he was more than satisfied – especially with her striking manoeuvrability. Sweet and sure in going about and lightning sharp to answer the helm in any circumstance, this was something to be treasured – only if the sail-handling could match it. He would make sure it did.

At midday he stood the hands down for dinner.

The afternoon generally would see one watch go below, but not today. These were the only precious days of independence away from the fleet he could count on.

'The men are going to smell powder now, Mr Hollis. Both watches, gun by gun.' He'd taken the precaution of consulting with the gunner about their practice allowance. As he'd suspected, there had been no expenditure for months while Parker had struggled to keep his hold on the ship.

He could feel the lieutenant's hostility.

'We'll start with a little dry practice. Mr Bowden?'

Among the waiting gun-crews there was a stillness, a naked loathing that radiated out.

'Carry on.'

He let them go for three 'rounds', then casually ordered, 'Sail trimmers to stand clear.'

The gun numbers detailed for going aloft in an action stood back, bewildered. To the remaining crew he rapped, 'Run out your guns!'

It brought gasps of dismay for the cold iron of the big guns was a preposterous mass for the reduced men at the tackle falls.

He waited with a grim smile to let them feel the impossibility, then stepped forward. 'You've never seen close action, you lubbers, have you? Let me tell you that calling away sail trimmers is no excuse for standing about idle while the enemy pounds us. When they go aloft it's every man on the falls, gun-captain included, and only after the gun's close up do they go back to their place. Let's have it done, Mr Bowden.'

Next he would see what an eighteen-pounder could do after *L'Aurore*'s twelves, a good one-third smaller weight of metal.

A target was knocked up: an empty barrel with a pole nailed to the side bearing a large red flag.

It went over the side, rapidly left bobbing jauntily astern until it was a tiny red blob on the face of the ocean.

'Larboard first, start from forward. Lay us to weather of the mark, four cables distant,' Kydd snapped at the sailing master, an unnaturally subdued Joyce.

He clattered down to the gun-deck and hurried forward to where the gun-captain of the first was making preparation. These long eighteens were a byword in the navy for accuracy at a distance, if served well, and had the weight to make themselves felt.

The gun-crew readied.

'In your own time, two rounds at your target.'

Kydd saw that Bowden was leaving the loading and pointing entirely to the gun-captains and silently approved, even if the young man was doing his best to ignore him.

These eighteens were big beasts, half as high as a man and over a dozen feet long and now the skills would turn from backbone and sinew to hand and eye . . . and of one man, the gun-captain.

Kydd, however, turned his attention away from the gun-captains – Bowden could be relied on to pick up shortcomings in working the gun. He was interested in the results, out there where the speck of red in the distance nodded cheekily to leeward.

The first gun banged out, the slam of concussion and then the reek of powder-smoke briefly enfolding him. It was a fair shot, twenty feet to one side but reasonable for elevation, and Kydd was impressed. Not with the marksmanship but the fact that these long eighteens had such a flat arc of fire – the white plume of first-strike was close to the target even at this range.

He felt the gun-captain's darted glance at him but he gave no notice and continued his gaze to seaward.

The second round was closer still but if the target had been extended to be an imaginary frigate it would have missed astern of it. 'Off the target, complete miss,' he growled.

The gunner made much of noting the expenditure of each ball but it was within allowance and Kydd ignored him.

Other guns on the larboard side did even worse, and after he had given orders to wear ship to bring the starboard side to bear, he paced grim-faced along.

The first two guns did not improve the showing. The third gun took its time but the result was dramatic – the sudden rise of the plume within only a couple of yards and perfect for elevation. Its second round was even better, the ball within feet of the flag, so close it fluttered in alarm.

He turned to congratulate the gun-captain, who looked back at him with a controlled blankness. It was Stirk, come up from his station as yeoman of the powder room.

'Well done, that gun,' he said loudly. Stirk folded his arms and gazed back without comment.

It was too much to expect the next gun to match up. Neither did the remainder on that side.

When it was all over Kydd summoned the gunner to him. 'Mr Darby,' he said acidly, knowing that his words were being overheard by all. 'Pray do explain to me why the Tygers are so wanting in the article of laying a gun. With one exception, that is.'

He knew very well, of course. Not only had he kept the

L'Aurores on their toes with exercises but they'd been in savage actions many times, while *Tyger* . . .

'Most would think it good practice, sir,' the gunner said woodenly.

'But I don't. The rest of the afternoon all gun-captains will muster in the fore-bay and take instruction from the yeoman of the powder room.' He waited, then said, 'And in the last dog-watch we'll try again.'

This time there were savage murmurs and he looked around sharply until they'd subsided. 'Carry on, Mr Hollis.'

It was unfortunate for them, what with all the impedimenta of live firing to set up yet again and in their own time, but he was well aware that these two days were the only ones he was going be free to do as he wished.

'Can't do it!' the gunner said, with a smirk.

'Oh?'

'We've shot away our allowance. Ain't none more!'

'Then we'll use next quarter's in advance!' Kydd retorted icily, turned on his heel and stalked away.

The next day was the last before arriving. With names noted previously he harried the first lieutenant to make changes, demotions, rating up the promising and reconfiguring watch and stations against the strengths and weaknesses he'd seen. Then he piled on more pressure at guns and sail.

They had to succeed!

There was some improvement, but apprehension crowded in on Kydd at the vision of a well-found French frigate circling for the kill – it was common knowledge that, with his battle fleets helpless in port, Bonaparte was taking the opportunity of sending his frigates to sea on predatory cruises with ample, picked crews against the short-handed and weather-ravaged British. The odds were against them from the start.

Kydd flopped into his chair in his cabin and held his head in his hands, thinking of his days in *L'Aurore*, the ship he had left so reluctantly, which had borne him to glory and distinction and in which he had put down so many memories.

'Come!' he called irritably, at a knock on the door that interrupted his thoughts.

It was Dillon, with a sheaf of papers. 'Sir Thomas, they're outstanding these five days—'

'Not now, Mr Dillon.'

'I do advise they are—'

'I said not now!'

'Sir, if another time is more convenient, I'd be happy to comply,' Dillon said, with quiet dignity.

'Damn it – just go!'

'Very well, sir.'

At the door Dillon hesitated, then turned to face Kydd. 'Sir, I'm your confidential secretary and – and I think there's something you should know.'

'I told you to leave. Now do so or I'll have you thrown out!'

Pale-faced, Dillon stood his ground. 'Touching as it does on your command of this vessel.'

Kydd shot to his feet, the chair knocked askew. 'What in Hades gives you the right to criticise *me*?' he barked in a fury. 'If you're not out of here in ten seconds I'll give you a spell in the bilboes, so help me!'

'Sir. The officers are convinced you're a glory-seeker, and the men that you're a blood-and-guts hellfire jack!'

Kydd went red and bawled for the sentry.

The marine entered, confused, looking from one to the other. Dillon slipped out past him.

'Go,' Kydd croaked at the sentry, who lost no time in making his exit.

Shaken by the episode, Kydd tried to think. His thoughts steadied as he realised that Dillon had risked a great deal by telling him what he thought – and that took back-bone. He'd felt that it was important Kydd should know the mood of the ship, and that could only have been motivated by a sense of respect and loyalty to him personally. In his black mood he'd wronged the young man.

And what Dillon had said – that the ship believed he was a despised glory-seeker, one who put personal vainglory first before the needs of the service – stung. From the choice of words he must have heard the seamen's verdict first-hand and it was a damning one. Nothing was held in more contempt and loathing than an officer who looked to honours and glory over the bloodied bodies of his recklessly sacrificed men.

Nobody, officer or man, in *Tyger* knew the full story of why he'd been sent to the ship. As far as they were concerned, the Admiralty had sent a known hero to turn around a muti-nous ship in the shortest possible time and he had – but he'd not left it there. His bullying haste to get the frigate to what they would see as impossible levels of perfection could only mean that his head had been turned by public adulation and he wanted more, no matter what it cost.

How ironic! He was doing it for his own very real reasons, but because of his single-minded and unforgiving drive even Bowden and Stirk, who knew him of old, must be persuaded of his glory-seeking.

Soon he'd lose any loyalty that was left, and end in the

forefront of the battle waving his sword but none following. He'd seen it happen in the Caribbean to another captain and squirmed at the thought that it could happen to him.

But if he slackened off not only would he lose his chance to bring *Tyger* to warlike readiness but the whole thing would be put down to tyranny and nit-picking over drill times.

If only Renzi were there to calmly dissect and analyse! In fact there was no one – not a soul – with whom he could talk at the level he needed.

But he had known that when he first boarded the ship and must live with it.

He summoned Tysoe. 'Find Mr Dillon and, with my compliments, if he is at leisure I should be happy to see him.'

Dillon entered, his expression set and defensive.

Kydd rose and, with a smile, indicated a chair. 'I've asked you here to offer my apologies for my unforgivable lapse in behaviour.'

'Sir.'

'Which was not occasioned by your good self, I hasten to add.'

It was not proving easy. 'A captain must have many worries.' The tone was careful, noncommittal.

'Ah, just so. As you of all must know.'

'Sir. May I speak plainly?'

'Please do.'

'What I've seen of you in these last weeks is not the Captain Kydd I know.'

'Go on.'

'I don't wish to pry but I'm of the mind that a matter of great personal moment lies upon you at this time, Sir Thomas.'

'That may be so.'

He continued, in a low voice, 'And of all men within the

234

compass of this vessel there is only one who does not have the comfort of . . . a friend. If it is of service to you, I would be honoured to share your burden, the matter most scrupulously to remain between us alone.'

Kydd sat back in astonishment. Not at what had been said, but that Dillon had found the moral courage to risk immediate condemnation for his impertinence.

'Why, that's handsome in you, Mr Dillon,' he found himself saying. He paused. 'Do you care for a sherry?'

There was intelligence, practicality and discretion on offer but was this friendship? He was drawn to the young man – personable, educated and with a depth of feeling. He would never be a Renzi but . . .

There was less than ten years' difference in their ages, but they were a world of experience apart. Could he ever bring himself to speak freely as a friend? If he did, like his administrative confidences, he knew it would be safe with Dillon.

There was an awkward moment, then Dillon said, 'You know, when I secured my position in *L'Aurore* in the first place, I can tell you now, it was more than a lust for travel that was urging me on.'

'Oh?'

'A young lady, of importunate ways who unaccountably set her cap in my direction. I raised the siege only by the time-honoured device of running away to sea,' Dillon added, with an amused smile.

'Ha! It was ever so,' Kydd said.

'Then when *L'Aurore* was no more and I had to return, the siege was laid in earnest. Only your timely summons to *Tyger* saved me from a dolorous fate.'

'Are you then contented with your choice? *Tyger* is a very different barky from *L'Aurore*.'

Dillon nodded, and Kydd felt encouraged to open up to him, to tell him of the misreporting that had led to the Admiralty's set against him, the dependence of a captain on favour and interest for employment, and the inevitable fate of those who ran athwart their lordships' hawse.

And of the last sanction: that he and his ship distinguish themselves to such a degree that it would be impolitic to take his ship from him.

Dillon listened sympathetically. After Kydd had finished he gave a twisted smile. 'Ah. I have it now. A pretty problem.'

They sipped their sherry. Then, in quite another voice, Dillon said, 'It does occur to me . . . would you wish to learn backgammon?'

'To—'

'A relaxing and harmless pursuit but a sovereign cure for solitude.'

'Why, perhaps I shall.' It was a thoughtful and practical suggestion and would provide an excuse to meet companionably.

Dillon returned quickly with the hinged box that Kydd had so often seen in wardrooms. He set out the black and white pieces and handed Kydd a leather cup and two dice. 'The idea is to go point to point to bear off all your stones before your opponent. These are the points and there is your home.'

There was more to follow and Kydd took it in gravely until they were ready to begin.

'Your throw.'

The pieces began their journey around the board.

'You think I've been too hard on the people,' Kydd said, in satisfaction seeing off one of Dillon's stones to the bar to begin its trek again.

'I can't but think you have been,' Dillon answered, positioning his pieces in a continuous mass.

'There's no alternative – *Tyger* has to be ready to meet the enemy.'

'I fear you'll lose them. Even if they knew of your difficulty they'd hardly feel it warranted to haze them so for that reason.'

The massing of pieces turned out to be an effective trap, holding Kydd until he could overcome it only by throwing a high number. He was learning.

'There's no other way.'

'Then you're at a stand. Press on this way and you've lost your crew. Ease away and the French might spring on us. Yet it does seem to me in my ignorance that the last is the least probable of the two.'

Two fours and he couldn't move. Kydd yielded his turn. 'So ease off on the beggars? What'll they think we've been doing this last week? I can't back down now.'

There was an opening – instead of moving both pieces he combined the numbers into a move by a single one and leaped ahead.

It was working: simply bringing it out and talking about it was sufficient to cut through the tangle of decision elements.

'A good one,' Dillon said, in admiration, but at the next throw sent two of Kydd's stones to the bar.

Tyger's captain was not put out – for in that instant he realised he knew what he had to do.

'Gentlemen,' Kydd said with a broad smile, looking about his table benignly. 'Our last night before we make port on the morrow.'

His officers regarded him with expressions varying from

suspicion to hostility but an invitation to dinner with the captain was not to be spurned.

'Wine with you all!' he declared, raising his glass.

There were scattered murmurs but nothing even approaching jollity. It was time to make his play. 'To *Tyger* – in whom I am well pleased!'

A ripple of barely concealed surprise went around.

'Yes – we've worked hard, damned hard, and don't think I haven't noticed. The enemy may pounce at any time, but I now declare that *Tyger* is ready for 'em.'

Hollis glared balefully but Bowden's face cleared. 'Sir, you mean—'

'I do. The only sure way to reach a true fighting spirit is to pitch in, heart and soul, however long it takes, until we're of one company and mind, and now we are.'

Their expressions held incredulity and cynicism.

'So as of this hour we step down to regular sea routine, confident we can meet anything the Frenchies throw at us.'

It was getting across: pleased smiles broke through and a dawning respect replaced the hostility.

'I've driven you hard but I've no regrets – the results speak for themselves. So I call on you now to toast our tight little frigate. To *Tyger*, and long may she cleave the seas!'

'To *Tyger*!' This time there was real feeling in it.

'In the forenoon tomorrow before we arrive I'll speak to the ship's company and tell 'em the same thing. It's been a tough claw to wind'd but we've made it!'

It was done.

The reality was that *Tyger* was far from ready, his words a mockery in his own ears, but now in his officers and later the crew there would be a morsel of pride, the beginnings of a belief in the ship and her captain.

But he was taking a risk by relaxing his efforts. He was gambling that, when the time came, *Tyger* would not let him down and would rise heroically to the challenge.

He'd done all he could. The rest was in the hands of *Tyger* and her company.

Chapter 15

Yarmouth Roads was alive with shipping – from brigs to sizeable ship-rigged vessels. In a sprawling mass at the assembly anchorage, they were protected to seaward by naval sloops and cutters of the local defences.

Kydd had never experienced a Baltic convoy – they were legendary for their size: one had set forth with over a thousand sail. This assemblage was of some hundreds. The stirring sight was a paradox: a thrilling testimony to Britain's trade supremacy and at the same time a frightening demonstration of vulnerability for an island nation.

A frigate and a number of sloops were in the naval anchorage, the escort for this argosy.

'Pennants of *Lively*, Cap'n Hozier,' Kydd was told.

The frigate was the same class as *Tyger* but the seniority of her captain was September 1802, and therefore predated Kydd's. He would thus have the command and the responsibility, not only for the safe arrival of this immensely valuable convoy but the heavy burden of producing the complex orders and signals, procedures and assignments, and their transcription into hundreds of sailing-order instructions. It was a tedious and lengthy task but had serious legal and financial implications, for Lloyds Insurance would be relieved of payment against a loss if a transgression of their strict provisions could be shown.

In the absence of a flag officer there was no ceremony and Kydd put out in his gig for *Lively* while *Tyger* secured from sea.

'Well, now, and we're honoured indeed, Sir T,' murmured Hozier, eyeing Kydd's sash and star. Kydd had hesitated about wearing them but he'd been led to understand that if he did not it would be assumed he did not value the honour.

'I was lucky enough to be in the right place,' he replied genially. 'As could happen anywhere.'

'Not here, old trout,' Hozier answered, with a small smile. 'Hard blows and a lee shore is all we can rely on.' He had a noble forehead and a languid, patrician drawl.

'And another month, another convoy.'

'Quite. You'll send me a lieutenant and brace of middies to bear a hand?'

'Lieutenant you shall have, reefers I've none.'

'To spare?'

'In any wight. I'm appointed into *Tyger* at short notice and the mids fled with the last captain.'

'Oh, yes. I recollect there was some to-do that—'

'Which is over now. I'll send my sailing master, if I may, for chart corrections and similar. Can I take it there'll be no difficulties on passage?'

'I'd say not. The Danes are very strict on their neutrality and run the Sound transit like a business – which I suppose it is to them. Once inside the Baltic there's nothing to fear, no Frenchy fleet or even cruisers, what with the Russians our ally and with ships-of-the-line to spare. We just let the convoy disperse about their business.

'As usual, Boney is rampaging away on some land campaign or other – the Prussians are taking a hammering, which means the southern Baltic shore is a scene of slaughter, but it's nothing to do with us. We keep our offing well out of it.'

'So a straightforward trip, nothing to—'

From above, a terrifying bellow interrupted them.

Hozier winced. 'My premier, a man of . . . plain manners. I've endeavoured to encourage a more gentlemanly address but I fear it's a lost cause with Mr Bray.'

Kydd gave a sympathetic nod and went on to conclude the meeting: 'I'm in reasonable fettle. Victualling and stores shouldn't take long. Have you a date of sailing?'

'Five days, subject to numbers made up to my list. Shall we meet again, perhaps for dinner? I've a tolerably inventive cook who knows his soufflés and I can promise you a capital evening . . .'

Piped over the side and in his gig, Kydd felt a glow of pleasure. In the past he would have felt intimidated by the man's effortless high-born gentility but now, with his honours and distinction, he need never fear it again.

But then came a rush of bleakness. Was he facing his last days at sea? From what he'd heard there'd be virtually no chance of a spectacular and distinguished action in this voyage.

Hollis was waiting for him, stiff and tense. 'You left no instructions regarding liberty, Sir Thomas, and I had to—'

'Harbour routine. At noon, starbowlines to liberty ashore,' Kydd snapped, irritated that the first lieutenant had not thought to ask before if he had concerns. 'Back aboard for the forenoon tomorrow.' He'd have pay-tickets made up and send for the clerk of the cheque. Then the seamen would have something in hand to raise a wind ashore.

He was not long back in his cabin when the boatswain reported.

'What is it, Mr Dawes?' If there were defects that prevented their sailing he'd need to know at once.

'Well, it's like this here,' the man mumbled. 'I've got t' think how I stands.'

'What do you mean, sir?'

'It's m' bones, like. Never had it so bad, at me all night they is, a real trial.'

'Are you saying you're suffering a griping in the bones? What does the doctor say?'

'He weren't a help. See, it's not as I can show 'im and—'

'You're ill and worried that it's affecting your duties,' Kydd said smoothly, grasping what was going on, 'so you're informing me now. Right and proper it is for you to do so, Mr Dawes. Well, we must get you ashore to recover. Don't concern yourself about the ship, we'll find another to relieve you. I'll make arrangements with shoreside immediately.'

It worked well for both parties. The boatswain would remain 'ill' ashore until *Tyger* had sailed with a replacement, then emerge and take a more comfortable berth.

Kydd turned to other things. 'Tysoe, I've something I'd like you to do for me . . .' His stored sea furniture from *L'Aurore* would transform the great cabin from a bare monk's cell into something like gentle living.

His spirits rose, and he passed the word for his first lieutenant. 'Mr Hollis, I've a notion to priddy the ship before we put out. Kindly detail three good hands and I'll have the figurehead put to rights, gold leaf and the rest.'

'Sir.' There was still an underlying resentment in his tone – Kydd's necessary intervention in his first lieutenant's professional judgments had demeaned him in the eyes of the ship's company.

Kydd sent Bowden to assist Hozier; he had need of Brice's good sea sense in setting up the rigging while a new boatswain was found and it would get Bowden out of the ship for a while.

After the first day he knew he'd been right to award liberty, for there were few stragglers. His bracing talk to the hands, repeating in earthier terms what he'd said to the gun-room, must have had some effect, and the prospect of losing all prize money owed by deserting would have been an even greater deterrent.

Hozier's invitation to dinner duly came for Kydd, along with a note that four other captains would be joining them.

It was a pleasant evening, but the drumming of rain on the deck above told of a wet and chilly night for those on watch. Kydd knew two of the guests vaguely and Hozier had a ready fund of well-practised yarns. A marine violinist played soft airs just out of sight.

The cigars had come out and the talk was languorous when there was a sudden knock at the cabin door and a dark figure in streaming oilskins thrust in.

'Sir. Silent hours, master-at-arms says lights out an' the ladies are quiet 'tween decks,' was the growled report.

'Not now, Mr Bray, we're at dinner – I've company, can't you see?' Hozier glanced about apologetically at his guests.

'Two in bilboes, carpenter gives less'n a foot in the bilge and the red cutter still in the water.'

'Yes, Mr Bray, thank you, thank you. You can leave us now. Good night.'

Deep-set eyes flicked over the gathering. Then their owner left abruptly.

'Not as you'd say a paragon of politesse and I do apologise for him.' Hozier sighed. 'Shall we broach the cognac at all? I can vouch for it, as having come from a Frenchman who thought he was delivering it to Napoleon himself.'

Kydd dutifully tasted the delicate fire and joined in the appreciative murmurs – and was transfixed by a sudden thought. It grew and took hold and he delayed his departure until he was last to leave.

'A splendid time, David,' he said warmly. 'As gave me pause . . .'

'Oh? I do endeavour to please, old fellow.'

'Just a thought – you've heard *Tyger*'s seen a mort of pother, not to say a mutiny. My first was in the thick of it, poor fellow. A sensitive chap, comes from a good family, politeness itself and a first-class education. How he must have suffered for want of society, my other officers being of the more . . . ordinary sort.'

It brought a small frown, so he hurried on: 'What's more to be desired in a ship so recently in a moil is a plain-speaking, no quarter, hard horse as will brook no insolence. Rather like, shall we say, your Mr Bray?'

After a pause, Hozier smiled. 'Ah, I think I can see what you mean.'

'And I was thinking that—'

'They must both agree.'

'Of course!'

'Mr Hollis,' Kydd said, as early in the day as he decently could.

The officer braced himself.

'I've had an approach from the senior officer escorts – that is, Captain the Honourable David Hozier, father a species of viscount, you know. For some odd reason he's heard you're with me in *Tyger* and has a desire to exchange you into *Lively*. Of course I had to say that I have the highest regard for your service to this ship and can't possibly . . .'

The movement of lieutenants between ships to vacancies and flag posts was not uncommon and a simple exchange was even easier. *Tyger*'s new first lieutenant was aboard that same morning.

He was thick-set and imposing, with a ram-rod stiff bearing and restless glare.

'L'tenant Bray, Sir Thomas,' he rasped, with a quick bow, his eyes darting about the deck.

'I welcome you aboard *Tyger*, Mr Bray,' Kydd said politely, 'and can only apologise for the haste, not to say inconvenience of your removal from *Lively*.'

'My pleasure,' came back an instant growl, leaving no doubt that this officer regretted it not at all.

They shook hands with the understanding that introductions and taking up of post could wait until lunch and a meeting with the officers.

It was a cool affair: Bray's presence was large and disquieting and his dark features never once broke into a smile. His voice was a bear-like rumble. Kydd briefly wondered if he'd done the right thing but the man spoke civilly enough.

In the afternoon, accompanied by a distracted Brice, the big lieutenant took survey of the frigate from bowsprit to taffrail, watched surreptitiously by the seamen, and in the evening disappeared into his cabin with the watch and station bill.

This first was very different from the previous.

Kydd had to wait longer for his new boatswain. It was no trivial matter to summon one at such notice.

However, a sympathetic admiral's staff did their best and a boatswain for *Tyger* duly arrived.

A temporary Navy Board warrant had been made out to a Mr Herne, late of a frigate undergoing extensive repair in Sheerness. He came on board the day before they sailed, a neat and seaman-like figure, grey-haired and with the dignity of age.

It was going to be hard on the man – he had to take into charge all the rigging, stores and equipment on a bare handover, then acquaint himself with the ship so that on the next day he didn't make a fool of himself before his men.

And how would he get along with Bray? From what little Kydd had seen of Herne, he'd gained an impression of a cautious, quiet individual; Bray might want a more assertive creature, as the boatswain was a key figure in the first lieutenant's role of running and maintaining the ship for her captain.

As was now their practice, Dillon was waiting for him at day's end, ready to discuss events over a small repast, if invited, and subtly taking the opportunity to bring up matters for attention or diversion.

'You'll be passing content now, I believe,' he opened, as they sat down to supper.

'How's that?' Kydd answered, leaning over to take full advantage of the fresh butter while they were in port.

'It's not escaped my notice that as of this day you've achieved nothing less than a clean sweep, fore and aft. Since coming to *Tyger* you've had every officer, the boatswain and master replaced. I dare to say the gunner is now concerned for his position.'

'I suppose you're right. What do you think of our new premier?'

'Mr Bray? The gun-room thinks him a hard man and are giving him a broad lee.' It was gratifying to find Dillon striving for the sea lingo even if it did sometimes come out a mite curious.

'I asked what *you* thought of him, Edward.'

'So . . . I find him a stout enough specimen of the breed of mariner whose bite is undoubtedly worse than his bark.' He hesitated for a moment. 'Which is all to the better so far as your own good self is concerned.'

'Yes, I must admit it's a rattling fine thing to give an order and know it'll be carried out in every detail, even if it may be at the cost of the men's feelings.'

'I was rather thinking of another advantage – that from now on it will be Mr Bray who shall be reviled for his slave-driving ways while his captain stands back in saintly detachment.'

It was a good point, and a dry observation uncannily like those from the Renzi of old. Kydd nodded. 'As is right and proper in a first.' In quite another tone he added, 'Have you that account of our taking of the Dutchman squared away yet? It's legal evidence and I want it on the mail-boat tomorrow.'

'It'll be ready, sir.'

Their orders came later that night. *Tyger* was given the seaward approaches for the convoy assembly and sailing, which suited Kydd well. It meant an earlier sailing but his duty would be merely that of the slow cruising up and down several miles out to sea on deterrent patrol while the convoy was at its most vulnerable, forming up.

The morning saw more than the usual scurry and tension

before putting to sea, a tired Bowden returning on board at the last minute and boats plying to and fro even as the hour for departure approached.

Kydd thought it proper to give his new first lieutenant a chance to take the ship to sea, a straightforward enough exercise in Yarmouth Roads, and soon the deck was spurred into hasty activity by a series of uncompromising roars.

He stood back while all customary preparations were put in hand – there was every indication that Bray knew what he was doing and Kydd began to relax.

'Sir.' The gunner came closer and spoke quietly. 'Sir, I have t' tell you. My mate's not on board.'

'Your gunner's mate? This is a strange thing, Mr Darby.'

'I – I went to his berth an' found he . . . he's run. Taken his gear and skinned out, like.'

'He *deserted*?' Kydd said in disbelief. A gunner's mate was not a common foremast hand with nothing to lose but a well-respected warrant officer.

'Seems he did, sir,' Darby said uncomfortably.

'Then you're in a pretty pickle, I believe. Why did he do it, do you think?'

'Ah, I asked about, an' some o' the hands heard him swear as how after this convoy we're going into the ice again, an' he's not having anything t' do with that.'

'You know we're not going to get hold of another gunner's mate before we sail.'

'Aye, sir. Don't really know what's to do.'

'Put your mind at rest, Mr Darby. Are you not aware that your yeoman of the powder room was a gunner's mate? Let's see if Mr Stirk feels he's equal to the task just for now.'

Two hours later, *Tyger* put to sea without incident and settled to routine.

Chapter 16

The southern Baltic shore stank.

It wasn't the bodies – they'd been cleared away days before. It was the ever-present stench of East Prussia, with its flat, open plains broken with marshes and waterways, intensively farmed by fearful peasants who hadn't yet joined the flood of humanity eastwards, away from the rolling thunder of war.

Flügelleutnant Klaus Gürsten knew he should be used to it by now but, born and bred a Berliner, he couldn't warm to these lands, so much in thrall to a medieval past. The people stood about as he and his horse clattered into the farm courtyard, the men in long smocks, the women in stitch-worked dirndls, gaping in wonder at what was happening to their ageless existence.

He slipped from his mount, grunting at the pain of fatigued muscles as a soldier took the animal in hand.

The farmhouse, with its limply hanging *Leibfahne* flag of eagle and up-thrust sword, was the field headquarters of the Prussian commander, Generalleutnant von Hohenlau.

Gürsten marched smartly past the two sentries and into a low room. Seated at a large kitchen table spread with maps, von Hohenlau was conferring with his chief of general staff, Gerhard Scharnhorst, a handsome officer in fashionably high collar with a romantic curl of dark hair on his forehead.

Scharnhorst was standing and speaking in low tones. He looked round as Gürsten entered and acknowledged his clicked heels and bow with a terse nod. 'Yes?' he said, pausing. His campaign uniform was dark Prussian blue with the Brandenburg red cuffs but had little in the way of gold lacings, and Gürsten knew he was facing a soldier who had learned his trade and gained field promotion under the peerless Frederick the Great. He had an intimidating presence.

'From Feldmarschall Count von Bennigsen, Generalleutnant. Orders in respect of a possible flank attack.' He handed over a package and stepped back smartly.

Von Hohenlau grimaced as he sliced it open. Bennigsen was overall commander of the coalition forces – but he was a Russian and at the head of an army far superior in numbers to what remained of the Prussians.

'Is he still at Heilsberg?' he asked.

'He fears Davout and Soult will prove troublesome but he's brought Labanoff across his rear. Yes, sir, he's still there.'

'Humph.' Von Hohenlau extracted the papers and scanned them quickly. A dark frown appeared and he read again, more slowly.

'Do you know what this contains?'

As staff intermediary between the two allied commanders, there were few secrets Gürsten didn't know. 'The Feldmarschall has many concerns, sir, and—'

'He demands I extend my right until it reaches the sea.'

'To prevent the French turning your flank, sir.'

Scharnhorst leaned forward and murmured something to von Hohenlau, who said, 'He's aware that Bonaparte lurks beyond. Who would not be happier were I to lengthen my lines? The devil has an unemployed regiment of cavalry to play with, and if I were to be stretched thin in the manoeuvre it could all be up with us.'

'I'm sure he knows, sir, but is persuaded that Bonaparte must be checked in his advance until Oberst Tolstoi's reinforcements arrive.'

'Very well. It shall be done.'

Slapping down the orders, he looked up. 'Herr Gürsten, you've done your part – you should get your belly filled and rest while you can.'

He grunted peevishly and nodded to his chief of staff. 'So, Gerhard, shall we get up the plans? We've no time to lose.'

Gürsten was effectively dismissed. He threw off a smart salute, wheeled about and marched away.

In the fields a massed line of fusiliers was drilling, the red-faced *feldwebel* screaming orders at raw recruits, stumbling *landwehr* from the nearby war-torn and devastated countryside. Gürsten tried not to show his despair at the level to which the proud but heavily mauled army had sunk and made his way to the mess-tent.

The field-kitchens were at work and the odour of boiled mutton triggered sharp pangs of hunger. He had left Bennigsen's lines early that morning and eaten only biscuits and raisins on the way.

'Hey, now, the prodigal returns!' It was Engelhardt, his friend since those far-off days of peace.

'And sharp set – but naught that can't be remedied with a libation of the right sort, Willy.'

'Ho, the kellner!' Engelhardt called imperiously to the messman. 'A pair of schnapps – from the red bottle, mind.'

After the man had brought glasses of the golden liquid, they toasted each other, then Engelhardt leaned forward. 'Now, Klaus, you can tell me. How goes it in the centre? Will the Russkies stand?'

Gürsten hesitated, considering his response.

Prussia had a proud history and, since Frederick the Great's profound modernising of state and military, it had looked to itself as pre-eminent on the continent – until the ferocity of, first, the French Revolution, then the genius of Napoleon Bonaparte had transformed the scene.

Staying cautiously neutral, the Prussian King Friedrich Wilhelm III had secured peace for his realm, but when the battle of Trafalgar had confined Bonaparte to a European cage the emperor had been compelled to look east for new conquests. The Austrians and the Holy Roman Empire stood in his way and Bonaparte did not hesitate, striking into its heart. Yet instead of joining with their fellow Germans against the erupting force, the king had decided on a retreat into neutrality.

Gürsten knew Friedrich had blundered but with the absolute autocracy of the Hohenzollern court it would be madness for him to say so, especially to his friend, a loyal and unquestioning officer of the traditional kind.

The result of the king's action was decisive. After the spectacular defeat at Austerlitz, despite the entry of Russia to aid the Austrians, a collapse of the coalition against Bonaparte became inevitable.

During an uneasy peace a general rearrangement of borders and alignments followed, but it was clear that with the Confederation of the Rhine, Bonaparte was intent on destabilising the centuries-old patchwork of kingdoms and principalities. Friedrich had reconsidered his neutrality and blundered again into disaster.

With confidence born of an unbroken tradition of Prussian military discipline and success, he had declared war on the French empire, his well-trained armies outnumbering Bonaparte's rag-tag allies and auxiliaries, but it was a fatal misjudgment. Impatient for glory, he did not wait for the distant Russians to join and two giants faced each other on the battlefield.

Bonaparte moved on them efficiently. In the twin battles of Jena and Auerstedt he succeeded in encircling and comprehensively obliterating his opponent in a victory so complete it effectively removed Prussia as a player from the world stage.

Within nineteen days of those opening scenes, Emperor Napoleon was riding into Berlin a conqueror. Two members of the Prussian royal family had been mortally wounded on the battlefield and the rest were in headlong flight, with the pitiful remnants of the army. Only the approach of winter and the need to consolidate his triumph kept Bonaparte from continuing.

The Russian Army, marching heroically through the mud and snow, reached the frontier in Poland and dug winter quarters opposite the French lines in preparation for the spring. Surviving Prussian generals had pulled together something of an army but it was a shadow of what it had been and joined the Russians very much as the lesser partner, von Hohenlau agreeing to serve under their commander, Bennigsen.

It couldn't last: even in the freezing hell of a Polish winter manoeuvres turned into aggressive thrusts and the two armies became locked together in a bitter struggle on the plains of the Vistula around a little village called Eylau.

Gürsten shuddered at the memory – it had been only a few months ago and he recalled it as yesterday. A titanic ebb and flow of hundreds of thousands over treacherous terrain in the cruel bitterness of howling snowstorms. Forced marches and last stands against merciless artillery as stolid Russian peasant soldiers came on against the unbending will of Bonaparte in a conflict that lasted agonising days.

It stopped Bonaparte in a bloody stalemate but at what cost? Never again did he want to see the ghastliness of frozen corpses and piteous wounded strewn over the wreckage of battle, some piled together, others littering the landscape in every direction. In the fields around Eylau alone no less than fifty thousand casualties lay in an appalling scene of slaughter.

Then Bennigsen, suspecting a trap, had retreated and yielded to Bonaparte. Since then it had been a steady falling back.

Bennigsen had taken the centre of the line, with von Hohenlau and the Prussians on his right, the Austrians tying down Massena on his left, and as spring turned to summer they had contested every mile, every yard as they fell back towards Königsberg.

There, the royal family and government in exile had set up on the last piece of unconquered Prussia and that was the situation now: a straggling line across East Prussia with vast armies manoeuvring and clashing in savage encounters, half starved and desperate.

Somewhere out there as they supped, not far beyond the enemy lines, Bonaparte held state in his forward imperial headquarters, controlling his marshals and their divisions like chess pieces. Victor, Soult and Davout, Murat and Ney, young sons of the revolution, determined on glory and fame at any cost.

Gürsten pulled himself together and told his friend, 'Bennigsen stands – he must. He's too many enemies at court to show cowardice.'

That much was safe to say. Tsar Alexander was too ambitious by half: if it were in his interest to turn his coat he would, and with it take all the military resources of Russia.

'And we?'

'We face Victor and his seven divisions with our one and a half. But, yes, we'll stand. I know von Hohenlau, one of the best. Old school from the glory times. If he gets orders to stand, he will, count on it.'

'He's on the march, Klaus.'

'Orders to extend to the right to meet the sea and stop Victor turning his flank.'

'Risky.'

'Yes.'

Gürsten downed the last of his schnapps. 'If you'll excuse me, Willy, I really must rest.'

At first light he was a-horse, with von Hohenlau's acknowledgement to Bennigsen, riding across the adjacent field in the damp, misty morning to the rutted Liebdorff road east.

At first he made good time, threading through the tents and artillery parks of von Hohenlau's rear until he reached the deserted countryside beyond, where he turned parallel to the lines.

Breaking into a canter he relaxed into the rhythm of the movement – until an hour further on something intruded into his senses. It was deathly quiet but on the air there was the faintest disturbance. He reined in and tried to listen above the snorting and snuffling of his horse. Wanting to hear better, he dismounted and walked away a little.

Over to the south-west, in the direction of the lines, there were signs of vague disorder, rising dust and the faint, muffled sounds of battle, an engagement of sorts – well to the rear, where it had no right to be. He knelt down, put his ear to the ground and heard the subliminal thunder of many horses.

He felt a cold wash of fear. It could only be that the French had observed the Prussian move to the sea and, knowing that their line would be stretched, had thrown a flying column in the other direction to smash a wedge between the allies.

It would be heavy cavalry first to punch through – that was what he must be hearing – and it was open country: they would be moving fast.

He looked around helplessly – the road stretched on for miles, nothing in sight on these God-forsaken plains. A wind-breaking hedge followed the road and on the far side there was a ditch, the field beyond nothing but a mass of wild-growing nettles.

The drumming of hoofs was now viscerally perceptible. Cavalry warhorses would soon catch his slightly built mount, but if he was seen on foot out in the open he'd be instantly cut to pieces.

The skyline was now stippled with movement, trumpets braying faintly amid a ragged tapping of musketry. In an agony of despair he tore loose his sabretache and dived into the base of the hedge, wriggling frantically until he reached the ditch the other side.

It was running in jet-black slime and oozed effluvium. As the drumming turned to thunder he ripped the dispatches to pieces and thrust them deep into the mud then snatched a look through the hedge.

The whole horizon to his front was alive with galloping cuirassiers in shining breastplates and their distinctive curved, plumed helmets, intoxicated with the charge that had carried them deep into the enemy lines. Their heavy sabres glittered in the wan sun; each had hate on his face.

There was only one chance: he crouched, then thrust himself face down into the ditch and lay still.

The thunder turned into an avalanche of noise – in the next few seconds he would either live or die. The terrible hoofbeats grew louder, overwhelming – then strangely cut off as the cavalrymen launched themselves over the hedge to crash down beyond the ditch and away.

He kept deathly motionless, his back crawling as he tensed for a casual brutal hacking with a sabre as they passed over him. It went on and on until the last stragglers had gone.

It had worked: he was grateful for his concealing dark blue uniform, its frogging and ornamentation out of sight under him. If he'd been seen it was likely he'd been taken for a stale corpse not worth the sticking.

He knew better than to make any move just yet for they'd penetrated deeply and must now regroup and return. Sure enough, they milled about in the field for a space and then, with hoarse shouts and a blare of trumpets, made off in a body to the south.

Still not daring to stir he waited until the jingling tumult had died away and carefully raised his head.

They were nearly out of sight and he got to his feet slowly, surveying the trampled hedge and field. His horse was lost, of course, and he faced the prospect of a long tramp in his heavy riding boots until he saw the beast about a quarter of a mile away, calmly cropping the nettles.

Heart still thudding he mounted and rode off at desperate speed back whence he'd come.

He burst in on von Hohenlau, who was surrounded by excited staff officers; obviously his news was not unexpected. He told a distracted Scharnhorst the details, then withdrew to change his filthy uniform.

When he returned there was a different atmosphere: a grave and serious quiet.

'Sir?' he enquired, of a despondent artillery *hauptfach*.

'They're through – Soult threw five squadrons of heavy cavalry at our left and he's pouring a column of his finest through after them. Klaus, it means we're cut off from Bennigsen – and we'll have to shorten our lines to face the bastards.'

Always it was the same: a restless probing of the front, and at any weakness, Bonaparte would pounce, sending instant marching orders to a tried and trusted marshal and supporting orders to others. It took masterly staff-work but Bonaparte's veterans could be relied on.

Later in the evening, when lamps threw soft gold on tired faces, and supper lay uneaten, worse news came.

'Sir. Soult is deep into our lines. We've now reports that he's wheeling left – sir, he intends to cut us off, isolate us. We must pull back, retire on Kreuznicke.'

Scharnhorst nodded slowly. 'It must be done quickly.'

Von Hohenlau shook his head. 'No.'

'Sir?'

'My last orders were to stand and that is what I will do.'

'Sir, if we don't retire we'll be cut off, encircled! We must—'

'Silence! Have I not a staff officer with a shred of honour? We've lost communication with our field commander, whose orders to us were to stand fast. He's in the belief that we've obeyed his last order and therefore remain in post to halt any advance in this sector. Do we now as Prussians betray that trust?'

'If we are surrounded we will be put to the siege and—'

'Sir! This is of no account. Recollect, if you will, that Pomeranian Kolberg still defies the tyrant under siege, near two hundred miles behind Bonaparte's lines. Are we so craven that we fear to do the same?'

Scharnhorst pulled himself erect. 'There is a difference, sir, which it would be folly to overlook.'

'Yes?' von Hohenlau snapped, his expression flinty.

'At Kolberg they are two, three thousand. Here we are sixteen thousand. Without we have supply and—'

'Noted. And dismissed. We do not move. I shall want plans to safeguard our perimeter and take all necessary steps by daybreak.'

'Very well, Generalleutnant.'

By mid-morning it was clear the French had achieved their objective – the Prussians were now isolated from the rest of the line and were left to their own resources for rations, ammunition and stores.

An entire division and more – how long could it last?

Gürsten received a summons to Headquarters. Von Hohenlau and Scharnhorst were together conferring and looked up to regard him gravely.

'Flügelleutnant Gürsten, I know your father and your uncle. It is because of them I feel able to make the request I do.'

'Sir?'

'Our situation must be made known to the higher authorities, in detail, that decisions may be made.'

'I understand, sir.'

'This is a mission of the utmost importance and of extreme peril.'

'Sir.'

'You will pass through the enemy lines and make your way to Königsberg.'

'Not to Feldmarschall Bennigsen, sir?'

'To Königsberg – to His Majesty and his ministers. There you will lay before him our entire disposition. If he gives leave for me to retire I shall do so but, on my honour, will obey no other.'

'I will do it willingly, sir.' The odds of his slipping through an alerted besieging force were slim but the stakes could not be higher.

'How you will achieve this must be left to you, Herr Gürsten. If there's anything we can do to assist . . .'

Outside he set out to find his friend.

'I honour you for it, Klaus, with all my heart,' Engelhardt murmured, shaking him by the hand. The two sat down and began to plot.

Towards evening, a shabby figure and another in a junior officer's uniform made their way to the last outposts before the enemy.

Near a pig-sty there was an old out-of-use wooden barrel. Gürsten was helped into it and after it was upended his friend left.

In the suffocating black airlessness Gürsten crouched and waited. Voices rose and fell. He heard muffled commands and the rumbling of a wagon or two – then quiet.

Hours came and went. His cramped body was a torture but there was no alternative.

Longer. It must be getting close to daybreak by now.

Then . . . voices.

He couldn't make them out and strained to hear. Hoarse,

peasant muttering. Polish – no, some other . . . If he chose wrongly, it could be a vile death from some looting band.

It wasn't meant to be like this!

The plan had seemed a good one: this spot was contained within a salient of the Prussian perimeter that was scheduled to be drawn in as lines were shortened, leaving him concealed in his barrel. As the French pressed in it would be overtaken and he'd find himself behind their line, at which he'd safely give himself up, a Prussian deserter.

He froze in shock as someone casually kicked against his hideaway, then heard a distant impatient order – in French.

With a convulsive heave he capsized the barrel and scrambled out before a goggling soldier in a French uniform. He lifted up his hands and gave a twisted smile as the man shouted, bringing at the run a French *poilu*, a sergeant.

'Who the fuck are you?'

'Isn't it obvious?' Gürsten drawled, in deliberately bad French. 'I've had enough of being on the wrong side. I'm giving it away.'

'Ha! You left it a bit late, *fripouille Prussien*. We're going to wipe the floor with you lot before long. Still, if you're coming over we'll find some use for you. Take him to the adjutant.'

With a pair of soldiers on each side he was marched to the rear. He knew he would be interrogated but was prepared.

'I'm Corporal Baker Höpfner of the third Potsdamers – but precious little could I bake!'

They quickly lost interest in one who could have no knowledge of the larger picture and he was handed on to others to process.

'Can't take you on here, m' friend,' a jolly staff sergeant told him. 'It's a tidy trot to Headquarters for you.'

262

'Kind sir, have you a crust and a taste of wine first? It's cruel hard times I've had and . . .'

The corporal was sent to get some small victuals and Gürsten wolfed them.

When he had finished, he looked up with gratitude. 'What corps should I join, do you think?' he asked eagerly. 'I'm rare skilled on breads – pumpernickel, Bauernbrot, Zwieback and similar.'

It caused spirited discussion between the two, and by the time they'd concluded, Gürsten had a considerable appreciation of the quality and reliability of Bonaparte's troops, quite unmatchable by the most meticulous observations.

A paper was made out: a pass for one Höpfner to travel to Saaldenz, Marshal Ney's headquarters, to join up as an auxiliary. He was given a simple knapsack with basic rations and a blanket, and two discontented soldiers were told to escort him there.

Against all the odds it was working!

They set off on the march: thirty-five miles along badly rutted roads and bare tracks over marshy, directionless moorland and heath.

Gürsten had no intention of completing it for he had what he wanted: a legitimate paper accounting for his presence. He slipped away at the first opportunity and made off at a sharp angle to the north – towards the Russians.

He skirted one village and unexpectedly found himself in an apple orchard. So close to the front line it was doing service as an under-cover artillery park. He turned to go but found his way blocked by a fiercely grinning gunner who held a heavy sword to his throat. Others approached to see the fun.

'A poxy spy!' he growled, flicking the tip of the sword

under Gürsten's throat. 'As will be strung up when we find a tree!'

An officer in a gold-laced shako came up, knocking aside the man's sword. 'Who are you and what are you doing here?' he demanded.

'Oh, s-sir,' Gürsten stammered, 'I – I think I'm lost.' He rummaged about in his undeniably French-issue knapsack and produced his paper. 'It says here I'm t-to join Marshal Ney's German auxiliary.'

The officer took it suspiciously. 'Where's your escort?'

Gürsten looked down, shamefaced. 'We were at an inn and, er, they didn't wake up in the morning, and I thought I'd better—'

'They got drunk,' the officer sneered. 'Not your fault. You did right – but Ney's over there, not here. You go any further in this direction and the Russkies will have your hide on a fence.'

The gunners about him chortled.

'Get going.' He thrust the paper at him. 'It's not safe to be so near the fighting. On your way, little man!'

With profuse thanks, Gürsten scuttled off.

He had to think – and quickly. No carefully laid plan could get him through the terrible danger of the opposing lines this time.

At some distance from the village there were the shattered ruins of a farmyard. It would give shelter until night fell when he could move under cover of darkness. But before he could slip away from his hideout there was the flash of guns and horses galloping past, other noises. It would be lunacy to go out but he would not get a second chance – and the value of his information was fading with every hour he was delayed.

The confusion and disorder had still not settled as the cold light of a new day appeared. He was now in very considerable danger and had to make a move.

He peered through the splintered timbers of the barn into the meadow. All the farm animals had been carried off for food but a stolid, hairy-footed old plough-horse remained, calmly snatching at tufts of overgrown grass.

For some reason his heart went out to the loyal creature in a world of madness caused by men – and he was struck by a thought equally as crazy.

In the strengthening light he scrabbled around in the rubbish of the barn until he found what he was looking for: a dusty grey farming smock and hat, even trousers still hanging on the hook where their owner had left them.

With rising hope he pulled aside the fallen beams and saw in the dark end of the barn a wondrous sight: a cart with a load of hay. It was rank-smelling but it was all he needed.

He drew on the ancient clothing and trudged out to the horse, lumbering, head down and with the pain of age.

The beast looked up at him mildly, tossing its head as he secured the straps but obediently followed him to the barn. Gürsten used it to haul away an exit for the cart, then backed it into the shafts and finished the job with bumping heart, expecting a sharp challenge at any moment.

He heaved himself into the rickety seat and clicked the horse into motion. A scene from earlier times drew into the daylight – an old farmer taking hay out to his animals as he'd done every new morning of his life. No war was going to stop him. That he was bent and his head drooping, his track an aimless meander, clearly pointed to the loss of his wits in this murderous war: he was piteously taking refuge in doing what he had always done for his creatures.

Gürsten's hands on the traces were slack, letting the horse choose his way. A subtle tug every now and then pointed the nodding head resolutely towards the lines and they continued on, the wobbling wheels complaining loudly.

There was no challenge, even as he could see the emplacements with their troops lying at the ready, some staring at him as if at a ghost.

There was now a spectral quiet as he rattled on; no musket fired on him, no shouts or warnings. A tranquil vision of another age had entered their existence of blood and struggle and nobody had the heart to disturb it by harming the old man.

Steadily they progressed over the gently undulating hillocks, the horse knowing to avoid the muddy hollows, patiently plodding on.

Incredibly this must be the open country between the lines – and still nothing.

His flesh crawled with anticipation of a suspicious volley but in the unnatural quiet he shambled on and on. There were other men now, staring out at him but in a different dress, which he recognised – Uvarov's Smolensk Grenadiers.

Keeping up his pretence he let the horse amble on until a kindly Jaeger sergeant took the bridle. 'You can rest now, old man, you're safe with us,' he said, holding out an arm to help him.

Briskly, he threw aside his smock and slid down.

'Take me to your officer,' he demanded in perfect Russian.

He had done it.

'His Majesty is dining and may not be disturbed on any account,' the haughty major-domo said icily.

The politesse of the Hohenzollern court-in-exile was not

about to be put aside for an unannounced arrival, no matter the gravity of his news, and Gürsten was taken to a reception room. He fumed. It had already taken three hours to find and borrow the required dress uniform, and now this!

He had reported to Bennigsen, his headquarters lying on the way to Königsberg, and then with a courier's warrant had galloped madly to the Pregel river and the city. Von Blücher, the military aide-de-camp, had been grateful for his report but all decisions lay with His Imperial Majesty King Friedrich Wilhelm, Elector of Brandenburg, and nothing could be done until his pleasure was known.

'Flügelleutnant Klaus Gürsten,' the equerry intoned at last.

He entered with every expression of respect – whatever his faults, his sovereign was heir to Frederick the Great.

'Your Majesty,' he murmured, from the depths of an elaborate bow. He straightened and made an elegant but lesser bow to the Queen, the much-admired Luise of Mecklenburg-Strelitz.

Friedrich frowned, but then his noble brow cleared. 'We are always minded to hear from our loyal officers, Leutnant. Do you have news for us at all?'

'Majesty, I'm to report from Generalleutnant von Hohenlau with much urgency. He is at present under siege from the French and—'

'Siege? How can this be?'

'Sire, we were ordered to extend our lines to the sea and while so extended Marshal Soult pierced our flank and, with superior forces, continued on to encircle us. We are now beleaguered.'

'And you crossed the lines to tell us so?'

'Sire.'

'A brave and entirely meritorious act. Be assured I shall

267

remember this at the next levée, which I believe shall be no later than—'

'Majesty, the Generalleutnant is desiring to know your wishes in respect of his position. Should he fall back on Heilungen or stand as ordered?'

'Ah, Leutnant Gürsten, I know von Hohenlau well, the stubborn old fellow, and if it is a question of orders he would as soon die as yield. He will stand and I honour him for it.'

'Sire, it's an entire division and more he has with him that—'

'Leutnant! You have done your duty in reporting. Leave us to the strategicals. Right, Blücher?'

'Your Majesty, the leutnant is no doubt alluding to the parlous situation of any army left to its own devices. If it's not supplied it must fall, no matter what heights of courage are shown.'

'I put it to you, sire, that if we cannot supply he must necessarily break out, and at immeasurable cost. I cannot at all see how it is possible to divert a sizeable portion of our remaining troops to force a corridor through to von Hohenlau.'

'Good God, Blücher! First you say that he cannot retire without ruinous loss, now you say he cannot be supplied! Are you seriously demanding I order a capitulation?' The King's pale face reddened.

The bluff general stood erect, splendid in his dark blue full-dress uniform and silver epaulettes, his eyes fierce, and said nothing.

'Sire, there may be an alternative,' dared Gürsten.

'What did you say?'

'Sire, Generalleutnant von Hohenlau has extended to the sea. Cannot we make supply with boats?'

'Ha!' spat Blücher. 'You've forgotten something. The Prussian Navy in Rostock was trapped when Bernadotte took Pomerania. We've nothing left will protect your boats, sir!'

'We have nothing, but our allies have, sir.'

'Who?'

'The English are masters of the seas. Cannot we ask them to—'

'It'll be too late. By the time we get word to London . . .'

'I wasn't thinking of such, sir.'

'Then what?'

'They trade much in the Baltic, and guard their ships well. Should we request a service of their men-o'-war, I'm certain they'll come to the aid of an ally.'

'A fine idea,' Friedrich said, looking relieved. 'As may well prevent a regrettable humiliation.'

Blücher glowered. 'And just how do you propose to ask 'em? Wave some sort of flag as they go past? Do you know where they are?'

'Sire,' Gürsten said stiffly, 'I request permission to requisition a vessel to sail out and find the nearest English ship of war to aid us.'

'Granted.'

There was no shortage of vessels. Coastwise trade had been paralysed and he was able to choose a fast-looking two-master.

'Where do you wish to go, Leutnant?' the captain asked respectfully.

'Why, out to meet an English cruiser!'

269

Chapter 17

At precisely the right position in the middle of the Baltic Sea, *Lively* struck her foremast pennant and the convoy ceased to be. They had reached the dispersal point and the merchantmen quickly clapped on sail and made for their various destinations, with their cargoes of cheap muslins, quiltings, dimities and crockery, tinware, machinery, boots and woollens. They were headed to Memel in the Grand Duchy of Lithuania, Riga in Livonia and Reval – old Hanseatic ports trading freely and profitably with Britain in defiance of Bonaparte.

Lively and her escorts, however, lay to, for their job was not yet done. There would be a returning Baltic convoy. The ancient medieval towns were trading timber, hemp, iron and tallow, vital supplies in keeping the Royal Navy defiantly at sea, England's wooden walls and the last defence of the islands.

For *Tyger* it had been an uneventful five days on passage. Kydd had exercised the men but with a regular honing, not a harsh forging. While there was clear improvement there had been no real challenges in the Baltic.

There was little to do as they lay comfortably a-weather. It was the smaller cutters and brigs that did the hard work, bustling about to shepherd their charges, issue upcoming sailing-order instructions and see to convoy details while the two frigates remained as the unmoving visible centre of preparations.

The convoy was shaping up well in assembly when, one morning, *Lively* hung out *Tyger*'s pennants. This was unusual: the two frigate captains had taken to dining each other out alternately, exchanging whatever news there was at that time.

Aboard *Lively* Hozier greeted Kydd warmly, then went on, 'Dear fellow, I've been handed something of a puzzler. I've a German cove come aboard from a merchantman – all in the right rig, as far as I can tell – who claims he's an emissary of the King of Prussia and is in a bit of a heat over some army they seem to have stranded. Not much English, but demanding our assistance as an ally. They are, aren't they?'

'Didn't they stay out of Pitt's coalition? If so, they're not.'

'Ah, but recollect, the new one we started last year?'

'I'm no lawyer, David, but I'd wager a coalition is not an alliance anyway. We're not bound to get tangled in their problems – and, besides, what the devil can we do to save an army? I'd say we send the beggar away with our warmest regrets and stay with our main duty.'

'They're fighting the French, and must tie down an awful lot of Boney's best. Seems a pity we can't do something for 'em.'

'What? We're a navy the last time I looked, not an army.'

Hozier fiddled with his pen. 'At least let's hear the chap. I'll send for him.'

The young man was arrayed in dark blue with silver facings

and red trim, his plumed shako under his arm in deference to the low deckhead. 'Lieutenant Gürsten of the Prussian Army.'

His intense gaze passed from one man to the other as he pleaded in painfully slow English: 'Honoured sirs. Ze tyrant Napoleon, he crush all of Europe! We cannot stand against him alone. If—'

'*Avez-vous le français, Lieutenant?*' Kydd broke in.

Relieved, Gürsten answered in a fluent stream that left Hozier, who had no French, blinking and Kydd frowning.

'He's saying that Boney is winning not only over the Austrians and themselves but now the Russians, who've suffered slaughter. They've all fallen back almost to the end of Prussia and their king and court are removed to Königsberg at the border.'

There was more impassioned French.

'A large part of their army has been outflanked and cut off from the main and he's saying that if it's forced to capitulate it'll bring shame and dishonour to their flag, besides removing a substantial portion from the order of battle facing Bonaparte.'

'So what does he want us to do?'

'They'll hold out if they can be supplied along the coast using boats and only desire that these come under our protection.'

'Sounds reasonable enough.'

'Except there's no way we can help 'em,' Kydd said, with asperity. 'We've got a return convoy in a few days and—'

'Yes, so we have. Hmm. It does cross my mind –'

'We can't get involved, David!'

'– that it would go ill with one who, when begged for assistance by the king of one of our coalition partners, refused and thereby caused the surrender and humiliation of his army. The government would throw a fit! No, we have to do what we can, do you not feel?'

'Well, send one of the cutters?' Kydd said weakly.

'I was rather thinking of a pair . . . and a frigate to watch over 'em.'

Meaning *Tyger*. Kydd was no stranger to armies and their battlefields, but the last time he'd been swept up in one was in Buenos Aires, which had ended in misery and defeat, and he had no desire at all to be sucked into another. 'No! You can't – your escort for a damnably valuable convoy cut by half? This is too much!'

'It won't be so arduous, I'd believe. Lie off and watch the boats bring relief, that sort of thing.'

'I – I'm not sure of the Tygers yet. They need more time to settle.'

'This isn't as who's to say a fleet engagement, old chap! As you said, it's more armies smiting each other mightily while you look on. Oh, and try not to be too long.'

As *Tyger* got under weigh, Kydd gloomily stared at his orders, written out at his insistence. 'To render such assistance to the military forces of the King of Prussia in furtherance of the relief of his army in Ermeland as shall be within your power, saving always that the interests of His Majesty shall not thereby be imperilled.'

Nothing about the extent of his aid, the hazarding of his command, the length of time he should spend in the defence. He'd heard of sieges going on for years but realised there must be a natural end to it, which would be when his own victuals ran out. And, of course, when Hozier reported to Admiral Russell what he'd done, there could very well be an abrupt reversal of orders or at the very least a relief sent.

He had to make the best of it, and he would insist that not a single one of *Tyger*'s company set foot on land. There would be no hauling guns, hopeless armed parties, heroic rearguards. The task was clear and unequivocal: to safeguard the supply boats and nothing else.

He'd been given *Dart* cutter and *Stoat* armed ketch, and they were dutifully following in his wake. They would form the inshore guard while he lay to seaward as a deterrent.

He let Dillon babble happily away with Gürsten in their gruff Germanic – he'd make sure his secretary was on hand when he made his number with the Prussian king.

The merchant brig led the way and the next day they raised the south Baltic coast. As his charts were rudimentary, Kydd was grateful for this guide ahead. Better ones would be the first thing he asked for, along with finding out just what resources were available.

The shoreline was uniformly flat and well wooded, with a fringing buff-coloured beach extending for miles. There were few settlements and nothing to indicate that in the interior vast armies were locked in a ferocious struggle, not even the usual nondescript far-off rising cloud of dust and dun haze that seemed always to hang over a battle.

At an opening in the line of coast, Dillon pointed. 'Klaus says that's Pillau, the entrance to the Pregel river, and Königsberg lies within.'

Two things roused misgivings in Kydd. The first was the complete absence of any kind of water-craft. The second was that Königsberg lay up the river. There was no way he was going to hazard his ship in a channel no more than a quarter-mile across – and, besides, a star-shaped fort, fat and menacing, dominated the entrance.

Yet he had to make contact and discover the situation. He should send a lieutenant on ahead but knew their second-hand report would not be enough. He'd go himself: it was not impossible that the whole thing was an elaborate French plot to set a trap for any British warship gulled into coming.

'Mr Bray, I'm heading ashore in the merchantman to see what I can. Your orders are to stand off and on until I return. Should you sight signals requiring you to enter harbour you are to ignore them. Failing my return in twenty-four hours you are to sail immediately to acquaint Admiral Russell of the circumstances. Clear?'

The deep-set eyes looked back at him, guarded, alert. 'Aye aye, sir.' There was no attempt to wish him well but neither was there any hidden satisfaction that he could detect.

'Very well. Mr Dillon to accompany me. Carry on, please.'

It was a complete unknown he was going into, on the word of a foreigner with no credentials he was in a position to recognise. He allowed Tysoe to array him in full-dress uniform with star and ribbon. Then, with Gürsten and a quiet Dillon, he boarded the merchantman.

They passed the citadel. Kydd saw the line of shore to the right fall away into a broad stretch of water before it closed again, and after some hours they made out the city of Königsberg with its medieval spires and palaces, canals and opera houses, and a waterfront choked with idle shipping.

Kydd was keyed up for anything but this was not what he was expecting. Here was a great city with, no doubt, a great army – that needed rescuing. Vaguely he remembered figures of half a million or more under arms in the titanic striving taking place not so far distant. How could a single frigate make a difference in this convulsion?

Gürsten insisted on being first on shore, determined that Kydd should have the state carriage and escort of troopers suitable for the saviour of their army.

A crowd gathered while it was being prepared, marvelling at Kydd's exotic uniform, and he grew increasingly uncomfortable, albeit relieved that this showed Gürsten was indeed what he seemed. He nodded gravely, doffing his gold-laced hat to this one or that, and they set off through the streets, the splendour and jingle of their escort attracting stares and comment on all sides.

They eventually arrived at a palace.

'Königsberg Castle,' Gürsten proudly announced. 'Ze Order of Teutonic Knights an' . . . an' . . .'

Seeing that his English was not equal to his passion, Dillon intervened, then relayed to Kydd that the forbidding conical tower had been there since the 1200s and was now the seat of the Hohenzollern reigning monarch. He added that this was the home city of the recently deceased Immanuel Kant, he of *The Critique of Pure Reason*, and of the mathematician Leonhard Euler, whose solving of the Seven Bridges of Königsberg puzzle had ensured his immortality.

That only increased Kydd's feeling of helplessness: this was no quaint medieval town or decayed magnificence, such as Naples, but the capital of a great power. The legend of the invincible Royal Navy had led this nation to seek him out for its deliverance.

He was ushered into the presence of King Friedrich Wilhelm of Prussia, Elector of Brandenburg, in the imperial reception chamber. A tall, reserved figure, the monarch was arrayed in military full dress, dark blue with a red blaze and massive silver epaulettes. His sword was an imposing cavalry sabre.

Gürsten introduced him – it sounded suspiciously like 'Tamas von Kydd' – and he managed as elegant a leg as he could muster.

Once again Kydd was grateful to Renzi's tutelage in French. He'd learned the language in the tedium of the blockade of Toulon those distant years ago and remembered Renzi saying that all the crowned heads of Europe spoke French to each other.

'I'm honoured indeed to be welcomed by Your Majesty into his palace,' he tried.

'The honour is all mine,' Friedrich replied easily, in the language, 'as providing me with the opportunity of making the acquaintance of a very gallant officer . . .'

Kydd bowed wordlessly. What did 'gallant' imply?

'. . . who comes to succour us in these harrowing times.'

'Your Majesty, I will endeavour to render such service as my ship can provide.'

'Ah. As it happens, there is a measure of assistance that we would be grateful should you perform for us, a mere trifle I'm sure to one of Nelson's tribe.'

'Sir?'

'Time presses – it were better you hear it directly from our distinguished servant, Generalleutnant von Blücher.'

The stern and moustachioed figure in the background stamped forward and, with a click of his heels, bowed jerkily. 'Just so, Kapitan,' he said, in heavily accented French.

He backed away from the presence, bowing, and led Kydd down a richly ornamented hallway until he came to a guarded door.

'The war room,' he snapped, as a young officer hastily flung wide the door.

Inside a vast table bore a single map, tended by staff

officers who crashed to attention. At barked words in German they resumed their business.

Blücher went immediately to one side and peered down at the complexity of lines and pointers. An officer obligingly pulled down a lamp cluster cunningly suspended with counter-weights.

'There!' He gestured.

Kydd moved forward and studied it, his first sight of the real situation, aware of the steely eyes of the Prussian on him.

It was a military map, the hachures and topography unfamiliar and the names unpronounceable. It meant nothing to him.

He nodded, with what he hoped was a wise expression, and asked if a smaller-scale map was available to place it in context.

One was brought and Blücher stood back with folded arms as Gürsten nervously explained it.

Kydd began to take it in: this was central Europe and, with the Baltic to anchor his position, he looked on while Gürsten talked.

Prussia, it seemed, extended right from the borders of the Batavian Republic – Holland – beneath the peninsula of Denmark, on to two-thirds the extent of the Baltic to the border with the Grand Duchy of Lithuania. To the south Gürsten pointed out countries whose names meant little to Kydd: Saxony, Bohemia, Bavaria, others, all of which were apparently important to know.

He snatched a glance at Blücher. The general was impassive but his thin lips were beginning to curl in disdain at the incredible ignorance of the English officer, and Kydd reddened.

'Thank you, Mr Gürsten. Now be so good as to show me how much of Prussia is at present occupied by the French.'

The young officer slowly drew a finger from the Batavian Republic in the west on and on, through proud and ancient provinces to the east, Hanover, Brandenburg and Pomerania. Over rivers: the Rhine, the Elbe and the Oder. And cities: Hamburg, Berlin and Warsaw.

It did not cease until there remained only a small margin far up against the border to the east. It was then that Kydd understood.

Unless a miracle occurred they were facing extinction as a nation at the hands of Bonaparte. And they had come to him for help – in this grand scheme it was little enough to ask, and in that moment he resolved to do what he could for them.

'Thank you,' he said briskly. 'May we see the present situation again?'

They returned to the big map and Gürsten studied it for a moment. 'All of Pomerania has fallen and here we have the Vistula, which was crossed by the French some weeks ago. Our lines at the moment are so.' With the sea barely visible along the north edge he traced a line from it across to the south-east. 'In the centre is Feldmarschall Count von Bennigsen, our joint commander with the Russian forces, say ninety thousand only. He faces Ney, Victor, Grouchy and Lannes each with an entire corps, some hundred and fifty thousand. There is—'

'Where's Bonaparte?' Kydd said, fascinated by the gigantic scale of this picture of armies locked together in mortal striving.

Gürsten looked up in surprise. 'Sir, the imperial headquarters would be here, close to the rear where his lines of communication—'

'Yes, of course. Pray do continue.' Kydd's eyes, however, lingered on the place indicated, his imagination gripped by a vision of the tyrant emperor who held all Europe in thrall now from that little village with tentacles of command connecting him with his marshals and armies, invincible and ruthless.

'Königsberg lies here on the Pregel.' Gürsten pointed to the eastern edge of the map, almost to the last extremity before the border and uncomfortably close – by eye no more than forty miles from the fighting.

'And your trapped army?'

'Here.' He tapped at a point well within the advancing French lines. But it was on the coast in the north – next to the sea.

'Hmm. I see. Unless you are supplied you must capitulate.' Kydd stroked his chin. The distance to cover was not great, even if boats gave a wide berth to French guns before they swung inshore, and providing the weather held, there should be no difficulty in maintaining a continuous flow. There could be contrary currents or shoals but with local charts there should be no difficulty.

Then he recalled the suspicious absence of shipping and asked, 'When we arrived I saw all your vessels idle in port. What must this mean?'

'Oh. First, I could say that without our navy they're worried about privateers but mainly, well, there's no trade possible when every supply and market is in the hands of the enemy.'

It would be a rash privateer to try conclusions with *Tyger*, and a resupply would be a straightforward enough matter, with so many unused hulls to call upon.

Straightening with a smile, he said, with what he hoped was winning confidence, 'Very well, gentlemen, I shall help you. Your army will be relieved by boat, safely guarded by the Royal Navy.'

'*Gott in Himmel!*' Blücher spluttered. 'Have you any idea of the size of a supply column? For a division of ten thousand – and we have one and a half with von Hohenlau – it's two hundred wagons, five hundred men and a thousand horses, miles long. And how many more thousands to guard them? Pah! You'll never do that with rowing boats, Mr Sailor!'

Kydd kept his temper. If nothing else, this army general was going to learn what it was to have command of the sea. 'Sir, this we will do.' He bit his lip, then said firmly, 'And you have my word on it.'

Kydd collected a wide-eyed Dillon from outside, and they were given a small room to work in where Kydd sat, letting his thoughts focus.

Time was critical: Heaven knew how long it would take to get a system in place and, from what Gürsten had told him, the army would by now be on its last rations.

First things first. 'Mr Dillon, my compliments to Mr Bray and he is to detach a boat's crew in my service, as I shall be staying here for a while to set up the resupply. As well, I shall require the master and the purser to attend on me.'

'The purser?'

'Is what I said.'

A hovering Gürsten was sent to the harbour-master to secure a large-scale chart, another official to the Customs house for a list of vessels in port, their tonnage and capacities. While they were gone Kydd started to sketch out some ideas.

By the time they were back he had a usable plan. Ships of modest tonnage would voyage from Königsberg out to sea to avoid French guns, then back inshore to the location of the besieged army to anchor. Boats to take their stores on to the beach, unloaded by many willing army hands, and return. *Tyger* to sail slowly offshore, a more than adequate deterrent.

As long as the Königsberg authorities had the wit to manage the assembling of supplies on the quayside in a timely manner, there should not be too much difficulty.

At length Dillon returned with the others.

Kydd nodded. 'Gentlemen, please take a seat, we've much to do.'

The purser sat blinking and unsure, and the jovial master, Joyce, joined him, gingerly glancing up at the palace ornamentation. Gürsten came in, reporting that charts and lists would be sent along as soon as possible.

Kydd started by outlining the problem and his proposed response.

'Now I need detail. Loytn'nt . . . That is to say, Lieutenant Gürsten here will now tell us what rations and stores his army needs and we will shape our plans accordingly. We will start with bread. Sir?'

The young man concentrated. 'Shall we take a *per diem* figure, to multiply later? Then that will be twenty-five thousand loaves, every day.'

'And meat?'

'If they are granted such, a half-*pfund* is the usual measure, so ten thousand *pfunde* allowing for waste. Er, the English I do not know.'

'The daily rate for seamen is two pounds o' beef or one of pork,' Kydd said, adding, 'unless it be a banyan day. So we're saying that for every day for your sixteen thousand. And beer?'

'Essential for troops in the field without reliable water. Say two *nösel* each, which is to say a Dresden jar of, er, so big?' He mimed a container of about a quart in size. So that would be fifty thousand of those, and every day as well.

'Anything else?'

'We should provide oats, cheese, onions, sauerkraut, of course – the usual is to supply it by the ton . . .'

This was growing to an amazing amount – and it didn't take into account the munitions of war that were needed: powder and shot, replacement muskets, blankets and so forth. Kydd tried to visualise the mountain of stores this translated to and found himself aghast. No wonder the Prussian general, with his thousands of horses and wagons, had been so scornful.

There were merchantmen to be had but not all would be suitable and some not fit for sea. Would there be enough? Anxiety tugged at him.

'Right. Assuming one-third more for general stores and munitions, and we have a sizeable problem. Shall we now figure the number of bottoms we'll need?'

He drew up a pad and pencil. 'Assume your usual coastal brig. A cargo volume of say sixty feet long, ten broad and a fathom or so deep. How much can she stow? Mr Harman, the dimensions of a standard loaf of bread, if you please.'

'Sir?'

'Come, come, sir,' Kydd snapped irritably. 'You've twelve years in the service to tell you what a rack of soft tommy looks like.'

'Oh, yes. Er, your four-inch squared bread is eleven inches on the side.'

'You hear that, Mr Dillon? Get figuring and let's see how many loaves a brig may take, while we talk about beef. Remind me, Mr Harman, how many pieces of meat do we find in one barrel?'

'In one puncheon we've a hundred and seventy pieces, sir.'

Kydd brought to mind the stout provision casks. 'And what size are these?'

'Ah . . .?'

'Yes, Mr Joyce?' The sailing master had ultimate responsibility for stowage of provisions aboard a man-o'-war.

'I allows four foot f'r length an' two and a half on the bilge.'

'So for y'r brig, let's see . . . I make it sixteen alongwise, four across an' three down. Say two hundred.'

'So. One puncheon holds . . .?'

'One cow. That's my rule o' thumb.'

'Thank you for that, Mr Harman.'

'O' which we may say, of the fifteen hundred pounds of the beast we get seven hundred pounds as is usable.'

'Hmm. Therefore for our Prussian soldier we can find in each cask enough for fourteen hundred meals.'

'Aye, sir. So with two hundred, our brig is supplying near three hundred thousand – that's eighteen days' rations, I make it.'

And all in a single brig. It was looking much more possible.

'Twenty-five thousand.'

'I beg your pardon, Mr Dillon?'

'That's how many loaves of bread can be carried.'

Kydd thought of the endless lines of mules and carts needed to load such an impossible number and shook his head in wonder. 'I think we're getting somewhere. Say we load the same number of puncheons for beer. That would be—'

'Seventy-two gallon for the Millbrook tertian we usually ships, sir.'

'Yields a hundred and fifty rations. Two hundred barrels on our brig makes our thirty thousand.'

'You're in rattling good form, Mr Dillon. Gentlemen, what this is saying is that our resupply can be maintained with a convoy of some half-dozen brigs a week, or just one or two a day. I believe we can do it!'

After a Baltic convoy of some hundreds, each vessel many times bigger, this was easy.

'Well, now we know what's required you may withdraw, Mr Harman. Have the charts arrived?'

Gürsten fetched them and stood back respectfully as Kydd and Joyce spread them out.

There were two: one of Pillau at the entrance to the river and the other a detailed study of the approaches to Königsberg.

The words were in German and the soundings were in *klafters* – but these were as near as maybe to fathoms so the charts were perfectly understandable.

But what they revealed brought a wash of shock and dismay.

'L'tenant Gürsten,' he said heavily. 'You said your army extends to the sea. Do show me where.'

He leaned aside to let the young officer find the spot. 'Here, sir.' It was a substantial length of the coast that should have proved an ideal landing place, were it not for one thing.

'Pray tell me, then, what the devil is this?' Kydd pointed to a long spit that paralleled the land some three to four miles offshore and ranging as far as the chart boundary in both directions.

'Oh, it's of no account. A mere piece of sand a few hundred yards across only and going nowhere – of no military significance at all.'

'And this interior water it encloses?'

'This is the Frisches Haff, a brackish lagoon. The only entrance is at Pillau in our hands, so you need not fear—'

Kydd held up his hands wearily. 'L'tenant. You don't know it, but you've just killed any chance of saving your army.'

Gürsten looked appalled. 'I – I had no idea . . . Is there anything . . .?'

'I fear that this is a matter between myself and the sailing master. We'll call on you should we need anything further.'

He pulled the chart nearer and studied it intently, but there was no getting away from it. There would be no access to the army on the coast with that long spit barring the way the entire distance. Even if Pillau at the far northern end had an entrance, there were two very good reasons why their brigs could not sail inside down to the trapped army.

The first was obvious: the few soundings showed that no deep-laden ship could find depth of water to reach it in the near-tideless Baltic. The second was that the plan to sail out to sea to avoid the French artillery and in again to the locality of the besieged was no longer possible. Any approach inside the lagoon must inevitably pass close by the besieging enemy positions on the coast.

Joyce raised troubled eyes to his. 'Boats?' he murmured.

It made nonsense of all their calculations – boats full of rowers could carry little, nothing like the massive amounts needed, and would be terribly vulnerable to artillery fire.

'Camels?' the master ventured.

These were barrels open to the water, firmly lashed along the waterline of a vessel, then at the right moment baled out – a method of raising a ship up bodily to take shallow water. It could conceivably work but would make them slow and cumbersome and an unmissable target for the French guns. It was not a solution.

Kydd stared at the chart, willing some winning idea to

strike but none came. The coldness of defeat began closing in.

'Mr Gürsten.' The officer hurried to his side. 'This spit o' land. What's it like?'

'Ah, you will call it the "Vistula Spit" on account of the ancient and debased natives by that name living there. It has very few settlements and stretches for fifty miles or more.'

'My meaning was, what is the nature of the ground thereabouts?'

'It's still well wooded, for farming is hard in sand. I should say firm, suitable for troops on the march.'

'I see.' A glimmer of an answer was emerging. It would need much labour but there were hands to spare in the besieged army.

But first he had to see for himself.

His boat's crew were by the jetty, Halgren's bulk unmistakable. About them was a square of Prussian militia on guard. The subaltern screamed an order to bring them to quivering attention, then stamped about to salute him with his sword.

A few hours later Kydd's boat under sail had passed out of the Frisches Haff entrance to the open sea and turned left down the coast, touching bottom at the right spot opposite von Hohenlau's encampment out of sight across the lagoon.

Kydd trudged up the beach and found himself in a light wood, continuous for miles on both sides. Crossing to one tree he inspected it. A four-inch bole and, as was usual with Baltic timber, straight as a die. It would do.

He walked on into the wood. There was leaf litter but, underneath it, hard-packed sand. Further on, the trees thinned and there was the lagoon, and some few miles across he could see tents and banners, eddying wisps of cooking fires and what was probably a marching column.

Yes!

'I shall want to remove to Pillau to set up my headquarters,' he demanded on his return.

Soon he was installed on the top floor of a bastion in the Pillau Citadel, the star-shaped fort he'd seen. It commanded a formidable view down the length of the spit, a fine sight of the open sea to the right and the passage to Königsberg to the left.

Gürsten was set to produce a corps of runners, then was dispatched to make contact with General von Hohenlau, carrying a sheaf of written instructions for the resupply plan.

From *Tyger* Maynard, a master's mate, was sent for to man the rudimentary signal mast, arriving with a determined Tysoe bearing Kydd's necessaries and two wide-eyed ship's boys for general duties.

Then it was down to work.

Eight coastal ships were selected and prepared. Cargo holds were cleared, dunnage battens laid and on the wharf the first stores appeared ready for loading, according to the priorities relayed back by Gürsten.

And at the spit the pioneer battalions set to in earnest.

They fell on the timber, lopping down trees by the hundreds in a swathe from the sea to the lagoon. Some were fastened together as rafts, others laid to form a wooden road across the spit – and, astonishingly, they were ready!

Kydd was there when the first brig anchored in the offshore shallows.

Right away it started discharging into a waiting raft on one side, and when that was loaded, turned to another on the other side while the first was hauled ashore. Waiting carts took the stores across the spit and a raft was again loaded.

In the lagoon there were pairs of ship's boats manned by well-muscled Prussian sailors with a line each to the raft and a continuous relay was set up that rapidly had stores in a satisfactory flow. On their return the rafts carried a different cargo – wounded men, some ominously still, others writhing in pain, but mercifully on their way to Königsberg's hospital.

Opposite the Prussian Army, they could not be touched by French guns and the flow of relief could go on unimpeded. Now there were only two things that could stop it: an enemy attack from the sea or the weather.

With *Tyger*'s sturdy silhouette to seaward, there was vanishingly little likelihood of the first, and with summer approaching its height, the balmy breezes threatened nothing more than cloudless radiance.

It could only be reckoned a success. A workmanlike solution to a military problem in the best traditions of the service . . . but Kydd felt restless. It had all been too easy, too straightforward.

He fell exhausted into his cot at the citadel and did not wake until morning. Reassured that all was as it should be, his apprehension eased. He had done it. The army was relieved and he had performed what had been asked of him – but then he realised that this was only the first part, the establishing of a resupply route. What had been requested was the guarding of same.

Dart and *Stoat* were still with him but their value lay in inshore defence against daring strikes by privateers and such. *Tyger* had to be there to provide an unanswerable deterrent against whatever else could be brought against them, such as a determined swarm of the vermin.

There was nothing for it but to remain until *Tyger* was relieved. That shouldn't be long – his was a first-rank fighting frigate and the job could just as easily be done by a light frigate or ship-sloop. Three or four days to get word to Russell and, with a fair westerly, less to detach one of his force. If he was lucky, a week and he'd be on his way.

He should be making an appearance in *Tyger* but he'd been led to believe that an entertainment had been planned for this day in his honour and it would be churlish to absent himself. Besides, he knew Bray would be relishing his time in temporary command.

The reception at the Grand Palace was to be followed by an orchestral concert.

In his star and ribbon and full-dress uniform, Kydd cut an impressive figure as, with Gürsten at his side, he entered the glittering room, remembering to render obeisance to King Friedrich Wilhelm, then award bows of recognition this way and that. In a short while he was surrounded by admiring officers and ladies and the evening swept on in a swirl of gaiety and noise.

Yet underlying the exhilaration and animation he could detect a darker element lurking. Not two score miles away Napoleon Bonaparte and his legions were lying in encampment. Nothing stood between them and that host but Bennigsen and the Russians.

Chapter 18

Unusually, Kydd woke late but didn't hurry in his dressing. He'd return to *Tyger* some time after their dog-watch leisure-time and let the inevitable waiting paperwork slide to the next day. Meanwhile he and Dillon could walk off the previous night's excesses in the old city with Gürsten.

Königsberg was an agreeable place and they spent some hours in leisurely exploration of the old Hohenzollern capital. However, when they returned they were urgently hustled to the war room.

'There have been developments – not good. Come!' Blücher snapped, stamping towards an inner room.

He slammed the door and pointed to a map. 'Bonaparte – he manoeuvres to deceive us.'

Kydd looked down at the pencilled wavy line going to the south-east separating the two armies.

'We have spies. They say that in the rear, concealed from us, there have been large-scale movements across here by Davout and Soult. To the east!' Before Kydd could say anything, Blücher continued, 'This means we're to be outflanked. Bennigsen's stand is for nothing. He must pull back and face about. His orders now no longer have meaning. Von Hohenlau's role to stay in position and threaten Bonaparte's rear is absurd and I won't be bound by it.'

Blücher stood back, arms folded. He fixed Kydd with a steely glare. 'His Imperial Majesty concurs that our forces must be restored to us. Von Kydd, I request you will take off Generalleutnant von Hohenlau, his men, stores, horses and guns.'

Kydd was taken aback. This was an entirely different proposition from a resupply exercise, and even with his limited military experience he knew that a successful formal withdrawal involved great complexities and risks – flanks and rear shortening lines in a co-ordinated sequence to prevent a retreat turning into a rout, the gradual taking up of field guns in such a way that the enemy could not gain advantage, the preserving of as much impedimenta as could be retrieved. It was a dangerous and fraught time.

As if answering Kydd's unspoken questions, Blücher growled, 'I undertake to bring our army to the edge of the sea, no worry to you, Kapitan. Then you – your ships – will take them on board and away. Can you do it?'

This was far more than a handful of coastal brigs could handle. And when the French saw what was going on they would throw everything at them . . .

Kydd's expression was grave. 'I can – but only if we have regular military transports. They have the right gear and capacity to take men, horses and guns aboard in a short time.' Where the devil these could be found short of Portsmouth or Plymouth he had no idea, or whether they could be released, and on whose authority.

'I understand you,' Blücher responded crisply. 'We ask

Sweden. I know they have these at Stralsund and more at Karlskrona. It is a matter for diplomats. You will leave this with me. Do maintain your resupply until the transports arrive, four, five days.'

In a way it was a relief for Kydd, for now the end was in sight. This mass continental butchery was not to his liking and it would be good to get back to the blessed reassurance of sea routine.

Tyger, in her slow offshore cruising, had been able to put the time to good use. The new boatswain had tut-tutted about the condition of some of the rigging and fittings and set to with his mates to bring her to rights. Bray had made sure of an unvarying hour at the guns every morning and, on Kydd's instructions, this was followed by sail-handling.

Kydd had allowed his officers leave in pairs to Königsberg, as much to see something of what lay behind the strategics of the armies that were deciding Europe's fate as to make acquaintance of the ancient city.

But two days later catastrophe struck. The plan for taking off von Hohenlau's troops was uncovered, and before the transports could arrive, the French made their move in an intelligent and daring expedition.

A force of dragoons dragging field-pieces had crossed the marshy flatlands at the far end of the Frisches Haff on to the Vistula Spit. Now, along unused trails of the old native peoples, they were advancing rapidly up its length, followed by reinforcements of regular troops.

They would be at the resupply crossing in little more than a day.

The move was well thought-out and in keeping with the main outflanking thrust – it was in Bonaparte's interest to keep a full corps of his enemy in idle helplessness while he brought the Russians to battle.

At the council-of-war that evening it quickly became clear that to counter the manoeuvre in a formal way would be impossible. In the time they had, it would be hopeless to attempt to effect fortified works on the sandy terrain and therefore it would descend into a brutal hacking match, which, without cavalry, the Prussians would certainly lose. Besides, Blücher was bleakly insistent that the Prussian Army should be preserved for the cataclysmic battle at the gates of Königsberg, which was still to come.

The occupation of the spit would therefore not be contested. The army would once again be left isolated and under siege.

Blücher turned to Kydd. 'We don't know when the transports arrive. Can you maintain resupply along the Frisches Haff?'

He had been dreading the question. The shallows couldn't take a reasonable-sized ship, and now that both sides of the lagoon were occupied by the French with guns, any attempt by boats would make them sitting ducks.

But somehow it had to be done.

'I'll think on it, General,' he murmured, feeling eyes on him from around the room. It was no use giving false hope with impossible promises and he left quickly.

The French dragoons made good time and were in position opposite before the next morning was out. Now even communications with von Hohenlau were severed.

Kydd ordered *Stoat*, his armed ketch, to be readied.

Taken up by the Royal Navy desperate for anything that sailed, she was as elderly as her commander, her sharp stern giving her away as a native of the Baltic. A relic of the far-off days of peace, the varnish of her upper-works hardly concealed the dark weathering of her timbers underneath.

Rogers, an elderly master's mate, was her captain.

'I shall want to wake up the French guns, see where they're positioned, how many and so forth.'

'Aye aye, Sir Thomas.'

'No heroics, in and out only.'

'Sir. How long should I—'

'I shall be the judge of that, Mr Rogers, as I'll be aboard with you.'

They put out from Pillau and passed into the lagoon. *Stoat* glided slowly along.

There was no gunfire: to the right there would be no point in the French occupying any of the spit past the crossing point, and the left was still Prussian-held. It was calm and the watery expanse glittered in the sun, ruffled here and there by small flaws in the breeze.

It couldn't last. Well before they were anywhere near the besieged Prussians the shoreline to the south sprouted puffs of white. The thud and rumble of the guns followed soon after. It was at long range but, even so, balls skipped and flew, some of respectable size, eight-pounders, Kydd surmised. He smiled grimly. It would have been better for the French gunners to hold their fire and trap the little vessel.

He spotted the far-off besieged encampment well down the lagoon. His heart sank with the realisation that as the range closed they would not survive: the French would undoubtedly have worked out that this was the only way to relieve the army and brought up many more guns to make it impossible.

'Take us back, Mr Rogers,' he muttered.

The idea came to him as they went about to go alongside the jetty at Königsberg harbour, where the ships lay together in idleness. On the short walk to the Grand Palace it took form and detail. There was great risk. But it *could* work . . .

'The relief will resume in a day, General,' he said flatly, 'provided I shall have what I desire.'

It all depended on his observation that both sides of the lagoon were completely flat, no high ground of any sort. This had one priceless consequence: at night even in moonlight the width of reflecting water between the shores would appear narrow, and targeting an object with the majority of its silhouette invisible against the darkness of the opposite shore would be damned difficult.

The other part of his plan was to use harbour lighters for the cargo-carrying. These were simple hollow craft brought up to a merchant ship at anchor offshore to allow discharge of cargo into them. Fully laden, only a foot or two of their gunwales would show above water, a near-impossible target compared with anything carrying sail.

Finally he had to find an alternative to boats in towing them. His solution was simple but back-breaking. The boats would tow the lighters as far as they could, then cast off. Aboard each one, they would have two grapnels on a line. The idea was to cast them ahead as far as possible and on the little after-deck a makeshift windlass would haul in on the line, propelling the lighter ahead for the distance of the cast and length of the lighter. To keep a steady momentum, there would be one line on each side, out of sequence with each other.

That was the best he could do. Their silhouette would be very low but this was achingly slow work and it was to be expected that they'd be under fire most of the time. And without doubt they would take casualties.

The first four harbour lighters were fitted out and the next night they were loaded, the tow-lines passed. When all was in darkness they set off into the gloom.

Kydd was in the first boat and kept them together as they passed across the entrance by Pillau, only too conscious that tonight moonrise was scheduled for ten.

In the boats a heavy silence was broken only by the slither and thump of oars – no one was in doubt about what lay ahead for the lighter crews who squatted in readiness.

'Put some heavy in it, then!' Kydd growled. The men at the oars wouldn't understand a word of what he was saying but the deep-laden craft were going agonisingly slowly through the calm waters.

They would eventually be seen. The French would be expecting some sort of attempt and would be looking out for it. The only question was when.

The camp fires of the friendly Prussians fell away abruptly to an unrelieved darkness. This was the forbidden ground between the two armies.

On they crept, into the blackness and silence.

More camp fires. With a prickle of tension Kydd knew that these were enemy positions now and at any moment . . .

The moon emerged above low cloud and, although only quartering, the night had lost its cloak of anonymity. It bathed the tops of the woodland in silver and laid a sheen on the Haff that could only reveal the intrusion.

Feeling exposed in the unearthly shimmer, Kydd tensed.

First one gun, then several – and the whole shore burst into life with the thunder of cannon fire.

The boats could go no further. 'Cast off the tow. Good luck, you men!' he roared at the lighters.

He watched as they began their furious work with the

grapnels, slow at first, then increasing to one or two knots as they found their rhythm.

As they moved away Kydd saw that gun-flash at the emplacements was making nonsense of aimed fire. The low shapes would thus not have to suffer a concentrated barrage directed on them. On the other hand the scene was alive with the crash and skitter of shot, some of which must find a target.

His instructions were to advance the lighters together to minimise time of exposure but stagger them in order that one shot striking would not take another beyond. It was all very well in theory but these were desperate men who would care little about formation once the guns opened up on them.

Straining his eyes, he followed the creeping shadows until they faded into the dimness among the leaping splashes and skipping of ricochets. If they succeeded, the army was safe for another two days on iron rationing.

'Return,' he snapped, gesturing back. The men and lighters would stay with von Hohenlau: there was little point in braving the holocaust again to bring back the empties. With luck, there would be just one or two more of these heroic sallies before the transports came.

Next day word was returned that three of the four lighters had got through, the fourth taking a hit and sinking quickly. There had been no survivors.

Another gallant sortie had been completed when *Dart* came streaming in from seaward with signals flying. The transports!

Heaving to well out of sight of the enemy, as instructed, it was at last time to put the grand plan into operation.

'We move tonight!' grated Blücher, unrolling a map.

The general had kept his preparations a close secret but had promised to bring his army to the water's edge.

The plan was outlined with an economy of words. It was simple and brutal: a suicide battalion. A picked body of troopers with light guns would be landed at the unoccupied opposite tip of the spit. Their mission was to ride down its length until they met the French and by any means to drive them clear of Kydd's crossing point, then keep them back, whatever the cost.

Tyger would have a role: in the minutes before they clashed at the crossing the frigate would close with the shore and smash in a broadside at the French positions, go about and hammer them with the opposite side of guns, then keeping up a withering fire until the French had been driven clear and a line of defence for the crossing established.

This was the point where the transports would come in to take the first wave of troops that had been brought across on rafts.

It would be decided by the timings. The Prussian force would land on the spit in darkness and aim to begin their assault with the dawn at precisely the time *Tyger* opened fire and the first of the besieged put off in their rafts. The French at the crossing could not count on reinforcements down the far length of the spit for some time but if there were delays they could be expected to enter the battle decisively. There was every need for a smooth operation at the transports.

It would be a bloody affair – but, one way or the other, by the end of the next day it would be over, and *Tyger* could be quit of this unnatural existence.

Kydd had last words with Blücher, who was dismissive of his sincere wishes for good fortune, coldly dictating orders to his staff officers and neatly pencilling in marks on his battle-plan.

Gürsten had no further part to play, but when Kydd found him to say his farewell he insisted that they go to a private room.

In broken but passionate English, he thanked Kydd for his services to the Prussian nation and assured him that His Majesty would never forget such. He reached into his military satchel and drew out two glasses and a wicker-covered brown bottle. 'I am grateful, we toast to our tomorrow,' he said, with disturbing intensity. 'Pliss.'

Kydd held out his glass, which was filled with a light golden liquor.

'To the new day, and may it go down in history as a glorious occasion for the Prussian military.'

Kydd went to raise his glass but stopped when he saw Gürsten hesitate.

'Sir, I cannot. This is retreat, not victory. No one remember glorious retreat.'

'Then—'

'Sir Thomas, can we drink to we both spared, do all our duty to the end, and then meet again.'

'I gladly toast to that, Klaus,' he said, and drank deeply.

It was a mistake – the thick liqueur nearly took his breath away with its potency.

'You're not liking?' Gürsten asked in concern. 'It is our Bärenfang from here in Königsberg, much esteem in East Prussia. A vodka liqueur of honey. The bear-trapper,' he explained, pointing to the illustration on the label.

'Oh, it was . . . delightful – I was not ready for it.'

Kydd had to accept another but then made his excuses, pleading his need to return on board his ship without delay.

Almost shyly, Gürsten felt in his satchel and pressed a different bottle on him. 'Sir, when all is over, whatever fortune bring, I beg you will drink with your officers to our fighting, we together.'

'That's so kind in you, Klaus,' Kydd said, touched. 'And what is this, pray?'

'A fine *Kopskiekelwein*, much loved in Königsberg.'

'Which means?'

'Sir, pardon the Low German. They make with redcurrant, and its meaning, that you're too fond of it, you fall down head over . . .'

'I do promise on my honour we shall raise a glass to you, my friend.'

It started well. At dusk the troopers and their equipment were transported over from Pillau to the end of the spit, despite a four knot cross-current set up by an increasingly brisk south-westerly.

Tyger lay offshore, and Kydd watched developments through a night-glass.

He could make out where they assembled together, in every kind of uniform in a brave show – these were volunteers from every regiment, united in one heroic purpose. Cuirassiers in mustard with the white slash of baldrics and magnificently plumed helmets; hussars in elaborately frogged chests and a shako in silver; among them, too, the darker and more utilitarian garb of artillerymen.

One stood out. On a white horse and in full dress uniform he was everywhere, imperiously commanding, gesturing: the captain of this gallant band – whose bold appearance would hearten his men but would inevitably ensure he could not survive.

Formed up, they marched off, the dragoons walking beside their horses, sparing them for the last wild ride, the infantry in column, the field pieces and limbers following behind. Almost immediately they entered woodland and were lost to view. The next act would be when all the players came together at dawn.

During the night *Tyger* stood out to sea, lying with the transports to avoid giving the alarm.

Their task now was to rendezvous off the crossing at dawn. Kydd had been careful to reach an understanding for, while the military regarded it light enough for operations at anything up to half an hour before the sun rose, the navy's definition was the point at which the horizon itself could be distinguished.

Thus when the stars paled and visibility began to extend over a colourless sea, course was shaped inshore.

Even as the grey low-lying land firmed ahead, the masthead lookouts, then the quarterdeck, saw that the encounter had begun. The livid flash of guns and musketry had already started about the crossing and nothing would be gained by a stealthy approach.

With *Tyger* in the lead, the armada made directly for the firing. There was every hope that the French would see the approaching transports and assume that they were landing an overwhelming force and fall back, but as they sailed closer in the growing light there was no sign that this was the case.

Rounding to, with two leadsmen in the chains chanting soundings, the frigate steadied and ran down on her target.

It was easy to see the line of division between the opposing sides by the furious musket fire and the dead ground in between, and Kydd sent a message to the gun-captains that this would be their mark.

Coming up slowly on the French lines he waited for the right moment.

'Open fire, if you please.'

With a bellowing crash the double-shotted eighteen-pounders spoke as one, powder-smoke driven away downwind in time for the gunners to see the result. Hidden by the trees a storm of fragments and darker objects was flung into the air as the shot tore into the French positions in a rage of pitiless death.

Nothing could stand against it, and as it subsided, Kydd could see the fire had slackened significantly.

Tyger put about for her other broadside but from the absence of firing it was clear their quarry had taken heed of what was coming and fled their ground.

Shivering sail he slowed his approach in time for messengers to warn off the gun-captains to shift their aim to allow the Prussians to move forward. Then he moved in and *Tyger*'s guns blasted out in another smashing rampage of destruction.

There were no individual targets, for the enemy was concealed in the woods – but if they thought that would protect them they were sadly mistaken. The spit was only a few hundred yards across, perfectly flat, and at a low trajectory the heavy-calibre battering would be causing untold carnage.

Even as the sun began tentatively peeping above the flat land it appeared that the French had been beaten back.

But little could really be seen of what was going on – gun-smoke wreathing up through the evenly spaced tree-tops, occasional flashes and a faint but continuous din of battle, leaving the imagination to picture the hand-to-hand savagery that was taking place within the woodlands.

The first transport nosed in, kedges streamed, inclined ramps already lowering down its side. Men and horses began moving out to it in an orderly procession while the second transport prepared to go in.

It was all going to plan! This was what it was to have domination of the sea, to know its freedoms and power. In fact—

'*Deck hooo!* Sail to suth'ard, standing toward!'

It was not yet in sight from the deck but almost certainly it was his relief from the North Sea squadron attracted by the firing, and now there was really nothing for it to do.

Kydd turned back to see if there was need for a follow-up cannonade. The firing had died a little, which made it difficult to—

'Another sail astern of 'un!'

'What d'ye see?' Kydd hailed back.

'Both are ships!' Nothing below a frigate.

'*An' one more!*' The lookout's voice cracked with urgency.

'Take us out, Mr Joyce,' Kydd ordered. 'Quick as you like – I need to speak with those ships.'

They were coming on from the south-west with the wind that was paralleling the coast and were soon in sight from the deck.

Certainly frigates, but end-on it was difficult to make out who they were. Two respectably sized ones and a lighter vessel.

'Don't say as I knows 'em a-tall,' Joyce said, peering through the officer-of-the-watch's telescope. 'Smaller t'gallants, as is usual, less goring in the topsails, like.'

Uneasiness pricked at Kydd. There were no French frigates in the Baltic, or Dutch for that matter. He'd been assured that the only countries with ships of size in these waters were Russia and Sweden. After his time with the Russian Navy he knew what to look for but these were not at all similar: besides, the master had been struck by the marked rectangular shape of their sail, blocky and quite at variance with their own.

Swedes, come to look after their own transports? He doubted it. The Swedes had the gifted Fredrik af Chapman as naval architect in Karlskrona and his designs were sleek and smooth, unlike these more stern and frowning forequarters.

Tyger was close-hauled and necessarily crossing their bows, if at a distance, but something made him rap, 'Private signals!'

The confidential fleet challenge soared up, snapping in the increasingly boisterous winds.

There was no response. Neither were any colours aloft that could be seen.

Yet this was not necessarily an enemy – unless they were North Sea squadron, they wouldn't have access to the signal of the day and colours were not usually flown at sea out of sight of others to save wear and tear on expensive bunting.

Still, they were taking their time replying and getting closer all the time. If in the next few minutes—

'Sir? I've a man wishes to speak to you, urgently.' Brice stepped aside to let a seaman come forward.

'Able Seaman Haffner, sir.' He was one of the German seamen fleeing before Bonaparte's advance, taken on as a volunteer in Königsberg.

'What is it, Haffner? Smartly now.'

In broken English the story was quickly told. These frigates were Prussian. They had been taken with the rest of the small navy when the French had overrun the main naval ports of Wismar and Rostock. It was likely that they were manned by sending seamen overland from the idle blockaded fleets in French ports – which implied they had picked crews and men to spare.

The smaller one was *Albatros*, a light frigate similar to *L'Aurore*; the one with the dark patched foresail was *Odin* and the other *Preussen*. The lighter had twenty-eight twelve-pounders but the larger two had thirty-eight guns of eighteen-pounder equivalent each.

They had clearly been dispatched as a squadron to fall on and destroy the transports, evidence that the thwarting of the relief of von Hohenlau's army was a major concern: a force had been sent that could be relied upon to sweep aside the single frigate standing in their way.

Tyger was hopelessly out-classed: over a hundred guns to his twenty-six eighteen-pounders and six nines. It would be no dishonour to stand aside before this foe and simply harry where he could as they got on with their butchery.

There was nothing in his orders or implied by his agreement that he should sacrifice his ship in the face of such odds and, indeed, if he did and survived, he would then have to explain why he had robbed the Royal Navy of one of their most valuable assets in a hopeless confrontation.

On the other hand if he withdrew he would be condemning thousands to certain death or capture.

Yet if he stood fast, every soul in *Tyger* would be pitched into a mortal fight with no certain outcome.

Where did his duty lie? To the Prussians or his own men?

Kydd forced his mind to a deadly coolness. The answer must be at the higher level – the strategics of the situation. Which course would accomplish the greater goal?

He knew so little about this continental struggle but if the desperate stand against Bonaparte failed for lack of this army it would be England itself that would end the loser.

His duty was therefore clear: to oppose the squadron by whatever means he could.

'Mr Bray, I believe we cannot run. We must stand and fight.'

There was no reaction at first. Then the hard features were split by a tight smile, which widened. 'Aye aye, sir!' he growled happily. 'We'll give the beggars such a drubbing as will have 'em yowling for their mothers!'

Those who overheard it spread the news and in a very short time muffled cheers could be heard breaking out over the ship. It swelled to a roar, and Kydd realised that the deadly peril was achieving what he had not: the Tygers were coming together as a true ship's company to take up the monstrous challenge.

Chapter 19

The ship was already cleared for action, the men at quarters and guns run out. Even if he desired it, there was no time for Kydd to call the men aft for a rousing speech and the martial thunder of the drums had long since ceased. His Majesty's Ship *Tyger* was about to sail into her greatest time of trial without the smallest ceremony.

Should he go below and put on his sash and star to be like Nelson at Trafalgar? It would hearten the men at the guns but single him out to the enemy sharpshooters in the tops in just the same way. Then he recalled that the great admiral had only worn them because there had not been time to go below and shift into something else.

This was going to be a ferocious struggle and he needed every advantage he could contrive.

Usually a frigate duel began with a lengthy period of sizing up one's opponent, detecting weaknesses in sail-handling, their poorest point of sailing, over-eagerness or reluctance to engage – all quirks that could be noted and exploited later in the deadly game of war.

But he didn't have that luxury, for his action was of quite a different kind. The stakes were not winning or losing an encounter but the successful protecting of helpless transports. At all costs he must draw off the pack from their killing.

And for that he needed – craved – sea-room.

The enemy were under full sail, arrowing downwind head-long for the helpless transports with only *Tyger* between them and their prey. He could take on one but while they grappled this would allow the other two to begin their slaughter.

Only a bold move would—

'Helm alee, hard by the wind close as she'll lie on the larb'd tack!'

Heads turned in astonishment.

'Sir, that would take us—'

'Yes, Mr Bray – I know!'

In the face of the onrushing enemy they should be short-ening sail to topsails and placing themselves firmly in their path ready for the fight. Kydd had just ordered them to head off straight out to sea, away from them, leaving the trans-ports wide open to the charge.

Tyger began filling and standing out to sea, heeling in the stiff breeze and steadily putting distance between her, the transports and the enemy.

He watched carefully: there was no alteration of course in the three frigates, which sped on towards their objective, leaving *Tyger* to continue her tight close-hauled run ever further out to sea. Aboard the enemy, there would be shrugged shoulders and the despising of a frigate that had fled rather than stand and fight. This was exactly what he wanted.

A bulldog of a ship, *Tyger* excelled in the weather. Losing hardly an inch to leeward she met the increasing seas exploding on her bow with exhilarating bursts of spray and a purposeful roll.

Ignoring Bray's sharp stare at him, Kydd concentrated hard on angles, wind pressure and what he knew of the longshore current. At what he judged to be exactly the right time he snapped, 'Hands to 'bout ship!'

She went round like a top and on this tack ended angled back towards the coast – but very neatly astern of the racing frigates. They had fallen for it!

Now they would know that not only was *Tyger* upwind and ready to turn on them, but as well could dictate how the action would be joined. And he had thrown them a conundrum: they could never know which of them *Tyger* would single out, and thus there could be no occupying him with one while the others set about the transports.

If they decided to continue with their attack, any who did would leave an unprotected stern to be exposed to *Tyger*'s guns in a brutal raking. It was a risk no sane captain could take – so they had to turn about and deal with *Tyger* first.

One by one, they braced around and took to the wind close-hauled after him, two on one tack and one on the other.

Kydd gave a grim smile. He had achieved his first objective, drawn them away from the helpless transports. But now *Tyger* was a hunted creature. He had to find that vital searoom.

He had two advantages. *Tyger* was still upwind of them, the weather gage, and could manoeuvre in a way that forced them to respond to his motions. The other was that while he was at some miles distance there was no danger from a battle-losing crippling shot. While he had this freedom there was a chance.

Odin was making good speed but the other, *Preussen*, was lagging. They would want to stay together to concentrate their force and therefore be constrained to the speed of the slowest. *Albatros*, the light frigate, was visibly chafing at the restraint. Until the wind freshened, conditions were perfect for her and, like *L'Aurore*, she had the legs on anything present and would know it.

Colours were now a-fly on every ship. All three of his opponents had French tricolours aloft. *Tyger* had the ensign of the North Sea squadron at the mizzen peak and Union flags bravely streaming from the main-topmast stay and fore-topgallant stay. Would they be hauled down by the close of day?

Over miles of sea the chase continued and, with satisfaction, Kydd looked back and saw that *Dart* and *Stoat* had had the sense to stay with the transports and keep them moving while they could. The first of them had already put out, presumably with a full loading; a second came in to resume the evacuation. If only he could keep up the luring away . . .

It couldn't last, of course.

At some point the commander, probably in *Odin*, would realise that *Tyger* was leading them a merry dance, and that by turning about to resume their descent they would force *Tyger* to follow, to be left far behind.

There was no other recourse: sooner or later *Tyger* must face all three.

Albatros came about with all the vitality and liveliness of her breed. She took up on the other tack well before the others and slashed ahead in an exuberant display – and Kydd saw his chance.

'On my order, we brace around and run large.'

None of the men who raced to their stations could have

been unaware of what that meant: *Tyger* was now turning right around and, with a brisk wind behind her, was running down to meet her pursuers.

'Helm up – move!'

The deep, broad rudder that gave her such sure-footed manoeuvrability did not let Kydd down. Under its impetus she rotated as fast as the men could haul on the braces and, under full sail, she was heading straight for *Albatros*, separated by half a mile from the others.

As Kydd expected, the less experienced captain hesitated – he was now presented with the choice of taking on *Tyger* or turning tail and running for his larger brethren. The last would take time and for all of that his stern would be offered to *Tyger*'s cruel broadside as she came up.

When he decided to run, *Tyger*'s gunners had been tracking their pieces, and even at long range, when the guns spoke a forest of plumes shot up all around the light frigate, bringing hits on the distant squared-off stern, which must have caused havoc inside.

The first shots of the engagement had drawn blood.

Kydd put the helm over and allowed a minute for gun-captains on the opposite side to lay their weapons, then let them loose.

Nearer, more shots must have told among the white gouts, but he was quite unprepared for what happened next.

Gently turning, *Albatros* came up into the wind and stopped, caught flat aback and lying helpless.

Joyce tumbled to it first. 'Aye, and he's had his rudder struck off!' he said happily, as cheers and shouts of jubilation erupted from all about the ship.

In a stroke of sheer luck the vessel had been knocked out of the fight without firing a shot in return!

Kydd was tempted to continue and finish the job but he resisted: it was enough that the odds had shortened to two against one, and in any case he could never take possession of it.

Now to the real contest. He was confident that in an equal fight with either, even against a bigger foe, *Tyger* could win, but against two, not only did it divide his fire but the necessary manoeuvring would be hideously complicated. To avoid being caught between two fires yet lie alongside one or the other without interference would be his chief problem.

Meanwhile *Tyger* was closing fast, head to head with the two enemy, which sailed close together in mutual support for the coming exchange, *Preussen* to starboard, *Odin* opposite.

The valiant frigate charged down to confront her adversaries. This was the moment of truth, when fates and destinies would be decided.

Kydd raised his telescope. Aboard each of the enemy the courses were taken in, the big lower sails drawn up out of the way of gun-flash and burning wads.

'Shorten to topsails, sir?' came an anxious enquiry from Bray. Unless they did so, they would be caught with men still aloft when the guns began firing.

But Kydd had no intention of conforming to expectations. He was going to put his ship to the test as never before and issued his commands calmly but firmly.

Under a press of sail she raced onward. It would be a near-run thing but if it succeeded . . .

They would be expecting *Tyger* at the last moment to decide on one or the other, then range alongside on her outer side, backing sail to come to a stop and begin a furious cannonade as they lay locked together, the other forced to circle around before coming in to join the fight. He was going to disappoint them.

Still under full sail, he careered on, his bowsprit exactly centred on the narrow gap of sea between them as if delaying his decision to the last moment.

As the frigates closed at the speed of a galloping horse time seemed to hang breathlessly. Not a soul moved on deck, hypnotised by the onrush – and then it happened.

Kydd did not choose one or the other. He plunged directly between the two, facing the very thing he should avoid – being caught between two fires.

And it worked.

Expecting the outer battery to be engaged on either ship the wrong-footed French gunners had to cross the deck to man the inner – but were then presented with a sight picture of their consort. To fire on *Tyger* would be to maim and kill their own side.

The English frigate swashed into the gap and as she hurtled through her guns smashed out in a devastating sequence, at point-blank range impossible to miss. Smoke briefly filled the void between them, the sound of the guns echoing back in a cacophony of thunder – but only to the starboard side. To larboard there was silence as *Tyger*'s gunners held their fire and *Preussen* was unaccountably spared.

But not for long – clearing the gap, *Tyger* wheeled round to catch *Preussen* with a raking blast from her larboard guns, but her captain was quick-witted and put his own helm over. Nevertheless she was caught by savage close-range fire as her stern rotated past, smashing and splintering her ornate windows and carving as the balls created their hell within, muffled shrieks and cries testifying to their work.

Now there was no escaping it: they must suffer.

Kydd had done what he could. It was close-in, brutal pounding and *Preussen* had her outer broadside at the ready. While *Tyger*'s guns were reloaded with desperate speed these guns thundered out.

In an appalling avalanche, balls smashed across the short distance and into the ship in savage thuds felt through the deck, the storm of shot shrieking through the air, sending splinters that whirred viciously to find human flesh. From above, a rain of debris tumbled down, bouncing and falling on the netting over the quarterdeck.

He paced slowly along the deck, conscious of muskets in the enemy tops but a torrent of thoughts and calculations left him no time to dwell on them.

The wash of enemy gun-smoke engulfed them briefly as it was driven past by the stiff breeze, dry and reeking.

Kydd took stock of the first impact. Mercifully no serious hit that he could see, no ceasing in the furious activity around the guns, the boatswain thrusting forward with his mates to stopper a parted shroud, all sail drawing, though now blotched and scarred by shot-holes.

There was no pretence at broadsides now. *Tyger*'s guns crashed out as they readied at the bigger frigate barely thirty yards away and closing in a frenzied cannonade. Black holes were appearing in the enemy side, the gun-crews in a fierce race to load and fire first.

Kydd's earlier manoeuvre had deliberately placed *Tyger* to leeward of *Preussen*, commonly thought of as the inferior position, but he'd seized on something as they'd approached: *Preussen* was high in the water, probably because they'd stored for only this brief voyage and hadn't bothered with compensating ballast.

And now he was turning it to advantage. To be close-hauled in the brisk winds meant a distinct heel to leeward – fine for targeting the enemy but it hid a crucial flaw that a more experienced commander would have expected.

On a level deck, guns fired and recoiled inboard, placing them neatly for sponging out and reloading. *Preussen* now was finding she did not have that assistance: her guns after firing rolled out again under their own weight and must now be hauled uphill bodily and held while recharged with powder and shot, throwing out of rhythm any well-drilled sequence.

By the time the first reply came, *Tyger* had got in two, three shots – a massive advantage. Her weary hours of gun-drill were paying off. *Preussen* was finding she was facing not a lesser 32-gun frigate but one with the equivalent of sixty to ninety guns, that of a ship-of-the-line!

She was taking real punishment now, damage visible, ominous dribbles of blood coming down from beaten-in gun-ports. In any other circumstance Kydd would have allowed a feeling of triumph, but not now, not with what had to be endured still.

It was a short time only before the other frigate would emerge to turn the tables. He had to get in a settling blow before that happened or . . .

The roar of guns was a continuous din and he had to shout at a trembling youngster: 'Odd numbered guns to fire high, target the enemy's rigging!' The lad scrambled off to the gun-deck below to pass the message to the hatless Brice, maniacally shouting at his gun-crews.

It was British practice to smash and hammer at the hull at close range. This took time – the real battle-stoppers were masts falling, spars carrying away and this was what the French generally tried for. It had its own drawback: there was a lot of empty air between ropes and the chances of dealing a settling blow were slim and, of course, sails could still draw with holes in them.

Kydd had compromised but at the cost of half his guns taken from the task of battering the enemy into surrender.

His senses registered the sea darkening off *Preussen*'s bow and with a tightening heart knew what it was: the shadow of *Odin* at last entering the contest.

She burst into view and Kydd was left with a last decision: to leave his duel with *Preussen* unfinished and face a fresh adversary – or stay locked together and fight the two simultaneously.

As *Odin* curved about, the decision was taken for him. As though swept away like a spider's web *Preussen*'s fore-topmast staysail was shot away and with its gear it fell to the foredeck, the lines entangling and smothering.

Kydd reacted instantly, giving the orders to get under way.

It was not a deciding blow but it was a reprieve. Until *Preussen* could make repair she was unable to manoeuvre and her guns were falling silent as men were called away and she shivered into the wind. Now he had what he wanted: an even match, one on one.

This was no time for subtle navigating – *Tyger* had to be brought around to face *Odin* in the most advantageous way, which meant falling off the wind and putting distance between them and *Preussen*.

Odin reacted immediately and warily shaped course to intercept. Her captain could be counted on to be on the alert for any trick – he had seen what Kydd had done to *Preussen* – but he would know as well that Kydd needed to bring on the encounter as soon as possible, if he were to have any chance at a conclusion before *Preussen* rejoined the fight, her repairs complete.

They circled each other like prize-fighters, looking for an opening, but this gave Kydd precious time to reload guns on both sides.

He knew his men must be desperately tired and would recognise that they were up against a fresh and vengeful opponent, but any doubts he had vanished when a roar of cheering spread through the ship – some even hanging on the rigging and shaking their fists, shouting, goading their rival unmercifully.

It couldn't last and the two ships came together under topsails in an oblique fashion, making it impossible for either side to open fire on the other until they met, for their guns could not be pointed so far forward.

They straightened at fifty yards opposite each other and fire was opened simultaneously in a hell of shot and noise. Again the cruel hits and rain of debris – and Kydd saw a ball take one of the midships guns in a welter of splintered carriage and upturned barrel, the gun-crew brutally thrown aside.

Beside him, Dillon walked slowly, his face a mask of control, Bray on his other side, his expression tigerish. At the head-rails of the quarterdeck Kydd could see down into the infernal regions of the gun-deck where men strove and fought on in a nightmare of pain and fatigue.

At the wheel Halgren was blank-faced and calm. He was chewing tobacco, which Kydd had never seen him do before, his gaze fixed on some tranquil world beyond *Tyger*'s bowsprit. His eyes flicked up to the sails from time to time. Although in idleness, as they fought it out, he nevertheless had a duty to counter any wind flaw in the backed sails that might compromise their position.

With all his heart Kydd wished the man should survive

the day. In this time of courage and death, the helmsman's duty was both the most dangerous and the most helpless.

It went on and on – it was almost impossible to think. Kydd snatched a quick glance at *Preussen*, receding on their quarter. She had men swarming over her fore-part – how long before she could rejoin the fight?

But *Odin* drifted closer, her fire telling, and on both ships casualties steadily mounted.

The frigate loomed – was she closing in for the kill?

Tyger's gun-crews never faltered, in a manic frenzy serving their iron beasts to pound the enemy in a fight to the finish. It was grit and tenacity, fearlessness and pugnacity on a heroic scale, but in war this was seldom enough. So often fortune dictated the terms: one fatal ball, a worn rope giving way, a stray spark to powder – any could alter the course of the fray and put at nothing the valour of men.

And so it was that day. A chance eighteen-pounder ball shot from a gun with quoin removed to give maximum elevation fired up in the vague direction of the delicate tracery of lines and rigging found a mark: *Odin*'s foreyard, near the tops. The ball gouged and splintered and, with a massive crack that sounded above the din of battle, the big spar, with its brailed up fore-course, broke in half and gracefully hinged down in a chorus of twanging from severed ropes.

In itself it was not a catastrophe. The fore-course was not set and had little effect on manoeuvrability – the fight could go on. It was what followed that ended the contest.

The doused sail, loosed from its restraints opened and spread as it fell, smothering in canvas the first three guns of the frigate. Even this was no calamity: the sail and tangle of rigging could be cut away readily enough. It was the action of a single gun-captain that ended everything.

Knowing that his reloaded piece had, seconds previously, just been laid on the enemy, he'd fired the gun blindly through the fallen canvas.

In the heat of battle it was understandable – but it had fatal consequences.

The wads seating the powder and shot flew out of the muzzle with the ball but were caught in the loose canvas. Instantly there was a flaring up, spreading fast.

It had all happened so quickly. Kydd was held in horrified fascination as he saw the fire leap and catch in *Odin* – and then, without warning, there was a muffled *whoomf* and the entire fore-part of the vessel blazed up.

He knew what had happened and was sickened. Somewhere, trapped under the tangle, a powder monkey had been sent sprawling by the falling wreckage. His salt-box with its cartridge had been knocked open and when the flames reached the struggling boy it had gone off, incinerating the child – and dooming the ship.

As if in recognition of the awful moment *Tyger*'s guns fell silent and men stared at the spectacle, the increasing roar of the fire easily heard as the tarred lower rigging caught and spread paths of fire aloft.

'Get us out of here,' Kydd demanded hoarsely, aware that to leeward of the conflagration they were in deadly danger.

Tyger bore off slowly and, as the wind caught, slipped ahead, leaving the charnel house to its fate, for a reckoning was waiting.

Preussen was under way – she had set to rights her forestay by some epic feat of seamanship and now was to weather of *Tyger*, altering towards for the final sanction.

They couldn't abandon the scene for the enemy frigate was quite capable of single-handedly causing the destruction of the transports. And at the same time *Preussen* could not achieve this while *Tyger* remained at large to prevent it.

Logic demanded that they meet in single combat to decide the issue.

Kydd gave orders that saw *Tyger* fall off the wind and away. This was not flight, it was buying time, for the ship desperately needed relief to tend the wounded, clear the decks of the debris of battle and prepare an exhausted crew for a new onslaught.

There were few preliminaries. Kydd ordered *Tyger* to wheel about. The two ships approached to grapple, like two punch-drunk pugilists.

They met and the battle began again. This time it was clear that *Preussen*'s captain was determined on a quick finish. Closing inexorably, the frigate opened fire with all it had – great guns, swivels, muskets – a deathly storm of evil that staggered Kydd with its ferocity.

He forced his mind to absolute concentration – so much depended on it and this was too hot work to last long. Side by side, the ships moving at a slow walking pace while pounding shot into each other, it was a chaos of noise and destruction that beat at the senses, and out of it death could come at any instant.

Every detail of the enemy frigate could be seen through the eddying powder-smoke: the frantically labouring figures behind the gun-ports, the sadly scarred scroll-work and the glitter of blades as a boarding party readied.

Then her deck erupted in a lethal spray of splinters, scattering the assembled party in a welter of screams. His last order to fire high was sending shot upwards through the higher enemy deck.

It went on but Kydd could see that the tide of war was shifting. *Tyger*'s skill at arms – her matchless rate of fire – was telling. And with her guns charged double-shotted it must be near unendurable on the enemy decks.

Quite unexpectedly the picture changed: *Preussen* was slowing, slipping back! Amidships there was some sort of tangle of canvas where the staysail had been. In a wild leap of desperate hope he watched men struggle to deal with it. If this was another of Fortune's hands dealt against the enemy, then . . .

The ship slowed further and *Tyger* increasingly pulled ahead. In a glorious surge of feeling, he knew that this was the defining moment of the contest and made ready to act. But the reek of the gun-smoke was making his throat dry and the words stuck in his throat.

His glance happened to flick to the after end of *Preussen* and saw it was no lucky stroke that had crippled *Preussen* – it was a deliberate and clever ploy to end the fight!

The big fore and aft driver sail on the mizzen was being hauled out by tackle to the wrong side, against the wind. In sudden understanding his gaze shot back to the midships shambles. He focused carefully and saw what it was – the whole thing was a mockery, the men heaving and tugging aimlessly and achieving nothing.

They had nearly got away with it, but Kydd had their measure. Their captain was intelligent and cool – he was falling back in pretence of damage but using the occasion not to disengage from a bloody duel: at the right point he would abruptly put over the helm and, aided by the backed driver, slide around *Tyger*'s stern. And there he would be in a perfect position to send a broadside in a brutal raking fire down her entire length, a mortal wound.

Kydd hesitated but only for a moment. If they turned away it would make things worse, presenting her stern so much the quicker. There was only one course to take.

'Helm up! Put us across her bows!' he croaked urgently.

The quartermaster stared unbelievingly – *Preussen*'s bowsprit was only just passing opposite but Halgren at the helm acted instantly, the spokes whirling as he wound on turns.

Tyger obediently swung towards the enemy frigate, closer and closer and at an ever steeper angle until she was madly sheering across the bows. *Preussen*'s jib-boom speared across *Tyger*'s quarterdeck snapping and splintering in a crazy progression – but what Kydd had trusted to happen, did.

One by one, as they passed across, *Tyger*'s guns spoke in an endless hideous sequence, the balls smashing into the naked bow – he had turned the tables and raked *Preussen* instead.

His officers and men had nobly risen to the occasion and, on their own initiative, had held fire in anticipation of this crushing blow.

They passed to the other side but *Preussen* did not attempt to wheel and follow. She could not: the epic repair to the forestay had been shot through and the frigate once more was helpless.

With bursting emotion Kydd knew the day was theirs. The enemy was at his mercy.

Coldly, he gave the orders.

Tyger circled around until the angle was just right. Then she went in for the kill, arrow straight for *Preussen*'s stern.

There was nothing to stop him from pass after pass of raking fire into the helpless vessel until there were only corpses, but this was war and a battle could only be won by one side.

There were figures at the taffrail, brave men who could do nothing. They were waiting for release – death or their commander hauling down their flag in surrender.

Colours still flew, therefore the dread logic of war demanded Kydd do his duty and begin the slaughter.

Sail was shortened to bring *Tyger* to a slower pace to prolong the battering – but Kydd couldn't do it. These were men as brave as his own and deserved a better fate.

He sent word to the guns to hold their fire and sent for a speaking trumpet. As they passed the high stern he bellowed in French, 'Strike your flag, sir! You have done enough this day for the honour of your country.'

There was a thin cry in return and with a sinking heart Kydd heard the unknown captain passionately refuse.

They were past by now and he wore around slowly and came down once more on his mission of destruction but again held his fire and hailed – with the same refusal.

Bleakly Kydd brought *Tyger* round for the last time.

This then was the final act. He must perform his duty and—

'He's struck!' Bray roared hoarsely. 'The bastard's dousing his rag!'

Kydd saw that he was right: the proud tricolour at the mizzen halyards was slowly descending to half-staff.

The last frigate had surrendered to *Tyger*.

In a tidal wave of emotion he looked round at the sea battlefield that had seen so much blood and heroism, agony and death, and rocked with fatigue and relief.

Far off, the disabled *Albatros* drifted while over on their beam the wreck of *Odin* still burned fiercely. Nearby he could see *Stoat* and boats picking up survivors from the water.

And there, lying under their guns, was *Preussen*, fairly beaten in as harsh a combat as he'd ever in his life known.

'My barge, Mr Bray. And I'll trouble you for the butcher's bill on my return.'

With his coxswain at the helm, he stepped into the boat, still in his battle-stained dress. He settled into the sternsheets, barely hearing the quiet orders Halgren gave that had it bearing off and making for the enemy.

His towering exhaustion gave rise to a feeling of unreality, a floating of the mind outside the body that brought a calmness, a strange tranquillity. The men at the oars pulled slowly, their red eyes in pits of white against the grey of smeared powder-grime, their clothing torn and stained.

No one spoke. There was no exultation, no cheers as they approached the vanquished. Too much had happened.

The bowman hooked on at the main-chains and stood aside to let Kydd mount the side-steps.

This close, the marks of the recent encounter were stark and plain. Great shot-holes in the wales, an infinity of lesser scars, the brightness of shattered timber against the black hull, a snarl of forlorn ropes and blocks dangling from above and trailing in the water.

Weighed down by fatigue, he pulled himself slowly up the lacerated sides. On deck he found a group of officers, grey-slimed and red-eyed, but one held himself erect, thin-lipped and grim.

Kydd recognised the lace of a frigate captain and crossed to him, ignoring the others. The man's arm was in a sling and blood seeped but there was nothing in his cold, hard expression to betray his feeling.

For a long moment they faced each other without speaking, then the Frenchman bowed painfully.

'Capitaine de vaisseau Jean-Yves Marceau. I have the honour to command the French National Ship *Preussen*.' The

325

voice was husky, controlled, the eyes coolly taking Kydd's measure.

'Captain Sir Thomas Kydd, of His Majesty's Frigate *Tyger*.'

The expressionless gaze held, then eased a fraction. 'I should say that you have been favoured beyond the ordinary by the gods of war, Sir Thomas.'

Kydd inclined his head and waited. Behind him Halgren stood loosely, huge and impassive. Next to him were Clinton and three marines.

'But I will not. It has been a hard-fought action and against great odds – but this contest has been fairly won by you, sir, and I honour you for it.' There was a glimmer of a smile, then a sigh. 'So I do invite you to take possession of my ship, for it is yours by right of conquest.'

A lieutenant stepped up with rigid control, thrusting out a sword and scabbard.

Kydd ignored it. 'Sir, your ship fought to the very end. The outcome could have been very different. I cannot take the sword of a brave man.'

An unreadable shadow passed across the hard features, then wordlessly the man snapped to a low bow, which he held.

'I must nevertheless ask you for the key to the magazines, Capitaine,' Kydd said formally.

Another boat was already on its way. The rest of the business of the yielding of the vanquished could be left to others.

Chapter 20

Bray gravely handed Kydd a folded paper and *Tyger*'s captain sought the privacy of his cabin.

He'd instantly known what it was, the butcher's bill. Those who had turned to that morning after a tense sleep had been doing their damnedest for their captain, their messmates and their ship and had seen the day go against them. Some had been touched by death, others suffered mutilation, many condemned to . . . The rest of their shipmates had life and a future. Where was the meaning in all of this?

Kydd held the summary rigidly. In Bray's hasty scrawl were numbers that clutched at his heart – thirty-six of *Tyger*'s crew had been chosen by Fate: eleven killed, nine wounded severely and sixteen who in some way would be reminded of this day for the rest of their life.

The list was baldly stated and in no particular order.

Digby, the young and bright quartermaster's mate, who delighted in races to the tops – right leg shot away, an amputation. Even if he recovered he could now only look on as others raced by.

Borden, master's mate. Head taken off by a round-shot. Kydd recalled cursing his absence at one point and felt a twist of guilt.

Dawkins, a long-serving able seaman whose work with sennit was legendary. His seamed face had been the 'sea-daddy' memory that countless young seamen would take with them. A splinter in the lower abdomen, he'd lived for an hour.

Others . . .

The boatswain, Herne, had been savagely lacerated. Kydd had seen him imperturbably going about the bloody decks looking for damage. Twice he had spotted him through the smoke, steadily going aloft into the lethal storm on some urgent mission.

A carpenter's mate, Gordon. Taken by a splinter to the bowels while stemming a shot-hole with Legge, the carpenter. Kydd knew they were fast friends, always to be seen together stepping ashore. Not expected to live.

Legge himself had been wounded, probably by the same ball bursting into the dark of the hull. He was marked as continuing duty but what grief he would be carrying.

Three marines dead. Eight wounded. They had plied their muskets without flinching and had paid the price.

The master, Joyce. Wounded in the ear. So that was the bloody bandage he'd seen on him. His cheery attitude had never faltered.

Three gun-crew of number-five gun dead. He'd seen the ball strike and dismount the gun, the sprawling bodies. The gun-captain had been transfixed by hundreds of shards from the shattered gun carriage and was now below in the most hideous pain, craving death as a release from his torment.

Then . . . Stirk, gunner's mate. Kydd froze, his eyes pricking.

Not Toby Stirk! The big-hearted tar who'd known him since those unbelievably distant days when he'd been a raw landman in his first ship.

He blinked convulsively and read further.

Gravely concussed, still unconscious. If he lived there was every chance he'd end in Hoxton, the asylum for lunatics maintained by the navy for cases like his. What an end – and to the bravest, truest man he . . .

Kydd couldn't go on. Racking sobs seized him. He buried his face in his hands and wept like a child.

When it was over he sat back, shuddering waves of emotion receding – then he saw by his side a single glass of whisky. His eyes stung again at the realisation that Tysoe must have seen him in this state and left it there, then quietly withdrawn.

It pulled him together. This was no time to indulge his feelings: his ship needed him. He had no idea how much she had suffered: he had to find out urgently and act decisively.

'Tysoe,' he called. His valet was before him in seconds, grave and attentive.

'Desire Mr Bray to attend on me at his convenience.'

The first lieutenant arrived with suspicious promptness.

'The ship – I'll have a report by part-of-ship concerning all damage and—'

'Sir. I've the heads of the matter here. We're takin' water into the hold, the carpenter's down there now. The mizzen's in sad state – we've fished with capstan bars above the tops but I doubts if she'll—'

'Anything else as will cause concern, Mr Bray?'

'We can't set any sail on the mizzen – the backstays are both stranded. Mr Herne is taking hawsers to the masthead and swears this will answer. The larb'd main-wale has sixteen shot-holes as are being plugged now, there's a mort of splicing and we've only the barge and pinnace will swim.'

It could have been far worse. No grave structural damage, but the leak was worrying.

'So nothing as will see us embarrassed in the article of getting under way again?'

Bray went to speak, then looked away.

'What is it, Mr Bray?'

'Sir. I . . . that is, there's a mountain o' work needs doing afore we're square . . . but the people, they're dropping as dead with lack o' sleep, there on the decks, work in their hands and . . . well, I—'

A hot flush of shame washed over Kydd. A fire-eating driver like Bray caring more for his men than he. 'Leave it with me,' he snapped.

Dart and *Stoat* were summoned alongside and in short order they were secured astern and every man jack of their company was haled aboard to relieve the Tygers.

Head swimming, Kydd summoned their captains to his cabin and learned the full story.

They had correctly interpreted his actions and had stood by the transports, which had successfully taken off the army who were now marching to Königsberg from Pillau.

'And the rearguard, have they been retrieved?'

'No, sir. They's to be what stops the Crapauds from interfering with the embarkation. They're still there.'

'Still there?'

'That's to say, they's all dead, sir.'

A wave of desolation swept over Kydd.

'To the last man. Their captain, never forget him. Rode a white horse, full kit an' all so everyone can see him, the enemy as well. Got around to the men, they heard him an' followed him whatever he did. Brave as any I've ever seen.'

'Still there.'

'Aye, sir. I met the beggar several times. Seems he was somethin' in Headquarters, safe and all, but volunteered for the job.'

'What was his name?' he asked, with a sense of foreboding.

'Oh, it was Gussan, Gusten, something like. A right valiant sort, I'll give you that.'

The pity of war. The crying, howling pity of war.

'Th-thank you, gentlemen, for all your assistance to *Tyger* at this time. I find I'm overcome by fatigue. I beg you'll forgive me but I really think I should rest . . .'

HMS *Tyger*, under jury mizzen and an hour at the pumps every watch, took her leave of the Baltic shore. Her sick bay full of moaning, agonised humanity, splints and lashings keeping her sails aloft, she set course for home.

At three knots she painfully passed through the Sound, unchallenged by the officious Danes, and in lowering, blustery winds, sailed around the Skagen and into the wider world.

Days later they raised the North Sea squadron and Kydd reported to Russell.

'. . . and I pressed redcoats to do duty as prize crew until we could get 'em to Pillau.'

Russell leaned back, his eyes alight. 'And your Prussians, what do they think of it all? A right glorious occasion, I'd say!'

'They've other worries now, is my thinking, sir. Boney is making moves as will see him at the gates of their capital within the month. There's nowhere left they can run to, and what then?'

'Well, that's not our concern, of course. We keep well out of such, thank God. You'll be off to Sheerness for survey and repair, I believe. I can give you *Stoat* as escort, enough do you think?'

If *Tyger* foundered on her way, that was just a cutter to take off all her crew. 'I'd be happier with another, sir,' Kydd replied.

'Very well, you deserve the best. We'll ask *Lively*, even if it leaves me short a frigate.'

'I'm indebted to you, sir.'

The weather had not improved, and the blustery, ill-tempered easterly had set *Tyger* to an edgy roll that was trying their temporary repairs to their limits.

As so often in these waters the weather then changed. The clouds scampered away and sunshine beamed down as if to speed the injured vessel on her way.

But before the sun had gone to its rest it had changed again.

In cold gusts, the easterly took charge. Flat and hard, it had the feel of the unknown regions of the limitless land-mass of Asia about it. Coming in from astern, it strained the jury backstays and the multitude of other patches and repairs.

There was nothing for it but to take sail off her, but this brought other dangers. The pumps were holding for now but the carpenter had not yet found whatever other wounds *Tyger* had suffered in her bowels below the waterline. In the bracing weather in which the action had been fought, the ship had been rolling, exposing her hull, and shots would have struck between wind and water.

The ship with the wind aft and less steadying sail had a

lively roll once more – and this was bad news. As she heeled to whichever was the side of the shot strike, the wound would be plunged deeper, and on each roll the ingress of water would change from nothing to a hard waterfall directly into her innards.

It was a race against time and the weather.

Kydd remembered the harrowing struggle after Trafalgar when a storm had overtaken the battered fleet and their prizes. *Victory* herself had been threatened and battle-weary men had gone to their doom as shattered prizes foundered in the night.

For them, however, the reassuring bulk of *Lively* was out on their beam, heaving and lifting as she conformed to their reduced sail. He glanced up at the shot-torn sail that still fluttered and bellied and eased his thoughts. It would be an uncomfortable several days but they'd make harbour.

Only two hours later it was a different story. The sharp blow had turned to a fresh gale, something that *Tyger* would have scorned in normal circumstances – but these were not normal.

A gale-driven swell had risen with it and this had increased her movement and, therefore, the whipping strain on damaged shrouds and stays.

Kydd gave the order to take in more sail – there was little else that he could do.

This sent seamen up in grim conditions with more than the usual dangers. High aloft there would now be severed footropes, lines giving way that men placed their trust in, shattered spars with cruel timber spikes gouging their bellies while they reefed, and always the sullen roll.

As night fell there was no sign of the gale easing.

Lively sent lanthorns to each masthead telling of comforting

333

human presence nearby, but aboard *Tyger* there was misery and hardship. The galley fire could not be lit, and without good hot food the men must face the labour of saving their ship with hard tack and cheese on a mess-deck that swilled with water entering through so many shot-holes.

The glow of lights that were *Lively*'s lanthorns receded to pinpricks as the frigate kept at a cautious distance for it was all too easy in such a night to come to a disastrous encounter. Lookouts were posted in both ships with the sole duty to keep the precious lights in sight.

And those aboard *Tyger* endured.

Men whose bodies ached from their heroic exertions at the guns were now being asked to go to the pumps, the dreadful clanking monsters that needed brute force even to overcome the friction of the many valve parts, a heart-breaking grind.

For long hours *Tyger* heaved and fell in the increasing swell, the hard battering and dismal moan of the gale always with her as she fought on. On deck the watch stared into the night, slitting their salt-sore eyes into the storm.

Then came driving rain, in a hissing, stinging and miserable cold, invading oilskins and foul-weather gear.

Just after midnight the worst struck.

Kydd was with the group at the wheel as the middle watch coped with a split sail when, clear above the storm rack, a vicious crack sounded, followed immediately by a heavy slither as a hawser fell in a sprawling pile. Another quickly followed. Instantly Kydd bellowed, '*Forrard – go for your lives!*' They fled just in time. With a sickening splintering, like a falling tree, the fished mizzen topmast tumbled, driven awkwardly across to fall on the starboard side.

In the blackness of night and hammering rain, the tangle

334

of ropes and canvas had to be brought under control. From nowhere the boatswain appeared, a nightshirt under his oilskins, roaring for men to douse all sail before setting about the fearful snarl.

Tyger, without steerage way, began a helpless wallow broadside to the sea. A party got out a sea-anchor over the bows that brought her round, head to sea, but at the cost of halting their progress to safe harbour.

There was nothing for it but to await the dawn to see what they could do.

The report came up that the water was gaining in the hold. There was only one course left.

'Watch and watch,' Kydd ordered, condemning tired men to man the cranks continuously.

There was a chance that if the weather moderated he could get men from *Lively* who would spell them but until then they would know their labour and pain were saving the vessel.

In the cold grey of early light the full extent of the damage could be seen: the long spar lying on deck seeming so massive close to, had taken the driver gaff with it and in so doing had torn the big aft sail down to ruin.

The frigate could no longer cope with basic navigational matters, like a change in wind direction, for without leverage aft she could not tack about and most probably neither wear around.

'We've got to get sail on her aft, Mr Herne,' Kydd said, to the dull-eyed, exhausted man. 'Whatever it takes.'

He waited impatiently for the first sighting of *Lively*. They were so desperately in need of fresh men.

The report never came. Instead it was the age-old hail from the lookout at first light that normally would stand men down from the guns: '*Clear! On deck there – I have a clear horizon!*'

When they'd lost the topmast and come about to lie to a sea-anchor it had been in heavy rain and it was clear their plight had not been seen by their consort, who had sailed on.

It was no use to expect to be found eventually: the hard truth had to be accepted. They were on their own. If *Tyger* was to be saved it would be only themselves to do it, and if she wasn't, her name would join those recorded to history as having vanished at sea.

The boatswain, sailing master and carpenter huddled with Kydd in his cabin to try to find a way out of their situation. It was vitally necessary to get under way again, which meant some kind of rig on the stump mizzen with the same functioning as the driver.

It was Joyce, looking grey and old, who came up with the most promising plan.

A staysail secured at its peak to the topmast cap and reversed. At its lower end it was the clew that was affixed to the lower mast and the tack spread by a lower stunsail boom pressed for the service. A species of traveller could be contrived with two tackles at its end.

The new 'driver' could be goosewinged and, with other tricks, it would see them tolerably well placed to resume headway west.

After all, Herne remarked, they were before the wind the whole way . . . should the weather hold.

By mid-morning the strange-looking rig was spread abroad and the sea-anchor hove in. They wallowed around and took up on their old course under small canvas.

There was no sighting of the sun, and with their erratic movements dead reckoning was chancy, but a voyage to the Thames estuary was straightforward enough, no more than lying along the line of latitude of fifty and a half once they'd won their southing.

That wasn't Kydd's main worry. It had to be how long he could expect men to keep up the grinding toil at the pumps. There was a day or so to safe haven but to men on the edge it was an eternity – and there was not a thing he could do about it.

At the extremity of fatigue, men walked about the decks in a trance, staring at bulkheads, dropping where they stood. Yet not a word of complaint.

The following morning it was difficult to make out anything in the racing murk to leeward but the low coast of Kent could not be far off.

Then at last the carpenter formally reported that the water flooding in had overtaken their ability to pump it out.

Tyger was done for: at some point the rate would suddenly increase as the lower ports submerged and the gallant ship would sink beneath the waves for ever. And in this filthy weather, with no ships in sight, still less land, each and every one would go to his death unseen by the world of men.

The pitiless sea had won.

It was unbearable! To have come so far . . .

Kydd flogged his tired brain mercilessly but in the end it always came back to the same thing. Even with men giving their all, the pumping was not enough: the callous equation was final.

Then from somewhere his mind presented a desperate idea. If the capacity of the pumps was not enough, what if the speed of their operation increased? The net flow must, of course, increase – but this was crazy thinking!

Doggedly he pursued the thought: what if he sent every

man jack aboard to do a trick but this for only ten minutes at a time before spelling him, but at the same time expect a more furious rate?

His imagination visualised a long line of men waiting their turn. There were four places at the cranks along the main shaft. If each man was spelled in a staggered sequence the momentum would be kept up.

Yes – there was a chance!

In a short time he had explained it to Bray and the boatswain and left it to them to organise a means to work the ship from those coming off the pump before resuming their place in the line.

Meals? What could be held in the hand? Sleep? Snatched there and then on the deck. Respite? None!

'Form the line!' Kydd roared.

The first man stepped up ready.

It was the captain, who threw off his jacket and stood flexing his hands.

There was shuffling nearby – Bray, pushing aside Bowden. Behind him was Brice – the first four on the cranks would be the ship's officers.

'Take hold!'

Each grabbed a pitted iron handle and braced.

'Start!'

It was astonishingly difficult, winding up the long chain with the drag of their leather seals and Kydd's muscles burned with the effort. Panting, he drove around the cruel bar, now heaving it up, next pushing it down, in a dizzy cycle that left no room for thought.

'Faster!' he gasped, throwing himself into it.

Reluctantly the muffled rumble of the drive chain rose in tone a little, and then more. Sparing nothing, he worked like a madman until the note rose higher still. It was furious labour and a mesmerising rhythm took hold.

Standing by with a watch in his hands, the quartermaster called, 'Spell one!'

It didn't register in the flailing grind and Kydd felt a tap on his shoulder.

'Sir.' It was the boatswain demanding he yield his place.

Kydd fell back exhausted, tripping over and ending on his knees.

Half a dozen hands helped him up but his eyes were only for the pump.

Herne had caught the rhythm quickly and was bulling the crank around, now whirling at an astonishing speed.

Staying to catch the next handover, he prayed it was working. If anything was going to deliver them, this was it.

A wave of exhaustion swept over him in a dizzying flood. Just as he had so long ago, as a common foremast jack, he sought the ship's side and sat down, leaning against it. Folding his arms he put his head on his knees and let go of consciousness.

The morning brought two desperately desired things. The water had not only been halted but was down a full eight inches – and land was sighted, the low mudflats of Essex. They were just to the north of the Thames, with small miles to go. It was impossible, incredible, but release was only hours away.

But they were not home yet. Ahead were the notorious sandbars of the estuary, said to be the worst a seaman could face. Low in the water, *Tyger* would touch at the slightest mis-navigation and she could leave her bones within sight of her rest.

In the hard easterly there was little shipping and the pilot cutter came streaming out promptly, the grizzled old pilot mounting the side in astonishment.

'As you're *Tyger* an' all?' he said breathlessly.

'It is,' Kydd said wearily. 'You'll get your fee, never fear. Now I'll have you know we're well down on our marks, four feet or more, take mind of this, sir.'

'*Tyger*, begob!' He snatched off his sou'-wester and looked at Kydd in open admiration. 'An' the country's in a rare moil t' hear of your great fight. And to think I'm here to—'

'Sir. We have to make Sheerness with the greatest urgency. Do you—'

'So you shall, sir! You're grievous mauled an' will make port or I'm to swing for it!'

'One thing.'

'Anything you wants, sir!'

'Your cutter. Do send it into Sheerness dockyard directly and I want a hundred fresh men ready for me the soonest. Compree?'

Tyger crept ahead in the white slashed seas, the familiar bleak outlines of Sheppey firming with the dark silhouettes of the ships of the Nore in a long cluster to larboard.

What did he mean, the whole country alive with news of their engagement? It would have to be Admiral Russell sending an immediate dispatch by fast packet, which, with their slow progress, had given time for the news to spread.

A desolate curtain of rain enveloped them and drove down on the distant cliffs and marshes, obscuring the shoreline. When it lifted it revealed an astonishing sight. From Garrison Point, the fort, all along the foreshore there were people, hundreds, a thousand. Scorning the rain and winds and, without question, there to welcome them home!

The pilot cutter must have brought the exciting news and the whole town had turned out.

A firework soared up, then several. From the fort came the crump of guns – no naval salutes would greet a mere frigate. Boats could be seen putting off and by the time they'd rounded the point to reach shelter they were surrounded by yelling well-wishers, soaked to the skin.

Tyger came to and picked up moorings even as dockyard boats were putting out, filled with men.

'Get those men to work this instant!' Kydd bawled. It would be a sorry end after all that had passed to sink at their moorings.

He turned to the master shipwright, who stood respectfully but held up his hand. 'I've orders that give you the highest priority for a docking, sir. The master attendant is turning out *Hibernia* as we speak.'

'Thank you. I desire you will allow me to make use of your boats.'

'By all means.'

From below came a procession. Stretchers with wounded, pale and bloody. Some moaning, some very still. They were handed down into the boat with the utmost care and it put off.

Another piteous procession followed them. Five canvas shrouds. These were sent down with equal tenderness as *Tyger*'s company lined the side, taking off their hats. The milling boats quietened as they made way for men taking their last journey back to the land that had given them birth.

'Sir. The men are now all relieved at the pumps. We've . . . we've made it, sir.' Bray's voice had turned husky and Kydd was nearly overcome, it coming from such a lion-hearted soul.

'Ah, yes. You've just an hour to write liberty-tickets for the whole ship's company. They'll go ashore at once, do you hear?'

'Aye aye, sir.'

It was all so unreal, so dreamed of but never expected.

'Sir?' Bowden seemed to sense his mood and spoke quietly. 'Yes?'

'It's the admiral. Came aboard without we knew he was here. Will you see him?'

Kydd blinked. Admirals only came out to ships with much fuss, fanfare and good warning. Was this a matter of some urgency? Kydd hurried to greet him.

'Ah, Sir Thomas! My, are we glad to see you. Word from the North Sea squadron was that you were sore injured, and when *Lively* lost you, we thought you'd gone down.'

'I've the entire ship's company to thank that we didn't, sir.'

'I'm sure. Now, I know you're much overborne with matters but I can't allow that you will refuse me if I desire you to come to dinner very soon and tell me all about your great action.'

'I'd be glad to, sir, should I be at liberty to do so.'

'Splendid! Perhaps at—'

But Kydd's first lieutenant had come up and was standing by impatiently.

'Yes, Mr Bray?'

'Could I have a word, sir?'

They went to one side and Bray coughed in embarrassment, saying, 'I've never heard of it in all my years in the service.'

'What's that, then, Mr Bray?'

'It's like this, sir. When I told the clerk to prepare the liberty-tickets he said as how he'd been approached by the

342

men who said they'd be damned if they're to take their rest before the barky does. They'll not set foot ashore afore they sees *Tyger*'s safely at her ease in dock.'

'Thank you for telling me this, Mr Bray. They shall in course be allowed to stay aboard.'

The admiral looked on in concern and, when Kydd returned, asked, 'Not a case of worriment, I trust?'

'No, sir, just . . . nothing as can't be arranged.'

'Well, sir. If there's anything I can do, please tell. You're to be indulged, I believe, sir!'

In a surge of feeling, Kydd replied, 'Yes, sir, there is one service that would gratify me in full measure.'

'Do fill and stand on, sir!'

'The people conceive that they will not step ashore while *Tyger* awaits her rest. Their wish is to stay aboard until then. We're at a stand for comforts and so . . .'

'Yes?'

'I ask that you do send out the marines to every tavern, ordinary and hostelry in Sheerness. They're to bring back to *Tyger* a piping hot pie or similar, enough for all our company. This to be to my expense, of course.'

The admiral looked at him in astonishment, then leaned forward and barked, 'Impossible!'

'Sir?'

'I won't have it!'

'Sir.'

'This will be done – but to *my* expense.'

After Kydd had seen him over the side he called for Bray once more. 'The men to remain aboard. There's only one thing I can do.'

'Wives and sweethearts?'

'Just so.'

343

The word was passed and spread ashore. In a remarkably short time a joyous armada of boats put off and *Tyger* was invaded by a gay throng of womenfolk.

Kydd watched from the quarterdeck, his heart full. The mortal tiredness had receded and it was time to take joy in the hour.

He especially rejoiced at the news of gunner's mate Stirk. The tough old seaman had come to and, with no sign of derangement, was able to let his views be adequately known about being landed from *Tyger*.

Then across the thronging decks he saw a pair threading through, moving purposefully towards him – and rubbed his eyes in disbelief.

'Nicholas! Cecilia! Wha'?'

'Well, we were just passing by and—'

'My love, don't chouse Thomas so. Dear brother, your hero fight is known throughout the land these last days, since those dispatches. We heard even in Wiltshire, and Nicholas put a carriage on the road in the same hour, you must believe! He worked out that the nearest dockyard you'd make for would be Sheerness and he was right, the darling man, and here we are!'

To see his sister and her noble husband, his sea companion of years, was touching to a degree. He'd sent a terse message before he'd first joined *Tyger* under a cloud and they would have had no news since then.

'So this is your new ship, Thomas,' Cecilia said, looking around her curiously. Her striking dark good looks were arresting in such bare surroundings. 'It's so much bigger than *L'Aurore*.'

'Yes, sis. An eighteen-pounder o' the first water,' Kydd said proudly, then led them below to his cabin.

She saw the needlework sampler on the bulkhead and rose to read it.

> *Tyger Tyger, burning bright,*
> *In the forests of the night;*
> *What immortal hand or eye,*
> *Could frame thy fearful symmetry?*

'How intriguing!' she said in admiration. 'Who wrote these words, I wonder?'

They turned simultaneously to Renzi, who held up a hand and gave a wry smile.

'It was written while we two were in *Seaflower* cutter in the Caribbean. By a gentleman who was taken up for sedition on the eve of Trafalgar for saying, "Damn the King. The soldiers are all slaves!" Your William Blake is not to be claimed by those who set at an eminence England's crown and sceptre.'

'But Thomas's ship was named after this, I'm sure of it!'

'I feel that it is rather more the stout *Tyger* of Sir Francis Drake, as mentioned by Shakespeare, my love.'

'I'm keeping it anyway!' Kydd said rebelliously, and shepherded Cecilia back to her chair.

Tysoe entered with refreshments. The silver salver had an ugly twist and scoring on one side. 'My lord, I do apologise for its appearance. We did not entirely escape the malice of the enemy as you may see.'

'And I didn't like to remark it, Thomas, but your ship is sadly out of countenance. She must have suffered, poor creature.'

'No more than our gallant crew, Cec,' Kydd said, in a low voice. Then in a stronger tone he declared, 'But she's blooded now, and when she's set to rights we'll take the tight little barky out to meet the enemy and bid Boney do his worst!'

'I'll drink to that in a bumper!' Renzi said, raising a glass.

The three did so, then Renzi regarded Kydd with a quizzical look. 'Knowing you, old trout, I'm sanguine you've given no thought to what it is you've brought to pass.'

'We came through it without disgrace, Nicholas. That's all I desired.'

'As I thought. I beg you will understand that the world will no longer remember Sir Thomas of Curaçao. From now on, the frigate captain who faced three frigates and bested them will be ranked with Pellew and Blackwood, his name coupled with his ship, like Keats of the *Superb*, to the glory of this kingdom. It will be by his bare name that Kydd of the *Tyger* will be spoken of henceforth.'

Kydd coloured, but muttered darkly, 'As will give the Admiralty something to choke on!'

Renzi smiled gently. 'Dear fellow, forgive me if I point out some home truths. Your contretemps with Lord St Vincent is as nothing in the eyes of the world now. No one is listening to the old gentleman these days, for the navy and the world are quite changed and his views are sadly set at naught.'

'His friends their lordships, the damned villains, have a lot to answer for, Nicholas. Why, when—'

'A mort of perspective will ease your ire, my distinguished friend. You're as yet untutored in the dark arts of politics and power – do believe me when I say there are tides of animosity and adulation both of which swish about figures at an eminence. There are cabals and conspiracies, alliances and antagonisms that ebb and flow with the fevers of the hour.

'Inevitably you will be perceived as owing allegiance to one or another and therefore an enemy to the rest. I counsel you to accept your lot and pay no mind to the shrill cries of the other side, for at the height of your fame you may assuredly count on a quantity of the envious, the mal-prepensed, the petty to take pen and wit against you.

'Rest on your laurels, dear friend, for they're hard-earned, and do scorn these lesser creatures.'

Kydd reddened again, then looked up and spoke softly. 'Nicholas, my dear and true friend. Those times we were watch-on-deck together in *Artemis*, even through to the old *Tenacious* – do you remember? I took in a hill of your advice and it brought me to . . . to here, to this hour. How can I not hoist it aboard?'

There was a muffled sob as Cecilia got up and ran to Kydd, crushing him to her. 'You wonderful, wonderful man!' She gulped, tears starting.

'Er, sir?' It was Bowden, standing at the cabin door and somewhat at a loss at the sight.

'Yes?' Kydd managed to disengage himself.

'So sorry, sir, but you're wanted on deck.'

'What is it that . . .'

His words died away at the sight before him. Every one of the Tygers was silently standing there.

'Off hats!' roared the boatswain.

Bowden stepped forward. 'Sir Thomas, I'm desired by the ship's company of HMS *Tyger* to make presentation of this loyal address to you, captain of their ship and commander of same in the late battle.'

Dumbstruck, Kydd just had the wit to doff his own hat as Bowden unrolled the parchment written in a hand uncannily similar to Dillon's.

In ringing tones he declared:

'To his honour, Captain Sir Thomas Kydd of the Royal Navy. May it please you, sir. We, the dutiful and loyal ship's company of His Britannic Majesty's Ship Tyger *hereunder subscribed, do wish it known and witnessed our true and humble duty to you, our worthy and well-beloved captain, and pledge our undying devotion and obedience in whatsoever perils and adventure His Majesty commands his ship doth perform.*

   In this, our expression of fidelity and loyalty, we trust you will always be attended by success and happiness in the years to come.

   Signed this day . . .'.

He concluded with an elegant bow, which Kydd jerkily returned. The scroll was formally presented.

'Th-thank you, Mr Bowden. And I do thank you for this, the Tygers. From the bottom of my heart. I'll never forget you all—'

But Kydd couldn't go on and had to turn aside as his vision misted, for he now undeniably had the greatest prize he could ask for: *Tyger*'s heart and soul.

Author's Note

Of all the characters in history I've come across while researching the sixteen volumes in the Kydd series to date, there's been none like Rear Admiral Sir Home Riggs Popham KCB (as he eventually became). He served under the Duke of York in the army, was a scientist, secret-service manipulator, fellow of the Royal Society, inventor of Nelson's Trafalgar code of signals, originator of the Sea Fencibles and a Member of Parliament all through the time of his contact with Kydd – but never once did he take his ship against the enemy.

Yet, gifted as he was, for some reason he had a genius for making enemies – from the visceral hatred of St Vincent and nearly the entire Board of Admiralty to many of the highest in the land. The closest I could come to putting my finger on it is to conceive that he never bothered to conceal his intelligence in his dealings with lesser mortals. I kept coming across asides like 'incurably plausible' and 'he suffers from an excess of cleverality'. Whatever the reason, his court-martial was the sensation of the age, leaving none in the land without an opinion. It polarised the navy and Kydd's experiences were typical. You've not heard the last of this cryptic figure in Kydd's future adventures . . .

Despite his taking against my hero I've to confess much admiration for John Jervis, Earl St Vincent. Denied the life of a sailor by his parents, he nevertheless ran away to sea. His service spanned the Seven Years' War, the American War of Independence, the Revolutionary War, the Napoleonic War, and he was still standing at Waterloo. His devotion to the navy was intense and unwavering. When Britain was hysterical at the threat of invasion he famously said, 'I do not say, my lords, that the French will not come. I say only they will not come by sea!' His uncompromising stand on mutiny and discipline made him much feared, but the same approach nearly cost England the war when, as first lord of the Admiralty, he ruthlessly moved against corruption in the royal dockyards and the timber cartel that was manipulating prices for the most vital raw material of all. They responded essentially with an embargo, and the crusty lord, utterly refusing to give way, provoked an instant crisis. It took all the diplomacy of Nelson himself to resolve it. Such a man of indomitable black-and-white views was never going to be biddable in politics and he was removed from office subsequently.

And I couldn't resist the piquant tableau of the founder of Australia, Captain Arthur Phillip, in his old age acting the press-gang chief, hating it but doing his duty for his country in its time of peril. Incidentally, recent research has thrown up that, almost certainly, he was a paid secret agent of the Crown in deeds of derring-do that had considerable effect on the conduct of the war.

In the course of working on this tale I became particularly

fascinated by my Arctic research. There was indeed half-hearted thinking to resurrect Archangel to act as a fall-back port if the Danes sided with the French to close off the crucial Baltic trade, but as it turned out, events took another course. Nevertheless, with my modern charts and pilot to hand, I stand amazed and humbled at the sheer grit and fortitude of those who voyaged in these regions in days of sail. In conversation with W. K. De Vaney, an Arctic hand of no small experience, it was eye-opening to pore over the great narratives of the historic Arctic to reveal what had to be borne to allow routine human existence in those latitudes.

Trade ventures there in Kydd's day were mainly locally subscribed from England's north. One of these was merchant broker John Bellingham, whom Kydd meets in a Russian gaol. He'd gone to sea as a midshipman in an East Indiaman and been caught up in a mutiny that sent the ship ashore. On return home he set up as a factor and businessman and was signally unsuccessful, ending up in Archangel, where he got on the wrong side of the Dutch, who probably framed him. Languishing for years in prison, he conceived a violent hatred of the British government, which he believed had failed him, and in 1812 sought revenge by killing Spencer Perceval in the lobby of the House of Commons, the only prime minister in British history to be assassinated. His friends' attempts to have him declared insane failed and Bellingham was publicly hanged.

In this stage of Kydd's career the greatest military drama was undoubtedly Napoleon Bonaparte's campaign to the east of the continent, caused by Trafalgar and its consequences, which prevented his breaking out of Europe. A truly astonishing canvas of millions of men clashing under arms, spread over nearly a dozen countries, it was vastly bigger than the

Peninsular War that was to follow and only ended with Bonaparte's disastrous retreat from Moscow. The part Kydd plays in the fevered times before Friedland is based on contemporary events, the little-known heroism of the Royal Navy in the defence of Danzig and that of Kolberg at the time. England does not remember them but their part is certainly revered in Germany – Danzig eventually fell but the navy's desperate help, including the night spent navigating under fire of a powder barge to the besieged, is cherished, while with their help Kolberg held out to the end.

The Prussian hero of Kolberg, Gneisenau, has a grand statue still venerated in the now Polish city of Kołobrzeg. The brooding but talented Gerhard von Scharnhorst, whom we see as chief of general staff to Blücher, afterwards joined with him and a brilliant pupil, Carl von Clausewitz, to transform Prussian military culture into the most feared in Europe, going on to defeat France and enter Paris as a prelude to taking all of Germany under one flag.

Ironically, in the Second World War these men and their epics of resistance were commemorated by the German Navy in their famous battleships *charnhorst* and *Gneisenau* and were held out by Hitler as an example to follow in the most expensive Nazi film ever made, in the calamitous final year of the Third Reich – the Royal Navy, of course, kept to a humble walk-on part.

The Vistula Spit, the Polish *Mierzeja Wiślana*, as it is now known, is a noted vacation spot, but Pillau and Königsberg have had a different fate. The port is now within the Kaliningrad Oblast, a peculiar piece of cut-off Russian territory carved out of southern Lithuania for the sole purpose of securing Pillau – now Baltiysk – as an ice-free port for Russia's Baltic Fleet. Most of the town and its red star-shaped fort are therefore now forbidden to foreigners. Königsberg, with its rich heritage, now Kaliningrad, saw grievous tragedy in the Second World War but many relics of this past remain, despite strenuous efforts at Russification.

All in all I stand amazed at the range and breadth of what happened after Trafalgar in eastern Europe, with Napoleon at the height of his powers and astride these antique untouched lands, like a colossus. I can promise even more in the next tale, as Kydd and the navy are called upon to stand alone before the conqueror . . .

To all those who assisted me in the research for this book I am deeply grateful. My appreciation also goes to my editors at Hodder & Stoughton, Oliver Johnson and Anne Perry, and their creative art/design team; and copy editor Hazel Orme, who has brought her meticulous blue pencil to bear on the Kydd series right from the debut title. And, as always, heartfelt thanks to my wife and literary partner, Kathy – and my literary agent Carole Blake.

Glossary

a cable distant	a tenth of a sea mile, conventionally one hundred fathoms
Navy Board warrant	writ of authority from commissioners of the Admiralty necessary to officers under the rank of lieutenant; boatswain, carpenter, etc.
adze	two-handed horizontally bladed axe used for shaping flat and curving timberwork
athwart	crosswise, such as intersecting a ship's course, across one's bows
auger	long-shanked boring tool
barky	pet term for one's ship
bashaw	grandee, from Turkish *paşa*
blow out his gaff	have a riotous time ashore, sparing nothing
bulwarks	planking above the deck forming the side of the ship
butcher's bill	euphemism for list of casualties after an action
Channel Groper	rueful term for the Channel station after the number of fogs to be expected
chouse	tease
clerk of the cheque	dockyard representative of commissioners of the Admiralty with authority to disburse funds, e.g. payment to seamen
comprée	seize or grasp meaning, French *comprendre*
corvette	French equivalent to ship-sloop, larger and with more guns
cuirassier	mounted soldier with armoured torso
dirndl	colourful full-skirted dress with close-fitted bodice

dragoman	professional interpreter and cultural adviser
driver sail	fore and aft sail at the after end of a ship equivalent to merchant-service spanker
druxy	timber in advanced decay, soft and spongy with white spots and veins
élève	one put forward by interested sponsor, French *élève*, pupil
euphroe	piece of wood with holes to take lacing of awning or similar
feldwebel	sergeant
flank	the side of a military deployment contrasted with the front
fluyt	Dutch cargo vessel, full-bodied with shallow draught
garboard	range of strakes that abuts the keel
guardo	shabby trick, after reprehensible guardship practices on new-pressed men
gun-room	mess-room of warrant officers and midshipmen in larger ships; the wardroom of a frigate
Hamoaze	straight stretch of water at the estuary of the Tamar before it enters Plymouth Sound
hance	break in the line of deck at the quarterdeck, often decorated
hauptfach	army major
Hohenzollern	ruling house of Prussia since 1701
hugger-mugger	in confidence one with the other
kellner	officer's mess waiter
klafter	fathom (German)
landwehr	locally raised army, militia (German)
larb'd	larboard, left side of ship looking forward
liberty-ticket	issued to seamen going ashore as protection against press gangs
liebfahne	banner of highest expression of love of country
lighters	open craft with flat bottom for carrying goods to or from ships at anchor
middling repair, great repair	if middling, requires docking; if great, requires the ship to be taken out of commission
mort	a significantly large amount; from mortal
naught	nothing
nösel	quart of liquid (German)
pettifogging	quibbler; from petty and *voger* (German 'arranger')
pfund	pound (German)
points (of sailing)	all the angles that the ship can take with respect to the wind

popinjay	person of vain and pretentious character; like a green woodpecker
private signal	ship's identifying code known only to members of a given squadron or fleet, requiring secret reply
prize	vessel captured from an enemy state either by a man-o'-war or licensed privateer
puncheon	cask of 72-gallon capacity; can be filled with liquid or bulk
quarters	after a warship has cleared for action it closes up at quarters: men go to the guns
quoin	inclined wedge placed under breech of a gun to effect elevation
ran-tan	all out joyous run ashore; French *ran-tan*, knocking, banging
reefer	midshipman
row-guard	manning a boat and circling a ship slowly to discourage deserting
royster	general merriment at a tavern
rum do	strange happening
running rigging	the operating ropes of a ship as compared to standing rigging, which supports masts
rutter	old term for written sailing directions
Sami	peoples indigenous to Lapland, Finland, the Kola peninsula
sabretache	flat bag or pouch suspended below the sabre of mounted horseman
sennit	woven yarn or straw worked by sailors
ship-rigged	fully rigged; three masts with square sail on all
skiddy cock	smaller friend
strut-noddy	swaggering promenader who doesn't know he looks foolish
tertian	type of barrel traditionally used in the south-west of England
the *ton*	those adhering to high fashion, stylish; Latin *tonus*, tone
trots, the	piles sunk out in a river or waterway to allow a vessel to moor alongside without taking the ground at low water
yeoman of the powder room	an experienced hand in charge of powder stowage; keeps accounts on behalf of the gunner

Timeline

1773	Thomas Paine Kydd is born 20 June, in Guildford, Surrey, son of Walter and Fanny Kydd.
1789	The Storming of the Bastille, 14 July.
1793–1794	Louis XVI executed, 21 January 1793.

1793–1794 France declares war on England; Kydd, a wig-maker by trade, is press-ganged into the 98-gun ship of the line *Duke William*. **KYDD**

The Reign of Terror begins, 5 September 1793–28 July 1794. **ARTEMIS**

Transferred aboard the crack frigate *Artemis,* Kydd is now a true Jack Tar who comes to love the sea-going life.

1795 The Netherlands is invaded by France, **SEAFLOWER** 19 January, and becomes the Batavian Republic.

In the Caribbean, Kydd continues to grow as a prime seaman.

1797 Battle of Cape St Vincent, 14 February. Mutiny at the Nore, 17 April.

	Kydd is promoted to acting lieutenant at Battle of Camperdown, 11 October.	*MUTINY*
1798–1799	Kydd passes exam for lieutenancy; now he must become a gentleman.	*QUARTERDECK*
	From the Halifax station, Kydd and his ship are summoned to join Nelson on an urgent mission.	
	The Battle of the Nile, 1 August 1798. Britain takes Minorca as a naval base from Spain, 16 November 1798. Siege of Acre, March–May 1799.	*TENACIOUS*
1801–1802	Prime Minister Pitt resigns February 1801. Battle of Copenhagen, 2 April 1801. Kydd is made commander of brig-sloop *Teazer* but his jubilation is cut short when peace is declared and he finds himself unemployed.	
	Peace at Treaty of Amiens, 25 March 1802.	*COMMAND*
1803	War resumes 18 May, with Britain declaring war on the French.	
	Unexpectedly, Kydd finds himself back in command of his beloved *Teazer*.	*THE ADMIRAL'S DAUGHTER*
	Kydd is dismissed his ship in the Channel Islands station.	*TREACHERY*
1804	Napoleon's invasion plans are to the fore.	
	May, Pitt becomes Prime Minister again. Napoleon is crowned Emperor, 2 December 1804.	*INVASION*
1805	Kydd is made post-captain of *L'Aurore*.	
	The Battle of Trafalgar, 21 October 1805.	*VICTORY*
1806	The race to empire begins in South Africa. British forces take Cape Town, 12 January.	
	A bold attack on Buenos Aires is successful, 2 July 1806.	*CONQUEST*

Now read an extract from Julian Stockwin's thrilling novel

PASHA

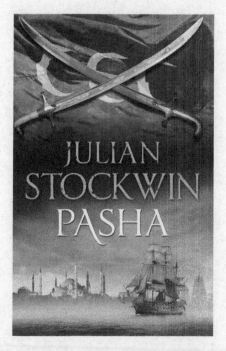

An Admiralty summons to England cuts short Thomas Kydd's service in the turquoise waters of the Caribbean. While the crew of *L'Aurore* can look forward to liberty and prize money, a shadow hangs over their captain: the impending court-martial of his one-time commander, Commodore Popham, who led a doomed attack on South America.

Following Nelson's death two years earlier, England is in desperate need of heroes and Kydd's Caribbean exploits are the talk of London. Feted by the king and a grateful country, Kydd is soon on detachment in a new and dangerous sphere of interest: the Dardanelles.

Chapter 1

It was as if the handsome frigate knew that she and her two-hundred-odd company were going home. After leaving the Caribbean she had quickly picked up a reliable westerly and now hitched up her skirt and flew, overtaking the broad Atlantic waves one by one in an eager swooping that had even old hands moving cautiously about the deck.

Channel fever was aboard and it gripped every soul. Soon after the chaos and drama of Trafalgar, HMS *L'Aurore* had been sent to join an expedition to wrest Cape Town from the Dutch. Success there had not been matched by the following ill-starred attempt at the South American colonies of Spain, and after capturing the capital, Buenos Aires, they had been forced to an ignominious surrender. Their later few months of service in the Caribbean had been abruptly terminated in an Admiralty summons to return to England. No doubt her captain was wanted at the vengeful court-martial to follow. But at last the handsome frigate and her crew were homeward bound.

Standing braced on the quarterdeck, Captain Thomas Kydd tried to take pleasure in the seething onrush of his fine command but he couldn't shake a feeling of foreboding.

A snatch of song floated aft. The men were in good heart. They had served nobly in all three actions and could rely on liberty and prize-money to spend while *L'Aurore* received overdue attentions from the dockyard. Her captain, however, could only look forward to—

'How now, old horse! Do I see you the only one aboard downcast at the prospect of England?'

His old friend and confidential secretary, Nicholas Renzi, had come on deck to join him. They'd shared countless adventures since they'd met as common seamen so long ago and had no secrets between them.

'England? Why, not at all – it's rather what's lying in wait there that troubles me.'

'The court-martial.'

'Quite. We gave it our best against the Spanish but lost. And our leader to be crucified for quitting station – if we'd prevailed it would have been overlooked, but the Admiralty will never forgive us now.' Kydd gave a bitter smile. 'There's above half a dozen captains who'll bear witness that I was in league with the commodore. It's beyond believing that they'll stop at only a single one to pay.'

'Possibly. But *L'Aurore* has done valiantly since, which should ease their lordships' wrath a trifle.'

'You think so? They won't yet have learned of our putting down the sugar-trade threat, and while we did stoutly at Curaçao, who's ever heard of the island, let alone Marie Galante? No, m' friend, after Trafalgar the country expects nothing less than victory, every time!'

'It might not be as bad as—'

'Don't top it the comforter, Nicholas. I'll take it, whatever comes. It's . . . it's just that it would grieve me beyond telling should I lose *L'Aurore*.'

'That would put us both in a pickle, I'm persuaded,' Renzi said. 'For at this particular time I'm obliged to say there are no shining prospects in store for me at all. I'll not hide that I'm disappointed my novel was not received more warmly. It did seem to me a sprightly little volume, but the public's taste is never to be commanded.'

'Well, I thought it a rattling good yarn, Nicholas! Are you sure?'

'It's been over a year and I've heard not a thing.' Renzi's head dropped. It was no use pining, though: he had to accept he was clearly not destined to be a novelist.

'But there's one thing you can look forward to.'

'Oh?'

'Nicholas, sometimes you try the patience of a saint! You seem to have forgotten your promise!'

'My . . . ?'

'Yes, your promise that when we touched port in England,' he ground out, 'you would that day post to Guildford and lay your heart before Cecilia.'

Nothing would please Kydd more than to see the long attachment between his sister and his particular friend brought to a satisfactory conclusion.

'Yes, of course,' Renzi said awkwardly. 'I'd not forgotten. But . . .'

'Yes?' Kydd said, his voice rising.

'Well, in the absence of prospects, I rather thought—'

'Nicholas, dear fellow,' he barked, 'if you're not on a Guildford coach within one hour of our casting lines ashore

I'll ask Mr Clinton for a file of marines who will personally escort you there. Am I being clear enough?'

It was the age-old excitement of landfall. A screamed hail from the volunteer masthead lookout, whose height-of-eye was more than that of the legitimate watch-keeper in the fore-top, sent pulses racing. The man would later claim his reward from the tots of his shipmates.

The pace of their homecoming quickened: now England would be in sight constantly, the well-known seamarks passing in succession until they reached the great anchorage at Portsmouth – Spithead.

The Needles, white and stark against the winter grey, were Kydd's reminder that within hours all would be made clear. The order that had reached out to him in the Caribbean would have been followed by another, now waiting in the port admiral's office. Relieved of his command pending court-martial? Open arrest?

Gulping, he realised that these last few sea-miles might very well be the last he would make under the ensign he had served since his youth.

Rounding Bembridge Point would bring Spithead into view and, if the fleet was in, he must make his report to the admiral afloat. If they were at sea, it would be to the port admiral in the dockyard. Gun salutes, of course, would be needed in either case.

The deck was crowded with men gazing at the passing shoreline, some thoughtful and silent, others babbling excitedly and laughing. It seemed the entire crew was on deck.

'Mr Oakley!' Kydd threw at the boatswain. 'Is this a pleasure cruise? Get those men to work this instant!'

L'Aurore had long since been willingly prettified to

satisfaction but she was a king's ship and had her standards. And he knew the real reason for his outburst and was sorry for it. Would the crew remember him fondly or . . . ?

The point soon yielded its view of the fleet anchorage – but four ships only and bare of any admiral's flag. Thus it would be the port admiral to whom he would make his number.

Her distinguishing pennants snapping at the mizzen halyards in an impeccable show, *L'Aurore* rounded to and her anchor plunged into the grey-green water.

Everyone knew what must follow but Kydd told them nevertheless. 'I shall report and return with orders, Mr Gilbey. No guardo tricks from the men while I'm gone or there'll be no liberty for any. Secure from sea and I want to see a good harbour stow. Carry on, please.'

With a tight stomach he boarded his barge, taking his place in the sternsheets and determined not to show any hint of anxiety.

'Bear off,' he growled at his coxswain, Poulden.

The boat's crew seemed to sense the tension and concentrated on their strokes even as they passed close by the raucous jollity of Portsmouth Point.

Reaching the familiar jetty oars were tossed in a faultless display and the boat glided in.

'Lay off, Poulden,' Kydd ordered, and stepped on to English soil for the first time in what had seemed so long. It had been nearly two years.

There was no point in delaying: he turned and strode briskly up the stone steps. At the top, unease gripped him as he saw a line of armed marines ahead.

Orders screamed out, muskets clashed, and an officer began marching smartly across.

'Captain Kydd. Sah!'

'I am he.'

'Sah!'

The port admiral, accompanied by his flag-lieutenant and other officers, appeared from behind the rigid line of red coats. 'Kydd, old fellow! Welcome to England! How are you?'

He held out his hand. 'We've been expecting you this age.'

The flag-lieutenant stood to one side in open admiration.

'Sah!'

'Oh, do inspect Cullin's guard, there's a good chap.'

There was nothing for it, and with a senior admiral at his side, Kydd did the honours, pacing down the line of marines wearing an expression of being suitably impressed, stopping with a word to one or two. At the end there was a flourish of swords and the party was released to go to the admiral's reception room.

'Sherry?'

A sense of unreality was creeping in: had they mistaken him for someone else? 'Sir. I thank you for your welcome, very pleasing to me. But might I enquire why . . . ?'

A small frown creased the port admiral's forehead. 'Do you think me a shab not to recognise a hero of the hour? Let me tell you, sir, since Boney set off his bombshell the public have sore need of same!'

'Hero?' Kydd said weakly.

'The papers have been in a frenzy for weeks. Curaçao – as dashing an exploit as any in our history! Throwing a few frigates against the might of a Dutchy naval base, sailing right into their harbour in the teeth of moored ships, forts and armies. Then every last captain takes boat, waves his sword amain and storms ashore to carry the day! How can it not thrill the hearts of the entire nation?'

'Well, it was a furious enough occasion, I'll grant you, but—'

'Nonsense! A smart action – and deserving of your prize-money,' he added, with a touch of envy.

'Sir.' Kydd paused. 'Are there orders for *L'Aurore* at all?'

The port admiral turned to his flag-lieutenant.

'Yes, sir. I'll get them instanter.'

He was back but not with a pack of detailed orders, just one, folded and sealed with the Admiralty cipher. Kydd signed for it, with only the slightest tremor to his hand.

'Do excuse me, sir,' he said, as he stepped aside to read.

It was short, almost to the point of rudeness. He was to place his ship under the temporary command of the port admiral forthwith pending refit while he should lose no time in presenting himself in person to the first lord of the Admiralty.

His heart bumped. There was a world of difference between a public hero and a naval delinquent and, without doubt, this was going to be the true reckoning.

'I'm to report to the first lord without delay. Do pardon me if I take my leave, sir. *L'Aurore* is to come under your flag until further orders – Lieutenant Gilbey, my premier, will be in command.'

THE
ADVENTURES
CONTINUE
ONLINE

Visit julianstockwin.com

Find Julian on Facebook

f /julian.stockwin

Follow Julian on Twitter

🐦 @julianstockwin